THE
SANTA
MONICA
SUICIDE
CLUB

JEREMY C. THOMAS

THE SANTA MONICA SUICIDE CLUB

First published in the United Kingdom in 2015 by Blue Baltic Press, a wholly owned trading
name of Blue Baltic Entertainment Ltd.

Set in Adobe Garamond Pro, 11.5 PT
ISBN 978-0-9933680-2-8

Supported using public funding by
ARTS COUNCIL ENGLAND
LOTTERY FUNDED

For the effervescent and ever patient, Jane.

And the twenty thousand unsung heroes who volunteer for the Samaritans.

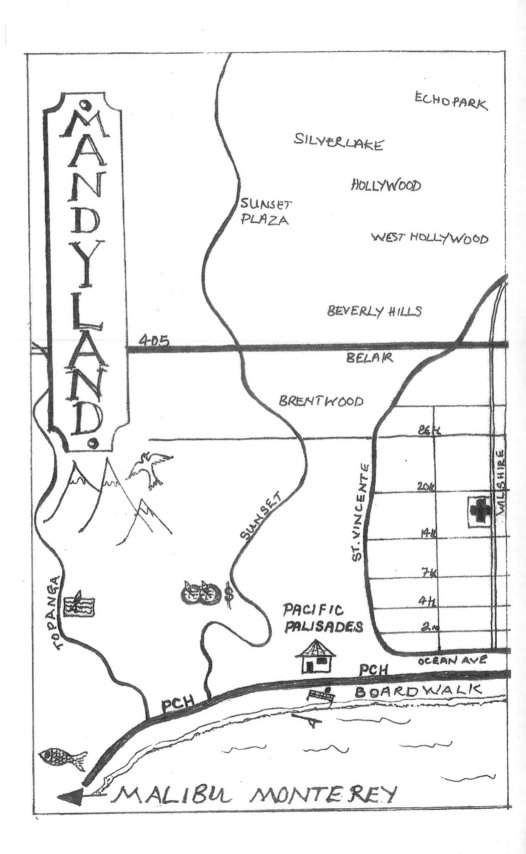

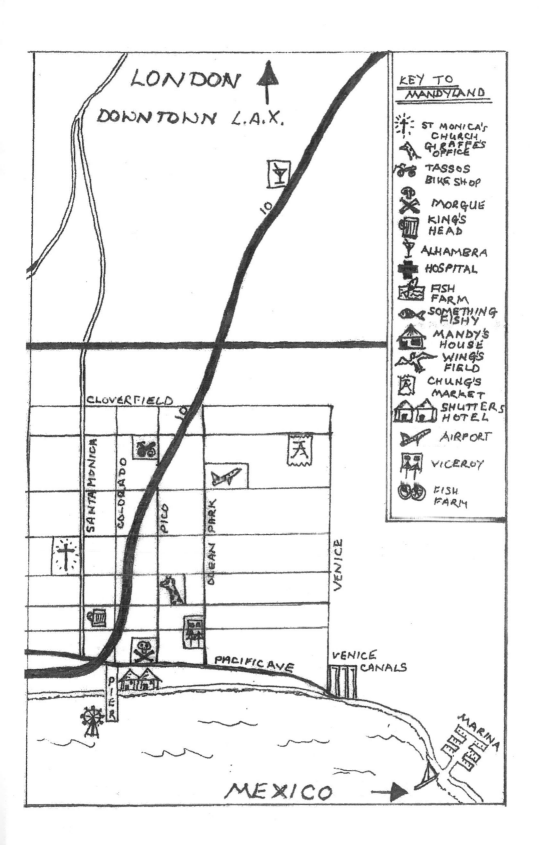

Dramatis Personae

Admiral Charles Mandy	Mandy's grandfather
Agent Anderson	Senior FBI agent
Agent O'Dowd	FBI agent
Alfonso García-Márquez	Pedro's younger brother
Alice and Caitlin	Terry's daughters
Anastasia	Dead Russian girl
Benny Tan	Owner of Fish Farm
Bradley Adams	Pedro's ex-teacher, volunteer at Ocean Park Homeless Shelter
Broadski and Dent	Santa Monica Police Department detectives
Dawn	Terry's wife
Dick Chain	Benny Tan's head of security
Dimitri Nabokov	Russian oligarch, prospective buyer of Fish Farm
Dominic Young	Retired musician, ex-boyfriend of Susan Green, AKA Dee Nitrate
Donna	Mandy's tenant and special friend
Dr Bates	Mandy's psychiatrist
Eduardo García-Márquez	Pedro's father
Fabienne	Assistant to the chief of police, AKA the Giraffe
Father Tony	British priest, on secondment to St Monica's Church
Foxy	Frank's assistant
Frank Polanski	Deputy assistant coroner
Harry and Carmen	Pedro's friends, away on holiday

Janet Lee	Benny Tan's No. 2
Javier Jones	Pedro's ex-lover
Joe and Marsha	Pedro's friends, away on holiday
Johnny and Sarah Sternwood	Pedro's close friends
Josefina	Nanny to the García-Márquez family
Kimberly	Javier Jones's girlfriend
Kurt	Intern at Fish Farm
Lucy Lack	Pedro's girlfriend
Mandy	Private investigator, owner of Endeavor Investigations
María García-Márquez	Pedro's sister
Memo	Polo player, godson of Mrs García-Márquez
Miguel García-Márquez	Pedro's younger brother
Nancy	Donna's sponsor
Ned	Mandy's cat
Pedro García-Márquez	Deceased, son of Eduardo García-Márquez
Pierre	Manager of Shutters Hotel
Quinn	Concierge at 200 Ocean Park Avenue
Samantha	Organizer of the speed-dating event at the Viceroy
Scottish Ray	Mandy's sidekick and actor friend in London
Susan Green, AKA Dee Nitrate	Dominic Young's ex-girlfriend and the singer with the Veil
Tamara Tyrer	A hooker from Sherman Oaks
Tassos	Mandy's Greek mechanic
Terry	Mandy's ex police partner
The Giraffe	Head of Santa Monica Police Department
The Swan Lakes	The Santa Monica Police Department Forensic Team
Valeria García-Márquez	Pedro's mother
Vanessa	Mandy's mother
Wayne Chung	Owner of Chung's Supermarket
Wing	Ex-Hell's Angel, old friend of Pedro

Prologue

6 p.m., 17 July

'Let us pray,' Father Tony said.

Mandy knelt in the dark wooden pew two-thirds from the front of St Monica's. The parquet-floored Spanish-style church was packed with at least two hundred people. He felt self-conscious and kept looking at the front-cover photo of the smartly printed service card and the smiling young man with his arm around a Dalmatian dog.

Two altar boys in white cassocks walked to the front row of the congregation and lit the candles held in each mourner's hands.

The choir struck up again. Mozart's Mass in C minor.

Mandy stared at the hem of Lucy Lack's dress above the back of her knees and then sat back. He inhaled Lucy's scent. Chanel No. 19. It wasn't his favourite, but it made his heart beat faster. What was it about being in church that made him think about sex? He clenched his bandaged fist to try to refocus on the requiem for the person he had never met. A feeling of being a fraud, uninvited, swept over him.

He was a private detective supposed to have the answers as to who killed Pedro. Yet he had none and was floundering.

Father Tony took a deep breath and looked up at St Monica's golden-domed ceiling, before starting on his eulogy to the dead man.

Mandy scanned the remaining faces of the expensively dressed congregation for any sign of complicity or guilt. Sarah Sternwood was nervously squeezing her husband's hand. Wing sat with his arms folded across his chest, his face dark and angry. Nearby, Javier Jones and girlfriend, Kimberly, were both dabbing their eyes with purple handkerchiefs.

Despite the air-conditioning, many people were fanning themselves with their service cards. Someone in that church knew something about why Pedro had died, maybe even more than that. Yet everyone looked inscrutable, poised, waiting for Father Tony to speak. Even the grief-stricken García-Márquez family looked silently up at the pulpit.

'As a priest, what I know is that God gave us free will, gave us the choice between good and evil.'

1

Eight days earlier, 3.45 p.m., 9 July

Mandy was driving along Pacific Coast Highway thinking life sucked. The road was black, the sea cobalt, the sky light turquoise, the temperature eighty-eight degrees Fahrenheit. An empty can of Coke lay on the passenger floor; a full one – ice-cold and unopened – sat clamped between his legs. A pork pie, past its sell-by date, lay on the seat beside him.

As he drove past the turning for Sunset, yet another news report from KCRW interrupted his thoughts: 'An award ceremony at the Viceroy Hotel ended in tragedy this morning . . .' Jesus. Not again. He felt bad enough already. He had been at the hotel only the previous night and was ashamed at what he'd done there.

He killed the radio and stared ahead at the open-topped Porsche in front as it slowed to a halt. As he braked, two massive new Range Rovers blocked him in. He glared at them. Smug fucking bastards. Both drivers tightened their grip on the steering wheel and stared straight ahead like he didn't exist.

He shrugged and stroked the warm dashboard of his 1968 Volvo Amazon like it was an old dog. The car was his castle in a foreign land – a constant companion in an inconstant world. It was him, the Amazon and his ex-police partner, Terry. The circle of trust.

The traffic began flowing again. A police roadblock at the McClure Tunnel was causing the back-up. Mandy turned off the highway and slotted the Amazon into a space overlooking the beach. He yanked up the handbrake, kept the engine running and breathed in the odd mix of fried chicken, dog shit and ozone. A black horsefly bounced off the rear-view like a pinball before settling on the windscreen. Mandy slapped his hand over it and flicked its remains onto the floor. Then he rested his left arm on the window in the sunlight and stole a glance at the bikini-clad girls playing volleyball. Despite all the warm, curvaceous flesh on display, he might as well have been in Siberia.

Santa Monica Beach – what better place to terminate your contract with life?

He had zero business and a bank account even a student would be embarrassed about. Failed actor, failed cop and about-to-be-failed private investigator. It couldn't get much worse. No wife, no girlfriend, an expiring lease on his rental, far more expenses than income, the occasional interaction with one female and ownership of one cat did not make for a happy life. Mr Micawber, reduced to finding people's missing dogs in Malibu.

'Jesus, give me some relief. Give me a break!' Mandy shouted up at the sky. He sat back and closed his eyes and fantasized, not for the first time, about attaching a hosepipe from the exhaust to the inside of the car. Mentally, he avoided the unpleasant detail about the attempts of people being left brain-damaged because of an inefficient vacuum for the carbon-monoxide fumes and fast-forwarded to his funeral. He touched a button on the dash and Mahler's 'Death in Venice' blared through the car's stereo. He allowed himself to go through the motions of viewing his own funeral. Weirdly, this was his way of staying alive. It was his method of *remaining*, not leaving but relishing a mild thrill in holding up two fingers to all those positive thinkers. Why should he have to smile and pretend that it was tickety-fucking-boo all the time when it wasn't?

Yes, his funeral: at least 150 attendees. A Cadillac hearse leading a cortege of black limos to St Monica's Church, which would be crammed with flowers. People trying to put on brave faces, shaking heads, fighting back tears. Gorgeous women, his gutless old agent, all those no-vision casting directors, cops, gang leaders, every last one of the ungrateful fuckers muttering, 'Such a nice guy. What a terrible waste.' His tearful ex-actress mother breathing in every breath of the drama, while his slug of a stepfather kept his head down. Yes, that would be a funeral to end a life well lived. And until he turned things around, he couldn't go anywhere.

The sound of happy shrieking from the beach caused the fantasy to stop. Opening his eyes, Mandy recalled a line from *Jerry Maguire* and yelled through the window to the girls playing volleyball, 'You had me at hello!' There was no reply or even acknowledgement. He grunted, changed the music to *Reservoir Dogs* and tore the wrapper off the old pork pie.

After a few moments of fast mastication, he pulled the Coke from between his thighs, yanked it open and took a well-earned gulp, nearly choking as 'I Feel Good' blasted from the passenger seat. It was his cell phone, but where the hell was it?

He scrambled under a jumble of unpaid bills, an art deco-style ashtray lifted from the Viceroy, Endeavor Investigations business cards, a torch and some half-filled notebooks. There it was – under last week's *National Enquirer*.

The call screen said, 'Fabienne.' He punched the 'answer' key.

'There's a stiff at 200 Ocean Avenue,' she said in her soft Southern voice.

'Sounds like you need an undertaker, then, not a private investigator ex-cop.'

'The victim is from the third-richest family in Mexico. Their lawyers have been on the phone – they want their own man.'

'And you think they'll choose me?'

'Don't you watch the news? Deputy Attorney General Griswold and Sergeant Powell are both dead, shot at the Viceroy this morning. All leave is cancelled. They're even taking on reservists.'

Mandy straightened his tie and brushed crumbs off his sleeve.

'OK, I'm listening.'

'And what they're not saying is that another, much younger cop was shot as well and a civilian . . . one of them not expected to make it.'

'Wrong place, wrong time. What's the story with the body?'

'Broadski and Dent have already been to the scene, made a verbal report about a weird food suicide.'

Mandy groaned. 'Not Broadski and Dent?'

Fabienne let out an impatient sigh. 'Get your pretty ass over there. I smell an opportunity.'

Mandy put the can of Coke down on the seat beside him. 'What about the Giraffe?'

'Off the record, it was the Gir— the Chief who put your name on the sheet. He's on three calls right now, but said to take a look, make notes but say absolutely nothing to no one. Two uniform rookies are guarding the place. He's going to call you later.'

'What about Frank and the Swan Lake crew?'

'Frank and Forensics are on their way. And it's apartment 70. Got that, Superman?'

'You're a doll, Fabienne.'

'Yeah, you wish,' she said, and hung up.

Minutes later he was slipping through the traffic, the Amazon's turbo engine purring, its red paint glowing in the bright sun. As he pulled up at a light to make the turn onto Ocean, a father and son wearing swim shorts, towels draped over their shoulders, jogged across the road together. They looked healthy, in control. Like nothing bad would ever happen to them.

His mouth started to feel dry. Multiple thought patterns were firing off in his head. He had not been to a serious crime scene in four years, and never as a private investigator. The Giraffe must be setting him up for a fall. More than most people in the force, the Giraffe knew all about how he'd screwed up the case with the gang and the girl, knew *exactly* what had happened. So why would he put Mandy's name forward?

'Stop churning – you're going to be great!' he shouted to himself, swerving onto the avenue.

Ocean was its usual opulent self: tall, anorexic palm trees; grass sidewalks where anxious owners trailed dogs with plastic bags; and sweaty chauffeurs polishing an endless line of luxury cars. Mandy found a space right outside number 200 – a swanky white stucco building – next to a double-parked squad car.

Showtime.

Stepping out of the elevator on the seventh floor, holding his own forensic kit – suit, shoe covers and latex gloves in a Something Fishy sushi bag – he inhaled the intoxicating blend of polished wood floors, fresh flowers, coffee and ironed clothes. It smelt like sanctuary. The same smell as his grandparents' home. The two uniformed youngsters were standing outside apartment 70, nervous, just as Fabienne had said. One of them held out the security log.

Mandy flashed his licence and scrawled his signature. They held up the blue-and-white tape for him to walk under.

'What's it like in there?'

'Two large bedrooms with en suites, big living room, a country-style fire-place, an awesome kitchen and a terrace with views to die for,' the shiny-faced rookie with the clipboard gushed.

Mandy raised his sunglasses and scowled. 'Are you police or real estate?'

The other new boy gritted his teeth and muttered, 'There's a dead body in the master bedroom.'

'Broadski and Dent are inside, right?'

'Left five minutes ago.'

'Damn! I needed to talk to them.'

The rookies exchanged glances.

'Lakers game,' the clipboard-holder said.

'Lucky them. Any sign of forced entry?'

'None that we know of.'

Mandy pulled on the latex gloves. *None that we know of?* The pair were as useless as a couple of lost golf balls.

Mandy fingered the dangling security chain, ran his hand down the side of the three bolt-locks and stepped inside the front door. No sign of damage to the locks. He climbed into his white pathology suit, put on the protective covers for his shoes and zipped up the hood. He could feel his heartbeat getting faster. Even when he had been a cop he'd never liked being alone in these circumstances.

He took a deep breath and stepped gingerly down the long, badly lit corridor. There was no sign of a struggle at the bedroom door; the carpet was good quality, thick, dark brown; the long drapes at the far end of the room were drawn and not shedding any afternoon light. He pushed the half-open panelled door and walked in. The bedroom was not huge by Ocean Avenue standards, but it was sumptuous. It felt sticky, with an aroma of coagulated blood, antiseptic and something else that Mandy was not altogether sure was human.

Would the Swan Lakes curse him for opening the curtains? Sod it, he needed the light. He took hold of the drapes; they were heavy and expensively lined. Blood pounded in his ears. Had Broadski and Dent even checked the place was empty? What if someone was behind the curtains, armed and dangerous?

He pulled them open, bracing himself for a shock, but there was no one.

Pure sunlight flooded the room and for the first time Mandy looked up at the ceiling, fully prepared for a fresco of dark jagged lines of blood-spray above the bed. But there was none, and none behind the bedhead either, or on the walls.

An old-fashioned TV stood on an antique table in a corner, and on top of a ship's chest of drawers were several smart looking bottles of aftershave. Otherwise the room was empty, apart from a bed and two doors, both open – one a walk-in closet, the other a luxurious bathroom.

He took a deep breath and stepped closer to the corpse.

It was lying on top of the bed in the shape of a crucifix. The body was a Latino male, athletic, good teeth, fashionably unshaven, wearing chinos, expensive black suede loafers and an Indian cotton shirt. The guy had been stabbed or skewered just beneath his sternum. He could see it might have been suicide, like Broadski and Dent had said, if the victim had been a serious masochist or skilled in hara-kiri.

But even the toughest suicide practitioner was unlikely to have covered themselves in a thick layer of tortilla chips afterwards. Blood had soaked through the chips, covering the solar plexus. The victim's eyes and mouth were open like a hungry but stunned baby bird. No obvious facial bruising except for a badly swollen lip.

Maybe he'd been killed somewhere else, then brought here and given the tortilla routine. There were no blood smears across the pillows or sheets, or drops on the carpet. No upturned lamps, no sign of any struggle. A white alarm clock, a hardback book and box of Kleenex lay undisturbed on the bedside table. The scene was too neat and tidy for this kind of body piercing. Unless the killer or killers travelled with their own clean-up team.

He looked at the man's face again – not much more than thirty. Only ten years younger than him. What had the poor guy done to deserve this? The air-conditioning had stopped any discolouration, and from the state of the body, Mandy guessed death most likely occurred early that morning. He scanned down the torso and noticed there were pools of blood on both sides of the lower back. There had to be a separate wound.

Mandy readjusted his latex gloves. He hated touching dead bodies and he knew it wasn't kosher to disturb a crime scene. But he didn't have a choice. He needed a head start on any information that could be gleaned from the scene if he was going to have a chance of getting this case – and solving it. He took an enormous breath and arched the nearest side of the torso slightly up in the air. Tortilla chips tumbled off the chest, stomach and legs as he peered underneath. Sure enough, there was a six-inch gash, matted with coagulated brown blood.

He lifted the torso higher and saw the same thing on the other side. Black felt-tip marking was above both wounds, which had been loosely sutured, the same way a sailor's nose used to be stitched before being buried at sea. More tortilla chips fell to the floor.

Now the air smelt of ammonia and rotting meat. Bile shot into his throat. He swallowed it, looked at the ceiling for reassurance and got back to it. Then he noticed one other thing. A soiled supermarket till receipt was stuck to the guy's neck. Using his thumb and forefinger, Mandy peeled it off. It was for eight dollars and twenty cents from one Chung's Supermarket. He bit his lip, knew he shouldn't, but still he pocketed it, and only just in time.

Someone was shouting at the rookies outside.

Fuck. Running out of time.

He laid the corpse back down and quickly but carefully restored all of the fallen tortilla chips. His back creaked as he straightened up. He patted his bulging stomach. Six feet two and two hundred and ten pounds. He needed to lose weight.

Three loud thumps on the front door and a muffled 'Sir, can you come out here right now?' The rookie sounded double-stressed. Behind him was the sound of a woman wailing in Spanish. Mandy rushed out of the bedroom, up the hall and to the front door.

Just inside the apartment, the rookies were struggling to restrain a stout, late-middle-aged Mexican woman. Dressed in black with dyed orange hair, she was shaking, choking back tears and holding up a basket of marigolds, a crucifix and a statue of the Virgin Mary. She must have snuck under the tape before the young cops could grab hold of her. He'd better get rid of her before Frank and the Swan Lakes arrived. Too wired to remember any real Spanish, he handed her a tissue, saying, '*Buenos días, señora,*' and then to the real-estate rookie, 'What's going on?'

'She was the one who found the body earlier today. Name of Josefina.'

The other rookie jumped in: 'She was the victim's nanny and wants to put these flowers and the cross on him right now.'

There wasn't time to think about the implications of nannies and thirty-year-old men. Mandy flipped to the Giraffe's guidance: observe, take notes and be discreet.

'Did this woman call it in to the PD? Did she make a statement to Broadski and Dent?' Mandy smiled at her sympathetically and whispered some Catholic solidarity: '*In nomine Patris . . .*'

The two rookies looked at one another for the answer.

'*Et filii et Spiritus Sancti*,' the woman mumbled, crossed herself, nodded her head and wailed again.

The real-estate rookie put a hand on her arm. 'Yeah, I think she did,' he said.

'Don't you know?' Mandy said, forgetting he was an unemployed PI, not their superior officer. The awkward silence was relieved by the mechanical whir of the elevator. No time to argue.

Mandy took hold of the basket, cross and statue. 'Listen, *señora*, I'm sorry for your loss, but this is a crime scene and you must leave now. You have my word that these will be put by—'

'Pedro,' the woman interrupted.

'Pedro, exactly,' said Mandy. 'Can one of you two men drive this lady home? Do you live far, *señora*?'

The woman moaned, shrugged and shook her head.

Mandy took out the last ten-dollar note in his wallet and handed it to her. 'Take a cab and get yourself home.'

The rookies took her arm and started walking her towards the blue-and-white tape.

The elevator pinged. Assistant Coroner Frank Polanski stepped out, as always carrying his brown leather bag. Frank reminded Mandy of his podgy Latin schoolmaster, with strands of hair swept over his bald head, his grey moustache and warm, toothy smile – more like a favourite uncle than someone who cut up dead bodies for a living. Due to being caught in a fire twenty years earlier, Frank's right ear was shrivelled, the same shape as a walnut, above which was a creepy-looking skin graft. Nevertheless, Mandy was relieved to see him. Frank was a true professional, a safe pair of hands with thirty-five years' serious experience, unlike the two useless rookies. Mandy would explain about the woman later. He raised his hand in greeting to Frank, then quickly walked back into the apartment, leaving the front door slightly ajar for Frank to follow him in.

He pulled the screwed-up plastic bag that contained his forensic suit from his pocket, spread it flat on the carpet next to an empty umbrella stand and set down the Virgin Mary, crucifix and basket of orange flowers. It looked like a roadside shrine. He wiped his nose with the back of his hand and sighed. The ten dollars he just gave to the nanny had better pay off as an investment, because, save for some loose change down the side of the sofa at home, it was the last money he had.

Suddenly he needed to pee. Bloody anxiety medication. He strode back into the victim's en suite and unzipped his flies.

Frank called, 'Mandy, you in there?'

'Come on in, Frank. Won't be a second!' he hollered.

He heard Frank enter, set down his case and close the bedroom door behind him. The sound of urinating seemed to fill the crime scene. Mandy cleared his throat, trying hard to finish.

A few moments later Frank's balding head peered round the bathroom door.

'How come every time I run into you, Mandy, you're taking a piss?'

'I drink two litres of water a day, Frank.'

'You wouldn't know two litres of water if it jumped up and bit you.'

Mandy forced a laugh and shook his penis, willing its flow to finally stop. He clenched his buttocks together and grinned at the mirror above the basin for inspiration. Only then did he notice the pair of pink panties on the backside of a young woman behind the shower curtain. She hadn't said anything during the peeing marathon. Not because she was shy or embarrassed, but because she was dead.

2

4.05 p.m., 9 July

Mandy gritted his teeth and wrenched the shower curtain to one side as if pulling a plaster from his chest. Another dead body. The dangling girl was curvy, dark-haired, with icing-sugar skin. For a few seconds, it felt like a bad joke. Some actress taking part in a *Twin Peaks* spoof.

But it was real. Her head was lolling to one side. Judging from her cheekbones, she was Eastern European. A silver chain with a crucifix was hanging from the back of her neck, partly obscured by her long hair. He moved closer; there was an inscription on the cross. Was his Russian up to it? 'Mama loves you.' Not even the girl's name. He looked down the length of her body. She was wearing a light blue bra that did not match her panties. And she had thick black lines inked on her lower back. What did they signify? Did they match up with the ones on the body lying on the bed next door?

Just then a hand slid onto his shoulder. Frank. He moved past Mandy and took hold of the woman's wrist.

'More dead than that pumice stone, right?' Mandy said.

Frank nodded.

Several loud voices outside meant the Swan Lake Forensics had arrived. Frank leant towards Mandy and said in a half-whisper, 'Just be cool and let everyone get on with their work. You've got a possible case here, so don't blow it by messing with the evidence. Unless there are other bodies, we'll only be an hour, an hour and a half tops. Get yourself a coffee in the kitchen and chill out.'

Mandy wiped the film of sweat from his forehead. He didn't want to be in the apartment with all the Swan Lake people, but there was nothing he could do about that, other than leave, and that would send the wrong message back to the Giraffe.

Within minutes the Swan Lakes had the apartment smelling of medical wipes, bad breath and failing deodorant. Banks of photographic lights were positioned in the hallway, main bedroom, en suite and the other bathroom. The six of them, four men and two women, were busy dusting and dropping fibres and crumbs of food into plastic bags. They were soon taking swabs, noting, measuring and filming each detail of forensic information as if their own lives depended on it.

Frank had been right: the only safe place to stand without getting in the way was the kitchen. White-walled and white-floored, the room was a tropical garden full of exotic palms and plants, with the latest appliances and a swanky coffee machine.

Mandy fixed himself a glass of water from the tap and sat down at the white marble kitchen table underneath a mosquito palm. He took out a pen and notebook, made a heading '*Tortilla Ocean Murders*' and the familiar subheadings '*Who?*', '*How?*', '*When?*', '*Entry*', '*Motive*', '*Robbery*', '*Finance*', '*Romance*' and '*Sex*'. So what if the list might appear biblical or old-fashioned? Most crimes were still committed out of jealousy, revenge or good old greed.

He gulped down a mouthful of water, stared at the list of motives and for the first time in months allowed himself to feel excited about being back in the saddle. And how good did it feel to be wanted, to know that others thought he was really worth something? Having a sense of purpose back again made him choke up. A decent case was worth more than all the Porsches and Range Rovers currently clogging the freeways in LA. Praise to all gods on duty that he would get hired. Hadn't he even given his last ten bucks away?

His cell phone vibrated in his pocket. Damn.

Live cell phones were forbidden on a crime scene. He flicked it open.

It was a text from the pushy blonde who'd run the speed dating at the Viceroy last night. Samantha. Mandy cringed. Ten tables, seven British females, one American, one Russian, one Australian, all twiddling pens and score cards. Six American guys, one British, three Canadian – all losers, including him. 'Girls Just Want to Have Fun' playing in the background. The women – Jane, Trudy, Lulu and 'What Do You Do?' Caroline. Everyone – including the organizer's small dog – with new haircuts except him. '*Were you ever in a rock band?*', '*Did you wear a suit and tie especially for tonight? You didn't?*' The one girl he fancied, Tamara, born and raised in Sherman Oaks, short dark hair, tall, big eyes, foxy – it turned out she worked at the hotel and did escort work on the side. Or was it the other way round?

Whatever. She seemed to like him too. But when he looked at those big eyes, he couldn't stop wondering whether he could have a thing with a girl who did it with other men for money, and then she whispered into his ear that she was being leant on by a pimp. Could he help her? Mandy remembered forcing a sympathetic smile. Who said romance was dead? But he'd given her his card. He needed all the work he could get, just like Tamara.

Frank and some of the CSI people walked past the kitchen door, heading for the big sitting room. He shoved the cell back in his pocket. As the voices trailed away, he read the text. 'Sorry you didn't find your soul mate! Please come again tomorrow. 25% discount for second-timers. Hugs, Samantha.' Mandy put his head in his hands. Speed dating had been an all-time low. Why hadn't the award ceremony for the LAPD been last night at the hotel, instead of this morning? He could have been in the right time, right place for once. He could have seen something, saved someone. Maybe.

He switched off his cell, poured himself another glass of water from the fridge, leant on the draining board and stared through the window at the surfers out on the ocean. The glass of water wasn't hitting the spot. Checking no one from the Swan Lake crew was peering round the door, he pulled a see-through bag of light blue anti-anxiety pills from his pocket, took out two and swallowed them.

He forced himself to focus on the first category in his notebook. '*Who?*' What about the girl? What had she been doing here? A call girl? A cleaner? He looked inside the tall kitchen cupboards nearest the door. Four of them. The first three were dull and full of polishing and cleaning machines, with only one humble broom in sight. The fourth was more interesting.

'Hello?' Mandy said quietly to himself, lifting a blue shirt and a pair of belted Levi's from a hook behind the door. He held the shirt to his face and breathed in an unfamiliar but fresh perfume. So that was what she smelt like when she was alive. He gulped at his trespass. Beside a smart vacuum cleaner, a pair of pink socks and trainers, and a brown handbag. He picked up the bag and nearly put it down without examining it. It felt like poking and prodding something sacred, something that the girl's parents should do first. But a voice said, 'You need the money. You need this job or you might end up sleeping in the Amazon.' He picked up the bag again.

It was a cheap copy of a Donna Karan. Definitely not a local call girl, then. In Santa Monica, *they* could afford the real thing. He opened it. Inside was a big blue bus pass, lipstick, cigarettes, three sets of house keys, a battered iPhone, a pink hairbrush and a leather purse with a loose, stained passport photo of the girl. No cell. And an empty envelope crushed at the bottom of the bag with the crumbs and old chewing gum. It was addressed to Anastasia Yu—, a smudged surname he couldn't decipher, no street or zip code. There were no credit cards, no driving licence and no social security card. Mandy pocketed the photo, dropped the purse into the bag and closed the cupboard door. Broadski and Dent had not only missed the Russian girl's body swinging from the shower; they hadn't found her clothes either. The rush to finish before the Lakers game had made them even more incompetent than usual.

He sat back down at the kitchen table and pictured the girl some hours earlier, getting off the bus, riding the lift to the apartment, changing into work clothes behind the kitchen door and then being murdered. Or could it be a genuine suicide? But why would a young woman, a cleaner, hang herself wearing only her underwear? It didn't smell right. He sat there, still, meditating on her life for a long time, the glare of the ocean filling the window.

When he heard the Swan Lake team packing up their equipment, he finally walked out of the sanctuary of the kitchen. Frank was in the hallway, drying his hands on a white face towel. Grimacing with a weariness that was slightly exaggerated, he began to take off his white bodysuit.

'Here, let me help you with that,' Mandy said.

Frank held up the palm of his hand. 'It's OK – I can do it. The male victim is confirmed as one Pedro García-Márquez.'

'García-Márquez, huh,' Mandy said. 'I knew he was called Pedro.'

Frank looked up enquiringly. Mandy explained about the woman with the basket of marigolds. Frank made no comment, but pointed to the umbrella stand, where the statue, marigolds and crucifix were wrapped in plastic evidence bags. Mandy took a step closer to the balding assistant coroner. He wanted to fess up about finding the photo and the cleaner's clothes, but changed his mind at the very last second. Any information that kept him ahead of Broadski and Dent was worth the risk. He needed to win. So he just said, 'Frank, what happened earlier has never happened to me before.'

The assistant coroner shrugged in bewilderment and stepped closer to Mandy. 'The kid in the shower?'

'Yes, the one with the pink and blue underwear.'

Frank threw the crumpled white suit into the police waste bag and shook his head. 'Stop beating yourself up. It was those two meatballs Broadski and Dent who missed it, not you.'

'Yeah, but I feel bad, Frank.'

'You feel bad because you think that no one's gonna hire you?'

'Maybe.'

'It'll be fine. Try to visualize being hired.'

Mandy almost gagged at the suggestion. He'd been visualizing since he was at drama school. It had been OK for acting but didn't work in real life. Must be something Frank had picked up at AA.

'This is my guess,' Mandy said. 'While someone was despatching poor old Pedro, his cleaner arrives to do her thing and disturbs them. They suffocate her and try to make it look like she was so distraught after killing her employer that she killed herself. So they rope her up to the showerhead and make it look like suicide.'

'I think we only got one murder here, Mandy, but nothing is certain until the 'topsies. How d'you know she wasn't just a miserable two-bit call girl?'

'Hookers usually have matching lingerie, you know,' Mandy said, thinking of Tamara from Sherman Oaks. 'At least, round here they do.'

'OK, maybe you're right, but to me this looks like a suicide or a sex game gone wrong. She stabs him by accident, panics, covers him in chips and then kills herself. Let's see what transpires.'

Frank picked up his leather bag, patted Mandy on the shoulder and walked across the carpet to the open front door.

'I think I'm right, Frank. I can smell it,' Mandy said.

Frank smiled a benevolent, almost patronizing, smile and walked out.

3

5.35 p.m., 9 July

The apartment empty of dead bodies, and the Swan Lakes gone, Mandy wandered down the corridor into the spacious sitting room. A painting of a girl in a late-night diner hung above the open fireplace. Jesus. Mandy peered at it. No doubt about it – it was an Edward Hopper. Jesus Christ. It was an *original* Hopper.

Whoever killed Pedro wasn't an art lover, then. It was worth a fortune. Mandy ran a covetous finger along the picture frame as he fantasized about accepting the Hopper in lieu of fees for solving the murder. Just as he suspected, no alarm sensors. It would've been an easy snatch. So this killing was personal.

Moving on, he opened a silver cigar box. CDs by Judy Garland, Antônio Carlos Jobim and the Pet Shop Boys. Not a Havana in sight. Based on that music, Pedro's sexual preference was probably not for girls. So the Russian had been, as he'd thought, just the cleaner. Frank was wrong about the suicide. There *were* two victims here.

He moved across to the fine art deco desk at the far end of the room. An iMac, a laptop and an iPhone, all tagged and stuffed inside plastic evidence bags, were standing on the walnut-veneered desk, waiting to be collected by Broadski and Dent after the game.

Shit. Mandy pulled the polythene tight round the cell, fingering the keys to see if he could figure out the last numbers dialled and received. It was turned off. On the desk, there was a white telephone, an old-fashioned Bakelite landline, and next to it, a photo of a smiling guy on a beach, his arms around a buxom, dark-haired girl dressed in a red bikini. Had Pedro batted for both sides?

He read out the inscription written round a hand-drawn heart: '*Lucy Lack loves Pedro García-Márquez in London – Santa Monica – Sayulita – Wherever!*'

The handwriting was sloping and assured. And the man who had been lying dead beneath the tortillas was clearly the same guy in the picture.

Pedro García-Márquez. He looked a whole lot happier on the beach than he did on the bed.

The Bakelite phone rang. The ring was loud – sacrilegious in the silent apartment. It was odd to realize whoever was ringing didn't know Pedro was sleeping the big sleep and would never reply. Mandy listened as the answering machine clicked.

'This is Pedro. Leave a message after the beep . . . Thanks.'

The dead man spoke in a firm, upper-class, no-nonsense voice with a hint of friendliness.

'It's Lucy! Pick up! Pick up! Why's your cell switched off? Pedro? British Airways 066 . . . If you're late, I'm going to kill you . . . I've had the journey from hell. A guy on the plane took an overdose.' The voice was confident, sexy, English and female. 'Me and an amazing priest – wait till you see him, gorgeous – saved his life and nearly drowned in vomit as a thank you . . .'

Lucy? *Lucy loves Pedro*? Lucy Lack? Mandy picked up the photograph. She was beautiful, and smiling. He smiled back at the photograph. There didn't seem to be anything lacking about her. And soon, after she'd picked up her luggage, she'd be waiting at LAX for a guy who was never going to arrive.

Checking the time on his watch, he headed back down the corridor and made himself walk into Pedro's bedroom. There was no body, no sheet, just an empty mattress, like in a hospital ward when someone has died. In the en suite, the girl in the shower had gone too. Suddenly the smell of death and the Swan Lakes' antiseptic wipes became overwhelming. He looked at the toilet bowl and felt like throwing up. He needed to get out. If he went now, he could make it in time . . .

'Thanks for your help, men,' he said, walking past the two young cops still waiting outside the front door.

Both rookies grinned and nodded their heads.

Mandy pulled off the latex gloves and switched his cell back on as the elevator reached the ground. The doors pinged open to reveal a large, ginger-haired concierge sitting behind his desk, scratching his arse.

'Are these working?' Mandy asked, waving a hand towards the security cameras placed around the lobby.

The concierge shrugged like he couldn't give a damn. Nice.

'Nope,' he said, offering him a waste-paper basket for the latex gloves with the same flabby paw he'd been using to scratch his arse. The guy was Irish-American.

'You are kidding, right?' Mandy said.

The guy shook his head.

'Those damn things look like they're on, but when you play the tape, there's nothing there. We've told them a hundred times now.'

'Them?'

'Lexington Property Group.'

'Could you give me their number or get them on the phone for me?'

'Happy to help,' the guy said sarcastically, slowly pulling out a thick sheaf of paper from an open desk drawer. Licking his finger with his tongue, he began turning the pages. 'Got the number somewhere. Can you hang on?'

'Don't you have it to hand? Isn't it on a sign somewhere?' Mandy said, surprised that such a well-heeled apartment building had such a dense oaf as its concierge. The man must be a temporary, summer-holiday replacement. The Irish guy suddenly leant his head back to sneeze, then carried on looking.

Mandy looked at his watch and took out a business card from his wallet. 'I don't have much time. Mind telling me your name?'

The man sighed, stopped sifting the papers, looked up. 'I can't seem to find the number, but it must be somewhere in the office.' Taking the card and examining it, he added, 'Oh, and everyone calls me Quinn.'

'Well, Mr Quinn, perhaps you could phone me with your employer's details? And also let me know exactly where you were in the last twenty-four hours? Yes?'

'No problem at all,' Quinn said, slotting the business card inside his shirt pocket, then added, 'But you're not actually a police officer, are you?'

Mandy shook his head as his cell started buzzing. Why was the guy being such an unhelpful jerk? He didn't appear to be shedding any tears or be remotely concerned that a resident had been found dead less than five hours ago. Remember: observe, take notes and be discreet. Quinn sloped off to a side office, where a TV was showing grim footage of the scene at the Viceroy Hotel.

Mandy flicked open the cell. He had received a text offering him a mortgage five times his salary. He squirmed, snapped the cell shut and sped out through the entrance. He'd conclude his enquiries with the ignorant, smart-arse concierge later. Maybe the time had come to do what Frank suggested and act as if he had already been hired.

4

6.50 p.m., 9 July

There must have been thirty drivers holding up signs outside the arrivals gate at LAX. Mandy hoped to God that Lucy Lack would spot his handwritten '*Lucy Lack*' placard. He wasn't sure whether to smile, look serious or morose, so he experimented with all three. For a moment it felt worse than being at an audition. And the last one of those had been two years ago. What on earth was he doing here? And why didn't he know how to act? A man was dead, for Christ's sake.

He was here, he told himself, because Fabienne had said he might get hired. Even the Giraffe might be willing to let bygones be bygones. And though it wasn't his job to tell Lucy Lack the bad news about Pedro, he wanted to observe her reaction.

That was a good enough excuse. And he could see how well she matched up to the photograph.

A dishevelled man, five feet eleven, in a stained corduroy jacket and a white dog collar strode confidently through the automatic door with a pale, semi-Oriental-looking female in her mid- to late twenties. To say Lucy Lack looked and sounded a lot better than any of last night's speed daters was an understatement. She didn't look exactly like the smiling, happy girl of the photograph, but close enough.

'Lucy Lack? Lucy Lack?' He flapped his home-made sign.

The girl stopped wheeling her trolley and looked everywhere but at him. The priest in the filthy jacket pointed out Mandy's sign and headed over. He had the same build as a professional tennis player, and the swept-back blond hair and blue eyes to go with it.

Up close, though, the priest smelt like he was wearing a litre of disinfectant. Mandy took an involuntary step backwards.

The guy gave an apologetic smile and looked Mandy straight in the eye.

'We've had rather a tricky flight, I'm afraid. The fellow sitting next to me took an overdose and it fell to us to help with the stomach pump.'

Mandy swallowed, shook hands and nodded.

The upmarket priest gestured to his companion. 'This is Lucy Lack, and I'm Father Tony.'

Up close and in the flesh, Lucy Lack was even prettier than in her photograph. Cleopatra with heavenly breasts and huge sunglasses perched on her head. She was tallish, elegant and mysterious, with piercing green eyes and a soft, vulnerable mouth.

'Are you here on behalf of Pedro?' she said.

Mandy swallowed again, felt for the see-through bag in his pocket, scratched his earlobe. None of it helped.

'Yes and no,' he began. 'Well, not exactly. I'm afraid I've got some bad news . . .'

5

7.20 p.m., 9 July

Mandy stuffed a mint into his mouth and tightened his grip on the steering wheel. Breaking the news of a loved one's death is never easy, but he'd never seen someone's face crumple in quite the way Lucy Lack's had. He felt bad. Expensive cars sped by either side of him.

'Fuck off,' he muttered to a passing Escalade.

In the rear-view mirror, he studied the girl, mascara smudged, staring through the window, right fist held up to her mouth like it'd keep all the pain out. Or in. Father Tony stroked his throat, a map of LA spread out on his lap, his other hand gripping Lucy's free hand tight. She had insisted the priest travel with her in the car, which Mandy thought was odd. Hadn't they only just met on the plane? Pastoral counselling in England had obviously improved, Mandy thought, as he counted the roadside billboards promoting summer films in which he could have had a minor role if his agent hadn't been so idle. Acting in anything was in his past now.

Another mile down the freeway, a rainbow appeared spanning the whole eight lanes. Mandy, smelling Lucy's perfume coming towards him, turned his head and saw her resting her chin on her hands on top of the passenger seat.

'Thank you for coming to tell me what happened to Pedro,' she said.

'It was the least I could do.'

'And don't worry about the cost of the hotel – if I have to be on my own, I want to stay somewhere special. Shutters will be fine.'

Mandy wondered if she was loaded or just bluffing. A basic suite at Shutters was $500 a night.

'Well, a lot of people would not be handling this as well as you are. You're being very brave.'

She smiled a sad smile and then mouthed a silent 'thanks'.

Was he a sucker, or was she really just bewitching?

Her perfumed hand touched his shoulder. 'Mind if I smoke? It would really help.'

Mandy never allowed anyone to smoke in the Amazon, except Terry when they'd been partners, and then only when they'd been on a stakeout and he couldn't kick Terry out of the car.

He nodded. 'Go ahead – I'll open a window.'

'Do you smoke?'

'I used to,' he said, with conviction. 'I know what it's like when you're desperate.'

He opened the back of the sunroof at an angle.

'Mind if I have one?' asked Father Tony, pulling a Marlboro from a soft pack. 'The air hostess gave me these during the crisis. I don't normally . . .'

'Father Tony, you know there's no smoking any more in St Monica's. They made the entire seminary no smoking.'

He checked the rear-view to see if that information rocked the priest's boat a little. It did not. Father Tony merely smiled, lit Lucy's cigarette and his own, and then sucked down a lungful.

A few seconds later he said, 'Mandy, can I ask you something?'

Mandy wiped a smear off the windscreen and looked in the rear-view at the priest. 'No harm in asking.'

The priest folded his map into his pocket, stubbed out his cigarette and leant forward. 'Are you British, by any chance?'

Mandy laughed. He knew that he could sound American at times, especially when it suited his purposes. But overall he had tried hard to retain his English accent, partly because it was still appreciated in America, good for business and getting out of trouble, and partly because it reminded him of who he really was. Inevitably, working with the cops and speaking the colloquial lingo had changed the way he spoke, but he still liked to be thought of as an Englishman abroad.

'You're spot on, Father Tony. Born and raised in Oxford. I've been here about fifteen years.'

'I had a feeling you might be English. So how do you come to be here, if I may ask?'

Father Tony wasn't suffering from an overdose of British reserve; should he tell the priest the whole truth or just some of it? Mandy shrugged and went for the midway point.

'I was an actor in London and decided to seek fame and fortune in Hollywood. Short version – it didn't quite go according to plan. I ended up researching a role in the TV show *NYPD* so joined the Santa Monica Police Department as a trainee. Never got the part, but I *was* fast-tracked into being a junior detective. I stayed in the force a while and then set up on my own as

Endeavor Investigations.' Mandy handed Father Tony a business card over his shoulder. 'You never know when you might need it.'

'My goodness, you've had quite a life, haven't you?'

'So far, not too bad.'

'Would I have seen you in anything on TV or in a film?'

'Doubtful.'

'Do you miss the acting?'

'No, not really. Not after all this time,' said Mandy.

Of course he bloody missed it.

'How did you guess I was English?'

'The Trebor mints.'

'Was that what gave me away?' Mandy said, impressed by the guy's deduction.

The priest was smiling, but Lucy Lack was staring morosely at the traffic, completely detached.

'Not just the mints. Your accent and the fact your name doesn't exactly match your physique.'

Mandy grunted to himself. The priest was the type to press for an explanation about his name. It was better to head the guy off at the pass. He turned round and said, 'My grandfather was Admiral Charles *Mundy*. I took his name because I respected him. He'd been a regular sailor, got to the top and never worried about anything, including what people thought of his name. He could make me laugh, sometimes without saying or doing anything. Do you have a problem with that?'

Father Tony held his hands up in the air as if someone had just pointed a gun at him. 'Goodness, not at all. I took the name Anthony when I became a priest. But feel free to call me Tony.'

Mandy briefly held up his hand in acknowledgement, annoyed for telling the priest too much about himself. How LA. He scratched his head to search for a riposte of some sort.

'I understand St Anthony or St *Tony* is the one people pray to when they have lost something?'

Father Tony stole a sideways glance at Lucy and nodded.

A silence ensued in which Mandy wondered what crime or sin the priest had committed to be sent over to work in Santa Monica.

The last sign for the freeway to Santa Monica reared up on the left. Mandy steered the car towards the exit road for the 10. The traffic had slowed right down to a crawl across four lanes. He flicked on the stereo. 'Teenage Wedding' belted out.

'Remember *Pulp Fiction*?' Mandy called out.

Father Tony nodded.

Lucy mimed every word of the song, her eyes shut. When the track was nearly at the end, she leant into Father Tony, sobbing. Mandy turned the music down, bit into another mint and clenched the wheel harder.

'This was our song!' Lucy blurted. 'The one Pedro and I danced to!'

Father Tony nodded and put his arm around her. Mandy crunched down on the mint. Lucy twisted out of Father Tony's arms and brought her fist down hard on the open window edge.

'Fuck! Fuck! Fuck!'

Tony squeezed her hand.

'I'm sorry, but did I get it wrong about you and Pedro?' Father Tony asked, a little hesitantly.

Mandy was glad that it was the priest who brought up the subject. He stole a glimpse at him in the rear-view, as if to register his agreement. He couldn't work out whether Lucy and Pedro had been lovers, friends or something in between.

Lucy let out a huge sigh and wiped her nose with the back of her hand. Mandy clocked her stylish ring and gold bangles.

'No, of course you didn't. He was gay. But that doesn't stop you getting married to someone, does it?'

It did tend to in Mandy's world. He switched off the radio. Father Tony lit another two cigarettes and handed one to Lucy.

'Go on,' he said. 'I'm listening.'

She dragged hard on the cigarette and blew out a long plume of smoke.

'Well, the story is a joke.' She turned to the open window.

'Why?' Father Tony said.

'A joke because if we had got married, it would've solved a whole heap of problems. Pedro is part of the García-Márquez family, one of the richest in Mexico. They have the monopoly on mobile phones and growing and selling avocadoes, as well as some serious real estate. Pedro was the eldest of four children. The family would never acknowledge in public he was gay. His mother and father didn't even say it in private. The father is tough, and very religious.'

'What about the mother?'

Lucy snorted. 'A polo-loving nightmare who's never lifted a finger in her life.'

'What about Pedro marrying you? Would she have been pleased?' Mandy asked over his shoulder.

'I met her a few times with Pedro and she'd always say we made such a pretty pair, but she used to tell Pedro privately that I was just good-looking trailer trash, not classy enough for him.'

Mandy slowed the Amazon right down. All four lanes of traffic ahead were at a virtual standstill. There must have been an accident. Maybe it was the Escalade. Mandy wound the window down and craned his neck. Three cop cars from the LA County Sheriff sped past in the emergency lane. It was a block where the 10 became Pacific Coast Highway – right where you could turn off for Pico . . . and Shutters.

'What the hell is going on? It wasn't like this last time,' Lucy said.

Mandy turned his head back towards Lucy and the priest.

'While you were on the plane this morning, two gunmen assassinated our deputy attorney general and a much-loved sergeant in the LAPD.'

'Why?'

'No one knows. They didn't leave a note.'

'How awful.'

'Never kill a cop in America – anyone else but not a cop. They've got every cop in the county working on this now.'

Lucy shook her head. 'You mean no one is interested in going after Pedro's killer?'

'No, I did not mean that. I'm just saying cops here look after their own.'

'Like most people,' Father Tony said.

There was a brief silence, punctuated by the siren coming from one of the cop cars in the early evening light.

Lucy gripped hold of the top of the passenger seat and pulled herself forward towards Mandy. 'I can't stop thinking . . . I mean . . . it's going to be some funeral . . . My God, Pedro's funeral! He hasn't been dead more than a few hours. What am I saying?'

'Grief comes and goes in waves,' Father Tony said.

She nodded.

'I wonder if everyone even knows he's dead.'

'The Police Department will have contacted his parents.'

'The family is so paranoid about security; they never do anything important by email or phone. Any sensitive information for Pedro is sent in the post to Josefina, their old nanny, who lives round the corner. Poor thing probably won't know what's happened until she gets a letter.'

Mandy said nothing but pictured the basket of marigolds shrink-wrapped in Swan Lake plastic. He made a large mental note to pay Josefina a visit the moment he was hired.

They drove on in silence. Lucy didn't go on with her story about her and Pedro getting married, even though Mandy prodded her for it a couple of times. Father Tony had finally shot him such a censorious look that he'd shut up and just drove. Eventually the Amazon swept into the grand entrance of Shutters and came to a halt.

Mandy gave a wave to the three valets preparing to open the car doors.

'Don't bother to garage it. I'm only here for a short while.'

'Sure thing – you got it, Mr Mandy.'

It felt good to be recognized as something other than a cab driver.

Father Tony and Lucy stood by the fireplace of the massive reception room. There was an East Coast, old-money, country-house feel to the hotel – perfect for a murder mystery to unfold. Numerous sofas, leather armchairs and occasional tables were dotted about the massive room in front of the long colonial windows leading out onto the beach. It was the place for the rich and famous to meet for pre-dinner drinks or nightcaps, or the not so rich but wannabe famous.

Mandy walked through from the lobby.

'May I introduce Pierre, the manager of Shutters,' he said. 'Father Tony is a top priest from England.'

Father Tony muttered, 'Hardly a top priest,' but the French manager was already ignoring him, saying, 'Ms Lack, we have prepared one of our best suites and will try to make your stay as comfortable as possible. If there is anything you need, day or night, contact me on my pager.'

The manager handed Lucy a card. She looked about to reply when he put his finger to his lips and added, 'Mandy suggested you may like to see a doctor in order to help you sleep?' He clasped his hands together in anticipation.

'I don't trust doctors, but I would like an acupuncturist if you can find one round here.' Pausing for breath, she continued, 'Also, I cannot stand pornography. Can you put a TV in my room without those channels?'

The manager blinked several times, stood up and bowed. 'I will arrange for what you have asked, Ms Lack, and thank you for staying at Shutters.'

Mandy smiled as the manager walked away. Nothing was too much trouble for his new, pretty guest.

'Smarmy French git,' he mumbled.

Lucy lifted her sunglasses and shot him a quizzical stare.

He handed her a card. 'This has my all my numbers – even the one marked with a dragon, which I reserve for my mother in London. Call me anytime.' Standing up and pushing back his hair, he asked, 'Would you like one of us to see you to your room?'

Lucy took off her sunglasses with a weary flourish. 'I can find my own way up, thank you.'

Mandy insisted on escorting her to the elevator; her luggage had already been taken up. As the doors opened, she dropped her arrivals card – she must have been clutching it the whole time. Mandy crouched down, retrieved it, stood up and handed it to her. She opened her mouth to say something, then changed her mind and put her lips together into a pout. The doors closed.

6

Mandy stopped the Amazon at 7th and Californian Avenue, close to St Monica's seminary, and offered his guest a Trebor.

Father Tony swivelled his athletic frame in the passenger seat and took one. They sat in silence for few seconds until a pink Chevy Impala drove up beside them with a sound system inside playing so loudly its bodywork was shaking. A tinted window on the driver's side opened. Vintage rap music like the Beastie Boys blasted out. The volume dropped.

Mandy turned to Father Tony. 'Nothing to worry about. This car's too old for a jacking.'

'Having worked in Belfast and Moss Side, not many things faze me.'

'Have you known Lucy for a long time?'

Father Tony stretched his arms behind his head and said, 'It certainly feels like it!'

'Uh-huh,' said Mandy. He'd wondered if the two of them had met before, given how Lucy insisted he travel with them.

'But no – we met on the plane when she volunteered her medical services.'

'Is she a doctor?'

Father Tony cleared his throat. 'Probably best if I let her tell you about her medical skills, I think.'

'Tell me what happened.'

Father Tony let out a tired-sounding laugh. The jet lag was kicking in.

'These things are always funny in retrospect, I suppose. A rather unpleasant man called Dominic Young sat next to me drinking a lot and telling me how much he hated religion. Said he was a retired musician. He had a charming satanic ring on his index finger. Not ideal company for a priest, or anybody else on a long-haul flight. I decided to watch the film rather than listen to him blather on. Mistakenly, during the next half-hour I thought he was cramming peanuts into his mouth . . .'

'When they turned out to be Diazepam?'

'How did you know? Did Lucy mention it?'

Mandy recalled the answerphone message in Pedro's apartment. 'A guess, that's all. So?'

'He'd taken forty tablets and was unconscious. I got the air hostess to ask the pilot to put out a call for help. Next thing, this glamorous young woman walks down the aisle, telling me she's a doctor.'

'And?'

'Well, let's just say despite her rather unusual methods, we managed to get him to be sick and saved his life. Lucy found a letter from his ex-girlfriend, which she read, something like he should never return to LA. He probably read it on the plane, thought about it and decided to kill himself, I don't know. Probably more to it, but a waste of a good plane ticket, really.'

'Do you remember the girlfriend's name?'

'Yes, it was Susan Green.'

'Good memory. You're in the wrong job,' Mandy said, scrawling the girl-friend's name in his notebook.

Father Tony smiled. 'Quite the right job, thank you.'

Mandy released the brake and drove another 200 yards. Father Tony got out of the car and took his bag out of the trunk without speaking.

Mandy called out, 'Please call me if you need any help or hear anything that might help the investigation.'

The priest stood by the double front door of the seminary, partially lit by the headlights of the Amazon.

'I'll know not to call the dragon's number . . .'

Father Tony from England didn't miss a trick. Mandy smiled and headed home.

7

9.15 p.m., 9 July

The Amazon coasted to a halt by the phoney garage door of Mandy's rent-controlled house. The two-storey duplex was modest compared to the other six-bedroom, three-garage houses in the Palisades. He'd been gifted it as a reward for saving a horse that belonged to an elderly actress from a forest fire in Topanga. An address on Castellammare Drive with ocean views was a good way of saying, 'Get stuffed,' to his doubters and detractors. You had to be a serious someone to live in the Pacific Palisades, let alone the high six-figure salary needed to pay the mortgage and gardener.

Despite the fact that his lease was due to expire in three months' time, it suited Mandy perfectly. The only downside was the young tenant he'd chosen to sublet the one-bedroom apartment downstairs. Donna was a cute, out-of-work make-up artist whom he had met in Narcotics Anonymous. He'd been checking up on behalf of some unhappy client as to whether her slippery husband had been attending NA or not. Mandy had spotted a tearful Donna during the meeting and offered to take her for a coffee afterwards. It turned out she was broke and hungry, struggling to get clean, being hit on by unsavoury freaks and sleeping on friends' floors. Mandy offered her the room downstairs for eight weeks, no charge, saying he believed she'd soon get back on her feet if she had somewhere decent to live. Then she could get a job and pay him a normal rent. That was thirteen months ago. Yes, Donna cleaned up, got a job and paid him a few months' rent, but then she was fired and went back on the candy. He wanted her to leave, but it was complicated.

Once inside, he pulled off his jacket and tie, dumped his notebook on the sofa, found a can of beer in the fridge, ripped it open, picked up the phone and flicked on the TV. The lead news story on Fox and CNN was the Viceroy assassinations. Two guys wearing crash helmets rushed from the hotel kitchens down through a staff-only corridor into the award ceremony, riddled the two

28

award recipients with bullets and ran out to a waiting motorbike. Was it terrorists? *Not everyone committing murder is a terrorist, you twats.* Cut to grey-haired wife of Sergeant Powell – only two weeks before he took retirement, she said. Between sobs.

Mandy looked away and dialled his answerphone: one missed call and seven messages. As they played, he flicked his remote for the main porn channels, telling himself it was just to check if Lucy Lack was among any of the earnest-looking actresses.

He recognized the number from the missed call: his mother in England and, as he'd expected, a slightly drunk Terry from a hotel in Vegas.

'Hey, fuckhead. You jerking off in front of the TV? I just want you to know that I knew Sergeant Powell, and he was a real dick. Not surprised someone took a shot at him – he had a big enough head. Shame about the deputy attorney general guy – he had balls. Have you found any work yet? Call me tomorrow, asshole.'

Mandy shook his head, took a swig of beer and laughed. Only Terry could be that funny, rude and unflinching with the truth. Next up Tassos, the cool Greek at his Colorado Avenue garage, rambling on about unpaid bills for work on the Amazon. The next two were terse – from the bank and then Fabienne, telling him, 'He wants you in his office at nine thirty in the morning, on the dot. Suggest you wear a clean shirt.'

Mandy took a longer slug of beer, scrawled, '*Flowers Fabi*,' on his wrist and ground his teeth as he imagined sitting opposite the Giraffe for the first time in four years. He clicked on the next message. Boring old Frank.

'Hey. Want to be my guest and come by the slab tomorrow for the autopsy of Pedro García-Márquez – about nine thirty?'

Mandy swilled beer round his mouth and swallowed. He hated autopsies and now had the perfect excuse not to swing by the mortuary until about ten forty-five, by which time Frank would be finished.

Donna was the last message. She sounded drunk, horny and belligerent.

'Hey. I wanna talk to you tonight. No, really I do. I'm not drunk or anything, just think it would be nice if we shared some time together.'

Mandy exhaled a long sigh and let another incoming call go straight to voicemail. It was probably Donna again, anyway, wanting him to collect her from some shitty bar on the beach. He padded back to the kitchen and took another beer from the fridge.

No way was he going to get involved in any shenanigans in lieu of rent with Donna that night. Imagining their confrontation, he shouted angrily, 'I just want to tell her to fuck off and leave. Here's a week's notice – now please find somewhere else to live and sod off.'

Just then Mandy heard the cat flap open and close in the back door. He sat down on the sofa and was about to kick off his shoes when he was aware he was no longer alone. He sniffed the scent of Donna. She'd sneaked through the unlocked kitchen door.

Without looking up, he said, 'Can I help you?'

'Sod off? Were you rehearsing your lines there to tell me to quit your shitty den downstairs?' Donna replied without missing a beat.

Mandy shook his head in despair and looked up.

Twenty-five-year-old Donna was perched on the edge of his favourite arm-chair, legs crossed at the knee, wearing a short T-shirt and holding a large, half-empty glass of wine. She had a fake-diamond stud in her tummy button and rings on both thumbs. Her long blonde hair fell over the pointed outline of her breasts, and her make-up was, as usual, immaculate. All five foot three of her smelt of recently used sheets, marijuana and peeled oranges.

'Thanks for letting yourself in, Donna. I couldn't be bothered to open the door.'

Mandy was pleased with himself for not being conciliatory. He was sick of pandering to her whims, the *acting out*, contrariness and hysteria.

But Donna wasn't listening.

'Oh my God, how gross can you get? You're watching people fucking!'

Mandy leant towards the screen, trying to disguise his embarrassment. 'Is that what they're doing?'

Donna flicked the ends of her hair back and forth, and then bent forward, holding out the palms of her hands.

'So?' she asked.

'So what?'

'Is "sod off" your pathetic way of telling me to get out?'

'Donna?'

'"Donna?"' Donna mimicked back, crossing and uncrossing her legs.

Mandy looked away and laughed. He was tired. The day's events were running through his mind far more than the tenant in the T-shirt gulping down wine.

'What's going through your mind, Mandy Pandy?' said Donna, swaying her head from side to side. 'Trying to decide if you want to fuck me or pretend you are – now, what did you call it? – oh yes, only fucking for the right reasons?'

Mandy wearily swung his right leg over the other. 'Donna, why don't you take your glass of wine back downstairs and go and do some more drugs until you fall asleep, then tomorrow morning apologize like you always do?'

Donna stood up and lurched forward as if to spit at him. 'Why don't you fuck off, curl up and die, you weasel? No wonder your wife left you, you cripple! You couldn't get an emotional hard-on if you tried, let alone anything else. And I don't buy your medication shit either, buster.'

Mandy drained the last drop of beer and crumpled the can in his hand. 'Donna, you're beginning to annoy me.'

'Oh!' Donna hollered sarcastically. 'I'm so scared! And you've got a gun on you and you could use it and say it was self-defence and all your stupid friends like Terry and Frank would back you up. Let me see now.' Donna pushed a finger into the cleft of her chin and made a chipmunk face with her teeth. 'Oh yes, how would I feel if my wife of two years was screwing our dentist? I mean, you can't have been much cop in bed if she had to send out for a takeout.'

Mandy thought back to the Donna he'd bought a coffee for after the NA meeting off Montana and 14th close to the Aero Cinema. How she'd bit her fingernail like a kid when he'd offered her the choice of a blueberry or a chocolate muffin. What a sweet, pretty, fucked-up, far-from-home kind of girl she once was.

He began reciting the names of the Major League baseball pitchers to stop himself from boiling over and smacking her backside with a yellow scuba flipper that had somehow found itself wedged under the coffee table.

It wasn't that he couldn't make himself find Donna attractive – clearly she was. But her return to her daily cocktail of cocaine, vodka, marijuana, Xanax and Prozac had made her behaviour so toxic he wasn't sure if she would ever get back to normal. He'd taken enough risks in letting her live downstairs. That was over a year ago, and her behaviour was becoming ever more unpredictable and dangerous. Business was bad enough without her adding a final nail in his financial coffin. He needed her out.

Donna was in full venomous flow, like she'd been saving it up for years.

'You're a joke, Mandy. Can't think why I ever let you stick your wiener in me.'

Mandy flicked through the channels on his remote till he found the highlights of the Lakers game. He turned the volume up as high as it would go. The Lakers were beating the Celtics by 107 to 91. They were beating the crap out of them. 'I said you were a joke and can't imagine why I ever, ever, ever let you stick your wiener—' Donna said.

Mandy stood up, holding up the flipper, no longer smiling. 'Donna? Shut the fuck up.'

'Make me.'

The saucepan of milk inside Mandy's head boiled over.

8

9.30 a.m., 10 July

'Take a seat,' said Fabienne, pointing to a leather sofa. 'You want coffee? He won't be long.'

'Coffee would be good – strong, white with one sugar,' Mandy said.

He couldn't stop yawning. Last night Donna had passed out as he was about to flay her backside with the flipper. He'd had to carry her downstairs and wait to check she was OK. Then he'd been too angry to sleep. She'd riled him up with her jibes about his marriage, leading to a familiar internal rant that Mandy had with himself. His ex-wife had confessed she had been seeing their dentist, but only admitted to this after the divorce had been granted by the judge. Mandy had just about got over the aspect of being cuckolded. It justified why they were getting a divorce and been for the best all round. In truth, he had married her largely because he needed some attractive stability, care and attention when he was working hard in the cops. She'd seen him as a good catch – tall, dark and handsome, with an English accent, someone who seemed so 'tough yet vulnerable'. He had become increasingly busy working alongside Terry and the cops, while she, being an underemployed model, had too much time on her hands. Time to go and have her teeth redone by her old high-school sweetheart. What really galled him was the fact that his ex was entitled to take all of the $95,000 proceeds from the sale of their apartment and that he had never played away from home, not even wanted anyone else during their two-year marriage.

And now he was too tired to meet the Giraffe. He sank into the sofa, aware that Fabienne was looking nicer than usual. Silver blonde, petite, cherry lips, pencil skirt and tight shirt.

In need of a distraction, he picked up the *LA Times* and the *Santa Monica Daily News* and scanned the front pages. The local rag had a collage of the smiling Powell family, the loved ones of the cop shot dead the day before. The

32

LA Times had a tribute to Deputy Attorney General Griswold and his crusade against the 'Mafia' of global crime, plus a photo mock-up of the two escaped gunmen, who looked way younger than Mandy had imagined.

Fabienne set down a coffee on a small glass table beside him, brushing her fingers against the back of his hand. 'One of our off-duty guys shot and wounded one of the gunmen as they escaped from the Viceroy,' she said. 'The *Times* got the photofits from his description, but no one's to know he took a bullet.'

'Did the shootings happen in the ballroom or outside at the back? Was anything picked up on CCTV?'

'I don't know, and even if I did, I couldn't tell you. Things are a little fraught round here. Anyway, let's change the subject – I feel confident something might happen with the case about the body on Ocean Avenue. Do you?'

Mandy nodded. Fabienne smiled and returned to her desk.

It was over four years since he'd been here. And it was one of the things about being a cop he did not miss at all. It was a very odd space, the lair of a deeply paranoid but wily chief of police, Clarence Spider, aka the Giraffe.

The office was huge – full of TV monitors showing black-and-white pictures of the station's open-plan detectives' room, front and back entrance, and the charge desk. The monitors flickered on and off.

Mandy took a sip of coffee; Fabienne sat back on her high-backed swivel chair and began to type on a PC the size of Mount Everest. Next to it was a framed photograph of a golden retriever. A tall but neat pile of manila-coloured files stood against one wall. An empty vase had fallen sideways beside them.

He folded the papers in two and ran the background on the Giraffe inside his head.

Clarence Spider was nearly seven foot tall. He'd been called 'the Giraffe' since he had developed vitiligo aged sixteen. One of the things Mandy learnt from Dr Bates, his shrink, was that though he admired the Giraffe, it was not obligatory to like him. This was lucky, because Mandy didn't like or trust him at all.

The Giraffe had stopped being interested in people after his wife was murdered by a crazy homeless person on the beach. That had been six years ago. Since the murder, the Giraffe never used email – for no real reason, he had taken against the Internet, didn't trust it and left that to Fabienne – and did his hiring and firing by telephone. All he wanted was to get through to the end of the year, become the longest-serving black commissioner in the history of the United States, then get the hell out with a big fat pension.

Not many people knew these things, but Mandy did, thanks to an evening with Fabienne six years earlier. She'd attracted the hell out of him that week – she still did, up to a point. So he'd asked her out and discovered, almost to his shame, she was a frighteningly cheap drunk – one who would tell more about her cold-hearted boss than she ought. So although the Giraffe knew everything Mandy had done wrong in his relatively short career, Mandy knew virtually everything in the Giraffe's long service too. Mandy'd never told anyone about that evening with Fabienne, or used the info, except once: to confirm with ex-partner, Terry, some necessary details, just to maintain the status quo between them all. And still Mandy had lost his job. But that was another story.

A buzzing on Fabienne's telephone jerked him back to the present. He watched her pick up the phone, nod and turn away from him.

'OK, I got it . . . OK . . . What?'

She was obviously talking to the Giraffe about something confidential.

She put down the phone, touched the side of her silver hair and said, 'You can go in now. I'll bring your coffee.'

Mandy stood up and straightened his tie. If he was lucky, the meeting wouldn't last long enough to drink a whole cup.

He walked over to the far side of the floor and through the half-open door. Inside the inner sanctum, the Giraffe – dressed in his usual beige suit – stood behind his teak desk with his back to Mandy, staring down at something across the street.

'Good morning,' Mandy said. 'I got your message yesterday.'

'Take a seat, young man.' The Giraffe enjoyed sounding like a grandee.

Mandy sat down on an uncomfortable chair by the desk. The Giraffe didn't move.

'Right, listen up. Mr Eduardo García-Márquez, the deceased's father, wants a private investigator. He's got issues' – the Giraffe spat out the word 'issues' – 'with local police detectives, which I am not even going to discuss. He thinks a PI is going to do a better job than us, so he's interviewing right now.' The Giraffe turned round at this point and laughed for few seconds like a weird version of Barry White.

Leaning his large hands on the desk, he said, 'And as we're overwhelmed with the shit going down at the Viceroy right now, and he's well connected, we're going to play ball. We'll treat it as a mysterious death, hold the funeral, pending a special toxicologist's report – a media blackout. What that means, Mandy, is that you've got seven days to come up with some answers. And you are going to keep the whole thing tighter than your asshole – more confidential than your medical reports. And if you get nowhere in the timeframe, you gonna be seeing more of those two detectives you're so fond of disrespecting. So go make your condolences and tell him you're going to find the sonovabitch who killed his son.'

Mandy nodded like he'd just been told by a solicitor in England that his mother was dead but had left him a million pounds. His brain was trying to compute all the possible outcomes, bearing in mind the state of the avocado market, the incompetence of the two detectives and that he might have a serious job, ergo proper money.

He gripped hold of the Giraffe's desk in unconscious mimicry and said, 'Is this for real? Straight up?'

'Mandy,' the Giraffe spat back, 'I'd press the gratitude button that your name came up in the mix. This case could restore your reputation; prove you've got what it takes. Prove you can take the pressure.'

Mandy bit his lip.

The Giraffe was known for his ability to taunt people into submission, get them to say something out of line. It was what had made him a successful cop in the first place.

'I'm in good shape, mentally and physically, sir. I'm ready. Thank you for the recommendation.'

He gave his most sarcastic grin. 'I didn't recommend you, Mandy. Believe me. Someone else did.'

There was a silence. Then the Giraffe grunted as he sat down in the high-backed leather chair behind his desk. He picked up the remote for the nearby TV and pumped the volume on the remote for CBS LA local news. A blast of commentary came through the television as footage showed people screaming in the aftermath of the Viceroy shootings. The Giraffe clicked off the remote and made a 'what the hell did they have to go and do that for?' face.

'García-Márquez will meet you at his house at number 1 Ocean Avenue. Midday. Got that? Now get outta here.'

Mandy drove slowly down Main Street, churning over whether he was being set up by the Giraffe. It felt too good to be true. What on earth was the Giraffe doing? Nobody hired a private dick for this kind of work unless they had incredible credentials. The Giraffe was acting like the puppet master, certain that Mandy would screw it up and then the family would have no choice but to hand the case over to the police or the FBI. And the Giraffe was highly experienced at steering the Feds away from a case he wanted for himself. He'd tell them it was personal, a matter of local police pride. But then again, maybe it was exactly as it seemed – because of the shootings at the Viceroy, there was no spare manpower to handle the enquiry, and the family didn't want them, anyway. Fabienne was no fool and he guessed she had in put the recommendation. Why not? Yeah, but then again, why?

Hell on wheels, was it even legal?

Still, no point worrying about that now. He needed cash. He needed a job. Why ask too hard where it came from?

He checked the wing mirror to see if he was being followed by Broadski and Dent. That would be their MO – let him do the work and then take the credit. But there was nobody there; maybe it was too soon. They were probably still stoned after the Lakers game.

Using his teeth to unwrap a packet of Trebors, he ruminated about the Giraffe again. The idea *must* be for him to make a fist of it so that the García-Márquez family would be forced to listen to the SMPD.

He crunched a Trebor and decided for now he'd focus on getting hired and being handed a cheque, whatever the outcome. But first he had to see Frank. He needed to be well informed prior to meeting Mr Big Avocado.

The changing room of the city morgue smelt as bad as it always did. Abandoned wet towels and decomposing Gorgonzola. It didn't improve Mandy's mood. He stamped his heels into white surgical boots, took two paces and pushed through the swing doors of the autopsy room.

'Sorry I'm late.'

Frank made a loud 'huh' noise. He was wearing a surgical mask, baseball hat and green gown and stood opposite a similarly attired redheaded female. They leant towards one another over the partially open chest cavity of a corpse that had until recently, Mandy assumed, been covered in tortilla chips.

The redhead raised her latex-gloved hand and mumbled, 'Hi.'

Mandy said a 'Hi there' back and looked at the three shrouded bodies waiting on gurneys. A queue of dead people. Nice.

Frank pushed the heavy-duty examination light away and said, 'Foxy, go and get yourself a coffee.'

Foxy started to pull off her gloves. 'Are you sure? I can finish off here while you go for coffee?'

Frank laughed. 'It's the last break you're gonna get for the next three hours.'

'I'm gone,' said Foxy.

Mandy's eyes followed the redhead's legs as she walked through the door.

Frank nudged him in the arm. 'You could do a lot worse . . . She's a peach.'

Mandy looked up into space and sighed. Frank never had any kids and was always looking to be Mandy's dad.

'Give me a break, would you?'

'My message said nine thirty, didn't it?'

'No excuse except for the psycho living in my house and the Giraffe.'

Frank nodded as his needle pierced the corpse's dead skin to make the final criss-cross stitches so that the chest cavity resembled a chest again.

'Tough love is what Donna needs.'

36

Mandy stepped away from the table, sniffed the handkerchief and exhaled. 'She's a witch.'

'She's an addict, I'm afraid.'

Mandy pitched the good news again. 'I saw the Giraffe just now. He suggested I meet the father, Mr Eduardo García-Márquez, at noon today. Number 1 Ocean Avenue. Every chance I'm going to get hired.'

'No kidding? Way to go, man!' Frank said, scratching his face with a retractor.

'Evidently the guy doesn't trust the police and wants a private investigator on the case. I wonder who tipped him off about Broadski and Dent's dedication to the job.'

'Be careful – you could be wandering into a trap.'

Mandy shook his head, smiled and rubbed his latex-covered hands together. 'No choice. I need the cash. Trap me now, trap me later.'

Frank returned to embroidering the corpse's chest.

Mandy stared at a table of surgical instruments. 'What killed Pedro García-Márquez?'

Frank didn't respond but tied the final stitch, respectfully lifted the sheet over the face of the corpse and said, 'Pedro García-Márquez was stabbed in the guts by someone using a very sharp blade – possibly a butcher's or surgical knife. He hadn't eaten any of those tortilla chips.'

'Does this look like the work of a gang from Mexico?'

Frank shook his head dismissively. 'He wasn't decapitated, and there was no stock-in-trade warning note.'

'But hasn't someone removed one of his kidneys?'

'What?' Frank raised one eyebrow quizzically.

'There was definitely bleeding from that area,' Mandy said.

Frank lifted the side of Pedro's dead torso up six inches.

Mandy noticed a small row of stitches on the victim's lower back, far neater than he remembered from the scene of the crime.

Frank sniffed. 'Look, maybe this is the work of some bombed-out Manson-type satanists drawing occult diagrams on their victims' torsos.'

'That's not what I thought at the scene,' Mandy said, scratching the back of his head.

Frank shook his head and sighed. 'I doubt it's a ritualistic killing. More like some sicko did it for kicks or a dare.'

'I think we might have an organ harvester on our hands.'

Frank lifted his baseball hat from his head and scratched his withered ear. 'You've been watching too many movies, Mandy. Keep it simple, bro.'

'Yeah, but what about the Russian girl in the shower? She had the same stencil markings on her back as Pedro whatever-his-name.'

'My bet remains the same. She was some hooker who'd already hung herself when the crazy people arrived and—'

'I thought you said it was a sex game that had backfired and not suicide?'

Judging by the turned-down corners of his mouth, Frank was getting irritated. He didn't like people interrupting his summations. He also disliked illegal immigrants and, in particular, Russians. It was like an obsession, his hatred of Russians. Considering how his own family had escaped from Poland in 1941 to Chicago and then moved to the sun in California in the 1970s, it was an odd prejudice for such a measured and kind man to have. A chink in Frank's perfect armour. Mandy'd never really figured it out.

'Some fruit loop thought it might be interesting to put markings on the girl showing where to take the kidneys out but changed their mind or was interrupted,' Frank said.

'I worked that out. So when are you are going to autopsy the Russian?'

'I'm not going to do her until I have her proper ID. You know how it works – you've been here long enough.'

'She's still a human being, for fuck's sake.'

It wasn't just Mandy's lack of sleep and his dislike of autopsies catching up with him. Leaving someone in a freezer because they had no formal ID was definitely wrong. It was time to shut up and wait until he'd been hired.

Frank held his arms up in mock surrender. 'Calm down, bro, calm down. You're going to be working the García-Márquez case, not the Russian.'

Mandy couldn't keep his mouth shut at the injustice of the situation.

'So Pedro counts and the dead girl doesn't? Is that it? They're obviously connected.'

Frank shook his head. 'Hey, like I said, cool your jets, big boy. I didn't make the rules. It's a job, Mandy, a job, not a vocation . . . We're not priests. Remember that.'

Mandy picked up a scalpel and let it drop to the floor. 'That's total crap and you know it, Frank,' he said, opening the autopsy room door.

Frank called to his retreating back, 'You got a great opportunity, so don't go boiling over and blowing it. People love you – remember?'

Back in the Amazon, Mandy calmed down. He needed to think what other information he could glean about the case before his visit to Eduardo García-Márquez. Fumbling in his pocket for a mint, his fingers brushed a crusted piece of paper. He pulled it out – the bloodstained receipt he'd taken from Pedro's body. He picked up his laptop from under the seat and typed the name of the Chinese supermarket on the receipt into Google. There was no website, only a local address on Cloverfield, and nothing on the Sacramento police files save for the name of the owner, Mr W. Chung. How original. Was it worth exploring? It seemed an uninspiring start.

He dialled Terry's number, but as he did so, remembered Terry and Dawn were coming back from vacation that afternoon, so he left a three-word message instead: 'Yo, Big Daddy.' He wanted to tell his old partner that he might be onto a case, a big case, that he'd managed to see the Giraffe without losing his cool, to speculate about the Viceroy killings. He smiled. Terry would probably say, 'Have you banked the cheque?' and, 'Course the bastards used the Viceroy. Someone high up somewhere is probably getting a free ocean-view suite there whenever they want.'

Some might call Terry a cynical old bastard. But in Mandy's experience he had not been wrong yet.

More's the pity.

Terry had known almost instantly that his cancer wasn't going to be as fluffy as the doctors kept pretending.

Sometimes having a keen eye for truth wasn't such a gift.

Hiding the laptop back beneath the *Enquirer* on the passenger seat, Mandy was ambushed by a memory. He grabbed the torch and bent down into the mucky depths to look under the seat. His fingers ferreted among the empty plastic water bottles, greasy rags, Coke cans, bottle of Martell brandy (for emergencies), enough Mars bar and Trebor wrappers to build an eagle's nest. Finally he pulled out what he was looking for – a black-and-yellow-spotted squash ball lying in the corner.

He stretched his arm and, using one of the empty water bottles, pushed the ball sideways until he could just manage to pick it up. It looked and felt like it had been in a chicken coop. He pulled his handkerchief from his pocket, spat on it and carefully wiped the gunk off its rubbery surface. Must be more than two years since they'd played a game of squash – Terry's illness was the cause, nothing else. Back when they were partners driving around in Terry's dark blue Lexus, Terry always kept racquets in the trunk of the car in case they were able to get in a game at the end of a shift.

Flashback. The crunch of Mandy dislocating the neck of a paedophile gangster on an airborne 727; when he got out of hospital, he was suddenly no longer a cop, no longer an actor, nothing but an English fish out of water.

Mandy squeezed the squash ball and smiled into the rear-view as he pictured blond-haired, blond-moustachioed Terry driving up in the Lexus every Sunday evening to pick him up from the house and take him to play squash at UCLA. Then, when they'd had their game, Terry'd take him back before driving another fifteen miles to Terry's own home in Echo Park.

It had been the one thing that Mandy looked forward to in his empty week. Slipping the ball into his pocket, Mandy made a mental note to play squash again soon. Hell, maybe Terry could referee until he could play again.

He pulled back the sleeve of his jacket, checked the time and took a deep breath. Lucy Lack answered on the first ring.

'I expected your voicemail,' he said, unable to stop himself from wondering what she was wearing. Negligee? Sloppy Joe's? Black dress and veil?

'I've been up for hours. There was a fire in my room last night.'

'What?'

'Two candles fell over in the bathroom and set fire to my make-up bag. I stopped the shower curtain from catching fire just in time.'

'Are you all right? Did you get help?'

'I was so scared that some weirdo was in there. I called Father Tony, as he's only up the road from here.'

Mandy pictured Father Tony and Lucy dressed in pyjama bottoms holding hands. The look on the priest's face was inscrutable. Pastoral care in the bedroom now – whatever next?

'Anyway, he wasn't there, so I had to put the fire out myself with a wet towel. No fire brigade, thank God.'

Mandy swallowed. At least Father Tony hadn't made it into her room. 'Why did you ring Father Tony? He's a priest, for God's sake.'

'I was frightened.'

'Call me next time. I know the area. I know how things work. Please?' Mandy yanked the stick shift from side to side.

'OK. Thank you,' she said, suddenly sounding gloomy.

Mandy felt a twinge of guilt. Poor kid, she was getting over the slaughter of her gay best friend; it can't be easy in a foreign place. And why not call handsome Father Tony? Hell, if he was female, he'd probably call the priest too.

'Listen,' he said, 'I know this is a bad time, but I do need to ask you some questions. Nothing too formal, but . . . would you mind meeting me for breakfast tomorrow?'

'I don't think I'm ready for questioning. Let me think.'

The line went dead.

Mandy stared at his cell wondering if they had been cut off, but as she didn't ring back, it was a deliberate dismissal. She was an odd mixture, Mandy thought, of strong and vulnerable. The type who start out as school swots, never put a foot out of place and then end up party animals having discovered sex games and mind-altering drugs. Or was Lucy Lack one of the ones who did it the other way round? Whatever, he hoped she wasn't mixed up in the murder.

9

11.54 a.m., 10 July

Mandy often recited 'Do Not Go Gentle Into That Good Night' when he was nervous. Like right now, when minus ten thousand was about to call on three billion. And the salt-and-pepper-haired figure of Adam Pollock was rushing down the steps of number 1 Ocean into a waiting car with a smile on his face wider than the Hollywood sign.

Shit! Someone had got in before him.

And it had to be Pollock, whose only talent was talking the talk. Drove a smart Audi, worked out every day and dressed in the latest schmutter, paid for by his wealthy wife. A guy who got by mumbling lines from *LA Confidential* at just the right time. Mandy couldn't picture Pollock doing store work, like he'd had to countless times when the overdraft had reached its expiry date. How come someone with an IQ of a frog had also been put up for this job?

Still, there wasn't time to ruminate. Frank's nagging voice came into his head: '*Visualize being hired.*' There was no choice. Mandy strode into the building as if he was high up on the payroll.

The po-faced, uniformed elevator guy avoided his eye. This was number 1 Ocean, after all, not just any apartment building. '*Visualize.*' The elevator sounded an expensive clunk of arrival.

'Penthouse floor. Please step this way, sir. You are expected.'

A beautiful, dark-haired Mexican woman in her late forties, wearing a black dress and flat ballet shoes, ushered Mandy into the two-storey apartment with a dignified sweep of her hand.

'They are upstairs,' she said, nodding calmly. A loyal and trusted personal assistant? No sign of the wailing nanny with the badly dyed hair here.

Mandy walked up the polished wooden stairs to the second sunlit floor, where he was greeted by an academic-looking guy in his mid-twenties, clearly uncomfortable in his black suit.

41

'Miguel García-Márquez,' the man said by way of introduction. Then he pointed to a man standing on the deck out through the open glass doors. 'My father is out here. Please come this way.'

The man on the deck – Eduardo García-Márquez himself – was built like a cross between a lifeguard and a Pontypridd prop forward. Immaculately dressed in a black suit, waistcoat and tie, he looked to be in his late sixties. He had a weathered face, a dark moustache and thick, slicked-back hair. He held the beads of a rosary curled round the fingers of his left hand and exuded power.

Mandy walked over and shook his outstretched hand. Judging from the grip, the guy enjoyed riding buffalo one-handed. Faint chatter, whistles and yelps were wafting over from the beach on a perfect breeze. It all felt surreal. Down there, the boardwalk. Up here, grief and power.

'Thank you for coming to see me,' García-Márquez said.

'I am very sorry for your loss.'

The words hung in the air.

Mandy looked across at Miguel for direction.

He inclined his head towards his father.

Eduardo García-Márquez nodded and motioned Mandy to stand next to him. Mandy inwardly winced. This was the moment when he was going to hear about other private investigators who had been hired and how he was to be kept waiting in the wings. They could afford a small army if they wanted. He needed to go on the attack before they made the wrong decision. It was now or never. Mandy held his hand up in the air. Eduardo and Miguel García-Márquez looked surprised, but angled their heads back to listen. Mandy cleared his throat and began.

'You will probably not hire me after I've said this, but I wonder why you should want to hire me, as opposed to some seriously proven ex-FBI guy. I want to do the job. I want to find the killer of your son, but I don't want to be the fall guy. I might not have the best record in town, but think I may be able to see things about this case that others can't. I've been through stuff other people haven't; sometimes it makes you see things they don't, is all . . .'

Mandy stepped backwards and immediately thought of all the other points he should have made, but it was too late. The speed with which the rosary beads were being swung told him he'd spoken for too long anyway.

Eduardo García-Márquez walked to the edge of the deck and the building, putting his large hands on the handrail. The penthouse was seven storeys high.

Mandy nervously placed his own hands on the rail nearby. Mandy stepped closer and selected a question carefully.

'Do you have any suspicions as to who might have done this, sir?'

García-Márquez took out a folded piece of paper from his inside jacket pocket.

'This is a list of all of Pedro's friends and associates.'

'Did anyone have a grudge against him?'

García-Márquez leant on the perimeter railing and looked out towards Catalina.

'My son chose to lead a different lifestyle from the rest of us . . .' The man's face suddenly looked troubled and he began swinging the rosary beads from one hand to the other.

Mandy wanted to offer some comfort about the acceptability and positive endorsement of homosexuality in towns like Santa Monica. Christ, even the new mayor was gay. Yet that hadn't appeared to have helped Pedro García-Márquez that much.

So because he badly needed the job, Mandy held his tongue and said, 'And do you think someone might have used this lifestyle against him? I'm not sure. Blackmail is quite an old-fashioned concept; people are very accepting of different lifestyles these days.'

García-Márquez tilted his head back and bared his teeth. 'People wanting money and being prepared to do anything to get it is in the Bible but still current, wouldn't you say?'

'Absolutely, and more so here in LA than anywhere else I know, other than New York and London, but I'm still not sure about the blackmail angle.'

'You forgot to add Mexico City, Washington and Los Angeles, Mr Mandy.'

They briefly smiled at each other.

'Oh, sir, please call me Mandy.'

García-Márquez flashed up the fingers of his left hand in recognition as the smile on his face disappeared.

'Is there anyone who loved or loathed Pedro not on your list? His old nanny, for example?'

'Josefina could be charged with loving my son too much but not with murder. But my daughter, María, and Pedro were not fans of one another. In fact, he threw her out of the apartment the night before he was murdered.'

'That's good to know, sir,' said Mandy, wishing he had the balls to do that with Donna. 'She was living with him, sharing the apartment?'

'No. She'd been paying him a visit, as it happens . . . But in case you're wondering,' García-Márquez added, 'María is not the type to hire a killer. She's a young lady whose bark is far worse than her bite. Here's the list of the friends. I don't suppose they are all possible suspects.'

García-Márquez handed Mandy the sheet of paper. Mandy opened it and read.

Lucy Lack

Harry and Carmen (friends on vacation in India)

43

Joseph and Marsha (friends on vacation in India)
Wing the falconer (ex-Hell's Angel)
Javier Jones (burns victim)
Johnny and Sarah Sternwood
Bradley Adams

Each name was followed by a contact number.

'Lucy Lack is in Santa Monica,' Mandy announced as if he was laying down three aces on a poker table.

'Staying at Shutters. We know.'

'Have you spoken to her?' Mandy asked, disappointed his revelation didn't carry more clout.

'No. This is a time for family and prayer. Although my son was very fond of Lucy, my wife is not. She thinks Lucy might have been responsible for . . .'

'Pedro's death?'

It was tactless but somebody needed to say it. Both García-Márquezes said nothing.

Mandy took out his notebook.

'I need to know if Pedro made a will and if he had any life insurance,' he said.

Eduardo and Miguel both laughed.

'Life insurance?' Miguel said.

'People insure their lives to benefit their families,' Mandy said, giving the most respectful of shrugs.

'The García-Márquez family has its own life insurance scheme set up by my great-grandfather. And anyway, Pedro had no children,' García-Márquez said, covering his eyes with his hand.

Mandy took a large breath – Jesus, these people were rich enough to *own* pension funds and insurance schemes – and asked again, 'Did Pedro make a will?'

'No,' Eduardo García-Márquez pronounced firmly. 'He was just twenty-nine years old. He didn't need to.'

'I think he did,' said Miguel.

Eduardo García-Márquez squeezed the rosary beads in one hand. Miguel was silent. Both men stared at Mandy. The roof terrace felt a few degrees hotter than it had.

'How do you know?' Eduardo asked.

'He mentioned that if anything happened, he wanted to make sure Josefina had some entitlement to the house on Montana,' Miguel said in a low voice. 'He wanted to make a will to reflect this.'

Eduardo García-Márquez gave an exhausted sigh. 'Miguel may be right.

44

Maybe he put something about this somewhere. We can all look. If we employ you, we want this business kept completely and utterly confidential and brought to a close as soon as possible. Do you understand me?'

'Of course, and I'll try to keep you as informed as I can.'

Eduardo inhaled. 'I make decisions based on instinct. You have four advantages to me. You are an honest man. You have been in the police force but now work as an outsider. You have failed in the past but are looking to restore your reputation. You are British and I suspect capable of seeing through some of Pedro's highly spoilt associates. Someone – I shan't say who – highly recommended you to us. We have considered one or two other options but have decided you are our man.'

Mandy squinted into the sunlight. The beach lovers laughed and cavorted. He had given his last ten bucks away and now he had a J-O-B. And they say there is no God.

'I'm very grateful for the chance to prove myself,' he said.

'I trust that you will.' The big man walked inside the penthouse and carried on speaking, Mandy and Miguel following like acolytes. 'Now, I don't want you to feel compromised, but I am offering a reward of $250,000 to anyone supplying information leading to a conviction. And providing you are still under contract to us when the killer or killers are caught, I will pay another $250,000 to a charity of your choice. And here is a cheque for one month in advance. We can set up a monthly payment into your bank and deal with your expenses on a monthly basis too. We do not deal in cash.'

Eduardo and Miguel García-Márquez then quickly conferred in Spanish. Mandy's Spanish was basic, or French, and he understood nothing of what they were saying. Eduardo turned back to him, his eyebrows raised questioningly.

'That sounds more than fair, sir,' Mandy said.

'Good. We are in business, then.' García-Márquez swung his rosary beads back and forth over his hand, and placed them in his pocket.

Mandy turned towards the boardwalk and gazed at the ocean, seeing large noughts and dollar signs water-skiing along its silky surface. He felt like cheering, weeping, but given the circumstances, decided against it.

10

1.35 p.m., 10 July

Pushing his last two quarters into the parking meter on 2nd Street, Mandy glared at the parking warden dawdling nearby. He walked into Continental, picked up a wire shopping basket from the side of the door and grinned at the glinting tins of food that lay on the shelves in front of him.

Caressing the bank receipt for the cheque in his trouser pocket as if it was the hand of the first girl he had ever fallen in love with, Mandy grabbed a large jar of Branston Pickle. His thoughts turned to a distant summer's afternoon in Oxford – Christchurch Meadow and a picnic of fresh prawns, soft-boiled eggs and mayonnaise, scones and Devonshire cream, and nearly consummated love. Mandy sniffed deeply, satisfied that he could completely recall the smell of the girl's perfumed skin and the grass on which they'd been lying.

His sense of smell was something he trusted. He wanted to create a library of smells. Not an oak-panelled one but a walk-in closet made of frosted glass and brass where inside, perched on parallel shelves, stood an assortment of chemistry bottles, each containing different memories: tobacco from his grandfather's pipe; the golden-coloured eiderdown at his mother's house; his first and only dog, sadly short-lived – a fox terrier that could play football; the garden shed he used to hide in from his stepfather; freshly grilled mackerel; his fingers after touching the inside of his first girlfriend's underwear; a bacon sandwich; the plastic seats of his first car; the ocean at Monterey; the sea at Land's End; bonfires in Oxford; a freshly mown lawn; a pint of Wadworth bitter; a shotgun that's just been oiled.

He walked up and down the aisles of the store, thinking about this library of smells, filling the basket with items that he did not need but seemed necessary compensation for the excruciating assignments he had had to take in the last years to make ends meet. Dreadful jobs that he didn't mention to anyone save his shrink, and even then not that often – he could only afford to see the

46

shrink twice a year. Keeping the cat in cat food and the Amazon maintained at the Swedish garage was sufficiently exorbitant.

And that did not take into account his back-up mechanic, Tassos, the rental on the Palisades house, the lack of Donna's rent, the disgraceful cost of insurance for being a PI, let alone the price of medication and quarterly blood tests. He could just about afford to pay medical insurance for Ned the cat, but not for himself.

'What would happen if anyone shoots you, darling?' his mother asked more than once. It was a good question. But he didn't have an answer.

Twenty minutes later he emerged into the hot sun, carrying two large brown paper bags full of food. Thank God the store took a post-dated cheque. He placed everything except for a small tray of strawberries and a tub of clotted cream in a large chilled bag in the trunk of the Amazon.

The traffic warden pushed a parking ticket beneath the windscreen wiper of the Amazon and stepped back as Mandy started the engine, then waved as if to say, 'Goodbye. Thank you so much for parking here.'

The smell of the strawberries and cream was strong and demanding of attention. So instead of driving away, he turned John Barry's *Zulu* soundtrack up loud, yanked a few green stalks from some strawberries and dunked them in the cream, placing one after the other slowly into his mouth as if it was a religious experience. Like taking first Holy Communion aged ten – sticking his tongue out and feeling the wafer mysteriously melt into the pores of his tongue.

He pulled out his cell, typed a text message to Terry – 'Have news re the man with the long neck. I might be in need of *your* paid consultancy. Call me as soon as' – and clicked 'send'. The mention of the Giraffe and money would prick up Terry's ears. There was another call he needed to make, to a man called Scottish Ray. But he was based in London. A late-night local call from here when Ray was up and about out of bed and having his Quaker Oats would do fine.

Mandy looked up at a Fox TV helicopter hovering overhead, its camera flashing as it sped off in the direction of sirens from somewhere like Sunset and PCH. He sat back in the car and wrote six Post-it notes of priority and stuck them over the display of dials and meters on the Amazon.

Flowers Fabienne
Collect Pedro's laptop from SMPD
Chase up García-M's list
Chung's Supermarket
Back-up team – Terry (local), Scottish Ray (UK)
Swim

Mandy fished out the García-Márquez list from his inside jacket pocket and ran his finger back and forth over Lucy Lack's name, before resting on another name . . . Wing the falconer (ex-Hell's Angel). Contact 310 . . .

He grimaced, picked up his cell and dialled the number, holding off on the last digit. The music in the car was close to the climax of *Zulu* the movie, as the hundred soldiers at Rorke's Drift are being taunted by five thousand chanting Zulus just before they charge. He pressed the last digit of Wing's number.

11

Wing didn't sound like a regular Hell's Angel to Mandy. Most Angels he'd encountered were intelligent but prone to talking about malfunctioning bikes, bad drugs and dangerous truckers. None of them could have been described as being on the sensitive side.

'Am I speaking to Wing?' Mandy said, wondering if the name denoted or meant a particular rank in the Hell's Angels Motorcycle Club.

The voice at the other end of the line sounded less grisly than expected.

'This is Wing. Who wants me?'

'My name's Mandy. I'm a private investigator with some bad news.'

Wing choked up completely once Mandy told him about Pedro.

'You are joking me, man! Pedro? Dead?'

'Yes, I'm sorry but it's true,' Mandy said. 'It must be a great shock . . . How about I call you back and arrange a time to meet? I've got some questions to ask you . . . Just routine.'

A short silence followed, punctuated by some angry sniffs. Wing cleared his throat.

'I don't want to meet you here in the Hills. I breed falcons and they can sense when someone has died and will get a bad vibe.' He spoke slowly like a choked-up cowboy. 'So I'll meet you tomorrow by the parking lot of the tar pits. I'll be riding a single-seated Harley. Three p.m. Don't be late. I can only leave my birds for so long.'

'I'll be driving a red Volvo Amazon.'

'What the fuck's that? Never heard of it,' Wing had said, and promptly hung up.

That was it. Mandy was in business; the investigation was underway. Moments later he was driving to Leafs on Lincoln and 4th. It was a plant store belonging to a man who he'd helped to reunite with his estranged father in Scotland.

'Put it on the slate,' the guy said, when Mandy explained the circumstances. So he bought Fabienne a large, white-flowered gardenia, stowed it in the trunk and drove back to Pedro's apartment. He'd deliver the flowers later, with a request to borrow the deceased's laptop.

Back on Ocean, Mandy found a meter with thirty minutes' free parking time. It didn't quite make up for the parking ticket, but it was better than a kick in the head. He straightened his tie and strode up to the entrance of 200 Ocean. He ran his finger down the chrome entry buzzers, some surnames printed in smart type, some blank, some with only a number. Pedro García-Márquez's name was still there, as if nothing had happened.

Mandy pressed the button marked, 'Caretaker.' No reply. He peered through the plate-glass entrance doors. The lobby and reception desk were empty. Maybe the concierge was in the side office. Mandy pressed the buzzer twice and waited. A well-dressed woman came out of the elevator and walked to the door, with a little dog on a lead. Mandy smiled and gestured that he wanted to get in. The woman pushed the door open, stepped out, blocking the door with her body.

'I do hope you are not a burglar or a fanatic,' she said in an Italian accent.

He felt uncharacteristically tongue-tied and handed her a business card. 'I'm looking for the concierge.'

'You mean Mr Quinn?'

'The Irish concierge who was on duty here yesterday afternoon?' Mandy blushed, aware he was making a meal of something simple. But a beautiful woman, whatever age, could do that.

The woman glanced at the card and handed it back. 'Mr Quinn has an abscess and is visiting the emergency dentist. He is a very busy man and in his spare time runs an over-fifties club called Mingle with a Christian.'

Mandy raised his eyebrows. Maybe Quinn was more goody two-shoes than he'd appeared.

'He was supposed to fix my dishwasher today. Always something else that comes before me. Why not call again?' she explained, closing the door shut behind her. 'I'm sorry, but we have to be very security-conscious at the moment – someone was killed here yesterday.'

Mandy grunted as he watched the woman walk off with her dog. He wrote a note on the business card, '*Contact me re Lexington details and the late Pedro G-M. URGENT,*' and posted it into the concierge's letterbox.

Back inside the car, he scribbled, '*Lexington – CCTV,*' in his notebook. He wasn't going to rely on Quinn but would google their address and email them later. Then he grabbed the last three strawberries from the pallet on the passenger seat, dunked them in warm cream and ate them in thirty unrestrained seconds.

According to Dr Bates, it was sometimes better to eat little and often, to replenish blood sugar levels when they might have dropped. Mandy didn't think it was that complicated. He was either hungry or simply being a greedy fuck. He double-checked the address on the bloodstained receipt inside its plastic evidence bag and drove off to the supermarket on Cloverfield Boulevard.

It took five tedious minutes to locate the shelf selling tortilla chips. Chung's was a big grocery store frequented by celebrity pilots before and after they flew their planes out from nearby Santa Monica Airport. Unlike Vons, at home in the Palisades, everything was overpriced.

Frustrated by the absurd array of chips, Mandy grabbed the largest bag from the shelf and walked down the aisle to the till. There was a queue of three women in front of him.

'Can I help you, sir?'

Mandy shook himself out of his irritation and looked up at a young Chinese-American man standing behind the cash till.

'I'm Mandy, Endeavor Investigations.' He flipped open his wallet to show his ID. 'I need to speak to whichever Chung owns this place.'

'I'm the Chung you need to talk to. Wayne Chung. Would you come this way?'

He led Mandy to the staffroom and offered him a chair, then disappeared off to see if one of the credit-card receipts for the day in question matched Mandy's photocopy of the till receipt. He returned, minutes later, with a red-covered ledger and a bulldog-clipped sheaf of receipts.

'I'm sorry, sir, but I can't see it here.' He looked up. 'You know, eight dollars twenty cents is not enough to put on a credit card? We usually enforce a ten-dollar limit. I think they would have paid cash.'

Mandy wiped his mouth with the back of his hand. He was feeling tetchy.

'Mr Chung, perhaps we could have a look at your CCTV footage for that afternoon. It was afternoon, wasn't it? Because it said, "17:05," on the receipt?'

'That's right, sir. Yes, I hadn't noticed. I'm sorry but the camera footage is kept elsewhere.'

'How far is elsewhere?'

'Chinatown.'

'Not exactly close. How come?'

'My grandfather has lived there since 1938.'

'Interesting, but why does he have the tapes?'

'He is the only one in the family with enough time to watch them.'

Mandy smiled as he pictured an elderly Chinese man in an armchair watching TV surrounded by piles of video tapes. Suppressing a flashback to a miserable time as a store detective, he stood up and said, 'Did you ever hear LA being described as seventy-two suburbs in search of a city? Ever been to the Viceroy?'

He dropped the last question in for devilment.

Chung didn't bat an eyelid, just shook his head.

Mandy shrugged, took a business card from his wallet and handed it over. 'Please call me tomorrow to confirm you have the tape.'

Chung looked up at the ceiling, held his fist against his chest and said, 'I promise that I will do my best, sir.'

The guy looked like he was swearing the Oath of Allegiance. He was nervous about something. Maybe he was worried he was going to get busted for health and safety. The back of the store looked pretty grimy. Mandy grabbed hold of his jumbo bag of tortilla chips, shook them up and down them in the air and said, 'Talk to you tomorrow.'

Wayne Chung held the office door open and sucked in his belly as he walked past.

Outside the store, the temperature was still burning hot. He walked quickly up Cloverfield Boulevard to the Amazon. He just needed to sort out Fabienne and the laptop, and then he could have a swim. Photocopying, then pinning up posters of the dead Russian girl would have to wait.

Where was Lucy Lack? Was she weeping in her room at Shutters waiting for the phone to ring, hoping it was Father Tony? He needed to process more people on the Eduardo García-Márquez list. Someone on it would lead him to the killer.

12

There were two living neighbours on one side of Benny Tan's Silver Lake house; all the ones on the other side were dead. His stunning-looking neighbours – the living ones, both female – relaxed at the end of the day by smoking marijuana on their back lawn. Benny Tan chose to unwind by reclining on a sofa analysing the financial press on his laptop and having his drink refreshed by Yale, the live-in ladyboy who acted as cook and housekeeper.

Benny was rehearsing for his upcoming membership interview at the Los Angeles Country Club. Ten years on the waiting list.

'Ask me the questions again, Yale.'

'Coming right up, sir.'

He always named his ladyboys after American universities. It made them seem more intelligent. But nonetheless he hated Yale's obsequiousness. Benny believed gratitude was a sickness only suffered by dogs.

Yale grabbed the clipboard resting on the chair next to Benny, pushed his fringe away from his eyes and began: 'How long were you married to your wife?'

'Twenty-seven years.'

'Would your late wife be in favour of you adopting children?'

'We talked about it a lot. Before she died, she told me to find a new wife and adopt as many children as I could support. She wanted me to give something back.'

Yale smiled as if he believed him.

'How long has your new wife been a resident of the US?'

'Three years, two months.'

'Have you fully considered the obligations and costs involved in being a member?'

'We have,' Benny said, stifling a yawn.

'Have you and your wife ever been turned down by a club in the US?' Yale took an anxious breath.

Benny shook his head a little and answered, 'Never.'

Yale waved his painted fingernails in the air and said with more emphasis, 'Will you swear on the flag of the United States that you believe in God and a Christian way of life?'

Benny shook his finger in self-admonition. 'I don't mind being a Christian, but I don't want to have anything to do with any Jews or Muslims.'

Yale clapped his hands and shook his head. 'Wrong answer. You must not say that – ever.'

The truth was, Benny disliked most people, and most domestic pets. But he desperately wanted to belong to the club.

'Mr Tan,' Yale's whiny voice interrupted his thoughts, 'I'm worried about the tuna I've been marinating all day. Would you mind?'

'Get on with it, then,' he said with a dismissive wave of his hand.

He watched Yale stagger back into the kitchen in his high-heels and went back to thinking about the adoption game. What else would he need to disclose? Financial information? He drove a five-year-old black BMW estate. It was only worth $7,000, but so what? His money was in real estate, boats and planes, not dumb cars. His business relied heavily on export. There was no need to be too specific. Anyway, he was giving the club a hefty donation, so figured they would end up playing ball.

Everything has its price.

Benny always needed the smell of the ocean. He'd had it growing up in Vancouver and when he'd been a croupier on ocean-going cruise ships before London. But Benny didn't like thinking about London too much. It had been a low time. One of the few things about which he still felt guilt. It wasn't until he moved to LA that his life improved. Actually, it didn't just improve; it went stratospheric. Life had been good to him in LA, and all because of fish. He'd started by selling exotic fish in plastic bags from the pier, then door to door, before opening his first little store fifteen years ago. He now owned three tropical fish shops outright, the largest in Santa Monica, and a thriving fish farm in Topanga. LA had indeed been good to him, and he'd tried to be good to it in return.

Yale appeared with the usual pot of cashew nuts, interrupting his thoughts again.

'Possible signs of a downturn!' Benny shouted in a mocking voice, throwing the *Wall Street Reporter* onto the floor.

'Why say "possible"?' Yale asked.

'It's been obvious for months!' Benny snorted. 'Stupid assholes!'

Yale smiled nervously and sprinkled some nuts into Benny's outstretched hand.

Benny prided himself on being able to spot a recession in the same way he could spot any form of theft or disloyalty at the office. A few days after Hurricane Katrina, he became certain there was going to be a downturn in the economy. That had been virtually three years earlier. He'd made sure he was prepared, but like everyone else made plenty of hay while the sun shone. Thank goodness he had not expanded his operation but decided to cut costs by concentrating on the local market.

Now, to his satisfaction, discussions regarding a takeover deal with the Russian Corporation were already at an advanced stage. Providing he could close the financial year with the increase in turnover he had forecast, the deal could be banked by October. Three months of hard work to go and then he could be out. Then he could concentrate properly on the Kids in Africa adoption programme.

Benny put down his copy of *Forbes*, listened to the mechanical digger at work next door in the cemetery and smiled. There was something about the sound of a grave being dug that he liked.

Six thirty in the evening was his favourite thinking time. He always ate dinner at seven, saying little but keeping watch on four plasma screens simultaneously: the Cartoon Network, CNBC, National Geographic and a split screen showing the key points of his showroom and offices.

His reverie was disturbed by the click-click of Yale's heels crossing the hardwood floor to the dining table. He stood up and stretched as Yale carefully unrolled the napkin resting by the side of the plate of tuna steak and salad.

Benny briefly smiled, sat down at the table and watched the anchorman for CNBC News. He was describing the scene in Marina del Ray where LAPD SWAT officers were surrounding a warehouse where the two Viceroy assassins were meant to be hiding out.

It didn't seem too likely to Benny.

Yale filled his glass from a bottle of Pinot Grigio. A grandfather clock in the hallway chimed seven. Benny sipped the wine and carried on listening to the news item, wondering if the assassins were already dead.

13

Mandy pushed open the door of the Evil Eye Café and spotted a table. The café was squeezed between a bike hire shop and a spaghetti restaurant behind Santa Monica Beach – and opposite Shutters. The place smelt of bagels and strawberry cheesecake. He shoved the crusty bottle of ketchup, sugar and packets of Sweet'N Low to the side of the tablecloth and sat down. It was a dump, but he liked it because it was a dump – and close to the boardwalk. It was also handy for spotting Lucy Lack with his binoculars, should she decide to slip out of Shutters the back way.

A waiter came over to the table.

Mandy looked up. 'Regular coffee and doughnut, please.'

'Coming right up.'

Mandy yawned and felt on the verge of falling asleep. Donna playing Joni Mitchell's 'Chelsea Morning' all night downstairs had kept him awake. The late-night calls to Pedro's friends in India hadn't helped either – made him feel like a bereavement counsellor. They coughed up nothing of real significance other than that Pedro had seemed to be keeping a low profile of late, not being too social and focusing on his charity work.

A loud gasp of steam from the espresso machine on the counter brought Mandy's attention back to the present.

A man with a grubby white T-shirt sat at a nearby table coughed, held up a copy of the *LA Sun Times* and read the back page. Mandy glimpsed a front-page headline of 'Viceroy Killers Escape Cops' above a colour picture of members of a heavily armed SWAT team staking out a building. He reckoned the two gunmen would probably be dead by now, or about to be shot by several LAPD marksmen while trying to escape. He smiled as he recalled what he'd said to Lucy Lack in the car: '*Cops here look after their own.*'

The media was still awash with coverage of the Viceroy, and increasing unrest that the killers remained at large. Jeez, even the Evil Eye had taped a 'Wanted' poster on the side of their coffee machine. The intensity of the coverage, and the media blackout requested by the family and the Police Department, meant that no report about Pedro's death had yet appeared on Twitter, Google, Yahoo, AP or in print, on the radio or TV.

The spokesman for the governor's office interviewed on KCRW that morning hinted a special visitor from Washington might be attending the double funeral in the cathedral downtown. Mandy pictured all the sharp shooters lining the rooftops along the procession route. But he needed to keep his mind on the case in hand. Pedro's murder.

None of the people he contacted yesterday had known about Pedro's death. He hadn't enjoyed breaking the news to them one bit – telling Lucy Lack and Wing had been bad enough. The four others he had rung were on holiday in different parts of India. All had said variations of 'I don't believe it. Is this some kind of joke? Oh my God!' All sounded tearful and had probably never experienced anyone die in their lives before. Not someone their own age. Someone close. Everyone saw people die all the time – on the news. Iraqis, poor people, Africans. They died and people drank their morning coffee.

The waiter set down Mandy's own morning coffee, iced water and doughnut. Mandy grunted, swigged on the coffee and went back to his thoughts. Maybe Pedro had been smoking pot, got the munchies, dropped into Chung's and brought home a homicidal Chinese-supermarket-shopping friend?

The options for going off piste away from García-Márquez's list were endless. He was better off returning to the safer ground of greed and envy rather than random killers. What if one of the friends in India had murdered Pedro and then made it back out there in the given time?

Unlikely.

But why not?

Maybe the killer was in LAX boarding a plane for Delhi at the same time as he was waiting to meet Lucy Lack and Father Tony.

Being halfway across the world was a good alibi.

He'd better contact Jim, his tame source at Horizon, to check Pedro's holidaying friends' cell-phone usage. Maybe Terry could get his connections at LAX Immigration to run a check on the passports at the exit and entry points. There could be $250,000 at stake. Which would mean a new start for Terry and him. New medications. New hope.

He stared through the window towards Shutters, in front of the grand hotel. On the boardwalk, a long-legged girl in purple shorts and T-shirt made a tricky manoeuvre and nearly fell over on her roller skates. No sign of Lucy. No message from her on his cell either.

Should he call her again to put some pressure on or cut her some slack? She was in mourning, after all. Or wasn't she? Mandy turned back to the table and clicked his pen on and off as he thought about his next appointment and the random nature of death.

14

10.20 a.m., 11 July

Mandy pressed Terry's entryphone, whistling a tune from his childhood that he'd found annoying even then. A young girl answered.

'Who is it, please?'

'It's Santa Claus.'

There was a pause as the girl conferred with someone else.

'You're too early. Can you come back in five months?'

'That's not convenient, miss.'

'Sorry but the rules are the rules.'

'What about if I said I was Spiderman?'

'Push the door, please!'

He walked in and down the hall knowing that he would be ambushed by Terry's daughters any second. Caitlin and Alice could have been identical twins except Alice was taller and older – eight and three-quarters to Caitlin's mere seven years. But both were dressed in nursing uniforms complete with upside-down watches and toy stethoscopes, each of their hats emblazoned with a red cross.

'Hey. How are you doing?' Mandy knelt down to give them a hug.

'Fine,' they trilled.

'Is your mom here?'

'No, she flew to Tokyo this morning.'

'Oh, Tokyo – that's near Detroit, isn't it?'

The girls shrieked in horror.

'It's the capital of Japan!' Alice said.

'Is there anything you two don't know?'

The girls stuck their tongues out at him.

He pictured Dawn handing out drinks aboard a United Airlines long-haul flight. Did she think about Terry's illness or just blank it out and get on? She didn't have too much choice. A small hand tugged at his pocket.

59

'When are we going to see your cat, Ned?'

'Soon.'

Mandy widened his smile as he and the girls walked into the converted downstairs den. He hated hospitals, but seeing his sick friend at home was different. Or so he told himself.

A faintly yellow-skinned Terry hunched himself up from the mattress of the raised medical bed and stuck his thumb in the air. He was holding a remote for the TV, wearing shorts, a white vest and a treasured Beastie Boys baseball cap. Both girls walked over, took hold of their father's arm and pretended to take his pulse. The room smelt medical and faintly of Camembert and Budweiser.

Terry played along, yelled, 'Hell on a stick, it's Big Mandy!'

Near the bed was a glass-fronted fridge that housed medicines and Terry's secret supply of beer. Next to that, two rocking chairs, a large TV showing a game-fishing programme, a two-seater sofa and, resting on an old desk, a melted car dashboard with police radio and corded microphone.

Imagining the beeps, call signs and static coming from the radio, Mandy remembered the dark blue Lexus was the last car Terry'd wrecked before having to take sick leave. But still Mandy preferred looking at the pale blue microphone of the old radio than the dripping tube of chemo going into Terry's arm.

Cancer of the kidneys. What a bastard.

Terry motioned that he wanted to whisper something in Mandy's ear.

'Would you like some of this? It's better than crack and I'm selling it cheap.'

Mandy pulled a face and said, 'You're sick, Mr Tibbs, you know that?'

Terry lay back on the pillow and smiled. 'Don't tell me I'm sick; tell me what's happening, you oversized, fucked-up banana.'

Mandy smiled. Insults were good.

'I'm gonna take the girls to see the cat and go hiking in a couple of weeks' time. Think Dawn will mind?'

'Are you kidding? She'd love it. We do like silence occasionally.'

Terry clicked his fingers in appreciation. 'What's the magic words, girls?'

'Thank you, Uncle Mandy!'

'Remember to bring your boots and special sun hats with the target on top,' Mandy said, standing to wag his finger in mock censure.

'Goodbye now, girls,' Terry said, pushing himself up in the bed.

The little nurses danced out of the room, shrieking, 'Boots and hats, boots and hats, hoooooooooray!'

Once Mandy was sure the girls were upstairs, he sat down at the end of the bed.

'They're great kids.'

Terry sighed. 'Yeah, I suppose so. At least they're not smoking crystal meth.'

Mandy groaned at Terry's humour.

'You are bad, so bad I can't believe it.'

'Cut the crap and tell me the news. There must be some because I've seen you smile at least three times today.'

Mandy flashed Terry the finger, sat down on the bed, picked up the remote, switched off the TV and took a deep breath.

'First off, I get a call from Fabienne – you remember her, the one who works for the Giraffe?'

'The one you almost—'

'Do you want to listen?'

'So the princess from Louisiana called you and . . .'

'Tipped me off about a suspicious death on Ocean. A rich young Mexican, Pedro García-Márquez, found dead at his apartment – an original Edward Hopper painting on the wall, and his Russian cleaner girl strangled, hanging from the showerhead in the en suite. Get the picture?'

'How was the guy killed? Strangled too?' Terry was sitting up, arms folded, gazing into space.

'He was stabbed through the guts and . . .'

'Yes?' Terry picked up on Mandy's hesitation.

'He was stabbed in the back as well,' Mandy lied, not wanting to tell his sick ex-partner about the missing kidney, not yet anyway. He swung the subject back onto safer ground. 'Broadski and Dent were supposed to be handling the case.'

'Those two jerks couldn't find the Grand Canyon,' Terry said, lobbing a crumpled V8 can across the room into the trash. At least he hadn't lost his touch at basketball.

'Well, they missed the dead Russian girl completely.'

'Wow! And how come?'

'The dead girl was hiding behind a shower curtain.'

'Hang on.' Terry's head dropped forward; his shoulders were shaking as he ran his hand through his hair several times.

Mandy stood up from the bed. 'Are you OK?'

Terry nodded, held his hand up as if he was trying to catch his breath.

Most times in a medical emergency there was barely time to think. But it was the medium-to-small ones that Mandy disliked because he was conscious of too many options.

Terry lay back on the pillow, slapped the mattress and laughed. There was nothing wrong: he'd been fooling around. Bastard.

'Praise the Lord! Do you mean to tell me that you've been hired to investigate this crime?' he said, slipping in and out of a Mississippi accent.

'Listen, fuckface.' Mandy cleared his throat and looked up at the clock on the wall. 'Don't do that again to me, OK? OK?'

Time was passing too quickly. He took off his jacket, rolled up his sleeves and walked round to the side of the bed where the chemo drip stand was.

'Eduardo García-Márquez has hired me to track down his son's killer. The family don't want to work with the cops. I've banked his cheque and the Giraffe has agreed that Pedro's death is going to be treated as unexplained for seven days. In which time we have to bring in a result before he opens the case up to his department. This is day two. Are we on the same page?'

'We?' Terry said, inclining his head like a parrot.

'Yes, you scumbag – we.'

'Three questions,' Terry said, stroking his moustache.

'Shoot.'

'I may not have worked for three years, but this case is not going to get solved in seven days.'

'I know, man, but let's think positive!'

Terry raised his eyebrows and smiled. 'They're super wealthy, aren't they? You sure no Mexican drug gang has been blackmailing the family?'

'I think the father would have said something. He's a decent guy.'

Terry winked. 'Decent guys'' children get kidnapped – particularly very wealthy ones. Maybe they just meant to take Pedro away and ask for a ransom, not kill him.'

Mandy thought of Pedro lying in the shape of a cross, bleeding and covered in tortilla chips while the Russian girl hung dead from the showerhead next door. What a shit-awful world. He gripped hold of the drip stand.

'I asked Frank when he was doing the autopsy whether it looked like a gang thing . . .' He stopped short.

Damn, Mandy really didn't want to mention the missing kidney.

Terry spotted the hesitation and said, 'You didn't say Frank did the autopsy.'

'Yeah, he did. He also told me that . . .' Mandy looked over at the TV screen and stalled.

'Told you what, bro?'

'He also told me that someone had removed one of Pedro's kidneys.'

Terry's mouth opened, but no words came out. His eyes were staring straight ahead.

Two seconds later he sniffed, wiped his mouth and laughed. 'Why didn't you say that before? Did you think it would piss me off?'

Mandy shuffled on his feet, still holding the drip. 'It didn't seem the most tactful thing to say, so yeah, I did.'

Terry eased himself back up on the pillow, looked at the virtually empty bottle of chemo, clipped the line off and carefully pulled the needle out of his vein. The needle was two inches long, thick, with a diagonal sharp end. Mandy clenched the drip stand, unable to stop watching as Terry deftly held his finger over the puncture mark, released it and expertly stuck a thick plaster over the hole. He grabbed some Kleenex from a box on the bed and wiped three bulbous droplets of blood from his arm.

'Don't feel bad, man. It's unlikely that Pedro and my kidneys are gonna match. I'm seriously elite, very exclusive. Please don't hide things from me – drives me mad when people do.'

Mandy drew a deep breath, bit the inside of his lip.

'This isn't a game, bud,' Terry said. 'Or some shitty film or something shit on TV. It's my shitty life and I want to keep it real. OK?'

'OK, Big Daddy, let's move on. What d'you reckon?'

Terry eased himself off the bed and held his arms out in front of him. 'I think there's a good chance you are being set up by the Giraffe or by somebody.'

'I agree, though my gut tells me Fabienne wouldn't give me a bad steer.'

Terry bit into a bar of opened chocolate and nodded. 'That's right too. Well, you've been paid, a month up front?'

'I have,' Mandy said with a satisfied smile.

'Fucking A! Well, I am on the case and will help in any way I can. Do you want me to have a word with my guy at the DEA?'

'Check the García-Márquez family are not selling nose candy instead of avocadoes?'

'Better safe than sorry.'

Mandy stuck a confirmatory thumb in the air.

'Anything else to tell me?'

Mandy looked at the clock. Ten fifty-five. He wanted time to do more background research on some of the people on García-Márquez's list.

'One or two things I need your help on, such as calling your contact at LAX and checking out Quinn the concierge at Pedro's building and some firm called Lexington Property Group?'

Terry scribbled the names down onto the margin of the *LA Times*.

'Next?'

'I forgot to tell you about Pedro's sort of girlfriend, the Catholic priest and the two items I borrowed from the crime scene.'

Terry's face contorted into a question mark. 'You took items from the crime scene? You serious?'

'Nothing that could be used as evidence.'

A shiver of anxiety shot up through Mandy's body as he pictured the bloody till receipt and Russian girl's bus-pass photo.

63

'OK, OK,' Terry said. 'So stop looking like I outed you. You're the boss on this case; I'm just the freelance brains.'

'Thanks, but regrettably there's every chance you can be my partner again.'

Terry smiled, gave Mandy the peace sign.

Mandy took a piece of paper from his jacket and held it up in his hand. 'I'm going keep processing this list of suspects that Pedro's father gave me.'

Terry ripped open a can of Coke, swigged it, wiped his mouth with the back of his hand and took hold of the list from Mandy. 'Good plan. Want me to look at it and play devil's advocate?'

15

2.15 p.m., 11 July

Dances with Wolves swept through the Amazon's stereo during the drive back from Echo Park to La Brea. It normally calmed Mandy down, centred his stress into a manageable ball. The seriousness of Terry's illness only really hit him once he got into the car and drove away from the house. The whole issue of friendship and work was becoming a double-edged sword.

He needed to solve the case and use some of the reward to sort out Terry's cancer. Problem with this particular disease was that money often made no difference.

Yet examining the list of suspects with Terry had brought mixed blessings. There had been an argument about why he hadn't disclosed information about Lucy Lack sooner. 'She's got to be involved somehow, dude,' Terry had said. 'Why are you not seeing her right now?'

Mandy told Terry he had the matter under control and to move on. Trouble with Terry was he always thought he was right. And the bigger trouble right now was maybe he was.

Even though Terry was talking like they were still cops, Mandy squirmed in his boots, knowing that he should have insisted on seeing Lucy the morning after he'd driven her to Shutters. Whatever, he'd allowed a fantasy to percolate inside his head. It was time to tighten his belt and sharpen his attitude to the delectable Miss Lack.

He parked up outside the museum of the tar pits on Curson and 6th. The whiff of methane and asphalt was compelling but made him want to gag. Wing, the ex-Hell's Angel and one of the suspects on García-Márquez's list, was not there.

Looking around the car park for a single-seated Harley but seeing none, Mandy walked off in the direction of the fenced-in pits. The bubbling ponds and leaf-strewn rocks reminded him of Leicester Square in London – a place people made out was far more interesting than it actually was. In Mandy's case, he had been to the tar pits twice: once as an actor to shoot a scene for a film that never came out, and the other time when he'd been patrolling with Terry and they'd saved the life of a Mexican backpacker hounded into the pits by three rednecks with nothing better to do.

He must have been staring at the bubbling tar for about five minutes when a loud, throaty motorbike noise filled the air. Wing, Mandy thought, as the rider dismounted. He wore black leather, thick biker boots, had tattoos on his neck and hands, and no smile.

Mandy didn't wait to be spotted.

He walked over, with a 'Hi there. I'm Mandy.' Close up, the guy was young – late twenties, far younger than Mandy anticipated – relatively short but muscular, and wore mirrored sunglasses. Wing removed his black helmet to reveal a shaved head.

'Shall we walk and talk?'

They walked in silence along a path next to a wire fence for about two minutes, stopping when they found a tar pit nobody else seemed interested in. Wing scratched his head and stared at the bubbling surface of Tar Pit 13, took off his biker jacket and held it over his shoulder with his hand, revealing tattooed muscles, an Iron Cross and crucifix dangling over a hard-man vest. Mandy wondered if the guy was remembering someone he buried there in the bubbling tar.

Eventually, after a moment, and without turning round, Wing said, 'I may be on medication, but I still belong to the Oakland Chapter and have been a Dead Head for years, so I ain't anyone's fool, OK? Who the fuck killed Pedro?'

'You?' Mandy asked.

Wing gripped hold of Mandy's right arm, swung round and grabbed the other arm. Jeez, the guy was strong. Despite having both arms in what felt like a vice, Mandy tried to repress the feeling that the depressed weightlifter was about to throw him over the fence into the tar pit. Clearly the dir-ect-questioning approach needed to be changed.

'I loved Pedro. I had nothing but love for the guy,' Wing yelled, causing all the ducks and other birds sitting on the rocks to fly away.

'OK, we don't want the world to hear us, so let's start again. Would you mind?' Mandy looked down at his arm.

Wing waited a second, released his grip, took a joint from his pocket and lit it.

'You sure that's wise?'

'Fuck, man!' Wing said, lighting the jay.

'I meant with all the methane – don't want to get blown up.'

Wing shrugged his shoulders, as in 'Do you think I give a flying fuck?'

'How did you come to know about Pedro?' he said.

'I was recommended to the family.'

Wing looked like he was going to spit something unpleasant from his mouth.

Mandy ignored the hostility and carried on. 'How did *you* meet Pedro? You moved in very different circles.'

'Why should I tell you?'

'I'm not a cop.'

Wing raised his eyes upwards and hung out his tongue. 'So?'

Mandy grabbed the joint and took a deep drag.

It was strong. He felt wiped out with only one hit, but managed to cover it with a fake laugh, and breathed in and out.

'Wing, I'm trying to help Pedro's family, not the LAPD.'

Wing looked at him and gave what might pass as a smile if you were a depressive. Mandy gave what he hoped was a tough but friendly smile back. Wing stopped walking and spat some gunk into the ground.

'Mandy whatever-your-fucking-name-is,' he said, 'I'm going to give you any help that I can.' He took the joint back, checked over his shoulder that no one was watching and inhaled on it as if it was his only form of life support.

Mandy waved away an offer of a further toke. 'So once more with feeling, how do you know Pedro?'

Wing gave a long sniff as if he'd just snorted a thick line of coke. 'Dude, it's not me you need to be questioning.'

'Who is it, then? Lucy Lack?' She'd been top of the list from Eduardo.

Mandy remembered the names that came after. 'Johnny Sternwood? The four people who were on holiday in India. Javier Jones? Wing? Who knew Pedro the best?'

'Never met the girl. She's English and pretty and . . .' He paused and shook his head as if clearing it. 'Wait a minute, I did meet her once.'

'And did you think she was cool?'

'Pedro loved her. I thought she was, you know, a little up herself, the way that English women can be. She was OK. Insecure, I guess.'

Mandy made a non-committal grunt. 'Did you form the impression she was after his money?'

'No, more that she kept touching him all the time like they were on their fucking honeymoon and in love; but that wasn't possible. No one could get near Pedro. I mean it – not guys and definitely not girls, not that way.' He took a huge hit on the jay. 'Well, maybe except her, I guess. I mean, they had an intimacy he didn't share with other people.'

For a depressed twenty-something, skunk-smoking Dead Head, Wing had insight.

'What about the two guys I mentioned?' Mandy said. 'Javier Jones and Johnny Sternwood?'

'Javier is a gay or bisexual friend of his who I thought was a jerk. The other guy, Sternwood, I never heard of. I think Javier was in love with him, but like an ego thing – you know, not real love. That's all I know.'

'And you?' asked Mandy. He wanted to open Wing up, sensed that he had more to tell. 'How did you know Pedro? Like I said, seems like you moved in very different circles.'

Wing picked up a stone and threw it into a pond. There was an echoing splat like a Boy Scout shitting into a latrine. Mandy screwed up his face, waiting for the tar pits security to rush over. Nobody seemed too concerned, not even the family group ten or fifteen yards away. Wing cleared his throat and held up his hands in a 'just listen the fuck up' kind of way.

'Pedro's little brother acquired a smack habit at the age of seventeen. Pedro kept it from the family by paying the dealer and stumped up for Alfonso to go into detox during his school vacations. It didn't work.'

'Mind if we keep walking? I don't want this to be overheard,' Mandy said.

'Somehow Pedro discovered I kept falcons. I think he hoped that Alfonso would clean up by learning to fly one. He thought the best of people, you see? But Alfonso couldn't fly a fucking paper kite, not unless his sister was helping him at one end of it.'

'Meaning what?'

Wing laughed and shook his head. 'You will have to find out about *that*. Pedro learnt to fly falcons, had his own bird for a while, reckoned it was the happiest he's ever been. Helped me get established. Four years ago. A real fucking gentleman, there's no other word for it.' Wing was choking back tears now. 'Send my condolences to Pedro's father – only met him once, but he was a real guy, and Pedro was the best.'

'That's been extremely helpful, thank you,' Mandy said, shaking Wing's hand firmly and turning to walk back to the car. It was an old trick of Terry's – wrong-footing an interviewee before they got to their point. A final verbal enema, so people spewed any information they might be holding back.

'Hey, man, where you going?' Wing called after him.

'I have to get on, Wing,' Mandy said, looking at his watch for effect. 'Have you anything really important to add?'

Wing wiped his mouth with the back of his hand. He looked like he was going to cut to the chase.

'Yes, I do! As I just said, if I were you, I would check out Alfonso . . . He's always hanging out with his sister.'

'Well, that's not a major crime in this state . . .'

'Plenty of other things are, though,' and Wing gave what Mandy reckoned was an ironic laugh.

16

4.45 p.m., 11 July

Mandy parked up next to a palm tree a few metres from 200 Ocean and opened the windows of the Amazon. The ocean breeze cooled both the interior of the car and his sweating face like the sweetest air-conditioning possible. He bit into a pork pie and gave thanks to Continental for having the widest selection of British comfort food in LA. The time in England was nearly 9 a.m. He decided to wait ten minutes before calling Scottish Ray, his permanently out-of-work actor pal.

Wing hadn't proved Terry wrong about Lucy but *had* pushed Mandy into thinking he needed an independent view. Insecure and up herself? All over Pedro like they were in love, when she knew he was gay? Wing did not appear to have an axe to grind, as far as Mandy could tell, other than wanting justice for his dead friend.

It was time to secure some extra help, and now that he had banked the García-Márquez cheque, he had the means to get it.

Meanwhile, he picked up his Steiner 8x30s from the passenger seat and trained them on the entrance of Pedro's apartment building. The binoculars were so powerful he could normally see two dogs screwing on Catalina, but today they saw nothing of Quinn the concierge. He hadn't been able to see Wayne Chung when he visited the supermarket after returning from the tar pits either. *'No, he's not coming in. Mr Chung's wife not well today, but he'll be in tomorrow for sure.'* The checkout lady sure had a strop on.

Stuffing the remaining bit of pork pie into his mouth, he fired up his laptop, typed the name 'Lucy Lack' in Google and pressed 'enter'. One entry next to a London firm: Steel Bond Futures. She was listed as a junior – it was probably an old listing. A random idea popped into his head. Remembering her request about a room with no porn channels, he added the words 'adult, British, porn, actress' beside her name and pressed 'search' again. A page of entries unfurled.

'Bloody hell.'

He checked each one. Tits, arses, orifices and assorted equipment flashed across the laptop's screen. Black Lucys, white Lucys, blonde ones – lots of blonde ones – a couple of Asian ones, but none of the entries were the Lucy Lack he'd met at LAX.

Shit. Pork pie finished, Mandy dialled a London number and, as it rang, pictured his friend lying in bed in his dingy basement flat in Fulham Broadway. It had been nine years since Mandy'd been back for a visit. Nine years!

'Hello? Who wants me?' Ray always answered the phone in a pretend gruff South London voice, an affectation that Mandy enjoyed, particularly as Ray was so Scottish.

'Central casting, West Hollywood,' Mandy said, brushing crumbs off his shirt onto the already filthy Amazon floor.

Ray grunted. 'Central casting, my arse!'

'We were rather hoping to use your entire body,' Mandy said.

'You wouldn't have enough budget,' said Ray, then slipping into his normal accent, 'How goes it in the fast lane, you old charlatan?'

'Fancy earning a few quid, Ray?'

Mandy heard a cigarette being inhaled, followed by a wheeze and a cough.

'Well, I am a bit busy rehearsing for a role in a new movie.'

Mandy's heart almost stopped in astonishment but quickly beat on.

'Shut up, you bullshitter. The nearest you're going to get to a film are the ones you put into Boots seven years ago.'

'That's such an old joke. Can't you do any better than that?'

'I am old.'

'Been having any surgery done, love?'

Mandy laughed, aware that Ray's grubby mind would probably be turning over the conditions for his services.

'How much are you paying, and can I come and sleep on your couch for a few weeks?'

Mandy gave Ray the background.

'So you see,' he said, 'I need you to check out this Lucy Lack girl – I'll give you five hundred dollars now, and then if you really produce some results, an air ticket to LA, another five hundred cash and ten days on my sofa or the apartment downstairs.'

'So what makes you think your girl is into something?'

'I don't know,' Mandy said. 'She's a murder suspect, and she has a thing about porn.'

'I like it. Is it just soft porn or hard-core?'

'No, she hates all of it.'

Mandy told Ray he strongly suspected Lucy Lack had once been duped into taking part in some kind of soft-porn scam.

'And you want me to check out when and where?'

Mandy pictured Ray licking his lips. He decided to play it down a little.

'She's a respectable girl, Ray. Classy.'

'They're always the worst, I'm told.'

Mandy grunted. 'She's beautiful and works in the futures business in the City.'

'Must be loaded. Got any photos?'

As Ray said it, Mandy realized he should have acquired some photos of Lucy or at least surreptitiously taken some himself. Maybe he could snap her through a zoom lens coming out of the hotel. What a cliché.

'No photos at this point, Ray. Get you some in the next twenty-four hours?'

'You're not mixing business with pleasure, are you?'

'Stop being an arsehole, Ray.'

'Sorry – that just slipped out. Go on.'

'So I need you to find out whatever you can – in the City, you know what I mean. Where does she live, and with whom? Is she loaded? Does she have many friends? She didn't call anyone in London when I told her about Pedro's death. Does she have any boyfriends? Maybe it was a dodgy old boyfriend who sold an intimate film of her to some porn outfit. This girl might be in serious trouble here, and I need to know whether she's been telling me the truth—'

'Hey,' Ray interrupted. 'I'm on it, no worries.'

'And anything to do with her and someone called Pedro García-Márquez. Written that down? . . . Speak later.'

Mandy hung up and bit into a Trebor, feeling confident his money was being well spent. Ray could be a dick sometimes, particularly when it came to spouting on about sex, but there was no better terrier than Ray for turning up stones and finding out information. Actors often worked far harder than junior police detectives when it came to doing the donkeywork on a case.

He wiped his mouth with a handkerchief and felt a shiver of guilt passing down his spine about doubting Lucy Lack. Fuck it, he thought. He needed this job to be a success. He wasn't her best friend. He just *fancied* her a little, didn't he?

Breathing in several lungfuls of sea air, Mandy pushed the seat into recline and closed his eyes; he hadn't worked this hard in months.

He dreamt he was sprinting through the surf on Zuma Beach, dressed in his suit, chasing some paparazzi who were running after a bikini-clad Lucy Lack. But before any conclusion was reached, James Brown started singing 'I Feel Good'.

He blearily pulled the phone from between his legs. He hadn't had a chance to say so much as 'hello' when Donna started wailing like a six-year-old kid lost in a department store.

Between her sobs, Mandy managed, 'Where are you?' and watched himself go boss-eyed in the rear-view mirror.

'Cross Creek,' Donna said.

She sounded two beats short of a breakdown. Something had happened; he wasn't about to ask what.

'Do you want to eat some sushi?'

Donna said a tearful 'Yes.'

'Hold on a moment.'

Mandy put the binoculars to his eyes and adjusted the focus to scan for any sign of life in the reception at 200 Ocean. Nada. There didn't even seem to be any lights on. He would come back and find Quinn tomorrow.

'Donna? I've got to collect a computer on Main Street and then I'm on my way. Grab yourself a coffee and don't talk to any strange men.'

By the time the turn-off for Malibu loomed up, Mandy was definitely not in the mood for any moaning. He was hungry, and there was a far more interesting dinner date sitting underneath his passenger seat – Pedro García-Márquez's laptop freshly picked up from the cop shop on Main Street.

He accelerated towards Malibu, heading for Something Fishy. The plan: grab a takeout, double back to Cross Creek, pick up Donna and find a shady spot to swim, eat and read Pedro's files. What a difference a day makes in LA.

At Something Fishy, the sushi looked sexy. Mandy always over-ordered and made the same excuse: buying extra for Ned. That Friday evening was no exception. Breezing back south on Pacific Coast Highway, he took a large bite of his California roll and turned left at the lights into Cross Creek. The sunlight was beginning to fade and the shadows of the buildings flickered across the windscreen. Just as he rounded a corner towards the meeting space outside the shopping mall, a silver VW van with foreign writing on its side pulled out in front of him.

Mandy slammed on the Amazon's anchors and screeched to a halt. The VW slid back into the drive. It was a near-miss. Mandy's mouth filled with saliva. It took a few seconds to swallow enough to wind down the window and shout, 'Sodding idiot!'

The driver of the van flashed his headlights and drove past. Relieved to have avoided an accident, he hardly registered that the couple in the VW van were two Asian medics.

When he finally found Donna, she got into the back seat of the Amazon and folded her arms. She was dressed in denim shorts, white pumps and a green halter-neck top, and was carrying a Miss Piggy shoulder bag. In the distance, she looked like jailbait. Close up, she appeared to be a deeply unhappy twenty-five-year-old.

'I had a bad experience with a company who I thought were offering me a make-up job,' she said, between scowls.

'Bad luck,' Mandy said, telling himself not to falter or change his mind about Donna *definitely* having to leave the apartment because of what he was about to hear.

'Story of my fucking life.'

'A little suggestion: might be wise to wear something slightly more formal for the next interview?'

Mandy handed her a compensatory box of sushi, said nothing more and drove back onto PCH, heading south. Donna ate. He breathed in what he believed to be the superior air of the ocean and thought back on the day.

Jesus – all the grovelling he'd done to get Pedro's laptop out of the station.

It had been a few years since he'd been in the evidence room of the SMPD, yet everyone behaved as if he was still on the force. Lucky, that. Even big-arsed Officer Marcia offered no resistance whatsoever to his request to have the laptop, other than her usual obsession with signatures: *I'm not blocking anything. Mandy, you can have whatever you need until I hear otherwise, but you have to sign here first, there and again over here as well.*

A strong whiff of ozone cut with carbon monoxide, and Donna's chewing, helped Mandy rejoin the present. The turn-off sign for Topanga Beach appeared in the near distance. He angled his head back towards Donna. 'Fancy going for a swim? Might do you good. I'm up for it.'

He watched Donna scowl in the back seat and say, 'Narrrr. I'm going to a meeting to get my head straight.'

Mandy looked up in the rear-view and saw that Donna was staring through the side window, sucking her thumb. Something else apart from possibly having to leave the apartment and the phoney employer was making her pissed off. Doubtless all would become clear. He guessed he should crack on with the laptop and suspect list, pass on the swimming, go home and finish up the sushi.

By the time he'd fed the cat, showered and changed into shorts and T-shirt, Donna's sponsor was beeping the horn of her VW Beetle outside. He waved through the kitchen window at the corkscrew-haired sponsor and breathed a sigh of relief as Donna got in the car. He had a call to make, to number six on the list – a married couple living near Venice Beach. The Sternwoods.

But first a look online for some minor research.

Sitting in front of the screen in his office, he ravaged his sushi box, cramming two pieces of salmon into his mouth with one hand, while the other felt underneath the table and took out a chilled can of Coke from the mini-fridge.

Opening it, he downed a few large gulps, quickly typed in 'Google' and then 'Lexington Property Group'. Fifty sites came up for the name, all based in Kentucky. Must be under another name. Mandy tried 'Lexington Property Management Services, Santa Monica' and pressed 'enter'. Nothing under that name, save for some real-estate office in Glendale selling apartments in Lexington House, a new development.

Did Quinn give him the right name or a fake one? No. Why should he? One more thing to ask Mr Quinn, when he could get hold of the slippery fish. Let Terry do it.

Move on; take another card.

He opened up Pedro's laptop, turned it on and typed in 'Last will and testament' and hit the search bar. He didn't expect to find more than a gnat's cock.

Pedro, whatever else he had been, had been as bumbling as most people about his laptop security.

There it was. In nice, crisp lettering on the screen.

'No shit!' yelled Mandy at the sushi box.

Yep, Pedro was as open as the rest of his family were cagey. Eight files, each numbered and titled 'The Last Will and Testament of Pedro García-Márquez' unfolded on the screen like a series of ancient scrolls with ribbons round them.

He highlighted the one with the most recent date and hit 'enter'.

Thirty seconds later he slapped the worktop and shouted, 'Lucy bloody Lack! No way!'

Pedro had not only 'bequeathed' Lucy Lack his holiday cottage in Sayulita, Mexico, but also the 1927 painting *Automat* by Edward Hopper. Mandy stood up and pictured a sun-kissed Lucy Lack lying with Pedro in the surf on a beach in Mexico.

'Pedro must have liked you one fuck of a lot or you are much cleverer than I'd realized . . .'

He gulped down the remaining Coke and, with a celebratory flourish, crushed the can between both hands.

17

9 a.m., 12 July

Mandy was cleaning his teeth when Miguel García-Márquez called round at the house at nine o'clock, completely unexpected.

'I wanted to meet you on your turf,' he said as he stood on the doorstep, adjusting the white cuffs of his shirt so they jutted out of his jacket sleeves. 'We are serious about security in the family and prefer not to use the telephone or Internet – so easily hacked nowadays.'

Despite saying little in their first meeting, Miguel was clearly senior vice-president of protocol. Using a towel to wipe toothpaste dribble from his chin, Mandy ushered his guest through the sitting room into his study, kicking the yellow flipper underneath the coffee table and praying that no stray underwear or other evidence of Donna would appear. Miguel stepped gingerly across the carpet, clutching his cell in one hand and car keys in the other. Mandy spotted the crested signet ring on his left little finger. Did he use a rosary like his father?

'Take a seat,' Mandy said, indicating a dusty director's chair in the corner of the room. 'Can I get you some coffee?'

Miguel shook his head. 'No, and I'd rather stand.' He took a step towards Mandy's computer, hands clasped behind his back. 'This looks familiar hand-writing,' he said, peering at his father's list of friends and suspects, which Mandy had Blu-tacked to the edge of the screen.

He looked even more uncomfortable than the day before.

Mandy picked up his pen and notebook, cleared his throat. Miguel García-Márquez began. He seemed peculiarly uncertain. Maybe it was being in such a small room with a relative stranger.

'My mother and Josefina, our old nanny, are currently in a clinic in Mexico City being treated for shock,' he said. 'They are not to be contacted under any circumstances. And go easy on Alfonso and María – they've taken the news pretty bad.'

Clearly the García-Márquez family look after their own, Mandy thought.

'I give you my word that information will go no further. How do I make contact with the family?'

'No one will ever answer their cell directly, but here are a set of numbers to text with – but only a number to call you back on. Again, it's too easy for a kidnapper to hack into mobile signals, and after what's happened . . .' Miguel held up a piece of paper.

Mandy copied the details into his notebook. Miguel folded the paper back into his wallet.

'When are your mother and Josefina returning to LA?'

Miguel gave the ghost of a smile. 'I really can't say at this time,' he said. 'I must go now.'

Mandy led the way back to the front door, grateful for Donna not making a guest appearance. There was little to say other than 'I will be in touch.' Miguel stood motionless on the doorstep for a few moments, eyeing him over. In his dark suit, white shirt and black tie, he was more buttoned up than a chesterfield sofa.

'I wish you good luck,' he said finally, 'but I do not share in my father's faith that you will bring my brother's killer to justice. The sooner the police are involved, the better. Nothing personal, Mandy.'

With that, Miguel García-Márquez walked over to his red Jaguar, got in, spun the wheels and drove off. As the Jaguar turned the corner out of Castellammare Drive, Mandy stood in the morning sunlight, glad that he had not volunteered what he had discovered about Lucy being a beneficiary in Pedro's will. He knew he should have told him, but an unconscious feeling to cover Lucy's back had prevented him coming clean. He would tell Eduardo García-Márquez in person and try not to take Miguel's last remark personally.

He strolled back inside the house and exhaled several times, like that'd help. Every family has its straight man, and he didn't mind betting that Miguel was the straightest and most repressed in the García-Márquez gang. Nothing wrong with that – difficult to get far without having a Ned Normal around.

Spending time with Miguel was like having to be on best behaviour while holding a hot knife between your knees. Mandy sighed. There was no way round it: Miguel's parting words had left a bad taste in Mandy's mouth. He needed to get out of the house and have a shot of caffeine at the Evil Eye.

Within minutes of Mandy reaching the boardwalk behind Santa Monica Beach another strange thing happened. If Mandy was a smidge more superstitious, he'd have run back to the ranch and hid under the duvet for a couple of days. A bare-chested black guy on roller skates, in blue shorts and headphones, was skating backwards. A heavily tattooed white female boarder was zigzagging forward. The inevitable happened.

They collided, clashed heads, smashing metal, flesh slapping against concrete. The black guy fell awkwardly onto his elbow, split open the inside of his wrist like a pod of pink peas.

'Whoops! Shit!' he called out cheerfully, and then passed out at exposed veins, muscle and gristle.

The skateboarder hit the deck hard too, but cushioned by her ample backside, sat up quickly. She took one look at the semi-conscious roller skater and yelled, 'You stupid motherfucker – look the fuck where you're going!'

It was, Mandy thought, like she was on automatic. Automatic bad mood. Like so many people nowadays. Where was the love? What happened to having fun?

By now a small crowd was gathering.

'Hold on!' Mandy called out. Instincts still a cop's, he stepped onto the boardwalk to help and bent by the unconscious man. 'Don't move him.'

A blond-haired man rollerbladed by, coming to an expert halt right next to them. 'I'm a doctor. Can someone call 911?'

Mandy raised his arm in acknowledgement, dialled the number and gave the location and idea of injuries to the paramedic service. He slammed his cell shut. 'Help is on the way.'

The crowd began to applaud. Everyone in LA liked a drama. Services no longer required, Mandy stood up and turned on his heel to go. Just then a familiar female voice called out his name. Fabienne with her golden retriever.

'Hey. What the hell are you doing here?' he said, rubbing the dog's head.

'Have you forgotten I only live six blocks from here?'

'Of course I haven't,' Mandy lied. 'Why aren't you at work?'

She smiled and gave the dog's lead a gentle shake. 'Walking doggie on the beach. Worked late four nights out of five on this crazy Viceroy thing. One morning off seems reasonable to me.'

'Do you want me to register my support with the Giraffe?'

She laughed. 'The only time I get to walk the dog now is late at night – pitch dark when the beach is full of weirdos.'

Mandy steered them towards the Evil Eye. As Fabienne walked, she smoothed down the short sleeve of her white cotton shirt with her hand. 'The Giraffe doesn't see why I can't live in the office. Cheaper rent, no travel costs, he once suggested – douchebag!' She chuckled to herself and patted her dog.

Mandy looked at his watch, wondered how much the Giraffe listened to Fabienne. What she needed was a man in her life. He picked up the beat.

'Viceroy must be close to wrapping now?'

'Don't bank on it. Supposedly there are orders to take the gunmen alive, but that's never going to happen, right?'

She linked arms with him. 'So how's it going? Got any suspects yet?'

He fished out García-Márquez's list. 'Quite a few. Four of them are on this list. Some from the father, some that I've added in along the way.'

'I haven't got my contacts in. Read out the names and I'll tell you who did it. Just for fun?'

'Like a kind of psychic helping with enquiries thing?' Mandy said.

She laughed. 'Even more random than that!'

He felt like a kid being asked to recite a rollcall at school. He adopted an aloof, nasally schoolmaster voice and read the names in random order. 'John and Sarah Sternwood, Wing, Javier Jones, Bradley Adams, Wayne Chung, Lucy Lack, Father Tony, Mrs García-Márquez and Mr Quinn. Oh, that excludes half of the gay meeting places in Santa Monica and anyone interested in eating or dissecting kidneys, any trainee Hannibal Lectors and all the medical schools in Los Angeles.'

'Kidneys?' Fabienne said, holding her hand under her chin, still laughing slightly at the way he read it.

That British thing gets 'em every time, Mandy thought. If only she'd been a casting agent.

'Yeah, someone took a kidney from the body. No one can say anything until the seven-day blackout is over.'

'The Giraffe never mentioned that. Jesus! I hope that's not going to become a pattern round here.'

'In Santa Monica? There's a market to steal Porsches and Range Rovers, not body parts. A gang with a full order book from Eastern Europe come in the middle of the night and winch the cars onto low-loader trailers and disappear. They've got plenty of their own body parts back home.'

Fabienne pulled a face as if she had just tasted sour milk. 'OK, three names on your list are doing it for me: Sternwood, Lucy Lack and Mrs García-Márquez.'

Mandy cleared his throat. 'Interesting choices.'

'I'm an interesting girl,' she said, fluttering her eyelashes.

'When I break this case open, I promise next time it will be considerably more than flowers.'

He put his arm tight around her shoulder and squeezed. He could tell by the way she kept looking at him that there was no man on the scene.

They had arrived outside the tatty exterior of the Evil Eye. He gestured to the entrance. 'Would you like to have a quick coffee?'

She laughed and shook her head. 'In that dump? My pooch wouldn't be seen dead there, let alone me. Why don't you come home and I'll make you one?'

Why not? It can't hurt, a voice inside Mandy's head said. But he liked her too much to lead her up any garden path. People always want what they cannot have. He and Fabienne had always had a flirty relationship, but he was careful not to cross the line.

'I don't think I will. Dumps are good . . . Suits me somehow . . .'

She nodded wistfully, reached up and kissed Mandy on the cheek. 'Let me know if there is anything I can do to help.' Holding the straining dog lead with both hands, she and her golden walked slowly off towards the beach.

He pushed open the door to the café. He could spend five minutes max on breakfast. He sat at his usual table and gave his order to the waiter, stroked the neck of the new bottle of ketchup and moved his foot over the hardened lumps of gum on the floor. He knew each lump by feel, and when someone had stuck a new one there. He'd probably be able to tell if anyone ever cleaned one away. But that was so unlikely it probably wasn't worth worrying about.

He took out ten blue six-by-four index cards from his jacket pocket and wrote down each suspect's name, giving them a number. The waiter set down coffee and a doughnut. He drank the coffee and after one bite of the doughnut decided he wasn't hungry.

No sign of Lucy Lack coming out of the back entrance of Shutters. He called her room, left a message on her voicemail. Best he could do.

Mandy stuffed his notebooks, index cards and pens into his pocket, and smiled. It would be just fine to find Pedro's killer and hire Fabienne as his assistant, if nothing else. She made him feel a better man, made him feel confident and good. The bad taste left in his mouth by what Miguel García-Márquez said earlier that morning had disappeared.

He stood up and visualized receiving an award and a cheque from the mayor of Santa Monica for solving the killings. It felt good. Maybe Frank was right and visualization wasn't just something rich hippies did about their Apple and Google share prices. He paid the check and walked out, a process that took less than twenty-nine seconds. Once outside, he peered at the address for his next appointment, Mr and Mrs Sternwood.

18

Midday, 12 July

The Sternwood house was close to the edge of the Howland Canal in Venice. It had a huge back lawn and flowerbeds full of red and white geraniums. A discreet 'House for Sale' sign hung from a white wooden gallows bracket by the entrance gate. Mandy reckoned the house must be worth over $2 million – not bad for a couple not yet turned thirty.

A tall guy wearing round tortoiseshell glasses answered the door, offered a clammy handshake and a fixed smile.

An image of Ripley, outwardly cool but inwardly a psycho, flashed onto Mandy's radar.

'I'm Johnny,' he said, ushering Mandy inside.

'It's good of you to see me at such short notice,' Mandy said, slightly over-doing the English accent. The house smelt of Kentish hops, but everywhere Mandy looked there were vases of red and yellow tulips. He followed Johnny through an open-plan living space into a ten-metre-long country kitchen where a blonde woman was sitting at the table.

He'd checked them both out en route on a laptop Google search in the slow traffic. Johnny Sternwood was an investment analyst; Sarah worked as CEO of an eco charity. How yin and yang. Maybe they squeezed each other's blackheads too.

'Hi. Good to meet you,' Sarah Sternwood said, getting up from the kitchen table. She was tanned and petite, dressed in a T-shirt, no bra, tight cotton skirt, standing in bare feet. An upper-class version of Donna without the sex appeal.

'We are so devastated about Pedro,' she said, swallowing heavily. 'I can't bear to think of him being dead. So was it really suicide, or did something else happen?'

Clearly rumours were already circulating around Pedro's nearest and dearest, despite the blackout on information.

'There are some questions over that,' he said, opening his notebook. He was itching to get the interview over and get the hell out of the uptight house of out-of-season, flown-in-that-morning tulips. 'Could you tell me what you were doing the night before and on the day Pedro died and how long you had both known Pedro?'

'As a couple, or me personally?' The woman was clearly in charge of talking. 'My husband has known Pedro since Junior High, haven't you, Johnny?'

Sternwood rested his backside on the corner of the table and murmured, 'Yes. He took off his glasses, blew on the lenses and polished them with the end of his checked shirt.

Sarah Sternwood added almost as an afterthought, 'And we'd been staying at my parents' house in Santa Barbara when the tragedy happened.'

Mandy waited until the glasses were back on Sternwood's face.

'You knew Pedro really well – can you think of any reason why he should take his own life?'

Sternwood cleared his throat, sat forward and said, 'As far as I know, Pedro didn't have anything bothering him, apart from being lonely.'

This time he was able to speak without any interruption from his wife.

Mandy sat down opposite on a kitchen chair at the table. 'Are you sure? How well did you really know him?'

'Since I was twelve years old. He was best man at my wedding. That's how well I knew him.'

'But that could mean that's how well he knew you . . .'

Sternwood shifted his position on the table. 'Whatever. Pedro is dead. Nothing we can do about him now, except . . .'

'Help me find the killer?'

Sarah Sternwood covered her mouth with her hand. 'Oh my God, you really think he was murdered?'

Mandy paused his reply to take in the expression on their faces. Johnny's face was entirely still, while his wife's eyes were blinking, her hand now covering her chin. He sensed both of them knew more than they were saying but could no longer justify the silence. He needed to catch them off guard.

'OK, completely off the record and between these four walls? I'm pretty well convinced Pedro García-Márquez was murdered.'

The Sternwoods stood up and hugged one another for what seemed like over a minute. Then they sat back down again and looked at each other in a way that reminded Mandy of two actors in *American Beauty*. He shrugged.

She touched the corner of her eye with her finger. 'Would you like to see some photos of when we were all last together?' she suggested. 'Might give you a better idea of how we really were . . . ?'

It was a change of direction, but Mandy had to go with it.

'They are on my Mac,' Sternwood said wearily. 'I'll go get them.'

'OK, honey.' She said it without looking at him and turned to Mandy. 'Would you like some home-made lemonade?'

Mandy nodded. He felt like asking for a cold beer, but given the circumstances . . . She got up, opened the fridge, then shut the door again without taking it out, and lifting herself up on tiptoes, took a photograph frame from under a pile of fashion magazines. She came over to the table and presented him with the picture. He took it in both hands . . . a laughing Pedro dressed in a dinner jacket being kissed on either cheek by Johnny and Sarah. How sweet.

'I found this earlier today. I had to put it away a few months ago, you see.'

'Why?' Mandy said, wondering what was keeping Sternwood. It was a big house, but it wasn't Siberia.

Sarah Sternwood put her fingers up to her lips and whispered, 'They had a bad falling-out.'

Mandy leant forward, cupped a sympathetic hand round his ear. 'About what?'

She exhaled. 'Dot-com money.' She said it like it was some kind of inevitability. Maybe living round here it was.

'Dot-com money?'

She nodded and went back to where she had been sitting.

'I noticed you are moving home. Going far?' Mandy said.

Sarah Sternwood flashed a nervous smile. Clearly he'd hit a raw spot.

'We're heading back east. I've got family in Boston. We thought it would be better to raise a family in Maine.'

'What was the dot-com business you mentioned?' asked Mandy, as heavy footsteps came down the stairs, along the wooden-floored corridor and back into the kitchen.

Sternwood placed an open Apple MacBook on the kitchen table. 'Here we are.'

Sarah Sternwood returned to the fridge and this time actually took out the lemonade.

'Would you like a drink too, honey?'

'Yes, please.' He was concentrating hard on scrolling down files of photos on his MacBook. 'Why did you just tell Mandy about the company, sweetheart?' he said, not even glancing at the photograph on the table.

'Honey,' she called out as she poured lemonade into a glass, 'don't you think it's better the issue is out in the open? Lucy's bound to say something sooner or later.'

'So was Lucy Lack a shareholder in your dot-com company?' Mandy asked.

There was a silence. Mandy moved to the edge of his chair. Sarah Sternwood brought over two glasses of lemonade. Under the table, Sternwood's right hand clenched into a fist.

'Well, you certainly put that out in the open, sweetie, that's for sure,' he said with a tight smile.

He turned towards Mandy, raised a glass of lemonade in a toast and laughed, clearly pissed off. 'If you hadn't got so *close* to Miss Lack, we wouldn't have to worry about any of that, would we?'

Sarah Sternwood blushed pink. For the first time she looked attractive rather than just well bred.

'Please,' she said. 'Can we not? It's not true. I don't know why you think it.'

Sternwood stood up and glared at his wife and, without looking at Mandy, said, 'Yes, she was, and she lost money too.'

He didn't seem very bothered by the fact. But then, Mandy guessed, it was OPM, 'other people's money'. He leant his elbows on the table and held his hands together in the shape of an A. The last thing he had anticipated was a domestic spat involving Lucy. For some reason, a wrong reason, he'd believed she only existed in Santa Monica with Pedro, not in anyone else's world.

'Could you tell me in plain English,' he said, 'what happened between the three or four of you?'

The Sternwoods folded their arms simultaneously. Both opened their mouths, but only a murmuring sigh came out.

Mandy scraped his chair back on the wooden floorboards. 'When did you last see Lucy Lack?'

Sarah Sternwood jumped in. 'We met two weeks ago at Loews Hotel.'

'Two weeks ago at Loews in Santa Monica?'

'Yes, and I'd say she was hurting badly for money.'

Mandy faked a coughing fit. Why hadn't Lucy mentioned this rather recent visit when he drove her to Shutters? He picked up the glass, swallowed a mouthful of lemonade and said, 'Mr and Mrs Sternwood, these things are often better out than in.'

Sternwood hesitated, held up the palm of his hand towards his wife and said, 'It's not how it looks, and it's not at all how it seems.'

Mandy took off his jacket and laid his notebook flat on the table. Without taking his gaze from his two hosts, he said, 'If I had a hundred dollars for every time that's been said to me, I could afford to be your neighbour. Just tell me the truth . . . It'll be quicker and less hassle in the end. Believe me.'

Mandy yanked the ignition key out of the lock and got out of the Amazon, not bothering to put money in the meter. He took off his jacket, loosened his collar and tie, and walked straight into Fat Sam's Burger Bar on Ocean Park Boulevard. He sat down at a table with a view of the TV, sipped a glass of iced water and shouted at the eponymous gut-bucketed owner behind the jump, 'Double cheeseburger, fries and French mustard – no onions – and a large Coke.'

Fat Sam, in his usual white outsized, short-sleeved shirt, repeated the order but did not take his eyes off the television. Mandy was so hot and frazzled from the two-hour-long Sternwood interview he hardly took in what was on the TV screen.

'One of the gunmen connected with the Viceroy Hotel shootings has been found dead in a Santa Monica parking structure. The LAPD are tight-lipped about the exact location of the body, cause of death and nationality. However, an officer, who did not wish to be identified, confirmed the dead man was found in a parking lot adjacent to Santa Monica City Hall. The source said the dead man is Vietnamese and lived in Long Beach. The other gunman is still at large.'

'Think they'll get the other guy?' Fat Sam asked, wiping his sweaty face with a cloth.

'You bet your life they will. The LAPD always get their man, especially when the men they shot were Sergeant Powell and the deputy attorney general of this state,' Mandy said. He felt like asking whether Fat Sam remembered the name of the Palestinian who shot Bobby Kennedy back in 1968 at the Ambassador. But he didn't bother. Fat Sam was a patriotic type who may take a reminder of another political slaying as a criticism of his country, and apart from anything, Mandy didn't want his burger burnt.

When his order was done, Fat Sam brought it over himself, with extra relish. As he bit into it, medium rare, he was glad he hadn't risked his cynical opinions.

Afterwards replete, Mandy drove north down Ocean Park, took a right and headed for Shutters at number 1 Pico. He was still flabbergasted by what he had been told by the couple with the $2-million house . . . He had to talk to Lucy Lack, right now. That girl sure had some questions to answer.

It had happened like this: ten minutes of cat-and-mouse and Sarah Sternwood had come clean. With her hands on her hips, she said, 'Truth is, although we're really attracted to each other, we like to pipe others on board to play, and that's the long and the short of it. Between these four walls, to use

85

your expression, we both became obsessed with Lucy. She was involved with us on quite an intimate basis, if you get my meaning. So we offered her the opportunity to invest in Johnny's new company. Trouble was, once the dot-com business collapsed, she blamed Johnny for losing her money and would not speak to either of us again. She even turned Pedro against us, especially when he found out what had been happening between us and her.'

It was as if she was commenting on the contrasting merits of eating linguine or fettuccine. Mandy was sure his face had flushed as a series of images of Lucy Lack and Johnny and Sarah Sternwood lying intertwined, naked on a blanket in Christchurch Meadow flashed up in his head. During his wife's frank confession, Johnny Sternwood had just sat there with his still-full lemonade glass in front of him. He looked like a balloon that was slowly deflating after a party.

So there was nothing for it but to confront Lucy Lack. Someone was not telling the truth. Or rather, lying by omission. As a lapsed Catholic, Mandy was somewhat familiar with this ruse. He hadn't been tough enough. Yes, yes, he said again to Terry's voice in his head. Yes, it was because she was hot.

It was going to be unpleasant, he knew it. He wanted to be the knight in shining armour, but he was just a grubby PI who had to scrabble about in the waste of other people's lives. That was how it was really. So he'd better get on with it.

But as the Shutters' car valets were parking the Amazon, and he was brushing down his jacket ready for the big confrontation, a taxi pulled away from the other entrance door.

He caught a glance of long, dark hair, and Jackie O sunglasses.

Lucy Lack.

Fortunately, he'd always tipped the car jockeys well. They'd know where the taxi was heading. But it turned out nobody knew, save that it had a nodding toy tiger in the back window. Because there were – what, a thousand? Two? – cabs in LA with one of those, right?

Mandy swore, grabbed back his keys and jumped into the car.

Must be somewhere local, he reckoned, steering the Volvo into the fast lane up Pico, the accelerator flat down to the floor.

By the time he reached the stop sign for the 12th Street crossing, he had a visual on a cab with a nodding tiger in the back ten cars or so ahead, heavy traffic in all lanes. He could see the back of Lucy's head; she was speaking into her cell, on the right of the rear of the cab.

One set of red traffic lights separated him from a full and frank conversation. Was she running away, en route to the airport? Was she heading towards a rendezvous with that handsome priest whom she'd said she'd only just met on the plane?

Mandy revved the Amazon, checked the rear-view for any sign of a cop. He needed to catch up with the cab before it turned off onto the freeway in six blocks' time. Despite the Amazon having a recon engine, it still lacked pace. Lucy could easily lose him in a cab on a six-lane highway.

The lights turned green; the traffic moved forward. All except for the stupid Toyota pickup right in front of his car, going absolutely nowhere. Damn it. He swivelled round and pointed to the driver behind that the guy in front had stalled. But the woman driver behind must've been stoned because she just kept staring straight ahead. Mandy reversed, engine gunning, while Lucy's cab moved past the green light.

'Back up, you moron!' he shouted, but the woman in the car behind did not move.

The lights turned red.

He watched Lucy's cab pull away into the distance.

He came off at the next exit and headed back to Santa Monica. At least he could find out where Father Tony was and what he really knew about Lucy.

Was it remotely possible that Lucy plotted and carried out a murder in return for a $3-million Edward Hopper painting and a nice little place in Mexico she'd stand to gain from the will? If you had lost enough dot-com money, maybe it was. If you were disappointed enough that a guy wouldn't marry you because of Mummy's disapproval, maybe it was. Heck, maybe she'd been planning it for years. Maybe the priest was looking to share in the proceeds. Surely not?

He ran into the St Monica's seminary and banged the bell on the oak reception desk. After an interminable minute a short, fat, balding man in a cassock appeared.

'I want to see Father Tony,' Mandy said, barely able to pretend to be civil.

'He's working at a homeless mission today,' the priest replied.

'Jesus,' Mandy yelled. 'What is going on? Nobody is there when they bloody well should be today.'

Back in the Amazon, he had begun polishing the dials on the dashboard when his cell buzzed. A text from Terry. 'Hey, schmuck! Will have a report back from the guys at LAX on frequent flyers to India, and the DEA are checking any gang interest in García-Márquez for me. OK, Big Daddy?'

Just a text from Terry calmed Mandy down. What had he been doing, swearing like that virtually inside a church? Jeezus. Stress City Arizona. Of course Father Tony wasn't in cahoots with Lucy.

It was time to move on and calm down. Mandy peered at the list. Jones was number five. There was a comment of 'burns victim' by his name, which was puzzling. Mandy pulled out his cell, dialled his number and, to his surprise, got straight through. The guy sounded as if he'd taken too much meow-meow.

'We got back ten minutes ago from seeing a private view at a gallery in Seattle, so we're a tiny bit fazed,' he said. 'Let's meet in five hours' time at Club Kafka off Main Street. I'll bring Kimberly – she's my art-dealer girlfriend – if that's OK.'

That was fine, Mandy said. Javier Jones. With the best will in the world the guy sounded like a jerk. Wing hadn't liked him much. But then Wing probably didn't like anybody much. So maybe Mandy and he would become best friends. Somehow he doubted it.

19

6 p.m., 12 July

At 6 p.m., Mandy drove across to Chung's Supermarket close to Santa Monica Airport. He really needed to lay his hands on those CCTV tapes, as all the other leads were drawing a blank. He'd already left two messages and had no call back. When he walked into the store, there was no sign of Chung whatsoever.

'He's sicky-sicky, sir, but will be in tomorrow,' a young Chinese checkout girl said with what appeared to be eye-blinking sincerity.

'Do you have his cell, home number or address?'

'Oh no, sir,' the salesgirl said, lowering her eyes.

Mandy clicked his fingers in angry disbelief and left an Endeavor business card on the till. As he walked out, he pushed several packets of tortilla chips to the ground, felt better and smiled. He still had enough time to shower and change before Javier Jones.

He drove back to the house, fed the cat, showered and changed his shirt. Donna was nowhere to be seen. He grabbed a beer from the fridge, tied his tie and saw a message flashing on his cell. Sod's Law – he'd just stepped into the shower when his cell rang in the bedroom.

When he'd dried and shaved, he picked up his cell, the voicemail alert blinking.

'Meet me at eight thirty a.m. tomorrow, in the outside – smoking – section of Shutters Bistro.' It was Lucy Lack. For some reason, she was whispering. She wouldn't try to ring him again, because she had meditation and was having an early night.

'"Come into my parlour," said the spider to the fly,' Mandy mused aloud, as he pressed the 'save' button. The only problem was, who was the spider, and who was the fly? He tried not to think sexy black widow and, like all things he tried not to think, couldn't stop thinking about it till he got into the Amazon.

At 11.01 p.m. he strolled into Club Kafka hoping he wasn't too early. He'd already preloaded his thoughts that it would be a low-lit club playing Moroccan trance and full of hookah pipes. But inside it was entirely the opposite: white with chandeliers and mirror balls, the only colour coming from the gold tassels on the performers' nipples, and the bottles from the well-lit bar. A couple of cool young Japanese people dressed up in futuristic designer suits were acting as hosts.

It took Mandy two minutes to squeeze between the closely positioned tables where Javier Jones was sitting.

Jones stood up and raised his long-fingered hand in a greeting. He was about five foot six, slightly built, boyish, dressed in a retro herringbone tweed jacket, buttoned-up white collarless shirt, gold bracelets on both wrists and a Muslim-type green-and-cream beaded hat on a head of thinning hair. One of those people, Mandy reckoned, who could look eighteen and forty-eight at the same time. There were raised scars at the side of his face that disappeared under the hat.

'Kimmy, this is Mandy, the man I was telling you about,' Jones said without actually greeting Mandy first.

Kimberly was a good ten years older than Jones. She looked like Morticia from the Addams family: long black hair, black lipstick and a skull-and-cross-patterned ring on her wedding finger. Her cheekbones were like razorblades.

'Good evening, Inspector,' she said in a faux-German drawl. She also sounded bombed out of her head.

Mandy smiled, sat down at the table next to Javier. Kimberly swung round in her seat so that her back was facing Mandy. Nice.

'So how was the private view?' Mandy asked her back.

Jones touched his beaded skullcap and gently prodded the silver bangle on his girlfriend's arm. 'I told Mandy you've just come back from a show.'

'Cool,' Kimberly said, scanning the other tables as if she was trying to find someone.

There was the sound of breaking glass and the music in the club suddenly went up several notches in volume. It was a techno remix of KC and the Sunshine Band's 'That's the Way . . .' with an echo effect on the girl singer's chanting 'Uh-huh, uh-huh' that Mandy liked.

Jones downed a glass of red wine and yelled, 'We always tried to help Pedro choose good paintings.'

Mandy projected his voice without shouting, 'So was Pedro really interested in art, or was it an affectation?'

'Owning a painting by Edward Hopper is not an affectation. It's a statement of belief. The beginning of Pedro's manifesto,' Kimberly said without turning round.

What a load of horseshit.

'I'm most obliged,' Mandy replied, trying to suppress his sarcasm. Then turning to Javier, he said, 'Is that your opinion too, Javier?'

Jones looked down at his empty glass, the scars on the side of his face still tight and raw. They would probably be tight and raw-looking for the rest of his life.

'He liked art, yes,' Jones said. 'But not as much as Kim and I do. He didn't live for it.'

'So what did he love, then?' Mandy said. 'What did he live for?'

Jones shut his eyes for a moment. He looked close to breaking. Then Mandy saw him steel himself, straighten his spine, shake his head as if dislodging a bothersome fly – a fly called grief? – and put on a smile. It was a ghastly kind of smile. More like heartbreak than anything else.

'It sounds corny, Mandy, but he believed in helping people, particularly people who came from a disadvantaged background.'

'People like his Russian cleaner, for example?'

'I didn't know he had a Russian one . . .' Javier said, pausing to put two red pills into his mouth and gulp some iced water. Stroking Kimberly's bare shoulder, he continued, 'Pedro had two sides to him – the philanthropist and the businessman.'

'Which side did he do best, do you think?'

'His ambition was to set up a social network site that would teach poor people basic financial housekeeping skills. Show them how to start up and run their own business.'

'Similar to the people doing micro-lending in India?'

'Yeah, along those lines.'

'So why didn't he do it?'

'He kept being sidetracked by other things.'

'Meaning what?'

'The family and various friends, in inverted commas – know what I mean? During the last year or so I think certain people close to him were taking all of his goodness and energy.'

'No kidding,' Mandy said.

There was one good thing about Jones being off his trolley: he was easy to lead. Then Mandy saw Kimberly put a hand on his back – she knew he was saying too much. Jones pushed it away and, like a kid asking a question to which they know the answer, carried on.

'Miguel is a stuffed buzzard but OK. His father is kind of cool but frightening, and Alfonso is kind of strung out. Have you met his mother and sister yet? The Witches of Toxic. Well, that will tell you why Pedro didn't spend too much time with his family.'

'What about Lucy Lack? Do you know her?'

Jones paused to rub his eyes. Mandy noticed the backs of both of his hands were a patchwork of raised shiny pink skin grafts, just like the patch of skin above Frank's ear.

'We met once or twice and that was enough . . . too painful for me. She's taken over . . . I used to be Pedro's number one, his favourite. Last time I saw Pedro was three months ago. He came here one night but left after an hour or so.'

'Why did he leave? Was Lucy with him?'

'No, he was on his own. He never liked just sitting around and people-watching. Not like us, I guess.'

'And you and Pedro . . . you were friends, or something more?'

'We were lovers,' Jones said wistfully. 'Not for long, before he ended it. But we stayed good friends.'

A fight broke out about ten tables away and took everyone's attention.

Jones pointed at the couple Kimberly had been staring at. The woman pointing her finger into her friend's face was wearing sky-blue garage overalls and had a brilliant-ginger beehive. The guy was pale, undernourished and had a thick black nest of hair that could have been a wig or dyed. He was in black, and reminded Mandy of the singer in the Cure. Although not audible over the music, they were pecking and shouting at one another like two wood-peckers competing for the same piece of tree trunk, jabbing fingers into each other's faces.

But then the woman stood up, threw her glass down onto the table, raised the palm of her hand into a 'Stop' sign and stalked off like a catwalk model on speed. The man picked up a napkin and dried his hair, swallowed whatever was in his glass and punched himself hard in the forehead.

Jones whistled and fanned his face with his hand. 'Wow! That guy looks like he just lost his Van Gogh.'

Kimberly swung round and grabbed hold of his hand. 'Forget about art, babe – that's Susan Green, aka Dee Nitrate, the singer with the Veil. Twelve years ago they could play three nights at the Civic and sell out. That crack-addled guy over there was the keyboard player – and Susan's the love of his life.'

'Wow, honey. You know everyone.'

Kimberly leant forward and kissed Jones on the mouth. 'I should have my own TV show called *Retrosexual*.'

Mandy was bored with witnessing histrionics from people past their sell-by date, people with too much sense of their own importance, acting out in a small goldfish bowl like Santa Monica. Also, something was bugging him about the name Susan Green, but he couldn't work out why. He needed to sleep. Would Donna be home and waiting to talk about staying even longer at his apartment? He hoped not.

'Just a final question, if that's all right,' he said. 'Where were you on the night Pedro was murdered?'

'We were at the Bukowski private view,' Kimberly said. 'Both of us – there are photos of us there, and at the club afterwards.'

Jones nodded. 'It seems so terrible now,' he said, 'that we were having so much fun while that was happening to Pedro.'

Mandy nodded and left them to it. They hardly even noticed him leave.

Could he cross Jones off his list of suspects? He wasn't sure. Both of them looked like they could do with an injection of cash. But of course that didn't mean they would kill someone to get it. If anything, Jones seemed too unco-ordinated to have slaughtered his ex-lover and his ex's cleaner. Underneath the cripplingly annoying affectations, Jones's eyes kept turning shy and even kind. Not only that but Mandy couldn't believe that Jones and Kimberly would have been able to leave the Edward Hopper painting on the wall. It would have been too much temptation.

20

1.45 a.m., 13 July

Benny had only been asleep for four hours when Dick Chain called. No mistaking his deep Texan drawl. There was an emergency with one of the vans. Not mechanical but human. Evidently, when they'd arrived on the beach, a passing homeless guy had threatened Dick with a bottle, rushed off and sprinted up and down the beach yelling things about the moon and his teeth.

'It took me ten minutes to tackle the guy, drag him back and tie him up in the passenger seat,' Dick said, as if he was talking about rounding up sheep on the farm.

'You didn't hurt him, did you?' Benny said.

'Don't think so,' Dick said unconvincingly.

'What's the problem, then?'

'Boss, I don't normally handle this area, just standing in for someone. I wasn't designed to deal with new clients—'

Already out of bed and half dressed, Benny interrupted, 'I hear you, Dick. Stay calm and wait there. I'm coming.'

Training was something that Benny took very seriously. Running a small business was like having a young family: someone had to get up in the middle of the night and deal with a crying child. In the case of Fish Farm, the buck stopped with Benny. And if there was a problem with one of the staff at two in the morning, and even if it involved a twenty-five-minute drive from Silver Lake and a risk of being identified, so be it. Benny cared.

When he reached the north end of Santa Monica Beach, Benny was pleased to notice that the silver VW dental van had been discreetly parked alongside a light blue lifeguard hut. Santa Monica Beach was a relatively new market for Fish Farm, and, like everything else to do with the company, it was vital not to draw attention from the wrong people, and in particular

94

any passing police car. Benny pulled on his latex Schwarzenegger mask, then dialled Dick's cell and asked him to step outside and brief him on the situation inside.

Dick was concise with his words. Benny was quick on the uptake. The new client, a young homeless lady from Des Moines, said she needed emergency treatment for toothache. 'You've come to the right place,' was what Dick said he'd said. They'd then given her the standard blood test to check out the grouping and given the young woman a cup of tea.

'So what's wrong?' Benny asked, rolling a pair of surgical gloves onto his hands.

Dick Chain hunched his enormous shoulders. 'There's something else. A message from Janet came through.'

Benny shone his torch straight into Dick's face. 'Yes, and what did the message say?' Benny clicked his fingers together impatiently. Dick's face creased like a bloodhound.

'Someone's back in town. Someone we don't like? Dominic Young? Trying to get back together with Susan?'

Benny Tan stood still and said nothing for a few seconds. Everything was calm and silent, save for the sea lapping onto the shore and the wind blowing spinnakers in the distance.

Dick spat tobacco juice from the side of his mouth and stepped towards his boss. 'Let me take care of it?'

Benny exhaled dismissively and handed the torch to Dick. 'That won't be necessary.'

He took hold of the cell and, using a ball-point pen, pressed the code for his executive assistant, Janet Lee. The number went straight to voicemail. Benny stepped away from Dick and left a message.

'I understand that our loose-cannon friend, Dominic, has returned to the US. Can you deal with it immediately, please?'

He slipped the cell back into his trouser pocket and turned to Dick Chain. 'I like your honesty about the new clients, Dick. You've been put in an awkward position, I can appreciate that. So just leave all this to me.'

Benny gently opened the back door of the VW and gasped at the sight of a white Scottish terrier lying on top of the patient.

'I'm sorry but it's unhygienic to have a dog in the treatment area,' said Benny, lifting the animal into the air. 'I'll put it with the driver. It'll be quite safe.'

The plump, blonde twenty-year-old tried to sit up on the treatment couch. 'My dog has to stay with me – he's my best friend. And you know what? I think my tooth is OK now.'

Benny smiled. The blue-eyed girl attempted to swing her legs off the treatment couch but discovered she couldn't move. The special tea she'd drunk was taking effect.

'What the hell's going on . . . ?' were the last words the young lady from Des Moines actually spoke.

To calm her and take away the fear in her eyes, he held the sleeping dog close to her face.

'You can see your woof-woof later tonight after surgery,' Benny said in one of his most reassuring tones.

The young woman's lips twitched and her eyes opened wide as eggcups. Benny guessed she was trying to say thank you but could no longer talk.

'Prepare the patient for surgery. I'll be back in two minutes.'

Dick Chain stood up, banging his head on the roof. Nurse Columbia stepped over from behind the patient's head, nodded and dangled a finger over the instrument tray as if selecting a candy. Benny lifted the security handle in the back door and climbed out of the van.

Clutching the sleepy terrier dog between his latex-gloved hands, he walked down to the shoreline. The white frothy sea reminded him of the medicated shampoo he always used when showering. His biometric head torch shone down on his rubber boots as they sloshed through the water. Some out-of-tune chanting from a group of drunken homeless kept wafting in and out on the wind from the other side of the pier. Benny turned round to double-check the VW van's headlights were off and that no people or police cars were in the near distance. It was 2.45 a.m. Santa Monica had gone to sleep. There were no cars on the road, no taxis, no speeding show-offs, not even the early morning garbage collectors.

Standing in seven inches or so of seawater, he spotted the dog had a shiny tag attached to its collar. He held the dog under his arm and twisted the tag round to see if there was anything too incriminating written on it. 'SNOWY. Please call 515-836-8636 if found.'

Benny mumbled the 515 phone code to himself. Ah yes. He remembered doing business with an undertaker in Des Moines with the same area code.

'Wow. You two are a long way from home, aren't you?' Benny said almost compassionately, deftly removing the dog's collar and tag.

The sleeping hound stirred but did not open his drugged eyes. Benny dropped the white terrier into the water. There was a splash and then another one as he lifted out his boot and clamped the dog down under the water until all splashing had stopped and the dog was quite still.

21

8.30 a.m., 13 July

Lucy Lack was wearing a black sleeveless dress with a thin black cardigan draped over her shoulders, a pair of sunglasses in front of her eyes. She was smoking her third cigarette. An untouched fresh orange juice sat in the sunlight next to a cup of black coffee.

A waiter set down a large plate of bacon and scrambled eggs in front of Mandy.

'Mind if I go ahead?'

She waved her well-manicured hand in assent and looked away. His fork bulldozed into the thick scrambled mess on his plate as if he hadn't seen food for days

'What questions have you got for me?' Lucy said, carefully not watching him eat. She took a long drag of her cigarette. 'Anything to keep my mind occupied. I feel as if I've been here for weeks.'

He finished his mouthful and took a sip of coffee. The coffee was good at Shutters, but he still preferred the Evil Eye.

'But you were only here two weeks ago, weren't you? Maybe that's why it's so dull for you.'

She lifted her sunglasses and touched the corner of her eye. Her eyes were suddenly windows with the blinds drawn.

'Exactly. That's quite right,' she said. 'Wonder who told you?'

Cool customer. Too cool for someone mourning the death of a loved one? But the eyes were red-rimmed and swollen as well as hostile. She began to scratch the tablecloth with her unused knife.

'Do you want to tell me what you were doing here two weeks ago?'

'Not really. I had some business here, nothing to do with Pedro . . .'

'I saw you yesterday afternoon,' Mandy said. 'In the back of a cab. I tried to catch you, but you seemed to be avoiding me.'

'I didn't see you – why didn't you wave? I was only picking up some photographs.'

He dabbed his mouth with a napkin. 'What is it that you do for a living exactly?' he said.

'I am a futures trader at Steel Bond Futures in the City of London. It's seriously stressful, and I'm surrounded by too much testosterone, but I make it work. I have to be tough as nails to do my job. I'm tougher than most men.' She lifted the cup of coffee to her lips and looked up at him. 'But not underneath. People like you are a thousand times tougher than me. That's why I was coming over to stay with Pedro.' She let out a nasally sob. 'Sorry.'

Mandy held a forkful of scrambled eggs in mid-air. 'Keep talking,' he said, without taking his eyes off her. Some of the egg made it onto the table. Some into his mouth.

She blew her nose into a tissue and rocked her head from side to side. He couldn't work her out: how much was genuine, and how much was carefully designed to manipulate?

'Pedro was such an extraordinary person. He gave everyone so much.'

'Where'd you meet him?'

'Five years ago, backstage at a charity concert in London. I'd had a row with my boyfriend; the idiot stormed off and left me on my own.' She pulled the cardigan tighter around her shoulders. 'For some reason, Pedro was there and he came over and asked if I was OK. We hit it off immediately, and do you know what?' She reached out and touched him on the arm. 'We have spoken on the phone every day since then.'

Her hand was warm, and disturbing. Was everything she did calculated? Terry would say yes. But Mandy wasn't sure. She took her hand back, and smiled sadly. 'It's quite something to have someone you can depend on, isn't it? Someone who makes you laugh every day and who doesn't count the cost of every word or gesture he makes towards you like some kind of emotional accountancy exercise.'

He nodded. 'Certainly is a big something.'

She picked up the fresh orange juice and took the smallest of sips. It took her a while to manage to swallow it. 'A waste of a beautiful man,' she said. 'God, I hope you find the bastard who did this.' She dabbed her eyes with a tissue.

'Was Pedro personally very wealthy?' Mandy asked.

She shrugged.

A waitress took away his plate.

Lucy leant backwards, as if talking about money was distasteful. 'He had a trust fund that gave him so much per year – easily enough for two people or even a family to live on. Anything else he had to go and ask his trustee for – the poor darling. He also owned the apartment on Ocean outright, a cottage in Sayulita – it's in Mexico – and a two-bedroom flat in London. I'm not telling you anything you can't find out yourself.'

Mandy coughed as he pictured Pedro's last will and testament on the laptop.

'A cottage in Sayulita? Really? Is the apartment at 200 Ocean the only one in Santa Monica that he or the family own?'

She leant towards him, revealing a deep shadow of cleavage. 'Apart from his father's place at number 1 Ocean, yes, I think so. Pedro didn't believe in owning property for the sake of it. I think he might also have owned the place that the old nanny, Josefina, lives in on Montana, but he never thought of that as his.'

'Do you know if Pedro had ever made a last will and testament?'

'He was only twenty-nine years old, so I think that's extremely unlikely. His father, Eduardo, will know.'

'Eduardo García-Márquez said he was ninety-nine per cent sure there wasn't one.'

Lucy lifted a teaspoon from her cup in front of her eyes and examined its shiny surface in the light. 'There you are, and if the one per cent of him that isn't sure proves to be right, we'll all be in for a big surprise, won't we?'

Lucy Lack was either the straightest shooter in town or one hell of an actress. Mandy swallowed a mouthful of coffee and decided it was time for one or two hot coals.

'Are you ready for some personal questions?'

'I can handle it.'

'So did you have sex with him?'

Her face went into a furious scowl immediately. It was as close as that girl would ever get to looking ugly. She jumped up from the table and took three steps to the exit, stopped and returned to her seat. Avoiding eye contact, she slipped back onto her seat, placed her elbows on the table and clenched her fists together.

'God, what the fuck is this? Fuck off, fuck off. You have no right . . .'

Mandy glared at the four film-types who were gawping over at their table until they resumed their conversation. Just like fishing off Malibu Pier, he decided to let out some line.

'OK, sorry, but someone's going to ask you – the police, Broadski and Dent. It won't be unasked, you must know that.'

'That's the police,' she said. 'You're just a PI – you're lucky I'm talking to you at all.'

'So you're doing me a favour?'

She shrugged. 'If you like . . .'

They stared at each other over the remains of their breakfasts. It was almost like being married.

'Look,' she said at last, 'I'm still here because I want to go to his funeral and I want someone to find out who killed him. He was my best friend. Why are you treating me like I'm a suspect? I wasn't even here when it happened, for God's sake.'

Mandy nodded. That was true. But there were always guns and knives to hire. If you knew how to. 'So when was the last time you spoke to him?'

She ran her hands slowly through her thick dark hair. 'Six days ago, but he was busy, so we made all the final arrangements for my visit via email. We use a secret Hotmail account in the name of Antonia and Carlos. I can show you on my BlackBerry.'

Mandy noted her use of the present tense and waved his hand dismissively. 'No need,' he said. 'No need.' And for a moment he felt dirty, but that was the job, wasn't it? Prying and reading things no one meant for you to read. That was what he was there for, after all. 'Do you think Pedro had any enemies? Was there anyone who resented him for having so much money?'

'He was careful not to flash his money about. No one hated Pedro. He had some disagreements with friends and family – sure – but we all do, don't we? I think he would have told me if there had been any serious problem.'

Mandy was sorely tempted to mention the matter of the bequeathed Hopper painting or lay the Sternwood card down but decided to wait – he'd get as much as possible with soft soap first. And being Mr Nice Guy. He upended the salt cellar instead.

'You said yesterday that you've met Pedro's parents and family. Had he met yours?'

'What family?' she asked, brushing the salt he'd spilt off the table. 'I'm an only child. My father left us when I was five.'

'Sorry to hear that.'

She paused, took a sip of orange juice. 'My mother and Pedro got on well,' she said, putting down the glass. She sighed. 'OK, the problem was, she thought I could get him to like me sexually. See, we were broke when I was growing up. Baked beans on toast one night, sardines the next. So my mother still latches on to anything that could provide security for me.'

'Even now? Even though you probably earn a few bucks?'

'Many bucks, yes. But my mother still thinks of me as a twelve-year-old.'

Mandy nodded. 'Mothers tend to do that,' he said. 'Was Pedro an active homosexual?'

'He wasn't the type to visit steam baths.'

'But he must have had some sex life? Going on dates with the odd man?'

'Why? Does everybody have to? Do you and your wife?'

At that he leant back in his chair and coughed so hard a waiter anxiously refilled his glass of water. She looked like a kitten but knew how to punch below the belt. No one except Donna had mentioned his ex-wife for some time. 'This isn't about me, Lucy.'

'I shouldn't have asked.' But she had a funny little smile at the corner of her mouth.

Mandy swallowed the remains of his coffee and shrugged.

'Didn't Pedro ever have a big love in his life?'

'No, one or two big loves when he was younger. Quite an intense affair once with a guy called Javier.'

'Jones?'

She nodded. 'But when Pedro left him, he poured petrol over his own head and set fire to himself. He didn't succeed in suicide, but he did put a stop to Pedro having any other relationships. Too scary, too much responsibility if someone's going to do that, I suppose . . .'

'Sure,' Mandy said, thinking back to his meeting with Jones. There was a loud ring of truth to what Lucy had just said. It had emotional smarts. He was aware that he didn't want the interview to end. Maybe that's why he couldn't bring himself to mention the Sternwoods and their accusations yet.

'Is there anything you haven't told me that might help find Pedro's killer?' he said, hoping to God she'd bring it up so he could be Mr Nice Guy.

She opened her mouth and kept it open as she ran a fingernail round the edge of her lips. 'What do you want from me, blood?'

'No, just the truth.'

'And nothing but the *whole* truth?'

'That's the idea.'

Mandy gestured to one of the waiters to bring the check. The waiter brought it over.

Mandy handed the guy forty dollars, picked up the receipt copy for himself and held up his hand to indicate he didn't want any change. It was a generous tip, but the guy was an out-of-work writer, so what the hell. He turned back to Lucy. She was slotting her cigarettes and lighter into her bag; she seemed to think the interview was over. She got up and brushed past him as he stood too. He smelt her skin, her scent and a series of wonderful carnal images exploded inside his head.

'Are you OK?' she said, peering up at him.

Did she know what had just passed through his mind? Probably. She was a beautiful woman, and old enough to have figured out what guys were like.

101

'Slight headache, nothing bad,' he said, screwing his fist into his temples as a phoney antidote. Shit, hell, damn, fuck and buggery. Terry'd be all for slapping the cuffs on her – and not in the way Mandy'd just envisaged in his head. So he put a hand on her bare shoulder and said, 'You know what? I don't see you as the killing type.'

'Well, thank you,' she said, managing a smile.

He felt her warm skin tingling beneath his hand. Five seconds felt like five minutes. But he had to stop playing Mr Nice and ask the awkward stuff. If he didn't, he might as well go back to finding people's lost pets.

He forced himself to lift his hand off Lucy's shoulder. 'But I don't think you've told me everything.'

She lifted her sunglasses and scowled. 'I've just told you my life story. What more do you want?'

An elderly couple was trying to get by. Mandy ushered Lucy out of the way several paces into the marble and wood-lined entrance hall to the restaurant.

'Well,' he said, 'the exact nature of your relationship with Johnny and Sarah Sternwood, and how come you were here two weeks ago in a different hotel would be a good place to start, if we're really being honest, wouldn't it?'

The effect of the question was instantaneous. Her face flushed ludicrous violet; her eyes screwed shut. Fury and shame. It was not a good look. She took two steps back, laid the palm of her hand flat against the wall as if she needed support. Her whole body was shaking. She was either laughing or crying. He couldn't tell which. The noise she was making was attracting a lot of attention. It took a great deal of effort to resist the urge to step forward and place a comforting arm around her.

Pierre, the manager, appeared out of nowhere – can't have the other rich guests disturbed – and took out a handkerchief. Lucy waved it away.

'Is everything OK here? Can I help you? Is this man bothering you?'

Lucy burst out laughing. It was a laugh on the edge of hysteria, if not beyond. 'Absolutely fine! Mandy just told me a very funny story.'

The manager clapped his hands together, not taking his eyes off her face. '*Voilà*. He is a very charming man, I think?'

Mandy stepped forward and unconsciously put his hand on Lucy's shoulder intending to make his excuses. But Lucy placed her hand on his and said, 'Thank you, Pierre. We're just going back up to the suite. The lift is over here, isn't it?'

Caught in the headlights, Mandy watched the manager usher them both round a corner to the open doors of a waiting elevator. She pressed 'five' on the control panel and the doors closed. Their faces multiplied around them in the mirrors.

As they began to rise, she pushed her finger against his lips. 'Wait till we get upstairs.'

The place was deadly quiet, save for the swishing of Lucy's dress as she stepped confidently along the carpet in her black high heels, one hand holding a key card. Every six or seven paces, she paused, as if she was trying to remember something in mid-step, balancing on the toe of her shoe, showing Mandy the crimson sole of her high heel. It was a game to check that he was watching her. That wasn't a problem, because he was watching everything.

There was something sacrosanct about the top floor of Shutters, mostly to do with having money, lots of money. The only sign of life was an abandoned breakfast tray on the floor outside one of the rooms. He gazed down at the used coffee cups, the bowl of uneaten fruit salad, the half-eaten croissant and the ten-dollar note left in the saucer as a tip. A broadly built Filipino woman, dressed in a light blue housekeeping uniform, rounded the corner.

'Good morning, ma'am. Good morning, sir.'

They nodded. Neither able to speak.

He took a deep breath to steady himself; there was only another ten seconds before the die was cast. Lucy's swaying backside was making it hard to concentrate. The white door of suite 6 was twelve feet away, a 'Do not disturb' hanging from the handle. A fantasy flooded his head – out-of-breath sex with Lucy on a chrome kitchen surface, and then doing it again standing against the refrigerator.

The sound of the expensive door clicking open dissolved the fantasy.

He followed her into the suite.

He took in the beige-and-white sitting room. Two sofas and a glass coffee table, two armchairs and a dining table. Other than a large brown teddy bear sitting on one of the sofas, similar to the one Donna had downstairs at home, the place looked as if it hadn't been occupied. At the far end of the suite, a pair of white shuttered doors led out to a balcony overlooking the ocean.

Mandy decided to test the water about Pedro's will once more. Maybe Pedro hadn't even shown it to her or mentioned it? Would he be opening a can of worms and adding a hornet's nest if he disclosed Pedro's bequests details? Whatever, it needed to be run up the flagpole.

'What an amazing suite. Far more David Hockney than Edward *Hopper*, wouldn't you say?'

'Yes, possibly. It does have a really calm atmosphere,' Lucy said, not appearing to register the Hopper reference as anything out of the usual. 'I'm going to change out of this dress. Please make yourself comfortable. Sorry about the mess.' She slinked off to the bedroom, a cat with its tail in the air.

He swallowed, took a few steps forward, hands tingling in anticipation.

The smell in the room was nearly the same as Pedro's apartment building: fresh flowers, freshly ironed clothes and instead of coffee, Lucy's expensive perfume.

'I can't see any mess at all,' Mandy called out.

'Oh, there's plenty,' she said, emerging from the far doorway, barefoot, wearing a cream cotton skirt and cashmere black V-neck jumper that exposed her bare midriff. 'I spend most of my time in the bedroom.'

The words hung in the air as she knelt on a chair by the wall to open the top half of a window. Her sweater rode up her back.

His mouth started to dry up.

'Do you?' he said, a little squeakily.

Lucy smiled, her mouth slightly open, and picked up a remote control from a side table.

Mandy took two steps towards her. She stroked the ends of her hair and took a step towards him. That must be a sign. He could take her in his arms, kiss her right now. He breathed in and out, building up steam to do it, but Terry nagging, '*She's got to be involved somehow*,' and a basic physical need overrode the carnal.

'Could I use your bathroom?'

She pointed to a door on his left. Had he ruined the moment? If so, thank God.

Inside the en suite, he shut the door and yanked out his cell. There was a text message from Scottish Ray – he must have missed it before. 'Searched electoral register, lives with mum in Battersea. Spoke to her. Chatty, needy, neurotic. Lucy's BMW covered in parking tickets. Hopefully meeting her day after tomorrow. No news yet from her work or on the porn front. Don't worry – will dig up some dirt soon. Be lucky, son. Ray.'

Then spotting a voicemail message from Terry, he held the cell to his ear. 'Yo, dude. Have you sorted out your grieving pretty lady friend yet?' Terry was drunk and rambling, Tennessee accent full-on. Dawn must still be away on her trip.

Mandy saved the message and looked at himself in the basin mirror, suddenly aware of loud music playing next door. Was it something sensual or some Gregorian chant from Father Tony? He couldn't tell. Couldn't tell what was what, right now.

His heart was beating faster. Too fast. He spat into the basin, let the taps run and washed his hands, pulled out a soft folded towel from a pile balanced on a chair behind him, dried his hands and closed the tap. Around the bath, seventy-five unlit night lights. He whistled in amazement as he took a pee. Propped against the far end of the bath was a beaming Pedro García-Márquez inside a twenty-by-thirty-inch mounted photograph, watching him with his happy, yet-to-be-murdered brown eyes.

In the living room, a high-pitched voice was singing 'I Don't Feel Like Dancing'. The volume was loud. Lucy was kneeling on one of the sofas, holding a glass of water, one hand behind her head, her eyes closed, jiggling her body in time with the music. In front of her, on the coffee table, was a glass vase full of white flowers, an Apple Mac computer and two speakers.

Mandy did not know whether he liked or disliked the music, but he had heard it through the floor courtesy of Donna. He walked over and deliberately stood in the light coming from the double doors. Lucy opened her eyes, swept her legs underneath her and yelled, 'Come and sit,' pressing the remote to bring the sound right down. He pulled a grim face about the music and sat down on the arm of the sofa near to Lucy.

'Bit too modern for you, Mandy?'

He grinned. 'Too modern? They sound like the old Bee Gees. Haven't you got anything else?'

She laughed, leant forward, revealing her cleavage, and slapped her knee. 'Good answer . . . So why exactly are we here? Now that Pierre is not bothering us?'

Her large green eyes were sparkling in the sunlight.

It was now or never. He knew he needed to ask questions before it was too late and he was in too deep to ask.

He folded his arms. 'Why are you really here, Lucy? Why not go back? Are you waiting for a payout from Pedro's estate?'

The smile dropped. 'Do you really have to be so offensive? And don't say you're just doing your job. I'm not stupid.'

'Listen, Lucy, we need to get certain things out of the way. I said before I didn't think you'd told me everything.'

'What else do you want to know?'

'Why didn't you say when we first met you were only here two weeks ago? That kind of thing makes people like me suspicious.'

She swung her legs off the sofa, so she was facing Mandy. 'You mean people who were once in the police, had some kind of a breakdown, a humiliating divorce and now sadly live on their own with a cat? Don't even bother to ask how I know – checking up on *you* was the best two hundred dollars I've spent in ages.'

He felt sick. That information had to have come from a person, not from the Internet. He waved his hand for more information. She rolled her eyes.

'Meanwhile,' she said, 'I guess you've been speaking to that devout, upright Christian couple the Sternwoods. Am I right?'

He nodded. She was going to pour everything out in one go, he could tell. Sometimes it happened like that. Like a faucet. On or off. No in between.

'Look,' she said, as she took a cigarette from her bag, lit it and pointed Mandy to the double doors leading to the terrace. He opened them. 'Let's cut to the chase,' she continued. 'Sternwood is a nasty, chinless wanker who talks a good talk. He couldn't change his mind, let alone a light bulb without the help of his controlling midget wife. God knows why Pedro and he were such great friends – similar background, maybe Pedro fancied him once – I don't know.'

She exhaled a long, unsteady plume of smoke. 'Sternwood took two hundred thousand dollars off Pedro and thirty thousand from me for his rock-solid, cannot-fail dot-com company, which died a total and utter death.'

Mandy cleared his throat. 'That's business, isn't it?' he said. 'Why feel so bad about it? All these Internet things are risky.'

She stubbed out her cigarette. 'The point is, there never was a proper company. It was a scam based on a smart, glossy brochure. Sternwood used Pedro and me as bait to attract other investors. He promised to pay us back, but by then it was too late. Pedro wouldn't press charges, didn't want anyone to know and so on, and eventually wrote it off.'

'What about you? What did you do?' Mandy said, slipping off the arm of the sofa onto a cushion, one away from the one on which Lucy was sitting.

'I wanted to go to the police, but Pedro wouldn't hear of it and gave me five thousand to ease the pain. I've been trying to get the balance back from those bastards ever since.'

She lifted the hem of her V-neck sweater and fanned it to cool herself, then sat back again, appearing to be the least self-conscious she'd ever been in his company. One last direct hit. He swivelled his body towards Lucy and angled his right shoe so it was underneath her left foot. At first, she didn't seem to notice or respond. 'Is that why you were staying at Loews Hotel two weeks ago?'

She nodded. 'Yes, I needed that money back. Thirty thousand may have seemed like pocket money to Pedro, but it's not to me.'

The seam of gold at last. Two more questions and it would all be over. 'Were you having a sexual relationship with Sarah or Johnny Sternwood?'

Lucy flung his leg hard away from her. 'How dare you! What sort of a person do you think I am?' she yelled, picking up the glass of water and throwing it in his face. She got up and ran to the door. 'Get out! Right now!'

It was as if he'd hit a geyser of scalding-hot steam.

'Get the fuck out of here before I call security!'

22

11.20 a.m., 13 July

Mandy sat inside the Amazon in a coin-op car wash on Ocean Avenue between Main Street and Neilson Way. He'd chosen the most expensive wash cycle, wishing he could experience the cleansing process too. As the enormous spray brushes dropped onto the hood and windscreen, he turned the *Gladiator* soundtrack up and watched the interior of the car darken as the windows were covered in suds and foam. Picking up a duster, he began carefully polishing the glass front of every dial on the dashboard. He could make this ritual last for five minutes or two hours.

The interview with Lucy Lack had been a fuck-up, whatever way he looked at it. He decided to do two things before driving to see number seven on Eduardo's list at the homeless shelter: write down everything that had happened in the restaurant and in Lucy's suite, and, more importantly, not do anything about Lucy, directly or indirectly, until he had finished questioning the other suspects that day. Whether Lucy Lack might make a complaint about his conduct to the Santa Monica Police was something he'd have to take in his stride. But he doubted it. She had something to hide. Grieving females, even in their late twenties from London, didn't normally hire private investigators in this town.

He gripped hold of the steering wheel, turned the ignition key, switched on the windscreen wipers and drove out of the cleansing chamber. His car may have looked great, but he still felt like shit. Hearing his past and present summed up so succinctly by Cleopatra the City trader left a bad taste in his mouth, all the way down to his gut. He'd not behaved like the perfect gentleman and had sprung some unpleasant surprises on Lucy in the suite. But that was his job, wasn't it? She certainly knew how to reciprocate and punch way above her weight. Mandy popped an anxo pill in his mouth, took a swig from the bottle of lukewarm water on the passenger seat and told himself to hold his nerve and carry on.

He parked in a forecourt space, got out and adjusted the wing mirrors and extended the aerial on the hood to full. A grey-haired man wearing a well-cut suit closed the door of a Ford parked eight feet away and walked towards him. Aged early fifties, he wore a white shirt, black tie, expensive, rimless glasses. The guy held up the palm of his hand to Mandy's face. Inside the hand was an FBI badge – Agent Anderson.

Mandy acknowledged the badge with a nod of his head and Anderson let his hand drop to his side. 'I know you are a busy man, sir, so we'll get straight to it. A part-time employee of the Viceroy Hotel died last night due to injuries sustained during the recent shooting at the LAPD Award Ceremony.'

Mandy's heartbeat increased. He wiped his mouth with his hand and attempted to look professional. FBI people made him feel nervous at the best of times – someone dying into the bargain was more than he required right now.

'Sorry to hear that, but . . .'

'Your business card was found in the deceased's handbag.'

A series of lights lit up in Mandy's brain. His stomach sank. 'You mean Tamara from Sherman Oaks?'

Anderson looked hard into Mandy's face. 'Tamara Tyrer, to be exact.'

'Dead?'

'Expired at eight forty-five last night.'

'What the hell was she doing at the award ceremony?'

'I thought you might be able to help us with that.'

'I only met her the night before. One night only.'

'But you were aware that Miss Tyrer was also a hooker?'

'Yes, I knew that. She asked for my help.'

'Why?'

'She was being leaned on by a pimp. That's why I gave her my card.'

Anderson seemed unconvinced. He held up a naked colour photograph of Tamara Tyrer draped in a white-, blue-and-red Russian flag. 'What exactly were you doing with this young woman that evening?'

Half an hour later Mandy let out a long yawn as he waited for suspect number seven, Bradley Adams, to reappear behind the homeless serving counter. The encounter with Anderson had not lasted long, but it had been intense. The FBI man had kept a straight face when Mandy explained about the speed dating and even appeared prepared to accept that it might have been just coincidence about Tamara and the Russian tricolour flag. 'We'll run some more background checks and see you again. Don't leave town without us,' he had said, handing Mandy a card.

Fuck it, Mandy wished he had never set foot in the Viceroy. The FBI would not go away so easily. Stupid fucking speed dating. And now Tamara from Sherman Oaks in a mortuary somewhere. He hoped she'd died before the devil knew she was dead.

He tapped his foot on the sandy stone floor of the canteen and returned to the present. Being at the busy homeless shelter was like being on a film set with no part to play. Like being a cop and making his first arrest – when Terry did it all.

'Trouble at mill?' Father Tony said from the far end of the counter.

'You can say that again,' Mandy replied, offering a casual 'how the fuck did you get to be here?' shrug to the priest. It was reassuring to hear an old English expression and particularly when pronounced in a perfect Northern accent. Must have learnt that from his time spent working on Moss Side.

Father Tony was wearing a dog collar, a short-sleeved black shirt and trousers, and a pair of old Timberland boots. He was pouring coffee from a catering flask into a cup for a tall, skinny homeless man, who had orange hair and was clutching a rucksack like it was a newborn baby. It flitted across Mandy's mind to ask whether he had seen Lucy Lack again, but after that morning's encounter at Shutters he thought better of it. Instead, he offered the priest a discreet thumbs-up of first-day-at-school solidarity – a gesture that was noticed and reciprocated by Father Tony, who called out an introduction to his new client. 'This is Stevie from Texas.'

Mandy didn't want to get involved but waved his hand and mouthed a 'hello', then stepped back towards the counter.

Bradley Adams, number seven on the García-Márquez list, had insisted on meeting at 'my place of work' – the Ocean Park Homeless Shelter. He was the only person on the list not to offer to meet at his home. 'It's too far away for the purposes of your investigation, and my wife's not well.'

Mandy knew that travelling from Santa Monica to Larchmont was a forty-minute drive, like driving from Oxford to Banbury, but in terms of California it was a trip round the block, so that was bullshit. Likewise, he'd learnt in his time in the cops never to trust people who don't want to meet you inside their home. But once Mandy was certain Adams had no involvement or connection to Pedro's murder, he would arrange for as many misleading clues to fall into Broadski and Dent's hands as possible. It was only a matter of time before they started to follow him, too lazy to do their own footwork and content to be lapdogs for the Giraffe.

The part of the shelter they were standing in had been a canteen for employees of the Santa Monica House and Boat Building Company, but that was back in the 1950s. In amid the rafters, varnished masts, tillers, oars, rudders and centre boards were glued like random bits of intestine and vital organs to the beams and roof in the same way strands of spaghetti stick to ceilings when flung there.

There were two long tables and chairs where people, or 'clients', could sit, rest and eat. It was possible to imagine the place as one large, cosy, noisy log cabin, save for the hygiene and anti-smoking posters shouting down from the walls, not to mention the whiff of human flesh that hasn't bathed in weeks or months.

Mandy didn't like the smell, knew it would catch in his clothes. The odour would not become an exhibit in his library.

Bradley Adams pushed through a swing door behind the counter. He dumped a heavy cardboard box onto the badly scratched wooden surface. 'So what exactly can I do for you?'

Not wishing to be rushed, especially after having been kept waiting, Mandy gazed down at the hundreds of initials carved into the wood. What had become of the carvers, and why were there so few arrows and hearts?

Bradley Adams coughed. 'Hello, Mr Mandy. I'm busy here?'

His voice was curt and professional. Mandy guessed he reserved that tone for people he thought were wasting his time. He sounded like Henry Kissinger.

Then again, maybe the guy was feeling bad about Pedro's death. Maybe he was a doctor volunteering his services, unemployed or offering to help get over a breakdown or depression. But Mandy guessed that was being too generous. Judging by his Ralph Lauren shirt and what looked like handmade shoes, he was either another of Pedro's wealthy friends or bought all his clothes from thrift shops in Malibu.

There had been no reference to occupation next to Adams on the list. But surely the guy didn't work here all the time?

Bradley Adams cleared his throat loudly.

Mandy came back to the present and pitched straight in. 'When was the last time you were at Pedro's apartment on Ocean?'

'Three months ago.'

'Did you notice anything odd about the place?'

'No.'

'Did you notice anything odd about Pedro?'

'No.'

'Did you have an argument with Pedro? You haven't been round there for three months since.'

Adams paused, seemed to think about the question. 'No!' he said, slitting open the masking tape fastening the flaps of the cardboard box together with a grey box-cutter.

'Any reason to believe that someone wanted to harm Pedro?'

'Yes. Of course!' Adams looked up and stared at Mandy as if he was stupid.

He lifted out ten or so plastic trays. At first, Mandy didn't recognize them, because he hadn't been on a plane for so long. 'Surplus to passenger requirements,' Adams said. 'We pick them up from LAX early evening. It stops them from throwing them away.'

'Good idea.'

The guy was clearly far happier talking about the shelter and how they operated than Pedro's death.

'Why are you so sure that someone might have wanted to harm Pedro?' Mandy said. 'I've not heard a bad word against him.'

Adams put the box-cutter down carefully on its side. 'I don't understand why I'm not talking to a cop or detective. You've been hired by the family?'

Mandy nodded. The door behind him pushed open; something metallic came through, probably somebody in a wheelchair. Mandy didn't turn round.

Adams leant forward and lowered his voice. 'Maybe they have something to hide.'

'I am not sure that I understand,' Mandy lied.

'Allow me to let you into a secret. I was Pedro's professor at Pepperdine. He wanted to master as a mature student in Chinese, but after two terms asked to be taught at home.'

'Interesting,' Mandy said, wondering if Lucy Lack spoke Mandarin or Cantonese.

Adams picked up the box-cutter and ran another deep cut along some masking tape. 'Pedro was a fascinating young man. Most people found him extremely kind and amusing, but . . . he could also be intensely oversensitive when it came to not having his own way. Coming from such a privileged family has its drawbacks.'

'He fired you because you wanted more money for coming to his apartment?'

It was a wild guess.

'In so many words, yes, and he also made a complaint to the dean – totally unjustified. He could just have said no to my request and ended our contract. It was petty. You could say it was the straw that broke my back.'

'I can now see where you are coming from.'

'I knew you would eventually, Mr Mandy. For the record, I am what you British would call a pacifist. Incapable of killing anyone, and despite my antipathy to young Mr García-Márquez, I never wished him any bodily harm.'

Without missing much of a beat, as if he was running an old-fashioned store, Adams walked round the end of the counter and greeted the priest. 'Father Tony, how's it going on the front line? I see you've met Stevie!'

Mandy swung round and saw Father Tony at a table with the red-haired skinny guy, who was now clinging on to a supermarket trolley filled with his worldly goods. Maybe the trolley garage had delivered it back to him after a thousand-mile service.

The door opened again and a fat woman carrying two full-to-bursting laundry bags walked in and yelled, 'Hello, Iraq. Hello Vietnam!' and burst out laughing. There was a brief silence.

Mandy grimaced, searched for a Trebor and wondered if he had met the woman before in hospital. Before he had time to come to a conclusion, the room came alive with laughter and conversation. Adams welcomed the new client with a handshake. He was clearly no longer interested in discussing his late student.

Mandy closed his notebook. It was refreshing to meet someone prepared to say they disliked Pedro. Speaking ill of the dead carried its own integrity. Suspect number seven, though slightly obnoxious, did not strike Mandy as much of a suspect. Perhaps it was time to look closer to home.

23

6 p.m., 13 July

'Follow me, please,' said the white-coated waiter at the Santa Monica Athletic Club, as he ushered Mandy to the far end of the twenty-metre rooftop pool. The twelve-storey club was set back from the hullabaloo of ocean life on the corner of Strand and Hotchkiss Park. A westerly wind was blowing over the surface of the pool and cheesy fairground music could be heard coming from the pier. The sun was at six o'clock, beginning to set, and only five people lay under sun umbrellas on loungers round the rippling water, and three of those were Japanese. No one was in the water.

Lowering his sunglasses, Mandy recognized an elderly con-man, well known to the cops. He was mid-sixties, stretched tanned skin, wraparound sunglasses on a polished head full of teeth, and a belly flopping over a white pair of Speedos. A man who'd relieved various local ladies of thousands of dollars but was now banned from all major hotels in Santa Monica. How the hell had he managed to get past security?

Mandy waved, best the man knew that the two young people he was about to sit down with were way off limits. The guy flashed Mandy an irritated smirk.

The Japanese trio began putting on white robes and making ready to go. Mandy squinted up into the sunlight and began hearing the theme to *Goldfinger* as an image of a naked woman covered in gold paint flashed on and off in his head. He aborted the fantasy, dropped down to one knee and retied his shoelaces.

The old waiter coughed politely and gestured towards two bodies lying on yellow towels spread over sunloungers under angled umbrellas. Mandy folded a five-dollar tip into the old guy's hand. 'I want to surprise them.'

'OK, sir,' the waiter said. 'But they are expecting you.'

He shrugged and walked on alone, to where Pedro's youngest brother, Alfonso, and his sister, María, lay side by side. Mandy expected Alfonso to be

113

sweating, wasted and skinny, or over-fed and obese. But as Mandy approached, he could see that in fact he was in good shape, late teens, toned and bearded. The only strange thing was three raised welts scarring his middle back.

María was pretty, freckled, plump but well proportioned. She had long black hair tied up with a bow and wore a red one-piece that displayed most of her back and compressed her ample breasts. For a split second, Mandy vaguely fancied her, but then remembered the age difference and that he was being employed by her father.

'How do you do.' Mandy offered his hand – formally as usual. 'I'm Mandy from Endeavor Investigations.'

'Hi,' Alfonso grunted but remained a motionless horizontal on the lounger.

María turned on her side, lowered her sunglasses and raised her hand in a disinterested wave.

Mandy stepped back, withdrew his hand and tried not to feel offended.

He squatted down onto his haunches – fuck, it was hot – wiped sweat from under his nose and tried again. 'Before we begin, I want to say how sorry I am about the loss of your brother.'

María sat up sharply, adjusted a loose shoulder strap of her swimsuit and said, 'Is what you've just said the same as offering your condolences in England?'

'Err, yes, I think it is,' Mandy said, unprepared for the snotty response.

'Only think? My father said you were from England, and my brother Miguel said that you might drop by.'

María smirked and stood up. Mandy got back on his feet, adjusted his shades and wondered if he had called at a bad time. Maybe he could buy them a cocktail to break the ice? He looked for the waiter. The rooftop was now empty – no Japanese, no waiter, no Romeo de Speedos. Alfonso hauled himself off the lounger and marched past him, leaving a jet stream of musk and suntan oil. Without any hesitation, he dived into the pool. It was a perfect dive, hardly making any splash at all. For a heroin addict, he was a powerful swimmer.

María tiptoed to the edge of the pool, folded her arms across her chest and yelled, 'Bravo, Alfie! Bravo, darling!'

Mandy stepped closer towards María, about to say something in favour of swimming, when María swung round on her heel. 'Don't even think about asking my brother any questions. It might not look like it, but he's totally griefed out.'

Mandy was about to say, 'Bollocks,' but María was too quick for him. 'I'm not asking, Mandy, I'm telling. And if you don't respect that, I am phoning my father this instant.' She jumped into the pool after Alfie, splashing Mandy in the process.

Taking two strides back into the shadow of Alfonso's umbrella, Mandy reached into his pocket for an anxo. In his suit he felt baked by the sun and like a child wearing the wrong clothes at a party. He wished he had changed into swimming trunks, lain down by the playboy con man, dived into the pool and then swum over to talk to María and Alfonso/Alfie. But he hadn't and he was stuck with the situation as it was.

Tempting though it was to walk off and go swim in the ocean, head home and sort out the farewell meeting with Donna, Mandy knew he had to tough it out. The more he knew about the case, the more he sympathized with Eduardo García-Márquez. But it was a thirsty sympathy – where was the pool waiter? Was this what Miguel had meant when he said to 'go easy' on them? Were they too consumed with grief to offer him a cold drink? They didn't look the average picture of grieving siblings, not even in Edward Hopper terms.

María and Alfonso got out of the pool. Alfonso took a towel from his sister and shook his head so that his hair emptied drops of water on her – she squealed. He dried himself quickly, all the time humming and smiling. He lay down on the lounger and cupped his hand round his cell screen.

María turned to Mandy and looked him up and down. He felt parched, sweaty and inexplicably horny.

'I take it you have interviewed Lucy Lack?' she said. 'If not, I would make that my very first call.'

'Thanks for the tip,' he said, adding with some reciprocal sarcasm, 'I take it you're not a big fan?'

María screwed up her face and shook her head pitifully as though Mandy or Lucy was a broken-down car in Compton. 'Alfie and I are the eyes and ears of the family – you should listen to us.'

Maybe she was beginning to thaw. Maybe she did want to find out who killed her brother after all.

'Your father told me that Pedro kicked you out of his apartment the night before he was found dead?'

'Yes, we had a big fight. We shouted and said bad things to one another. I feel terrible about that, but I didn't kill him, if that's what you think.'

María cocked her head at Mandy but was distracted by a motorbike roaring past, twelve floors down, on the road outside.

'What was the fight about?'

'I don't think I have to answer those sorts of questions,' María said, fishing a cigarette from a box of Virginia Slims. She lit it and took several fast drags, then noticing a club official waving at her from the right-hand side of the pool, inhaled massively and stubbed the cigarette out beneath the lounger. There

115

were some rules that even super-brats were apparently obliged to keep. She was acting fourteen but looking like twenty-two.

'Miguel said you were only asking basic questions, nothing intimate.'

Mandy covered his mouth with his hand in a deliberate fake yawn. 'Tell it to the cops, if you prefer. I'm trying to help find who killed your brother. And you know what they say – the truth will set you free.'

'What do you reckon, bro?' María asked her brother, as he thumbed a text message.

'I don't know. It's your life.'

María leant across and yanked a curly hair from her brother's hairy thigh. Alfonso shuddered and let out a long whistle.

Mandy cleared his throat and pointed to a rooftop on the shoreline. 'Lucy Lack is staying over there in Shutters.'

María and Alfonso smirked at each other. 'Uh, doh! The last person we want to run into is her.'

María swung her legs off the lounger and pulled her white Indian cotton shirt over her shoulders. 'OK, here it is. Lucy Lack is roadkill,' María said. 'Roadkill masquerading as prime steak. She's nothing but a bloodsucker who wants to get her hands on my brother's property and assets. The big fat fact is, she nearly got fired from her job a week ago, rang up all tears and weeping, and asked Pedro if she could come and stay. My mother told me that things were not well between Lucy and Pedro, and that apparently he'd recently had a fucking humdinger with her about money.'

'So you came round to intercede like a member of the UN?'

'I tried to explain to him what was happening, but he wouldn't listen to me. Threw me out on the street because he thought I was a "vicious, foul-mouthed airhead". I wish I could say I was that sort of person and then maybe I could have confronted Lucy Lack myself. It's too late now for Pedro, but I'm damned if she's going to get the better of us.'

For the first time Mandy watched María's mouth contort into an unhappy pout and her face soften. Instinctively he held out his hand in a gesture of solidarity.

She turned away, sniffed and half spoke, half sang, 'Sad. Really sad. Sad, sad, sad, *but it's too late, baby, now it's too late . . . though we really did try to make it . . .'*

Did she learn the Carole King song from Pedro, or did she have good taste in old pop songs? Whatever, for the first time he felt like he was dealing with a normal, screwed-up twenty-something. Mandy leant towards María to say something conciliatory, but Alfonso, sitting on his lounger, had begun to sneeze, repeatedly, like a person with hay fever or a bad coke habit.

116

María stood up and put her hand on her brother's heaving shoulders. 'Don't worry – you'll be OK.' Her face was returning to defensive. It was time to complete the questioning.

'So how do you know about Lucy Lack and her job?' Mandy said, over the sound of the convulsive sneezing.

María offered a vindictive smirk. 'I'd only been at Pedro's for ten minutes when an instant message came through on his Apple. It was obviously the drama queen calling. I could tell by the tone of her voice. So I said to my brother I'd go and take a shower. But I then needed to get some shampoo out of my bag, came back and by mistake overheard Lucy yelling, "I'm going to lose my fucking job!"'

Mandy beamed at María. 'Do let me know how you come to overhear somebody's conversation by mistake. It's a trick I'd like to learn . . .'

'Are we done?' María said angrily.

Mandy wanted to push her back into the swimming pool and not let her get out until she changed her attitude.

There was only a hint of a Mexican accent in her voice. No warmth, no emotion, just a spoilt, fucked-up rich kid. She was speaking like she'd abandoned her soul in a mid-Atlantic nasal dialect, which Mandy thought vapid and shallow. Pedro García-Márquez almost felt like a friend now. From what Mandy had learnt about him, he seemed the most fun and normal of the lot of them, someone who despite his background had managed to have a relatively normal life. Imagine having a brother and sister like that. María's divulgence about the row and the instant message was interesting, though, especially considering he also now knew the secret email address Pedro and Lucy had set up: antoniaandcarlos@hotmail.com. He just needed a password.

'You seem more upset about someone possibly stealing your brother's wealth than the fact he is dead. Don't you care?' said Mandy.

'I would rather my Pedro was alive, if that's what you mean. But there's nothing I can do right now to change anything . . . is there? I am not a sentimental person.'

Mandy inhaled and nodded. 'Probably not, no.' His instinctive dislike of her was becoming more acute by the second. What the hell was the funeral going to be like, a dysfunctional Gosforth Park on mescaline? 'People have been asking where the funeral is taking place,' Mandy lied.

'Nobody knows until the coroner issues a death certificate and releases the body. Until then poor old Pedro is stuck chilling in a refrigerator somewhere.'

María walked back to her lounger and stepped into her leather espadrilles. 'But knowing my father, the funeral will be held at St Monica's Church, followed by a reception with iced water and avocado and tomato tortillas in the rectory garden afterwards.' María chuckled, and continued, 'Knowing my mother, the funeral will be followed by a big party with cocktails either at her old ranch in the mountains or at a friend of my father's in Serra Retreat.'

Mandy must have looked perplexed or curious.

'You know the place where Mel Gibson used to live and where there's a Franciscan monastery?'

'Yeah, I know it. They have NA meetings up there,' Mandy said, loosening his tie and shirt collar.

María nodded. 'I pray we are not going there. The traffic on PCH is a nightmare these days . . .'

Alfonso lifted his head from the lounger. 'Yeah, tell Mom we're not going there, ever!'

Mandy looked at María and Alfonso, and then turned his head away the same way he did when he spent too much time with his stepfather. He stood up and felt a steady wave of sadness for Eduardo García-Márquez.

24

7.45 p.m., 13 July

Mandy unlocked the front door of his house, holding a bag of water with two goldfish inside. He'd driven to the pier and bought the fish from a smiling man in a wheelchair. Mandy was the last customer of the day, the guy said, and what the heck – he could have them for ten bucks, not twenty, and a free carton of fish food. Mandy had felt a flash of pity for the guy – and the fish. So he paid, shook the guy's hand, pleased to have met somebody normal, unlike María and Alfonso.

He closed the front door shut behind him and was startled by the sound of shrieking birds. He stepped into the sitting room. A nature documentary about Arctic penguins was showing on the TV; he had forgotten to switch it off that morning. He grabbed the remote, muted the sound and ignored the phone lying on the sofa. It felt better than good to be home. As he walked through the house, he kicked off his shoes, threw his jacket in a heap on the bed and strode into the kitchen.

Ned looked up from the bowl of dried food he'd been chomping from on the black-and-white tiled floor. Mandy grunted a greeting to the cat and took out a large Perspex bowl from a cupboard, set it down on the table and carefully poured the water and goldfish into it. The tangerine-coloured creatures started swimming immediately. Mandy cheered up at the sight of them.

Ned ate one more mouthful of food and climbed out through the cat flap. The daft cat hadn't even noticed the fish. Adding more water from the tap to the goldfish bowl, Mandy pulled open the refrigerator and took out a can of cold beer. For a split second, because of the need for a cool head with Donna, he considered drinking a can of Coke instead.

'Bollocks,' he said, as he ripped open the can of beer and drank it straight down, wiping his mouth with the back of his hand with a theatrical flourish. From now on, he said to himself, toughness begins at home.

It had been a crap day but one that had made him stronger. He had encountered Cleopatra in a luxury hotel suite, the homeless, billionaire rich, the spoilt, the arrogant, the FBI, the death of Tamara . . . What else? But it had refreshed his conscience about what he valued, what he wanted and what he did not. Crushing the beer can beneath the palm of his hand onto the table, he sprinkled some left-over breadcrumbs from the table onto the surface of the water in the bowl. The two goldfish were disinterested and ignored them.

It was going to be tough to get Donna to agree to leave the house this weekend, but no harder than what he had gone through already. At least, that's what he told himself.

He opened the kitchen door and stepped out onto the wooden deck. The sun was a darker orange than the goldfish and close to setting over the ocean. Joni Mitchell's 'All I Want' was playing downstairs in Donna's room and blending in with an orchestra of buzzing cicadas outside. It was showtime.

Mandy inhaled a deep breath of salty sea air and called out, 'Hey, Donna? Want to come up for a talk?'

He looked at his watch and decided to go downstairs, bang on her door and wait for her upstairs on the deck. He wanted it to be a brief conversation and on his territory. To his surprise, there was an unusually swift response. Donna bounded up the wooden steps dressed in a sleeveless cotton dress, pink scarf tied round her waist, wearing pink tennis shoes with the laces undone. She was holding a piece of paper and a half-eaten carrot, and looked like she'd spent the last twenty-four hours sleeping and doing yoga. Her long blonde hair was tied back; her tanned face looked less made-up, more natural, save for the usual mascara.

'Hi, Donna,' Mandy said with a weary smile. He'd already decided not to bring out the goldfish until she had agreed to the leaving date. 'Hi, big guy. You look like you've had a really shit day. *Qué pasa?*'

Mandy clutched at his throat and let out a sarcastic laugh. Donna was cute in more ways than one.

'I've had worse – about four years ago – but you know what? At least I'm being paid . . .'

Donna waggled her head. 'Oh, OK, I get it,' and then biting into a carrot, 'Like Elvis, you want to know when I am leaving the building – when I am going?'

Donna was either buying time for a sucker punch or about to loop the loop as usual. Should he just pick her up, put her in his car and leave her on a freeway like the traffic cop in *Short Cuts* did with some puppy? '*Incorrect answer; play it straight instead,*' his grandfather's voice spoke in his head.

Mandy held up the palms of his hands. 'I don't mean you any harm, Donna – quite the opposite.'

120

'I know that, Mandy,' Donna said, eating the carrot and brandishing the piece of paper. 'Guess what? Have I got a big surprise for you.'

'Nothing surprises me any more, Donna.'

'Hey! Be nice to me and lighten up! This is going to blow you away. Nancy, my sponsor – you know the one with the cool VW who is twenty years clean? She has offered me a room in her house for six months. She's coming over to help me move crack of dawn the day after tomorrow. And what is really *so* amazing?'

Donna sounded like she was twelve years old. Mandy stopped holding his breath and smiled. 'Tell me.'

'My sponsor also said that provided I get a job and stay clean for six months, she's going to introduce me to Joni fucking Mitchell!' Donna opened her mouth wide like she was screaming with joy. 'My sponsor's cousin and Sheryl Crow are really old friends. Sheryl is really close to Joni . . . Get it now?'

'Wow,' Mandy muttered, grinning. He knew enough about recovery to know that Donna was on a pink cloud and that one day soon she would come down with a bump. But right now a pink cloud was better than a dark one. This change in her could be a turning point to things getting better. He just needed one bit more of reassurance that this transformation was real. Within seconds it came.

Donna stepped forward and proudly pointed to the handwritten piece of paper, which he guessed had been written by Nancy the sponsor. Donna only knew how to write using a keyboard. 'This is my new address in Brentwood, my sponsor Nancy's number just in case you can't get hold of me, and here's my dad's address in China Lake. I apologized for cutting him out of my life and being an antisocial daughter and we've made up now. I doubt my mom will be so easy. Anyways, I want you to keep both addresses and numbers. In fact, give me your cell and I'll bang in all the details.'

Mandy raised his eyes upwards, smiled and pulled the phone from his pocket. Donna took it and using both of her ringed thumbs tapped in the details at breakneck speed.

'And Dad has agreed to pay off my back rent at two hundred and fifty dollars per month and wants you to send him *an account* and your bank details.' Donna paused for breath and a smile. 'And as you so often say, Mandy, nothing and nobody's perfect. But it's a good start, ain't it?' With that she returned the cell and held out her hand for Mandy to shake.

Mandy tried to hide the lump in his throat and shook Donna's small hand. 'Wait here, as there's something I want you to have.'

'Oh, and I have a little something for you too,' said Donna, skipping towards the stairs.

Minutes later Donna was cradling the fish bowl, blinking back tears, while Mandy stood by clutching a snorkel and a new pair of flippers and bottle of French wine Donna had given him.

'You'll have to be careful they don't jump out when you're taking them to Brentwood. I'll get you a lid to put over the bowl.'

Donna rested her hand above the water, staring at the fish as if they were babies in a crib. 'They're beautiful, Mandy. Thank you. I never had any pet fish. We had a cat once called Butch, but he got squashed by a truck when I was a kid.'

'Pets are good for your head. They help you to get out of yourself.'

'Is that why you bought them for me?'

'Maybe. What you have to remember, Donna, is that however hard things get, keep swimming like those goldfish.'

'That's why I bought you the snorkel and flippers, Mandy. Keep swimming yourself!' Donna twirled her finger over the surface of the water. 'I'm christening them Sparrow and Turner from *Pirates of the Caribbean.* They'll always remind me of you too.'

Working in the make-up department of *On Stranger Tides* had been the high point of Donna's career.

Mandy looked at Donna. 'I'm probably not going to sub let downstairs again but set it up as an Endeavor Investigations office instead. But I want to say . . .' he paused, cleared his throat and continued, 'thank you for being there during some of *my* black moments.'

A tearful Donna looked up at Mandy. 'Oh my God, thank you *so* much for saying that. I think I'm going to blub.'

Mandy put his arms around Donna and hugged her.

It was a long hug and one in which they told each other they were forgiven.

Eventually Donna eased her hand out of the embrace and ran her fingers down the side of the bottle. 'Can't we celebrate by having a tiny little glass of wine?'

Mandy let out a fake growl. 'I think it's best if we make that sparkling water instead, don't you?'

'Mandy, stop being so sensible, just for me, this once?'

25

5.45 a.m., 14 July

Mandy woke up feeling weird. He sank into the pillow unsure whether he wanted to be back in his dream about Lucy Lack or not. A soft American voice called, 'Uh, hello?'

He sniffed a fragrance of oranges and sex on the pillow beside him. His mind rushed to join a series of dots from the previous night, but before he could finish, the voice said, 'Are you going to take this from me? It's kinda hot?'

He hoisted himself up one elbow. Donna – naked – holding two mugs of steaming coffee in front of her breasts.

'That's great, thanks,' he said, taking one of the mugs. He sipped the coffee and burnt his tongue in the process.

Donna set her mug down, and her lightly tanned body slid under the cream-coloured duvet. Her foot slid all the way up the side of his leg. It felt good.

Donna enjoyed sex, wasn't shy or needing to have the lights out. Being in bed with him, she said, was where she felt safe, wanted and warm. Trouble was, there was no such a thing as a free lunch with Donna. And maybe there shouldn't be.

He thought about it while blowing on the scalding coffee and concluded that maybe, for her sake, it would be better if lunch cost a fortune. Truth was, he liked being in bed with her too.

'Let's go for a walk on the beach and come back and fool around?' she said, still perky. 'A special last-day treat?'

So she hadn't forgotten the conversation from last night?

Despite the affirmation of her departure, Mandy groaned. There were three things he hated about the beach: sand, seaweed and seagulls. Due to his current circumstances, he decided to be flexible. 'Fool around, then walk on the beach sounds like a better order of activity,' he said, gently running his hand over Donna's tummy stud.

By the time they had got up, a strong ocean wind was blowing along the footbridge spanning PCH between Castellammare Drive and the beach. Donna had run on ahead, to halfway along the bridge, and was leaning over the safety rail chanting a mantra to the eight lanes of moving traffic below. Mandy smiled and raised his eyes heavenwards at this latest fad. Something else her sponsor had suggested to keep on an even keel. *It works, if you work it.* Why not?

To mark the occasion, Donna was now wearing tight leather shorts, a shredded *Terminator 3* T-shirt and the same tennis shoes she'd been wearing the day before. Mandy's stopwatch was hanging from a cord round her neck. What was she doing with the stopwatch? The wind splayed her hair like a model in a shampoo commercial. She waved at him to catch her up.

She was smiling and swaying from side to side as if she was in a Sufi trance. Suddenly she stopped, turned to her left and yanked the stopwatch up to her eyes. He caught up with her and they walked slowly but determinedly across the bridge towards the metal staircase leading down to the beach.

As they walked down the steps, Mandy paused and grabbed hold of the stopwatch. 'Why have you brought this with you? Not being weird and timing our walk?'

Donna stood up on tiptoe on the second-to-last step from the beach and inhaled a deep hit of ozone being blown in from the ocean. 'I'm thinking about taking up running again. But it's crazy, really, because it's been years since I did anything.'

Mandy took hold of the cold handrail and squeezed Donna's shoulder. 'Come on – show me what you're made of. I bet you can do it and that it will all come back to you, just like tasting your grandmother's apple pie.'

'You mustn't laugh.'

'I promise there'll only be whoops of amazement.'

Donna lifted the cord and stopwatch over her head and passed them to Mandy. 'After a count of three, start timing me.'

Within two seconds Donna was running quickly along the beach with arms and elbows jabbing in and out like symmetrical pistons. Jeez. She was fast. It was not hard to believe that Donna had been a champion sprinter at high school in China Lake.

Mandy clicked on the stopwatch and yelled out a heavy cheer.

On the beach path, the air was salty, much warmer. He caught his breath and fished out his scope from his jacket to check where she had run off to. The only sound was the drone of the traffic passing behind him and seagulls screeching above. The left-hand side of the beach was deserted, save for a homeless guy wheeling a shopping trolley.

Mandy scanned to the right. There she was – the crazy diamond – still running at a good pace across the sand, heading towards what looked like a huge green suitcase or crate in the surf. For a few moments he was mesmerized by the rhythm of her speed, by her blonde hair bouncing on her shoulders. She looked innocent and beautiful.

Maybe he could leave Donna to discover her private moment of truth: maybe running was going to be her salvation, the way to happiness and sanity. Running the 880 in the park in Brentwood each day and feeding her goldfish was hopefully going to help her become the person she really wanted to be. Mandy was happy about that – a good bitter-sweet finale to her volatile tenancy. Yet a tiny sneaking Sod's Law feeling was also creeping into his gut that he didn't want her to leave after all. He breathed in a lungful of sea air, clicked the stopwatch and held it up to his face to check on Donna's speed.

But as he did so, a series of excited screams echoed out like a bad horror film. He swung round, placed the scope over his eye. Donna was wading through the surf towards the crate in the water, waving her arms at him to follow.

Mandy was thirty yards away from reaching Donna when he noticed she was crouched in the surf trying to catch her breath, staring at the sunlight glinting down on the cause of the trouble, an enormous green suitcase, the type favoured by travelling Asians.

He ran over to her.

'Hey,' he said. 'Are you OK? Are you all right?'

She didn't reply.

'It's cold, isn't it?' Mandy said. He took off his jacket and hung it around her shoulders. 'Let's get out of here.'

Donna knelt down by the suitcase, peering at the three locks.

'You don't really want to open the case, Donna, do you?' Mandy said, rolling back his cuffs. 'It's only going to have shitty seaweed in it.'

But as he spoke, the sound of three suitcase locks unlocking reverberated through the air. Mandy shrugged, looked up at the sky, aware that Donna was lifting the lid of the case. Impossible to stop Donna doing anything once she'd made up her mind.

But Donna wasn't saying anything.

She was hyperventilating, her eyes fixed and staring. Mandy stepped up beside her and looked down. The case was open all right. But something had flopped out as she'd opened it: a bruised and porous human leg.

He swallowed. At first sight the crumpled heap inside resembled a ventriloquist's dummy. But it wasn't a dummy.

It was a spiky-haired white guy, mid-thirties, dressed in a T-shirt and white boxer shorts with what looked like a British passport wedged between his teeth. Mandy forced himself to check if the tips of the fingers were present and correct – they were, and a ring with a silver skull and crossbones was on one of them. He wretched as a white maggot crawled out of the corpse's wet hair. Jesus. No serious work for four years, now three stiffs in one week. He looked at the pallid face. Something else was wrong. What was it?

Donna traced her finger above the man's eyebrows. Beneath her fingers, withered eyelids hung loose. That was wrong. Oh fuck.

The man's eyes had been taken out, leaving two fleshy, hollow sockets. And a severed tongue had been pinned to the bottom of the man's T-shirt – like a game of pin-the-donkey.

'Oh shit,' Mandy said, peering over her shoulder, and hoping Donna had not seen it.

But Donna had noticed the thick slab of flesh. She let out a birthing scream so loud every dawdling seagull flew for cover. Then she closed her eyes and screamed again – this time like an emptying party balloon – until she had no more breath with which to scream.

Mandy covered his mouth with his hand and yanked the passport from the guy's mouth, stood up, flicked open the back page: Dominic Young.

The name was extremely familiar. He closed the passport, turned his head. Donna was sprinting in a zigzag pattern across the beach, yelling like one of the witches in *Macbeth*. He decided to let her empty her tank, run herself back into some semblance of calm. Never easy with Donna, especially when she came face to face with a mutilated corpse.

He held the passport open again and stared at the photograph and then made himself look at the unhappy face of the stiff in the suitcase. It wasn't a perfect match, but there was no doubt about the identity. Just as he was about to stand up, he spotted a piece of rolled-up paper protruding from the man's nostril. Feeling squeamish, he took out a pen and a handkerchief from his pocket and manoeuvred the paper out without having to touch Dominic Young's cold, porous skin. The roll of paper was damp but not wet and made him remember bus tickets he used to collect as a child in Oxford. It only took a second for him to recognize it as a sales receipt from Chung's Supermarket. An image of Pedro García-Márquez covered in tortilla chips flashed through his head. This time, he wasn't going to pocket the receipt. Something stank, and it wasn't just rank seaweed or decomposing flesh. Two receipts on two bodies was not a coincidence.

He made a mental note of the Chung receipt date, items purchased, amount, then with his hand wrapped inside the handkerchief, shoved it back up the guy's nostril. Whoever sent Dominic Young on this package holiday wanted the identity of their passenger to be known. He stood up, balanced the passport on top of the dead man's head, stepped away from the suitcase and nearly threw up.

Donna had totally flipped out and was squatting and peeing in front of two worried-looking tourists. Inwardly, he cursed. When she was on the up, in her pink bubble, was often when she was most vulnerable. If anything went wrong, it would bring her crashing back down. Mandy needed to get her some help before the cops came and dragged her away to the state hospital. He needed someone who could offer immediate practical help for uninsured Donna. He couldn't ring up the sponsor and foist someone in that acute state on her; it wasn't fair to either of them. He needed someone who was used to dealing with people in acute mental distress, and strong enough themselves to cope with it. Three or four names came to mind, but he narrowed it down to one. Keeping a watchful eye on Donna, yelling obscenities at the tourists, Mandy pulled out his cell and dialled a number for Father Tony.

26

9.45 a.m., 14 July

Benny Tan stood up, stiffened his spine and breathed out through his nose. Yoga, fresh tuna and using worry beads instead of nicotine had saved his life. Eighteen months ago, before his heart attack, he would have sneered at anyone doing exercise or meditation, but not now. With success came pressure. What would be the point of selling if he didn't have his health?

He moved a pencil resting on top of his lined notepad so it was parallel to a paper clip and a felt-tip pen. A white PC and a split-screen CCTV monitor sat either side of his glass-topped desk. The only other items on it were a box of wipes, a colour photo of the African children he planned to adopt and his bible: *Dr Axelrod's Atlas of Freshwater Aquarium Fishes*. Benny disliked clutter, paper files and gadgets.

He glanced at the photographs on his walls and the two rows of City of Santa Monica Health and Safety Awards behind him. He sure had achieved a few things since being in LA.

A square squawk box hung four feet above the floor next to a partially unfurled Stars and Stripes. The box was already there when Benny joined the business twenty-two years ago, and probably forty-four years before that as well. It was teak with a green felt front. It was the one thing that he really cherished in his entire office. He could turn the sound off, but when it was on, it picked up all conversation in the reception and despatch areas.

Secretly, it reminded him of his time in London and the depressing betting shops with race commentary booming out of speaker boxes on sweaty walls. And of being a mini-cab driver and the hostile place they would have to sit to wait for jobs from the controller. That was why he hated England. Unfriendly, judgemental England, being broke, a grasping wife and ungrateful child, and a race of people who made him feel second class.

The old squawk box reminded him of how far he had come. It was a whip, a

128

way of driving him on to success, to never slip back to desperate times. He was staring at it when, after a burst of static, the receptionist's disembodied voice came over it telling a new intern to 'go on through and knock on Mr Tan's door'.

A gangly young man in the CCTV monitor, walking nervously down the corridor. Benny yanked the black worry beads from his pocket, wrapped them loosely round his right hand, flicked them back and forth like the tail of an irritable horse and sat back behind his desk. There was a knock on the half-open door.

'Mr Tan, may I come in, sir?'

'Come in and have a seat. Nothing to be worried about.'

Benny treated interns benevolently. He knew how it felt to be starting out with nothing. Sometimes he felt guilty about employing so many interns for no pay and assuaged this by giving each one a twenty-dollar note. In his mind, it was simple: if he didn't employ them, someone else would, and maybe in worse surroundings.

The young man sat down in the chair in front of the desk clutching a baseball cap. Benny moved the pencil so it was pointing at his interviewee.

'So you have met Janet and some of the team?'

'They were great, so helpful and—'

Benny held his hand up for silence. He didn't need to hear it. No time to waste when he was finalizing the buyout. He swung the worry beads and screwed his face into a smile.

'Kurt,' Benny said, jabbing his finger towards the young man, 'we like you. And subject to answering a few questions, you're set to join as an intern for six months, possibly a year.'

Kurt clenched his hands into tight fists. 'Awesome. Thank you!'

'Now, what about handling fish? Are you squeamish?'

The young guy smiled. 'No, sir. I grew up on a farm and helped wring the necks of countless turkeys and chickens.'

'Did you really do that?' For the first time in the interview Benny felt mildly impressed.

'Yes, sir, and I also used to catch trout with my bare hands too.'

Benny set down the worry beads and twiddled the pencil. 'Do you know many of the kinds of fish we sell, Kurt?'

'Well, sir, to be really honest, I can only name six tropical and six freshwater, but I will be able to learn the names of the other species within a few days of being here.'

'OK, step over here and tell me what the little guy is in this tank.' Benny guided Kurt to the far side of his office, where a row of five metre-wide tanks lined the wall. Benny loved the green glow their tasteful lighting gave out; it always calmed him.

Kurt examined the occupants and pointed to one. 'That's a baby nursing shark!'

'Correct, but look over here,' said Benny, pointing to another tank.

Kurt peered at a three-foot-long fish. 'It's got a huge head and looks kinda like a catfish, but I don't know.'

'Well, you've just met my favourite fish. Not a beauty, but a great character, often misunderstood by people and other fish. A *Hemibagruswyckii*. A ram among fish – the bull the other fish fear, and a champion breeder too.'

Kurt gave another polite smile. 'So people can buy these on the Internet and you ship around the world?' he asked.

'Sure, via our sales team,' Benny said. 'We also send out frozen samples to labs and frozen eggs and sperm to breeders.'

He did not add that, in fact, the dry-ice-filled polystyrene boxes had useful hollow compartments, or that fish covered the smell of anything else he liked to export – or import – in those compartments. This was something that Kurt didn't need to know. But Nabokov, the Russian buyer, would need to know. And Benny would enjoy telling him. It really worked as three-way traffic – like the slave trade his wife had been studying at night school all those years ago in shitty London. One type of sugar one way, fish another, and more – but different – candy back again. No waste. Not one drop of anything wasted.

Kurt blushed and suddenly looked younger than his twenty years. 'I hoped I could use my college experience to add something.'

'Which is?'

'Computer science.'

Benny looked at his computer screen. Its inner workings were more secret than those of the Pentagon. No way would the kid get his hands on that. Only his executive assistant and vice president, Janet Lee, and head of security, Dick Chain, got to see what was in there. And then only some of it.

'Well, maybe you can help me with something else while you're learning the ropes here,' Benny said. 'Are you a Christian?'

They walked back to Benny's desk.

'I guess,' Kurt said.

'Well, this company supports a charity that helps the less fortunate get free dental treatment – our way of putting something back.'

Kurt stood while Benny sat down.

'If you've got the right attitude, the sky's the limit. Helping others is a way of helping yourself.'

Kurt looked up and nodded his head earnestly. 'I'd like to know as much as possible – I want to be the best.'

Benny took a deep breath, switched on his internal censor and began an edited but similar speech he had given to Nabokov the first time the Russian declared he was serious about buying him out.

'What you see up here is for private clients. Fish Farm's main showroom is downstairs and there is a lower ground floor below for storage, administration and shipping. We have ninety tanks, some saltwater, mostly fresh. I have made us successful by having a special display of the top-ten-selling fish: people are sheep and buy what they see is popular. We do celebrity aquariums and ship all over the world. "No fish too small to ship" is our motto. But we don't just export fish; we import fish too. Waste not, want not.'

'Wow. I didn't know a store like this could operate worldwide,' Kurt said.

'There's a lot you don't know. Globalization is the only way forward. Staying local is death,' Benny said. 'Look in the parking lot out there – every member of our full-time staff drives a top-quality company car. Why? Because they've worked hard, earned my trust . . . and are worth it. Think you've got what it takes to make it at Fish Farm?'

'To be honest, sir, I never thought about working with fish in my life up until my first interview. But what you just said is so inspiring I want to work here and prove myself.'

Benny was only half listening as he peered into the CCTV screen. A flickering image of Janet Lee, reversing her three-month-old Range Rover into the car park.

'Yes. Let me just have a think for a moment,' said Benny, walking across to the window and raising one of the slats of the blind. The Range Rover pulled into Janet's designated space – shiny, buffed tyres still wet from the car wash, where she took it most days to be vacuumed and waxed.

Janet stepped out of the car, gym-toned, impeccably manicured but plain, holding her designer bag tucked beneath her arm and carefully touching the fringe and sides of her freshly cut hair.

Benny sucked his teeth as Janet clicked the remote locking device and went through her ritual of saying hello to the car-lot attendant, pointing out some dead flowers in the landscaping that required attention. Such a control freak.

He bit his tongue to remind himself he needed to speak with her about Dominic Young and walked back to his desk. Pretending to read from his notepad, he casually asked, 'Did you hear that a body was washed up on the beach?'

'I heard something about that, sir.'

'Yesterday, apparently.'

'I heard it was cut up into pieces and found in a suitcase.'

Benny swung his worry beads at a funeral pace. 'Everybody likes to embellish these stories. Being washed up dead on a beach is bad enough, isn't it?'

'You're right, sir. I'd like the world to get back to normal.'

'We can't allow these things to get us down,' Benny said, holding out his hand. 'Tidy yourself up, get your nails cut and Janet will take you through the orientation. OK? Welcome to Fish Farm.'

27

Three days later, 5.45 p.m., 17 July

Judging by St Monica's overflowing car park, the funeral was sold out. Mandy had had to park on Cloverfield and 3rd, pissed off at the distance, but pleased that when he collected the car later, it would act as a reminder to visit Wayne Chung. He hoped his new black suit was smart enough – thirty dollars at the Malibu thrift shop.

The late-afternoon heat felt overwhelming. Even after fifteen years in California, he still wasn't used to the high temperatures. He yearned for the cold, crisp air of an Oxfordshire autumn morning, the dead leaves of chestnut trees, the orderliness of hedges and the gravel underfoot.

On the steps of the church, an elderly priest and two burly civilians greeted the mourners. Afternoon starlings were chattering in the trees and shrieks of children having fun carried on gusts of wind from the beach. Just the time of day when Pedro García-Márquez might arise from a siesta and go for a walk in his expensive suede shoes, maybe call his best friend in London. But Pedro could no longer do that, because he was dead. And Mandy couldn't ignore the fact that the funeral was starting in fifteen minutes and he hadn't got a sniff of the killer yet. To make matters even worse, the Giraffe had declared open season and put Broadski and Dent on the case. Mandy exhaled. It was now only a matter of time before the media began fanning the flames of the story too.

At the bottom of the steps, he tried to shrug off the feeling of gloom and hopelessness. He adjusted his tie, pulled his jacket sleeves down and pictured Donna as she waved goodbye from inside the locked ward in Springfield Rehab. It was going to be a day of bad memories, he could tell.

The eyeless body on the beach was already the talk of the town. The effect on Donna: instantaneous freak-out, blown fuses, mental kettle boiled dry. Curiously and contrary to his experience of mental turmoil, Donna *was* aware of what was happening and actually wanted medication and a secure ward.

Her rescue and salvation had come about thanks to Father Tony's persuasive beachside manner. Whether it was his calm English accent or the way he smiled, Donna had really listened to the priest. And once Donna was safely inside the first-aid room in the seminary, Father Tony had telephoned a friend in San Francisco and got her a bed in Springfield. Once a ranch for a retired cattle baron, Springfield was now a three-storey mental health clinic in ten acres of Malibu Canyon. Funded by a Silicon Valley tycoon (an old family friend of Father Tony), the place had a no-nonsense Scandinavian feel that Mandy found reassuring on Donna's behalf.

'Promise you'll phone me, promise you'll visit me, and promise you'll not get someone else for my room?' she had said like a twelve-year-old girl. Was this the same person who regularly called him a 'fucking weasel' and a 'failure'?

Mandy recalled letting out a long sigh – this was an opportunity to finally ditch Donna. But he couldn't do that. No way. Not after the body on the beach, and her coming so close to grasping the nettle of recovery – he knew the score too well, through his own ups and downs. So he'd said, 'Sure I'll text you, and come and see you, but on two conditions.'

'What's that?' Donna asked tearfully.

'That you feed the goldfish and run round the grounds twice a day.'

'You got it, I will.'

At least that was one good deed done, he thought, as he climbed St Monica's grand stone steps, the last seventy-two uncoiling in his head like an unpleasant matinee. The one significant development was that Father Tony had told him Lucy Lack had removed a letter from Dominic Young's unconscious body on the plane. 'I just assumed she would have told you,' he'd said. When they had visited the seminary, Donna's hysterical description of Dominic's mutilated body triggered the priest's confession.

Graphic accounts of Dominic Young's corpse and jokes about Mafia-style penile dismemberment circulated Santa Monica like wildfire – almost as if a celebrity had been killed. It was odd the way people joked about death, the grimmer the better – as if that would stop its power. Odd, too, the way everyone seemed to know exactly who was to blame for the dead body on the beach. Even the guy cutting Lucy Lack's hair yesterday knew it was the Mexican Mafia.

'I'm just surprised the guy hadn't had his head cut off – that's what they normally do,' he'd said.

Mandy had gone round to Shutters to confront Lucy Lack about the letter she'd taken from Dominic. Discovered she was having her hair done. When he walked in, Lucy screwed up her face and dismissively brushed bits of wet hair from her white gown. She kept ignoring him as he waited for her in the white-leathered Shutters salon. In the end, she sent the criminologist hairdresser to ask what he wanted.

'The letter once belonging to Dominic Young that you pocketed on the plane,' he'd 'projected' RADA-style.

Ashamed or not wanting the hairdresser to know more, Lucy leapt up, got the letter and shoved it right into his wounded right hand.

This returned him to – yep – the injured right hand. He glanced at it as he laboured up the last church steps – a massive white paw against the black suit.

Another bit of the last seventy-two hours he'd like not to remember but couldn't forget – as the portly old priest took it and squeezed it at the top of the stairs.

'Welcome,' he said. 'Are you family or friend?'

Mandy gave a squeak of pain and nursed his injured hand.

It had happened like this.

An hour before getting the letter at Shutters, he had met the Giraffe at his office. The Giraffe stood, arms folded, within the door frame to his office, his width and height completely filling the gap, and warned Mandy off any murder other than Pedro's, like Mandy was some rank amateur.

'The Brit on the beach is police only,' he boomed. 'And if I were you, I would keep my fat fucking nose out of it.'

There was more, but that was the central thrust. It had pissed Mandy off badly. Hell, in a way that was good. Sometimes Mandy forgot he'd been a good detective before the child-porn case. Before he'd got ill.

A good one. But the Giraffe did not want to remember that. 'Broadski and Dent are now officially back on the García-Márquez case and handling the Dominic Young murder too. They specifically asked to. So don't even fucking think about playing Philip Marlowe, 'cos you are nothing to do with it,' he said.

To emphasize his point, and to make sure there were no witnesses, he handed Fabienne a ten-dollar bill and sent her out for fresh doughnuts. Then he turned back with a pissed-off look on his face, strode over to the chair by the desk and grabbed Mandy by the lapels. 'I don't like dead bodies on my beach. The sunbathers get squeamish.'

Mandy's tolerance snapped. 'What the hell did you just say? What drugs have you been taking?' he yelled, unwisely jabbing a finger towards the Giraffe's face. 'Don't accuse me of fucking up something I had no control over. It was right place, right time, that's all.'

The Giraffe bared his nostrils like a TV evangelist sniffing cash. He yanked open his desk drawer – a screech of timber on wood – and pointed to a manila-coloured file with a crime photo attached by a paper clip to the top of it. 'Take the picture out – someone you might remember.'

Mandy hesitated, more humiliation, but the urge to see it was far too strong. Something told him it was not going to be a snapshot of a nude Tamara from the Viceroy. It was something from his past. He reached inside the drawer, grabbed hold of the card. The Giraffe slammed the drawer just as he was pulling out his hand. Severe pain. Mandy fought back the instant scream. Not wishing to look like he was hurt or in pain.

Looking the Giraffe full in the face, he slowly spelt out, 'What d'you do that for, you c-u-n-t?'

A serious insult. The Giraffe smiled.

Mandy risked a glance at his injured paw – the skin beneath his knuckles was ripped open, an inch of blood-spotted pink-white flesh. Blood was beginning to drop onto the desk top. The photo was still between his fingers. He flipped the glossy colour print round in his fingers and stared at it. It was as if it had only happened yesterday, not four years and nine months ago. It had been taken on a film set of a porno film. The picture almost looked innocent. An underaged teenage girl was playing cards with a man sat next to her in an aeroplane seat – nothing too weird, except he was forty-five and they were naked.

He hadn't seen any of the photographic evidence of the incident before, just remembered every single detail of that day in his head. Terry had come home and dealt with the rumours going round the force. Kept up a stream of disinformation so the details were blurred; not even Fabienne knew exactly what had happened. Once Mandy'd agreed to leave the force, the Giraffe ensured the case became classified as secret. Someone standing next to him made sure of that. Oh yes, this was his warning that it might easily become declassified. Thanks. The Giraffe stood – his back to him, arms folded – watching an aerobics class in the building opposite as if nothing had happened. It had been a trick, a warning and his way of saying, 'Back the fuck off.'

Mandy squinted down at his bleeding knuckle. It hurt. Some crack dealer in Venice Beach had slammed a car door on his hand once; it felt pretty similar.

The Giraffe forced a grin and carried on watching the aerobics. Then Fabienne was in the open doorway with a carton of doughnuts, staring at Mandy's hand, a shocked expression on her face.

She cleared her throat. 'The commissioner is waiting for you to return his call, sir; it's about the Viceroy – urgent. And your colonoscopy appointment is in one hour's time, Cedars Sinai,' she said, no hint in her voice that anything was wrong. Ice cool in a crisis. Mandy'd always liked that in people, especially her.

'Is that all?' the Giraffe said.

'Yes, sir.'

2713

Macdonald, H

'Get him out of here.' The Giraffe flicked his hand down his sleeve as if getting rid of some unpleasant muck.

Fabienne guided Mandy out through the door, pulling it tight closed behind her. 'Let me put some antiseptic cream on that hand and bandage it up.'

Mandy groaned at the memory as he walked into the church foyer, clutching the Fabienne-dressed hand. He had to forget about it and focus on the positive. The one consolation was there had been no reference to Tamara Tyrer's death at the Viceroy. A damning report from Agent Anderson and the FBI would have been handing the Giraffe a hammer to nail the nails into his coffin. Strange that Anderson had not made contact again. Maybe he was being followed, kept out of the loop until they had more evidence. But what evidence?

Thank God for Fabienne. After the expert bandaging, she came down in the elevator, offered to keep him informed of any developments apropos Broadski and Dent, providing Mandy would agree to eat dinner at her place soon. 'No come for dinner, no info,' she said with a smile, stroking her perfect silver hair.

Back in the orderly queue of mourners, Mandy smiled, closed his eyes and breathed in as if he was a sommelier. The foyer was dominated by four cream-and-orange flower arrangements, gardenias and marigolds. Arrangements so big, so wide they looked like they each contained a dead child.

The flowers smelt of apricots, vanilla and ouzo.

'Excuse me, sir. Would you care for a service card?'

He opened his eyes. A warden was handing him a Requiem Mass booklet. He took it. On the front, a black-bordered photograph: Pedro laughing on a beach, his arm round an old Dalmatian dog.

He slipped the booklet into his pocket. What if the killing had been an accident, the wrong apartment, like the Manson family killing Sharon Tate by mistake? What if García-Márquez's suspect list was just one big red herring, full of the usual petty family rivalries and jealousies?

A familiar voice began directing the guests in front of him.

'Hello, Tío Juan and Tía Consuela. Dad would like you to sit opposite their pew at the front on the left.'

Miguel, the head of protocol for the family. Miguel nodded at Mandy in recognition.

Mandy pointed up to the gallery. 'OK for me to bed down with the choir, so I can see the congregation?'

Miguel paused mid-step and shook his head, his expression changing faster than a chameleon changes colour. 'We are only allowing members of the choir to be upstairs – security. Besides, my father would be upset if you were not part of the Mass for Pedro.' He emphasized the word 'father'.

Mandy shrugged. He wanted to be able to observe, not feel self-conscious turning this way and that to watch. But it was clearly pointless to argue. Miguel beckoned to his younger brother to come over, a maître d' summoning a waiter.

'Alfie? Would you show Mandy to row eight on the right? Make sure he gets a good seat.'

A loud cough came from behind. Against the back wall of the church lurked an unpleasant surprise: Broadski and Dent – arms folded, black-suited, trying to look sombre, cool and tough. One chewing gum, the other picking his moustache. So what? Of course they'd be here. The Giraffe would've told them. And made them wear the suits as well. Why was he even vaguely freaking? García-Márquez would never have invited Broadski and Dent.

No, it was Miguel. He'd always wanted the police in on the case, from the very start. But that still didn't completely explain the Giraffe's attack yesterday. No doubt about it, Mandy was in deep shit. Maybe the Giraffe would force Eduardo García-Márquez to terminate Mandy's only lifeline. Shit. He needed this case. He needed it. It was more than just *money*, for Christ's sake; this was his one chance to put himself back on the playing field. Back in the line-up and out of Loser's Meadow. But he also needed it to keep his house. Badly. And if Broadski and Dent were always gonna be over his shoulder, well, he just had to suck it up.

He followed Alfonso two-thirds of the way down the aisle. There was nervousness among the congregation. People turned to look at him, pretending to be looking at something else. But there was no stage – just a black coffin resting on a plinth at the end of the aisle. Alfonso gestured to the aisle seat in row eight. Mandy checked his watch: six o'clock.

Showtime.

Two altar boys in pure-white cassocks walked before the altar and genuflected. The atmosphere suddenly became breathlessly sad. Pedro's coffin, the thought of what lay inside – a twenty-nine-year-old man murdered and covered in tortilla chips eight days before.

He turned his head towards the exit and began his first survey of the congregation. Most were fanning themselves with their funeral cards, eyes on the altar. One kid wearing earphones, two adults on iPads. The business of social networking went on even while they buried a man. A few were kneeling in prayer. Others stared up into space as if waiting for a bus or something equally mundane.

Mandy squinted at the couple on his right: Kimberly, from Club Kafka – who wanted to make a TV show called *Retrosexual* – and, looking more closely at the bouffant-haired man beside her, Javier Jones. His eyes were bloodshot.

'I am wearing a wig, you know,' Jones whispered to him. His breath stank of lemon vodka.

Mandy nodded as if this was the most natural thing in the world. Jones was just who he wanted to speak to. Hadn't Kimberly and he known Dominic Young? But even in California, where life stories were exchanged at the drop of a charge card, it was wrong to whisper and gossip during a funeral – well, in his book, anyway.

In front of him was a two-space gap he presumed was being kept for the ushers. Next to it was the classy blonde head of Sarah Sternwood and Johnny, fidgeting with a bundle of scrawled-on cards.

Far ahead in the front row, the forlorn figure of Eduardo García-Márquez clutching a rosary. Beside him, Pedro's sister, María, in a black dress, her hair up, looking vulnerable, and Alfonso, the portrait of a sullen, privileged nineteen-year-old. Bolt upright was the woman Mandy knew must be Valeria García-Márquez, their mother. She did not, to put it mildly, seem like the motherly type. Ramrod straight, thin, beautiful golden hair, dark eyes, severe.

The orchestra in the gallery played the introductory notes of Mozart's Mass in C minor and twenty-two mixed voices filled the church, transforming the atmosphere. The congregation rose; the music swelled. For a moment the huge space felt full of expectation. But what expectations could anyone have? There were none left for Pedro; all that was gone. The only hope was to find his killer.

Some small justice.

Mandy tightened his fist. An unwelcome lump came into his throat as Father Tony and his acolytes proceeded up the aisle. The English priest walked solemnly, hands in front of his chest; behind him, two Mexican altar girls and a priest swinging an incense holder. At the coffin, Father Tony took hold of the smoking thurible and shook it three times. The beauty of the ancient ritual made the lump in Mandy's throat grow. Father Tony smiled as he accepted the jug of holy water from the altar girls and sprayed each end of the coffin with its garland of yellow roses and silver crucifix.

The church was breath-silent. The García-Márquezes stood sideways to face the procession. Whatever their differences, they were a united front, each one with a hand on another's shoulder or round their waist. Father Tony uttered an inaudible prayer, then walked through the gate to the altar, the holy of holies. He bowed deeply and was met by two altar boys. The musicians and choir stopped.

In the silence, waiting for the Mass itself to begin, Mandy picked up the prayer book and felt a jab in the arm: Javier Jones.

'Will you be at the party afterwards?' Jones hissed.

Mandy mouthed, 'Obviously.' As he did so, there was a gust of air – the church door opening, whispered voices and heels clacking on the stone floor.

Sarah Sternwood half rotated her head in the pew two rows in front of him. As she recognized him, her expression changed to open-mouthed surprise, a passenger on a cruise hit by an iceberg. She tugged on her husband's sleeve. Sternwood gave a faint smile. But not at Mandy – at the latecomers: Lucy Lack in a tailored jacket and dress, nearly too short for decency, high heels and a veil, her hand resting on the outstretched leather-jacketed arm of Wing.

Lucy saw the space in front of Mandy and was about to sit down when she noticed Sarah Sternwood. She gesticulated to Wing to sit down first. Wing obliged, looking more like a bodyguard than Mandy remembered.

The couple's entrance took no more than thirty seconds. But by the time she lifted her veil and knelt down, everyone in the church knew exactly who she was: the English girl who was meant to have been engaged to Pedro.

Mandy inwardly laughed as he looked at the freshly styled hair and the sunglasses balanced beneath her veil. Lucy had real style and front, and for that, if for nothing else, he wanted to applaud – and go to bed – with her.

Then he noticed something. The track of a tear beneath her veil, like the trail of a diamond on her perfect skin. Perhaps she was not the hard-faced bitch she seemed. Mandy's heart twisted in his chest.

Twenty-five minutes of the service passed in a daze of guilt at not finding the killer, desire, Lucy's minxy dress and the general grief that every funeral brought for all those Mandy had known who were dead.

Then Father Tony turned at the altar and said, 'In a moment one of Pedro's oldest friends will tell us more about Pedro's contribution to life. But before that let us remember Pedro well today.' Father Tony took a deep breath and looked up at St Monica's golden-domed ceiling.

Mandy scanned the faces of the expensively dressed congregation for any sign of complicity or guilt. Despite the air-conditioning, many people were fanning themselves with their service cards. Someone in that church knew something about why Pedro had died, maybe even more than that. Yet everyone looked inscrutable, poised and waiting for Father Tony to continue speaking. Even the grief-stricken García-Márquez family were silently looking up at the pulpit.

'As a priest, what I know is that God gave us free will, gave us the choice between good and evil.'

Lucy Lack was leaning forward, her shoulders heaving, holding her sunglasses and quietly sobbing.

'Sadly I never met Pedro, but I have had the pleasure of meeting his father,

Eduardo, his family and some of you. And I have learnt that this young man was decent, kind, loving and well informed about the world and his place in it. A caring person who gave so much to other people.'

A young man sitting in the same row as Mandy took out a purple handkerchief and wiped his streaming eyes.

'Pedro was fortunate. In my experience, highly fortunate young men often choose to focus their time, their lives on wanting and getting more – more money, more property, more status, more cars, more sex, more me, myself and I. You could say that we live in a society that endorses and encourages that approach, that no longer views human beings as sacred but as something to use and plunder. Our society only measures people by how much more than others they have got. But Pedro chose a path of love, of helping others. He gave to charities, helped his fellow countrymen to stand on their own feet and by all accounts was a loyal, generous friend. Let us pray for him and his family in their terrible loss.'

In the ensuing silence an anxious-looking Johnny Sternwood manoeuvred himself past Wing and Lucy, clutching his handwritten speech. Head bowed, sweating profusely, Sternwood trudged towards the altar. As he climbed the steps to the pulpit, Mandy put his hand on Lucy's shoulder. He did it without thinking. Lucy leant back and patted it. Then Johnny Sternwood was standing behind the lectern.

'Pedro was the best man at my wedding and I stand here today at his funeral. I wish it was the other way round. I am guilty . . .' Sternwood went ghostly white. He swayed a little.

'Sorry,' he muttered. A thin stream of vomit trailed out of his mouth. His eyes rolled into the back of his head and he went down.

Twenty-seven words. Twenty-seven words that had given him the mother of all heart attacks.

28

7.30 p.m., 17 July

Benny Tan knelt beside the glass tank of delphinium-coloured guppies and brushed flakes of skin into a dustpan. Coldplay played through the store's hidden speakers. Earlier, via the CCTV system Benny had spotted a customer picking at a patch of psoriasis, dropping bits onto the floor. He had let it pass at the time, as the woman spent $2,000 a month, but now he had to do something about it.

The wooden floor was always vacuumed first thing, the tanks polished four times a day. It was probably unnecessary, but 'probably' was not a word in Benny's dictionary. It either was or it wasn't, and if something needed doing, then it should be done. Besides which, he was expecting an important visitor that evening who needed to be sure attention to detail was one hundred per cent.

Benny held up his wrist to the light: seven thirty-one p.m. Dimitri Nabokov, beard and black glasses, Russian accent, precise in judgement, due at seven forty-five. Based on the last three meetings, Nabokov would be five minutes late.

Maybe it was a sign of good manners in Moscow. When he arrived, Benny'd show him around showroom, office and maybe the lower ground floor and some of the more select spreadsheets.

But not all.

Benny liked to hold something back, get what he wanted in the deal before agreeing to get into bed and be fucked. They needed him as much as he needed them. Right?

Benny shook his head.

No. Not true. He wanted out and they were his passport, ticket and plane. They had other choices. He had to make them believe he had other options too. No, sir, he wasn't desperate, whatever language you spoke. And Fish Farm was unique. Nobody on the West Coast had a business like his.

How did people like Nabokov get to the position he had and legally work in the US so quickly?

Was it the size of the man's brain or greasing somebody's palm? It had taken Benny more than fifteen years of hard work, greasing palms and, of course, the size of his brain.

He depressed the volume on the remote and cocked his ear to the ceiling, wondering if he heard an incoming call on his cell lying on his desk upstairs.

Why hadn't Dick Chain called? He stood up, used the remote to dim the lights and began pacing up and down the corridor of illuminated fish tanks. The hum of electricity and the bubbles from the oxygen pipes were the only sounds. It reminded him of diving. Peaceful and private. Fish made no noise.

Inside the fish tanks tonight, there was no fighting, not even from the large salt tank of barracudas. Maybe captivity deadened their aggression. Benny knew his fish were spoilt – they were fed on the best protein he could get hold of. And that was his big breeding secret, why Fish Farm made so many sales to people all over the world.

He looked down the showroom. At the far end was a red security rope, hanging between two chrome posts in front of the piranhas – the most viewed tank and the favourite of Janet Lee. Benny hated piranhas. They were stupid, vicious and ugly. And at the moment he hated Janet too. He was pissed, to put it mildly, with Janet for the way she had dealt with the loose cannon. What was her problem? Was she trying to take over by proving she could be more effective than him? She was lucky to be a number two. Janet Lee would not last seven days in a regular office, no way. He doubted she would survive the takeover. He hoped it wouldn't be too painful for her. But if it was . . . well, too bad.

Benny moved the rope aside and laid the palms of his hands flat against the tank. Several piranhas swam into the glass, triangular razor teeth tapping against it. Benny pulled out a concealed drawer, took out a scooping net and poked it down the feeding hatch. The fish scattered.

Face close to the side of the tank, he waited until a brave one swam towards him and, with a sudden swoop, hooked the fish into the net and pulled it out. He held the thrashing occupant above the open feeding hatch, until every drop of water fell back into the tank. The remaining piranhas swirled and darted into a tight, frenzied circle. Benny yanked the remote from his pocket and pumped up the volume to 'High Speed'.

He held the stranded fish higher, its slimy skin shining in the tank light. Higher still, then splayed his feet apart in readiness for when the fish decided to flip and jump out of the net as its last chance. This was the special moment.

Benny's legs and feet were shaking, half to the music and half in anticipation of the sole of his shoe crushing the little fish, feeling it burst through its skin.

Yes, yes, yes.

Heart racing, face hot, he dropped the motionless fish back into the tank, shakily replaced the hatch lid, put the net into the drawer, closed it, stepped back and wiped a tear from his eye. The other piranhas tore the dead fish apart in seconds.

He turned round and stared at the four rows of glimmering fish tanks. For a moment, it felt as if he was being condemned by the witnessing eyes of hundreds of fish. He suddenly felt uncertain, afraid.

A second later the echoing ring tone of his cell from his desk on the floor above provided the answer. Tan ran out of the showroom and up the stairs for all he was worth.

Slamming his office door behind him, he grabbed the cell: Dick Chain.

'What the fuck is happening?'

'We're here, waiting for her, as agreed. You OK, boss?'

'Concentrate on what you are doing, not me,' Benny spat, yanking his arm out of the shirt sleeve. 'So both of you are outside the entrance to the motel? You and that weirdo assistant you keep using?'

Benny went into his private bathroom, holding his cell to his ear.

'Yes, but if she doesn't show before midnight, we're going to take it in shifts, so that we function tomorrow.'

Benny pulled out a clean white shirt from the shelf of the bathroom closet. 'OK,' he said. 'You're sure you've not missed her?'

'We saw her go in, boss, no problem. She's a pretty distinctive redhead, if you know what I mean.'

'Dick? This job needs to be handled discreetly. Touch base in a few hours, but if anything happens before, call me.'

Five minutes later, smartly dressed and smiling, Benny Tan held out his hand to welcome Dimitri Nabokov.

Everything was back under control.

29

7.30 p.m., 17 July

Mandy followed the line of funeral cars northwards along 7th Street, direc-
tions face up on the passenger seat. The inside of the Amazon was like a sauna.
He hadn't seen Lucy Lack, Wing and Broadski and Dent come out: they
must have used a side exit to leave the church. What he had seen was Johnny
Sternwood being helped, almost pushed into one of the waiting García-
Márquez limousines and driven off, almost as fast as dying President Kennedy
had been whisked away from Grassy Knoll. The major difference was that
Jackie Kennedy appeared to do all she could to save her husband, while Sarah
Sternwood had travelled arms folded, looking mildly annoyed in a separate
car. Mandy had decided to pay the Sternwoods a visit in hospital as soon as he
was done being at the wake.

He crossed San Vicente, down West Channel Road, turned right onto
PCH, then right onto Sunset and made a left turn up Marquez Avenue, past
the Lycée Français de Los Angeles, close to the pristine Marquez Elementary
School. Jesus. Did the family own the whole district? This was Wealth with a
capital W.

He drove on for a mile or so up the winding Lachman Lane, to where the
landscape changed from ordered and urban to wild and mountainous, carried
on until the indicator lights of the cars ahead blinked in the dusk, and turned
right up a dirt track. He wound down the window as he went over a cattle grid
and through a large set of gates manned by uniformed guards. The warm air
smelt of burnt toast and horse shit. The crickets and frogs were competing so
loudly it sounded like they were preparing to take part in a revolution. Other
than the ranch house on the Will Rogers estate and the García-Márquez house,
there were no private houses allowed to be so close to the state park. Mandy
grabbed the last Trebor from a packet on the dash, changed down a gear. No
doubt about it, a few million dollars' endowment of a school had probably

secured Mrs García-Márquez the right to build. Clearly the main issue on the agenda with Eduardo García-Márquez was going to be Johnny Sternwood's collapse and what he intended to confess. Mandy's gut said that Sternwood's confession was more likely to be about setting up a scam and defrauding Pedro than killing him.

He yanked up the handbrake close to the exit of the temporary car park, wanting to get away quickly if necessary. It reminded him of an English point-to-point with his grandfather, only far warmer, with less mud and way more expensive cars. He stepped out of the Amazon and followed the other guests towards a glow of electric light.

The house itself was well camouflaged – protected behind a dense line of oak trees and sage shrubs three metres tall. Passing under the trees, he spotted a tarmac path with a rope handrail either side. He stopped and looked at the building in front of him.

The venue for Pedro's wake was a ranch house not much smaller than the place where Donna was staying with nineteen other patients. It was in need of a paint job and not like the perfect ones Mandy saw in the property-porn magazines shoved through his door every week. There was also a large stable block. He grunted. Six open stable doors on each side of a concrete yard and twelve horses poking out their heads.

Outside the slatted white wooden steps to the entrance was the same woman who had greeted him at the García-Márquez penthouse apartment on Ocean. 'Welcome, sir. Please go straight up and to your left, where Mr García-Márquez is waiting for you.'

Mandy walked up the steps, already nervous about having a conversation with the Big Avocado. He needed to marshal his thoughts. To buy time, he bent down on the top step of the entrance porch and pretended to retie his shoelaces. He fiddled with his laces, trying to figure out how to tackle García-Márquez's questions.

Once inside the enormous stone-flagged hallway, Mandy exhaled slowly and told himself to stay calm.

A middle-aged waiter tapped him on the arm and pointed down the corridor. Mandy knocked on the half-open door. The unmistakable voice of the head of the García-Márquez family called out, 'Come in.' Eduardo García-Márquez's face looked sombre and as if he had been weeping.

30

Nabokov stared at the entrance to the Viceroy, then at Benny. A LATV camera crew appeared to be filming an interview with a heavily decorated LAPD officer standing on the steps of the hotel.

'I thought we were going to Chez Jay,' he said. 'I don't like surprises. I hope your accounts – the real ones – don't have any.'

Benny hesitated for a second. He wasn't used to people being rude. 'Trust me, you'll like this place. And my accounts are pristine, I can assure you.'

Nabokov shrugged and got out of the car. Three silver-coloured police trucks were parked in a line fifty metres away. Benny followed, handed his BMW keys to the car valet, eyeballed the receipt ticket and gestured to Nabokov to follow him into the hotel. He kept a smile on his face as they walked into the mirrored lobby, nodding to staff as if he knew them. He reckoned once the Russian had a steak in front of him, noticed the ocean and was checking out a pretty actress or model, he would forget all about the change of plan. Chez Jay was for losers, anyway.

The bellboys and liveried staff behind the reception desk were trying to give a cool-headed impression that it was business as usual, yet the atmosphere in the hotel was tense and prickly. Benny and Nabokov paused as they walked past the three strands of blue-and-white police tape tied across the entrance to the hotel ballroom. Benny tried hard to catch the expression in Nabokov's eyes and face. But Nabokov's cell rang and the Russian rushed outside to take it in the smoking area.

Benny stood waiting in the foyer, trying to avoid the gaze of the two policemen standing by a sign requesting information regarding the 'fatalities' following the recent LAPD Award Ceremony. So rude. Still, Nabokov obviously had some friends in high places, maybe some of the same ones Benny had. So he didn't want to piss him off. Not before Nabokov gave him his money. Didn't he deserve it after all these years of hard work? All these years of chasing the American Dream?

'Trouble in the old country,' Nabokov said, reeking of smoke. 'Sorry about that.'

Benny shook his head. 'No trouble,' he said. 'No trouble at all.'

They both knew he was pissed off. They both ignored it.

A waiter showed them to a discreet beach table under a palm tree where you were unofficially allowed to smoke and handed them a menu.

'What can I get you gentlemen to drink?'

Nabokov pushed the menu to one side and pulled at his beard. 'A bottle of the Côtes-du-Rhône, rack of ribs, Greek salad and fries.'

Benny blinked and coughed, trying to hide his surprise at Nabokov's abruptness. This wasn't a burger joint; this was the Viceroy. But then the Russians weren't known for mincing their words. Canadian Chinese, like Benny, were not exactly verbose, but well-mannered – unsentimental perhaps, but they always had an elegant way of doing things. The Russians were something else. Nothing was sacred. Except, Benny hoped, business.

'A tonic and a twist for me,' Benny said, opening and closing the menu, 'and a tuna steak, medium rare, and a fava bean and pecorino salad.'

'And bring me a big Heineken to get started,' Nabokov added, lighting up a cigarette.

The waiter threaded his way back through the crowded tables, tropical plants and gas heaters. A nearby table of four Germans – all beautiful blonde women – began clapping the salsa band on the small stage close to the hotel side of the restaurant. They were slightly drunk.

Nabokov grunted and grabbed a chunk of bread from the table.

'Do you like music?' Benny said, for want of something better to say. He didn't really have much small talk. Business took up all the space in his head. Business and business. That was pretty much it for Benny.

Nabokov didn't reply. He obviously didn't do small talk either.

He was chewing some bread and drowning another chunk in a plate of olive oil.

Eventually, wiping his lips and beard with a napkin, he said, 'Tell me, why did you choose *this* place for your surprise? There are plenty of other restaurants, plenty of other hotels in this town. Shutters or Casa del Mar or even Georgio's on West Channel? Why here?'

Benny coughed and stared at the lights of the Ferris wheel on the pier. The evening wasn't going well.

'Well?' Nabokov said, blowing smoke in Benny's direction, pressing yet more bread into the oil.

'I think this is a smart hotel,' Benny said. 'They used it for a G20 conference. Good food, pretty women, nice atmosphere. I like it, and I thought you'd like it too.'

'And that's the only reason you chose this place, is it?'

'Would you rather go somewhere Russian?'

Nabokov rolled his eyes. 'Now you're just being crazy,' the Russian said. 'You know a congressman and cop were shot here . . . and a call girl?'

'Killed by some Vietnamese illegals. Yes, I know.'

The waiter arrived with the Heineken and the tonic'n'slice.

Nabokov poured the beer down his throat. He banged the empty glass on the table, laughed and slapped Benny on the shoulder. 'Bravo! So no other reason?'

Benny shook his head.

'Good. Let's enjoy ourselves, then!'

Benny faked a laugh and raised his tonic water in a toast. His radar was on full alert.

He knew a little bit more than he wanted to know about Nabokov now. The congressman must have refused to have his palms greased; maybe the dead cop too. Either way, with the Russians, you often ended up dead. He hoped to God that Dick was sorting out the remaining loose cannon scenario. Even faded rock stars needed to be silenced.

'Yes, to good times,' Benny said.

But Nabokov's attention was entirely for the German women. Bizarrely – and that was when Benny realized just how drunk they must have been – they were smiling back and gesturing for Nabokov to come over to their table.

The big Russian needed no second bidding.

Benny sipped on his tonic, thankful that Nabokov was now squatting by the side of the tourists' table, holding the hand of a tanned blonde lady, dressed in a white sleeveless dress, with gold bracelets and earrings. He had cocked his head at the woman like a little bear looking at food.

He pulled out a crumpled piece of paper from his pocket, flattened it on the table and started to write down plus and minus points about the deal and then screwed it up into a ball. It made him nervous to think ahead like this. Not just because of the endgame, but because of the whole process of Nabokov and his firm undertaking the final due diligence.

Janet was a safe pair of hands when it came to accounting. But she still had to explain the $100,000 missing from Chung's inventory. He didn't think the Russians would accept that as a staff issue. It'd be Benny's head on the line.

And then the loose cannon: Susan Green.

Nabokov had already told him that there could be no trouble, no loose ends, because it was the goodwill inherent in the associated business that was going to cost the Russians the most, the trade routes that Benny had established so smoothly, of course.

The German woman was dragging Nabokov back to Benny's table.

'He's such a darling,' she said to Benny. 'What a guy – bought us a bottle of Cristal.'

Benny smiled. The champagne would be on his bill, of course.

Nabokov gave him an evil grin. 'I knew you wouldn't mind, Benny,' he said. 'For a beautiful woman.'

The waiter arrived with their food.

'*Nostrovia*,' Nabokov said tersely, raising his glass.

Benny clinked his glass against Nabokov's.

Nabokov bit the meat off two ribs, chewed them and washed them down with a glass of Côtes-du-Rhône. Wiping his mouth with a napkin, and refilling his glass from the bottle, he leant towards Benny and said, 'There's something that doesn't make sense about your business.'

For the first time in a long time, Benny felt a shiver of fear tingle his spine.

'Oh, what's that?' said Benny, trying to sound unperturbed.

Nabokov shifted his chair so he was looking directly at Benny and began chewing on a large rib. The pretty German lady was no longer on his menu.

Benny knew he was small fry compared to the organization Nabokov *really* worked for. But he was in it now. Whatever had happened, he was going to make this deal work. He needed to go on the attack.

'What doesn't make sense, Dimitri?'

'Your business depends very heavily on export, doesn't it?'

Benny nodded and sipped his tonic. Nabokov arched his eyebrows. Benny grinned to signify his understanding that coded conversation was about to begin.

Nabokov poured some salt on a rib but set it down before continuing. 'There are time limits to the export of precious fish, Benny . . . Considering how rare and expensive some of your merchandise is, why not establish your own hotel complex so people can fly in, *relax* and choose their fish here?'

The Russian had correctly spotted the weak spot of the operation. There could be triple the amount of customers. Yet to set up a new operation was fraught with difficulties. It was something Benny had tried to camouflage. He needed to respond with a positive.

'You are absolutely right, Dimitri. That would have been my plan, but lack of cash and the difficulties with the law in California made it impossible for me. That's why you are here tonight, isn't it? Making the impossible possible?' Benny lifted his glass again to the Russian. 'To success,' he said.

Nabokov smiled, clearly pleased at Benny's answer, and raised his glass too. 'Yes, here's to success and no skeletons in the cupboards.'

31

8.30 p.m., 17 July

Eduardo García-Márquez heaved himself out of a swivel chair behind a large desk and greeted Mandy with a handshake. The high-ceilinged room had a large fireplace and smelt of old dogs and cinnamon. Despite itching to discover what had happened to Sternwood, Mandy took out his notebook and waited for his employer to speak. García-Márquez ran his hand through his thick grey hair and pointed to a wall of certificates and rosettes on his left.

'This house has been in my wife's family for a hundred and eighty-five years,' he said. 'They were given this land by the king of Spain.'

So Valeria García-Márquez was also loaded in her own right. A marriage of two wealthy families, hence the *name*.

'Did they build what became Santa Monica?'

Eduardo García-Márquez's sombre face lightened. He appeared relieved to be discussing history – something different from the death of his son.

'No, but they developed land from here down through the Palisades to the ocean and to north of Sunset.' García-Márquez pointed to the right of the fireplace. 'And all these medals and certificates are for the matches my wife has won. Sometimes I think she loves playing polo more than anything else.'

There were two broken polo sticks in an old fire bucket by the door.

Up close, García-Márquez's eyes looked weary and bloodshot, and exactly as if he had just been to his eldest son's funeral, with a wife who preferred polo sticks, even broken ones.

García-Márquez gestured Mandy to a high-backed chair in front of him. García-Márquez sat down and picked up a pair of gold reading glasses. Mandy watched him struggle to place one broken arm of the glasses behind his right ear. It was either a temporary pair kept in the house or one that mattered a lot to him. Mandy flicked over a page in his notebook, as if this was something he did every day of his life. He decided to open the batting.

151

'I'm making good progress investigating your list of suspects and suggest we deal first with Johnny Sternwood's performance in church.'

'Well?' García-Márquez said, his tone now stern and businesslike.

'My guess is, he was about to say he was guilty of cheating Pedro out of a lot of money and of betraying him, but not of being his killer.'

'The Sternwood boy told you about his dot-com company?'

'His wife did,' Mandy said.

García-Márquez's face gave away nothing as he took out a handwritten letter from his inside pocket and laid it flat on the desk.

'Well, this eloquent plea for forgiveness was delivered to me yesterday. I told him to ask for forgiveness from Pedro at his funeral. And I suppose he was trying to do exactly that.'

Mandy underlined Sternwood's name in his notebook. 'Was it a heart attack?'

García-Márquez smiled briefly. 'An extreme panic attack caused what is known as a hysterical syncope. He requires a few days' rest and . . . to spend some time contemplating his and his wife's conduct.'

'He sounds like he has the luck of the devil. May I make a copy?'

García-Márquez nodded but kept hold of the piece of paper. 'Do you think Mr and Mrs Sternwood are capable of murder?'

'No,' Mandy said. 'Greedy and stupid, yes. Killers, no.'

García-Márquez flicked the letter across the desk. Mandy carefully folded the letter and tucked it into his notebook, aware the atmosphere was growing darker.

'I'm flying with my son's body tonight for burial in Mexico. Our plane's waiting at Santa Monica Airport. My wife insisted the Sternwoods travel with us too and be treated at her clinic in Mexico. She never liked Johnny. The remaining family and close friends are following tomorrow.'

García-Márquez lifted a plastic file of papers from the desk and pulled out several loose pages.

Mandy nodded, patting the outside of his pocket for the plastic bag with the light blue anxo pill. It was in his other suit. He needed to say something to reassure García-Márquez that he had chosen the right man.

'I discovered the body of an Englishman on Santa Monica Beach three days ago.'

'I heard about it. Why is that relevant?'

Mandy edged his chair forward. 'The Santa Monica Police Department are not releasing this information to the public, but the man had his eyes and tongue removed.'

García-Márquez shrugged. 'You are not telling me anything I or anyone else in this town doesn't already know. What else?'

'The dead man turns out to be the same guy who was sitting next to Father Tony, the new priest at St Monica's, on his flight to LA eight days ago.'

He didn't mention Lucy Lack's role in Dominic Young's recovery from his in-flight suicide attempt.

'And you're making a connection because he said Mass at Pedro's funeral?'

'It's an odd coincidence, you have to admit.'

'And Lucy Lack was also on the same flight?' García-Márquez said with a sneer.

Mandy swallowed. His employer seemed to know everything that he did. He was wading towards a swamp of unemployment and needed to fight back. It was time to disclose the details of Pedro's last will and testament. He placed both hands on the arms of his chair and took a deep breath.

But before he had a chance to speak, García-Márquez took out three ten-by-eight colour photographs from a brown envelope and laid them face down on the desk. 'Have a look and tell me if you still believe what you said when we last met about blackmail being quite an old-fashioned concept.'

Mandy stood up, wiped his sweaty fingers on his trousers and turned over the first photo. It was an amateur soft-porn bondage photo, not like the ones he'd had to see while a cop but in magazines and on the Internet. Pedro García-Márquez crouched on all fours wearing nothing but a studded dog collar being spanked by Lucy Lack dressed in bondage kit. So Pedro liked a little S&M. Mandy let out a professional grunt like a dentist examining a patient's teeth and turned over the second and third pictures. The instant Mandy absorbed their content he wanted to exclaim, 'What the fuck?' but he told himself to act professionally and not display any reaction. A buck-naked, athletic Latino was standing sideways and opposite and caressing Lucy's naked breasts with both hands. Kneeling and performing oral sex on them beneath were Pedro and Sarah Sternwood.

'Goodness gracious me,' were the only words that came out of Mandy's mouth.

Eduardo García-Márquez carried on as if he'd just shown Mandy a gardening catalogue.

'It turns out Pedro couriered the pictures to my wife ten days before he was killed. You see, my wife could never accept or admit Pedro was homosexual. So he wanted her to see them just in case they suddenly appeared on the Internet. To his credit, he was not prepared to be bullied or blackmailed.'

'Any idea who took the photos?'

García-Márquez sighed and shook his head. 'I don't know but am guessing it's Mr Johnny Sternwood. He's not in any of the pictures.'

'Do you know who the other man in the photo is?'

García-Márquez cleared his throat and flattened his hand over the third photograph. 'The other man in the photo is my wife's close friend and godson. She didn't want to show them to me, but Sternwood's behaviour at the funeral this evening changed her mind.'

'May I keep one? It may help to get to the truth of who killed Pedro.'

'No, I want to keep them. If you need a reference, use your phone to take a picture now, otherwise they, along with Sternwood's computer, are going to be burnt.'

Mandy knew he looked like a paparazzo by an open grave in a cemetery but nonetheless took out his cell and snapped each of the images on the desk.

García-Márquez set the glasses down, looked Mandy in the eye and then turned his gaze towards a figure standing in the doorway. It was Miguel.

'Your presence would be greatly appreciated next door. Everyone is here.'

'Everyone?' Eduardo García-Márquez said.

Miguel shot Mandy a look of disdain. 'Maybe some people decided it was better not to come after all,' he said.

'We will join you in one minute.'

As Miguel closed the door behind him, his father turned back to Mandy. 'Anything else?'

'Well, there is something, yes . . .'

'Lucy Lack?' García-Márquez said. 'My wife has banned her from coming to the wake. Yet Pedro would have wanted her to be here.'

'Do you think Lucy Lack may have had something to do with Pedro's death?'

García-Márquez spread his large hand over his eyes and forehead, and shook his head. 'I don't know,' he said. 'Perhaps.' He took off his glasses and became absorbed in lifting the damaged arm up and down as if it was the wing of a small bird.

Mandy turned back the page of his notebook and drew a deep breath. 'You may remember we discussed whether Pedro made a will?'

García-Márquez nodded but carried on staring at the malfunctioning arm of his glasses.

'I discovered Pedro's last will and testament on his laptop.' Mandy hesitated. 'In it, he appears to make a large bequest to Lucy Lack of an Edward Hopper painting and his cottage in Sayulita. But I've not discovered anything legal, witnessed, so . . .'

García-Márquez's large shoulders shook as he coughed. He recovered his composure. 'I received a copy of the will you are referring to from Pedro's lawyers yesterday. They thought it appropriate to wait until his funeral. It had been witnessed by two people living in his apartment building and counter-signed by Pedro's lawyer. It is legal, but I've not told my wife or anyone else, so do not mention it to anyone yet. In fact, I don't want you questioning my wife at all.'

But I need to ask your polo-playing wife some important questions.

Alarm bells were ringing in Mandy's head. There was something decadent, old Hollywood, white mischief in Kenya about Mrs García-Márquez that he wanted to pursue. But owing to the look of anguish on García-Márquez's face, he decided to comply and return to the subject of Pedro's will. Maybe the prospect of losing the Hopper painting was troubling the man.

'I am sorry, sir – the bequests to Lack must have come as a shock,' Mandy said.

García-Márquez clasped his hands tightly together as if he was trying to strangle some invisible evil force. 'Pedro was entitled to leave his possessions to whoever he chose. However, I do not want the person or persons who murdered him to benefit in any way from his will. Pedro's problem wasn't that he was gay, but that he came from a rich family. Whatever he did or has done, he was my son, my first child, whom I loved very much.' He covered his mouth with his fist as his voice faltered. 'And always will.'

Grief, treachery and too little sleep had caught up with him. Like a heavyweight boxer knocked nearly senseless, García-Márquez slowly rose to his feet and pulled his rosary from his pocket.

'I want to believe Pedro had good judgement. I am willing to accept I am wrong. I have no faith in Clarence Spider or his police force. But I have faith in you, Mandy – faith that you will be fearless in finding out the truth. Please do not disappoint me.'

García-Márquez gestured for Mandy to follow him into the reception. The meeting was clearly over. Mandy strode beside García-Márquez, inwardly pleased to have survived the ordeal but full of admiration for his employer's intelligence and integrity.

The long, beamed reception room was full of people, a little salsa music playing; it could have been a cocktail party. Within seconds García-Márquez was surrounded by friends and relations – not exactly a feeding frenzy but close.

Mandy felt like an unwanted carnival goldfish, truly out of his element, in his thrift shop suit. No one was interested in who he was. Reminding himself of the benefits of anonymity, he peered over the heads of the guests, hoping to locate Father Tony, Wing or Mrs García-Márquez. But he couldn't see any of them.

He lifted a glass of wine from a tray and ambled to a nearby wall to study a painting of a horse. The horse was just a horse, so he took two paces sideways and stood in front of the roses that had lain on Pedro's coffin. He tuned into a conversation behind him.

'It was his body's way of telling him he needed to rest.'

'That motherfucker had guilt written all over his chest.'

Mandy swung round to try and identify the speakers, but they had moved on. He spotted Javier and Kimberly standing across the room by a window. He headed over.

'Good turnout,' he said.

'What do you expect?' Javier Jones said, putting his nearly empty glass to his mouth. 'Pedro was loved.'

'By some,' Kimberly said. 'But someone obviously didn't like him too much.'

'Shut up,' Javier spat. His wig had developed a pronounced tilt. The scars across his head were on show.

'It may be just a coincidence,' Mandy began, 'but I think you know Dominic Young is linked to Pedro.'

'How so?' Kimberly said.

'He was on a plane with Lucy Lack, and I found a letter from the woman he was arguing with the other night at the Kafka.' He paused. 'That was Dominic Young with the woman at the Kafka, wasn't it?'

'Dee Nitrate?' Javier asked.

'Susan Green is her real name,' Kimberly added, picking a smoked salmon canapé off a tray proffered by a passing waiter. 'Yes, that was Dominic all right.'

'Scumbag,' Javier Jones said. 'A real douchebag.' He put his hand to his mouth and leant towards Mandy. 'Alfonso knew him, you know. They had similar *habits* . . .'

'Can you help me get hold of her?' Mandy asked. 'I need to talk to her.'

Javier put down his glass on the nearest table and took Kimberly's arm. 'We can't help you,' he said. 'I doubt it has anything to do with Pedro or I would. But I don't want to get mixed up in this shit. It's too heavy.'

'How about if you just tell Susan Green I'm looking for her?' Mandy asked.

'Sure,' Javier called over his shoulder, pulling Kimberly to the door. 'I'll try.'

Mandy stood, still clutching his wine glass. He hadn't seen people leave that fast since watching people in a restaurant hear the earthquake alarm. Definitely a lead worth following – Giraffe warning or not.

'That was typically weird of them,' a voice said near his shoulder.

He turned.

María, Pedro's little sister.

'How are you?' he said.

She looked prettier than she had in St Monica's Church.

'Very sad.'

The girl actually now looked as if she had just lost her brother. Maybe it had needed some time to sink it. Quite different to when they'd met at the Santa Monica Athletic Club.

'How's Alfonso?'

'OK, I guess,' she said, then paused. 'Well, kinda depressed. Sorry but I have to mingle with my relations.'

'Do you know where Josefina is at all?'

María gave a funny little smile. 'Kitchen, I'd expect. She's happiest in there – reminds her of better times, I suppose.' She pointed towards a small door at the far end of the room. 'Through there.'

Mandy headed to the door.

Father Tony was just arriving with his film-star smile. A small crowd of women gathered round him. Mandy waved his hand above the heads of the ladies, managed to catch his eye and projected his old actor voice. 'Good to see you, Father. Beautiful eulogy.'

An instant chorus of agreement and approval came from the entourage. Father Tony managed a humble smile and thank you, then mouthed to Mandy, 'How's Donna? Any progress?'

'Donna's doing fine, staying up on the horse,' Mandy said, sticking his thumb in the air to emphasize the point.

The popular priest smiled and nodded back, while being swept along to meet Pedro's grieving mother. Valeria García-Márquez was holding a framed photograph of a polo player while leaning on the beautiful grand piano, a glass of whisky in her hand.

'Memo is so amazing,' she was saying. 'My godson – twice world champion. I adore him. Such a shame he can't be here tonight, silly boy.'

She took a slug of her drink. 'Now, why couldn't Pedro have taken an interest in polo? It's not like he didn't have the opportunity.' She shook her head sadly. 'Or Alfie.'

Yet she was gazing all goo-eyed at the photo as if at a newborn child. *Woman's Weekly* were not going to vote her 'Mother of the Year', that was for sure.

Just then Father Tony stepped forward to shake her hand, uttering his condolences. Valeria García-Márquez rested the photo frame on the piano, shook his hand and deftly manoeuvred the priest in the direction of where her husband was standing.

Mandy stepped over and peered at the handsome man in the photo. Perfectly groomed, dark hair, cheesy white-toothed smile and tight-fitting trousers. It only took a second for Mandy to clock on. Memo the polo player was the same guy Pedro was giving head to in the blackmail photograph. That's why he wasn't able to come to the party. Eduardo García-Márquez must have banned him, probably had him shot, just like she had banned Lucy Lack. No wonder he looked so distraught and shattered.

Mandy pushed open the little door and walked into a kitchen the same size as the ground floor of his house. In the centre was a wonderful old white table that would seat twenty-five.

Josefina stood up from this table with her arms folded tightly around her chest, as though she had to hold in her shaking body in case it fell apart. He walked towards her with his palms open and outstretched, the way Terry trained him to do whenever they had to deal with a jumper or anyone psychotic, dangerous or wacked out on drugs.

'I need to ask you some questions, Josefina.'

She shuddered and gave a nod.

Mandy sighed and sat down at the table opposite her.

'You do understand that Pedro was murdered, Josefina?'

She looked down at her hands and opened her mouth to speak, but nothing came out. 'You saw the body, didn't you, Josefina? Remember you told me when we met outside Pedro's apartment and I took the flowers, crucifix and statue inside? The police officers said you were the person who discovered the body.'

Her eyes clamped shut. 'I don't want to think about it.'

'Well, you have to think about it, don't you? It looks to me like it's almost all you *can* think about right now.'

Was he pushing too far? He didn't think so.

'Why have to think?' she asked, giving him a defensive stare.

She wasn't a likely murderess. Anyone with nerves like hers would've given themselves a heart attack, and she clearly adored the family. No. It was something else. Someone else . . .

He dipped his hand into a barrel of odd thoughts and pulled one out.

'You know more about this family than anyone, don't you?' he said softly.

Josefina slapped her hand over her mouth, ran to the nearest white sink and retched.

It was a curious reaction to his question.

Mandy stood up, handed her a tea towel. She began to dab her eyes with it.

'I understand that after the funeral this must be very distressing for you,' Mandy said in the same intimate tone. 'Come and sit down.'

She crumpled onto the hard chair and placed both hands flat on the table.

'Pedro was a very good boy really, considering—' She stopped in mid-sentence.

'I'm sure that's right – please go on,' Mandy said encouragingly.

A loud voice behind him said, '*Considering* some of his terrible friends.'

The voice had the same power as a centre-court serve. It shot past Mandy's head into the net of Josefina's ear.

The quiet and unassuming Mrs García-Márquez.

'You don't need to speak to Mr Mandy any more, Josefina,' the voice continued, confident, arrogant. 'You can leave now.'

Mrs García-Márquez rested her hand on the table and, as Josefina stood up from her chair, said, 'She is too upset to answer any more questions, Mandy. Please have the decency to wait. Can't you see she's distressed?'

Her dark brown eyes bored into him, daring him to argue. Josefina scurried out of the room. Terrified.

Mrs García-Márquez stood with her back to Mandy, took out a bottle of whisky from a cupboard and topped up her glass to halfway.

Mandy smiled. This made his own mother look like a Bisto commercial. 'And when will that be, Mrs García-Márquez?' he asked.

Mrs Eduardo García-Márquez took a large gulp from her glass and dabbed at the corners of her mouth with two heavily jewelled fingers.

'My husband and I are for leaving for Mexico tonight. Now, Mr Mandy, if I were you, I would come and interview Josefina in a few days' time,' Valeria García-Márquez said, putting the bottle back in the cupboard. 'You can also interview me if you like, and the three gardeners, the cook, my ponies, the two maids and . . . Mr and Mrs Sternwood.'

'I'm most obliged, Mrs García-Márquez.'

'And while we are on the subject, have you properly interviewed that little slut from London Lucy Lack?'

Mandy thanked the maid holding the front door for him and stepped out into the warm night air of the Santa Monica Mountains. It was good to get out of that hothouse. He walked back to the car park and punched in the code for Terry, who answered after several rings.

'Whassup, Big Mandy?'

Mandy opened the door of the Amazon, found a toothpick on the passenger seat and began picking his teeth with it.

'I need you to get some background on a Mexican polo player called Memo and Mrs García-Márquez.'

'OK, I've made a note of that, sir. Just so you know, the DEA confirmed the García-Márquez family have no connection to drug gangs, cartels or crime whatsoever. Clean as Fabienne's underwear.'

Terry'd been smoking weed or was on the mescal.

'That's what I thought. How about Quinn?'

'Have to wait till I'm back from Florida.'

'What?' Mandy screwed up his face.

'Yeah, taking a break from the chemo here and we're giving the kids a vacation with Dawn's parents in Tampa.'

Terry did not get on with his in-laws. Must have been some deal with Dawn about him making more effort with her parents.

'Since when?'

'We decided to do it at the last minute. No big deal.'

'Are you OK with that?'

'Yeah, I'm good. And it's the right thing to do.'

Terry signed off, coughing his guts out.

Mandy couldn't imagine it was going to be much of a holiday. It wasn't until he was driving down the poorly lit Lachman Lane that he realized he'd forgotten to question Wayne Chung. But it was too late; both Chung and Quinn would have to wait till tomorrow. What he could do tonight was make contact with Lucy Lack.

32

9.45 p.m., 17 July

Mandy was dog-tired as he drove up a quiet Castellammare Drive and parked the Amazon by the phoney garage door. He leant back over the passenger seat and pushed open the chrome ashtray stuck in the side door. Using his thumb and bandaged forefinger as pincers, he removed a half-smoked cigarette, its filter smudged in lipstick.

He sat back in the driver's seat, held the butt against his lips and sniffed it repeatedly, certain it contained Lucy's perfume. It did, but not Chanel this time. This was something else – a scent from one of those bespoke perfumiers springing up in New York, he guessed. It also contained her DNA. He dropped it into a small plastic evidence bag, wrote, 'LL,' on the label and put it in his pocket.

Hot, tired and sweaty, he unlocked the front door and threw his keys on the sitting-room table. Four messages flashing on his machine – probably all cold callers offering him crap. He grunted, 'Fuck off,' walked into the kitchen, yanked open the refrigerator and poured two cans of beer into an iced pint glass and drank it in one go.

Thirst dealt with, he ripped open a tin of beans, poured them into a bowl, pulled a pork pie in half, added that and a dollop of mayonnaise, then stirred. He needed something to take away the bad taste that had been left in his mouth since attending the wake. He reached inside his jacket pocket and pulled out his cell and the handwritten envelope addressed to Dominic Young.

He selected the picture of Sarah Sternwood going down on Lucy Lack and leant the phone against the kettle behind his bowl of mayo beans. Then he poured himself another beer, took several gulps, opened the envelope and unfolded the letter. He sat down at the breakfast bar.

The letter was written in a feminine slant, signed, '*Susan, with the best and last of my love.*' Mandy spooned more mayo beans into his mouth and read the last part of the letter again.

I am not just warning you to stay away, I am FUCKING telling you. These people may look civilized but they are not. Nor are they stupid or forgiving. You are an asshole for doing what you did to them and to me! Thanks, buddy. Thanks, my old, solid, once-dependable English chum, eh, doh. Stay where you are, get help, claim social security – don't be so fucking proud. You are only going to end up in jail. I am done – d-o-n-e – done and out of your picture, and if they ever catch you, so will you be . . .

Mandy put the letter down beside the kettle, took a swig of beer and briefly thought of how he actually missed hearing Donna playing Joni Mitchell's music downstairs. He yawned, closed his eyes and started laying down a random set of case notes in his head.

Susan Green had been in a relationship and at one time in a band with Dominic Young. Lucy Lack was on the same plane as Dominic Young from London to LA, where she had – for some weird reason – pretended to be a doctor.

Why the fuck hadn't he ever asked her about that?

Lust, he supposed. Lovely old-fashioned lust.

He opened his eyes and began cross-examining the photo of Lucy astride Pedro. You also phoned from the plane and left a message on Pedro's answerphone, he thought. I was standing there in the apartment when you left it, for fuck's sake. But did you already know that he was dead and were you just covering your tracks?

Lucy, sat in front of him, was clearly not as innocent as he first thought. He needed to get her back on speaking terms. He slapped his suit pockets for his notebook. Shit, left it in the car. He closed his eyes again and thought back to Club Kafka and the fight between the couple – the red-haired woman and the guy who looked like the singer in the Cure. Javier and Kimberly confirmed it had been Dominic Young. That had been twenty-four hours before his grisly end. The letter had warned Young not to come back to Santa Monica. Yet Dominic Young had come back to LA. So what changed his mind?

Money. It was nearly always money.

Love or money. Finance or romance.

Both could be dangerously addictive.

He began to pace the checked lino of the kitchen floor. Should he offer the letter to the Giraffe or make contact with the Met back in London? Young had been a UK citizen, after all. And the Met didn't have anything against him. Whereas the Giraffe was just waiting for an excuse to have him kicked off the job – especially if he went near the Young case.

The cat flap flipped open: Ned meowing for food. Damn. He'd forgotten to buy some cat food. The cat wound round his legs, leaning in and rubbing and purring as if he hadn't been fed in days.

He took out a tin of tuna and emptied it into the cat's bowl. With the cat chewing and purring louder, Mandy padded to the bathroom and threw cold water over his face. It cooled his boiling head.

Calmer, he went into the sitting room, chucked his jacket over a chair, fell back on the sofa and clicked on CNN. After watching for a few moments, he pressed the mute button and flicked on his phone messages.

The first was Tassos, asking about the unpaid bills again and why he never visited his garage any more. Tassos was a chilled-out Greek who ran a garage on Colorado and 17th. Mandy made a mental note to pay him a call. The second was Terry, about Caitlin and Alice coming over when they were back from Florida, and the third was a long, whispered message from Fabienne.

'So guess what?' she began. 'You are coming over for dinner very soon. Broadski and Dent have made a phoney appointment with a realtor tomorrow at four p.m. to view a house sale by the Howland Canal in Venice. Something fishy going on, I can smell it. I thought you'd want to be there . . .'

Mandy clapped his hands together and laughed. Fabienne was highly adept at watching his back. Going round for dinner was a modest reward for that piece of information. Broadski and Dent had figured out a semi-legit way of how to search the Sternwoods' house. The reward for finding Pedro's killer uppermost in their thoughts?

He picked up his cell from the table and tapped a text message to Fabienne: 'Thank you for Venice. Dinner any night you choose. Mx'

Four steps forward, three steps back.

He grabbed a dusty bottle of tequila from the bookshelf, pulled out whatever it was digging into his arse from beneath him. The yellow flipper from the other night. He lobbed it towards the front door, took a long pull on the tequila and felt an almost thermal glow as the spirit passed down his gullet into his belly; it had been a long while since he had swallowed that sort of intensity.

The cat leapt onto the sofa, licking its paws. Its attitude reminded Mandy of Lucy Lack watching Johnny Sternwood's collapse.

Without thinking, he picked up his cell again and dialled a number for the twenty-four-hour flower place on Wilshire and arranged for a large bunch of yellow and white roses to be sent to Lucy at Shutters with a note saying, *'Hope the funeral wasn't too difficult. Belated apologies for my insensitive remarks at Shutters. Have got some information. Please call. M.'* He took another slug of tequila. It was his best shot at reversing the spider-and-the-fly routine. It had been fucked up the way he hadn't stopped thinking about Lucy. Had it fucked up the case too? Made him blind to what had really happened? He drank more slugs of the liquor, tried not to think too much about anything and fell asleep.

Later – he didn't know how long – his phone rang. He picked it up, groggy from beans, mayo, pie and tequila.

'Is that Mandy?'

A Californian-sounding female.

Donna calling from Malibu?

'Yes,' he said, picking the tequila bottle up from the floor and putting it back on the glass-topped table.

'This is Susan Green. Dominic Young's ex?'

'Christ!' he said, nearly dropping the phone. She certainly knew how to get a guy's attention. 'How did you get this number?'

'Javier gave it to me. Please don't ask any more questions. I don't have time. We need to meet tomorrow morning . . . It's an emergency – no kidding about.'

'How about the Getty?' Clients liked meeting there, as it was local, public and safe.

'No way!' She paused for a moment. 'I'll meet you at the chapel in LAX departures at nine a.m.'

'OK, I'll be there.'

'Don't tell anyone you are meeting me. This isn't a joke.'

'I understand the situation, Susan.'

He put down the phone. Time to find his gun and holster.

33

9 a.m., 18 July

Mandy switched his cell to 'silent' and pushed open the LAX chapel door. Nine days since he had driven to LAX to meet Lucy and Father Tony.

Ten pews either side of an aisle leading to a bland, ecumenical altar – Amish-plain, a white cloth over sandstone and a thin wooden cross on the wall behind. The place was dimly lit – only three other people: a pilot genuflecting on his way out; a bald man dressed in a cream suit; and a woman with a bright orange beehive sitting in the front right-hand-side pew.

Mandy knelt down in the nearest pew and double-checked the place. Everything normal but for an upended black carry-on case next to the woman he hoped was Susan Green. She looked vaguely familiar from the Kafka. Maybe it was the crucifixion scenes in the stained-glass windows, but some instinct told him she had more enemies than friends.

He stood up, hands sweating in anticipation, and walked towards the brightly coloured hair. Underneath it was a woman in her thirties with swimming-pool eyes and a forearm covered in scratches. The lady he'd seen in Club Kafka, but decidedly less glamorous and a lot more scared.

'Is this your letter?' Mandy whispered, holding an envelope with a baked-bean stain.

'Yeah, I wrote it,' she said, touching the address with a pale freckled hand.

'I'm Mandy. How can I help?'

'My flight is boarding in less than an hour.'

'I'm listening.'

She didn't look at him but kept her eyes straight ahead.

He sat down next to her and she started. 'Ten years ago Dominic and I had a band in London. Eventually, it ran out of gas. He couldn't accept nobody wanted us any more, so we moved over here. I come from here anyway, and we still had a following. It was good for a while. We had a good few years.' She

165

drew breath and adjusted her grip on her handbag.

'Uh-huh,' Mandy said. So far it matched what Javier Jones had told him.

'When that dried up, I got a job and he became addicted to crack and heroin. His luck ran out six months ago when I finally kicked him out of my apartment.' She paused, opened her bag and pulled out a packet of tissues.

Mandy caught a glimpse of an airline ticket and passport. An image of Donna running wild on Santa Monica Beach, then another of Dominic Young's eyeless face flashed across his mind. Maybe Green was fleeing LA for a good reason, or maybe identifying Young's mutilated body had flipped her lid. It had certainly blown Donna's right off.

'It must have been a terrible shock.'

'That's British understatement, isn't it?' she said, wiping a tear from each eye.

Mandy detected the faintest draught of air on the back of his neck – the entrance door pushed open behind them: two tall guys, holding cowboy hats, wearing suede jackets, boots, in their late fifties, both clasping prayer books.

He whispered, 'How did Dominic support his habit?'

'That's what I was talking about in that letter. He'd been working as a courier for some bad people.'

Mandy closed his eyes. 'Is this why you wanted to meet?'

Susan pushed a piece of chewing gum into her mouth. 'I managed to persuade him to get out of the country, but not before Dominic *borrowed* some of the merchandise. A hundred grand's worth. Get the picture?'

'How do you know? Did he tell you?'

'I discovered it and tried to make him take it back. I even drove him to Topanga to return it. But he wouldn't go through with it. And that's when I met the boss's assistant.'

'OK.'

Susan blew on a tissue and turned her head away. 'We began a relationship, I suppose. It was purely physical, or at least for me. It was a bargain, a deal I had to make to ensure Dominic could get out of the country . . .'

'Tricky.' Mandy grinned nervously.

'Sometimes you don't have a choice: me going with her kept him alive.'

She wiped a finger through a band of sweat from above her lip. A real note of fear was in her voice now. *Me going with her?*

'So having got out of the country, the idiot decided he was going to come back. Said he'd fallen in love with me again and could he could move back in. I wrote him that letter. Told him no. Not to come back. It was too risky for him and . . .'

'But he did come back, didn't he?' said Mandy, grappling over what words in the letter had pushed Dominic Young over the edge on that plane journey.

Susan clutched at her chest. 'People like him always come back. But once I'm outta here, I'll never come back, because if I did, my tongue would be cut off too.'

Mandy grabbed hold of her wrist. 'Tell me who murdered him. I can arrange for twenty-four-hour protection.'

Susan gave him a childlike stare that said, 'Are you kidding?' and knelt down on the prayer stool with a long, faltering sigh. 'What a mess.'

Mandy knelt down next to her. 'Let's walk and talk. You could be next.'

'Thanks,' Susan hissed. 'Like I didn't know that already?'

He slid his hand along the top of the pew until it was on top of hers. 'Give me the information and I'll walk you to the gate.'

She sat back in her seat for a few seconds, wiped a tear from her eye and said, 'OK.'

Mandy sat back in the pew and took out his notebook. Susan sat down next to him again.

'Did you know Pedro García-Márquez as well?' he asked.

She shook her head. 'No, but Dominic knew his brother . . . Two of a kind, except for the bank accounts, you know.'

Dominic, Susan and Alfonso, three degrees of separation.

Susan raised her hand to speak.

Mandy felt someone tap him on the shoulder. He turned round. It was the larger of the two guys he had seen enter the chapel earlier.

'Sir,' the man said, 'would you mind holding this so I can light a candle?'

'Sure,' Mandy said, taking hold of the book.

But there were no candles. What the fuck?

'*Don't!*' screamed Susan into what seemed like an echo chamber.

His tongue felt like molten lava, and his front teeth hurt. The bed was hard. No, not a bed. A bench? He put his fingers in his mouth to check his teeth had not been bent back. They were OK, but the inside of his upper lip was bleeding. His nostrils stung, his lips felt as if he'd been chewing chilli, and his stomach wanted to expel the fried eggs he'd eaten for breakfast.

'You've been here a while; everyone thought you were asleep.'

The voice came from above.

Mandy opened his eyes. A priest was standing above him. He ran his fingers over the back of his aching head. No blood. No bump. Good. It felt like he'd been kicked in the kisser and swallowed a ton of dental anaesthetic.

'Where's everyone gone? Where's Susan?' He sat up.

'Susan?' the priest said. 'You were asking for someone called Lucy a moment ago. How many girls you got, my friend?'

Mandy struggled to his feet. He patted his jacket, relieved at the bulge of his cell and wallet. A man punching his face, Susan screaming, an envelope and suitcase, a cream-coloured ten-gallon hat, a genuflecting airline pilot and Jesus on the cross churned in his head back and forth.

Oversized Texans in a chapel. Why hadn't he sensed danger earlier? That was stupid. Really stupid. Rookie-stupid. The guy saying he was lighting a candle when there were none, punching like a boxer.

And now where the hell was Susan, the woman he'd promised he'd protect?

He managed a wan smile at the priest.

'Did you see a girl with big orange hair or two older, cowboy-looking guys?'

'No, you were already asleep when I came in – that was about an hour ago.'

Mandy looked at his watch and scowled. It was already ten past twelve.

'Thanks for your help.'

No sign of the black suitcase, he made a quick search among the pews for anything she might have left. Her chewing-gum wrapper. He put it inside his notebook, nodded at the duty priest and headed out into the bustle of the airport. Weaving through the sea of queuing passengers, he dialled Terry. The phone went straight to answer.

'Big Daddy,' he said, 'I need your contact at LAX security. Urgent.'

He slowed down. He'd have to wait for that name; no one would get inside security without it.

His stomach heaved; a knock-out blow and fried-egg sandwich was not a great combination. The men's room – he made it into a cubicle and threw up, washed his face and emerged back onto the departures concourse to the beep of a text on his cell.

'Officer Gomez. Returning to LA today; in-laws and me are a bad mix.'

The second-floor wasp's nest of LAX security was buzzing. Three amber alerts and a lost child. He found Gomez, a tall Hispanic guy with too many teeth, looking over footage of the lost child, a blonde girl clutching a toy donkey.

Gomez looked up. 'You a friend of Terry's?'

Mandy nodded. 'Ex-partners, SMPD.'

'Tell us what you need, man.'

'I think I've got a kidnapping on my hands. Do you have any record of a Susan Green boarding a plane in the last two hours?'

Gomez lifted his arms up in the air. There was a flurry of typing.

A young officer yelled out, 'Susan *Green?*'

'Yes!' said Mandy. 'Checked in online for the eleven fifteen a.m. United to London, hand luggage only but never boarded the plane. Economy ticket, non-transferable.'

'Maybe she booked another ticket?'

More typing, more clicking of a mouse.

'Not on our system.'

Gomez stepped in: 'Maybe she just changed her mind.'

'No,' Mandy said, remembering Susan's prophecy about her tongue. 'Two guys changed it for her.'

'Anything else we can do for you?'

Mandy rubbed his aching jaw and pondered for a few seconds. 'Where would unattended luggage be taken, if it was found in the chapel?'

Gomez picked up a phone. 'Want me to call them?'

'Please.'

Gomez punched in the number and held his hand over the speaker. 'This is a one-off favour to Terry. Don't come back expecting the same treatment.'

'Understood and appreciated,' Mandy said.

'Hello. This is Gomez. You been given any merchandise from the chapel today?'

34

4 p.m., 18 July

Mandy pressed the sockets of his binoculars to his eyes and focused on the lower-floor windows of the Sternwoods' Venice home. Susan Green's black carry-on case stood on the pavement beside him like an obedient dog. Once he'd retrieved the case from Gomez's lost-luggage contact, he'd locked himself in a cubicle of the nearest men's room and searched through the unlocked bag for any helpful clues. Other than clothes, make-up and stuff to do with her stay in London – that was genuine, at least – there was zilch. Nothing except for two photographs of a middle-aged woman with a Mary Quant hairstyle, one bearing a dedication: '*To dearest Susan, so happy to spend time with you. Affectionately, Janet.*' The other just the same, save for '*most affectionately*' and a double x.

A sixth sense told him to keep hold of the photos but to ditch the suitcase as soon as possible. Who could be better to hand the suitcase over to than Broadski and Dent?

The glare of the sun was making it difficult to see anything. He considered leaving the case on the doorstep or even on the roof of Broadski's Lexus. No, some nosy neighbour would report him and his registration number for dumping it. It was that kind of neighbourhood.

He briefly considered doubling back to the SMPD's lost-and-found counter, but didn't fancy the paperwork. He pondered a false name and address, but people knew him at the station. It would only make things worse with the Giraffe.

Wait for the clowns to emerge from the house and hand them the case. It could be their problem then.

A small biplane flew overhead, trailing a long white banner advertising dancing on the pier. He tracked it for a while. Pier dancing sounded so innocent; it almost made him want to do it. When he refocused the binoculars, four people were standing in the doorway.

He couldn't see Sternwood's face – just his feet – but Sarah Sternwood had her arms folded across a white T-shirt looking up at Broadski and Dent on the doorstep.

The two detectives stepped onto the porch, turned and said something. Sarah Sternwood nodded and closed the door. From the sickening bonhomie, it looked like a visit from a couple of interior designers. What was going on? Or had Broadski and Dent drastically improved their interviewing technique?

The detectives pointed to a few houses down the road as they ambled off, probably wondering how much they'd have to make in greased palms to afford one. Mandy grinned. They hadn't noticed the case on their car yet.

He got out and stepped over to the car and began patting the case as if it was a very well-behaved, and deserving, dog.

Broadski was laughing about something, but he stopped short when he saw Mandy and the case resting on the roof of his Lexus. Both looked over their shoulders, presumably to check that the Sternwoods couldn't see anything, then strode over. Broadski was first out of the trap.

'Mandy, you fuckhead, what you doing here?' Broadski's usual greeting.

Dent screwed up his rat-face and pointed at the case. 'An offer we can't refuse?'

Mandy smiled, grateful that he had remembered to take off the latex gloves he had worn to search the case.

'Always a great honour to be in the presence of eminent detectives.'

'Fuck off. What you doing here?'

'I am only going to say this once, so don't interrupt. The Giraffe told me I was to have nothing to do with the Dominic Young job. This suitcase belongs to Susan Green, his ex-girlfriend. I met her in a chapel this morning but she disappeared and left it there while we were praying together. It could be vital evidence, so I'm giving it to you. Straight up, no chaser.'

'How do you know it belongs to her? Been through it with your toothcomb?'

'I wouldn't go through a lady's bag, underwear and stuff, tamper with the evidence, if that's what you mean. I'm a gentleman just like you guys.'

'Like hell. You told anyone else about this?'

'I phoned my contact at KCRW. Told them she'd gone missing from the airport, vanished into thin air. Maybe I fell asleep and she had a diabetic hypo or was kidnapped by some weird obsessive fan. She was a singer once in a band who made it big round here in the 1990s, so they were more than interested to help find her.'

Broadski grunted. 'You told KCRW? Why didn't you go on TV and tell everyone?'

'I just did what any normal citizen might do under the circumstances,' Mandy said.

The sarcasm went unnoticed by Dent. Judging by the suspicious scowl on Broadski's face, though, he was catching on that they'd been stitched up. Whatever happened now, Susan Green's disappearance was not going to go unnoticed. Unless there were CCTV cameras in the airport chapel or toilet, there was nothing to indicate Mandy's involvement; his hands were clean. Now the media had been alerted, Broadski and Dent would be obliged to spend some of their time finding out about the missing suitcase, leaving him free to pursue Lucy Lack and discover just how well she knew Susan Green, or the charming Texan who'd knocked him unconscious in the chapel. That was the plan.

Dent wrapped a handkerchief round the suitcase handle and fetched it down to the ground.

Broadski took off his shades and read the luggage tag. '"Susan Green, Santa Monica, USA." What use is that to man or beast?'

The afternoon sun was bearing down. Mandy walked over to the Amazon, opened the car door, got in and called out, 'She told me she was travelling to London. I'm only trying to play according to the rules – make sure you tell the Giraffe that.'

Broadski replaced his sunglasses, stood up and peered hard at Mandy. 'How d'you know we were here?'

Although he could probably tap-dance and justify making the disclosure about their whereabouts, he didn't want to risk mentioning Fabienne as his source. He switched on the ignition, revved the engine and yelled back, 'Just a lucky guess. Did you get anywhere with Johnny and Sarah Sternwood? Find what you were looking for? Anything you want to share with me?'

Broadski and Dent both smiled and turned away.

Mandy drove off in silence. What should have felt like a tactical victory now felt like a fuck-up. Why hadn't he just left the case at the airport and not tried to be so smart? The cat was now among the pigeons, but the pigeons might be about to peck the cat's eyes out. He wanted a cigarette so badly, he considered lighting up the butt smoked by Lucy Lack in the evidence bag in his pocket but settled instead for a sugar fix. He yanked out a half-melted Mars bar from the glove compartment, ate it and then pulled out another and ate that too, flinging both wrappers onto the floor. He switched on KCRW. The DJ was talking over the back end of some miserable-sounding song.

'You're listening to Harry Shearer in Santa Monica, home of the homeless. It's twenty-six minutes past four and you've been listening to the Veil. Thanks for the calls regarding their elusive singer. Wherever you are, Dee or Susan, your fans love you, so come back – all is forgiven. Traffic on the 10 and 405 heading south is still bad, and this is a track from the Eels.'

Mandy killed the radio and cheered. Harry had come through and delivered the goods. The cat felt back in charge of the pigeons.

35

5.43 p.m., 18 July

By the time he hit Shutters, the clock in the lobby with the entwined gold anchors said it was five forty-five. Three receptionists were taking an age to register details of eight new arrivals; the lobby was awash with baggage trolleys and bellboys, and a faint smell of chlorine and suntan oil.

He couldn't see Pierre, so could not fast-track to answers on the whereabouts of Miss Lack. He could hear him on a telephone in the back office. Maybe he should just head straight up to Lucy's suite? Trouble was, Shutters had high-summer security goons who didn't let *anyone* in the elevators without a valid key card. So Mandy would have to wait for Pierre to stop jabbering. He took his cell from his pocket; nothing except a message from Donna. 'Rehab sucks. Please come rescue me. Dxxx'

And if Lucy wasn't here, where would she be? A technicolour image of her arms wrapped around Wing's waist roaring up PCH on a Harley-Davidson filled his mind. He pressed 'pause'. Maybe Wing had known Lucy a lot better than he suggested when they met at the tar pits.

Maybe he and the Sternwoods were involved together – but no, Wing was too rough a character for them. And they were pretty much everything Wing would hate. Then again, anything was possible, if it had money connected to it; everything had its price – coprophilia, snuff movies, dogs, sheep, desecrating graves in remote cemeteries at night for a satanic mass. Just ordinary people finding ways to pay the mortgage, the rent, the credit-card repayment, the down payment for a new Mazda or set of golf clubs. Or to finance a habit.

Mandy coughed and cleared his throat. Three guests registered and moved away from the counter as if he were contagious. Mandy advanced to the front of the queue.

'Can I help?' asked the bald desk receptionist.

Mandy laid the palms of his hands flat down on the cold marble counter.

174

'Yes. I spoke to one of your colleagues earlier about a guest – Miss Lucy Lack. They said they thought she may have checked out – would you mind looking for me?'

The guy ran a flourish of fingers over a keyboard while data unfolded on his computer screen. 'Yep, checked out this morning.'

'She did? Do you know what time?' Mandy flashed his private investigator ID badge.

'Twelve eighteen.'

'Did she say where she was going?'

'I wasn't there at the time, sir.'

'Could you find out if she left a note for me?'

For good measure, Mandy flashed the badge again.

The receptionist pushed open the door of the back reception area, where Pierre's voice was still speaking, and disappeared inside. He returned with a large spray of yellow and white roses covered in cellophane and laid them on the counter. An envelope with his name scrawled on it was taped to the bouquet.

'Thanks for your help,' Mandy said, clamping the flowers and the envelope in the same hand. Jeez, Jilted John. It was a relief to get out into the sunlight and look for a garbage bin.

The regular car valet, Reynaldo, drove the Amazon up from the garage.

'Hey, Reynaldo,' Mandy said. 'What time did you start work today?'

'Eight a.m.'

Mandy threw the flowers onto the passenger seat.

'Did you get a cab for a guest called Lucy Lack, tall, late twenties, long dark hair, been here about ten days, British, cute?'

Reynaldo looked blank. 'I don't think so. Very busy today. I can check.'

Cars were being driven up from the underground garage and lining up behind the Amazon.

Mandy got in, closed the door and stuck his head out of the open window when another thought occurred to him.

'Don't bother – just one more thing. Have you seen Mr Pollock round here lately? You know who I mean, don't you – the private detective?'

He gesticulated with his hands to indicate well dressed, groomed and swanky.

Reynaldo thought about it and shook his head. 'A few days ago maybe, but not today.'

Horns were sounding behind him. Mandy put the car in gear and handed the flowers through the window. 'For your girlfriend or your wife.'

Reynaldo put the cellophane up to his face, touched the roses and sniffed. 'Mr Mandy, they are beautiful.'

'Better watch out because they need water . . .'

175

'No worries – my wife loves pressing dead flowers and giving them as presents.'

'I didn't think they were actually dead.'

The Mexican nodded.

Mandy looked at himself in the rear-view. Sixty dollars' worth of dead flowers. Where was the ungrateful recipient? He needed to read the card.

'Have a good day, Reynaldo,' he called, accelerating out of Shutters with an unintentional squeal of tyres that felt pretty satisfying after the tragic bouquet. He drove round the corner, parked and ripped open the envelope.

The card was a print of another Edward Hopper painting, which he recognized as *Movie*, a painting of an unhappy blonde-haired usherette deep in thought leaning against a wall in a corridor of a cinema while the movie played. The handwriting was the same as the dedication on the photograph he had seen in the photo frame in Pedro's apartment: *Lucy Lack loves Pedro García-Márquez in London – Santa Monica – Sayulita – wherever!*

Dear Mandy,

Thanks for being supportive behind me in the church. The funeral was just about bearable, but what happened afterwards made me want to give up. I am not going to dignify the Sternwoods' or Pedro's mother's behaviour by making any comment. So I'm checking out, staying with a friend and maybe going to Mexico, maybe home to London – maybe, maybe, maybe, who knows. I'll let you know what I decide and . . . thank you for the flowers. Hope they'll find a good home . . . OK.

Mandy found a bottle of water under the passenger seat and took a swig. If he was Dr Freud, he'd have said the card was chosen deliberately – get me out of this scenario, please. For the first time, Lucy Lack was taking the lead by leaving Shutters. He couldn't stop her, and nor, he presumed, had Broadski and Dent even tried – though if he was in their shoes as cops, he would have issued a strong caution not to leave town without their say-so. Bit late for that now – she could be back in London in fourteen hours or Mexico in less than four: both out of the jurisdiction of the Santa Monica DA. Mandy chucked the bottle of water onto the mottled passenger seat and turned the ignition key.

He leant forward, pressed John Barry's 'You Only Live Twice' on the stereo and sat gently revving the accelerator. To his knowledge, she could be with one of three people: Wing, Father Tony or, as a long-shot bet, the private detective she claimed to have hired. He didn't believe she was going to go back to

London – what for? She might not have a job, and Lucy Lack would be making far more fuss if she was going home, wouldn't she? He checked his watch and swung the car round in an illegal turn back towards Venice.

Along Ocean Avenue, the palm trees acting like members of a jury, Mandy tried to consider Lucy Lack as dispassionately as possible. He repressed the thought that she should have called him last night, once she received the flowers, jumped into a cab and spent the night with him spilling beans, drinking tequila and sleeping with him. Whether or not Lucy was a psychopathic actress or an innocent abroad whose friend had been murdered and whose character, trust and reputation had been abused, she had been boxed into a corner of one sort or another and needed a shoulder to cry on.

So whose shoulder had she chosen? The leather-jacketed one belonging to Wing? That's how it might have looked to someone else, but that's not what he thought.

There were more than a dozen people standing in line outside the Ocean Park Homeless Shelter when he got there a quarter of an hour later. Some black guys, some white guys, some women, most aged between forty and sixty, but also two young couples, clearly from out of town.

Mandy called out, 'FBI,' and walked straight past the line, ignoring the jibes and comments – 'Hey, man, get to the back of the line!'; 'You special or different or something, soldier?' – and stood on the doorstep behind a long-haired balding guy with a moustache and a dirty red backpack bearing the sign *Broken pack on a broken back* and holding a small dog in his arms.

A familiar voice called out over the noise of the people eating inside, 'You can't have a dog in here, sir. No pets permitted where people are eating. Just tie him up to the post by the water bowls and come right on back to the front of the line.'

Bradley Adams again. The professor of Chinese who'd briefly taught Pedro, and number seven on the list.

The guy dropped his head and sighed.

'It's a she, and her name is Ecco,' he said as he stepped off the doorstep and shuffled towards a shaded wall where two dogs were already crouched down on the ground. Although Mandy didn't want to admit it, the guy's hair and pained walk reminded him of Terry.

Adams's voice boomed out, 'Have you come to help or ask more questions about Pedro?'

Adams was standing behind the counter wearing a white apron over a smart blue shirt and ladling stew from a large saucepan. The canteen was already full;

the queue must have been for the second sitting.

Two long tables were packed with homeless 'clients' talking and eating from plastic airline trays. The atmosphere was boisterous but good-humoured – like families could be on Christmas Day for the half an hour of lunch or present-giving, just before something kicked off.

Mandy walked over to Adams. Something about the man's tone stuck in his craw. But fuck it, deep down his instincts were telling him that although the guy might be a supercilious twat, he was not a murderer. Still, it was worth a passing shot.

'I didn't see you at Pedro's funeral yesterday,' Mandy said, stepping further into the room and scanning the people serving behind the counter.

'I am not in the habit of attending funerals of people I didn't care for.'

'Oh yes, I'd forgotten – you're not a hypocrite, are you?'

'I try not to be, Mr Mandy. Now, if you'll excuse me, I must go and find someone to murder. Only joking – a little British irony, ha, ha?'

Mandy didn't reply. He did a 360-degree sweep of the room. One glance told him Lucy was not there. But Father Tony was – carrying an armful of food trays from the kitchen. Mandy caught his eye and gestured with his bandaged fingers to have a word in an empty corner of the room. Father Tony set down the airline meals and inclined his head towards the end of the counter, where there was an open hatch. Mandy walked over.

'I would shake hands, but my gloves are covered in muck,' said Father Tony.

Mandy nodded. 'A slightly different party to last night.'

'Yes, you could say that. This is a bit more cheerful, though.' Father Tony nodded towards his greasy latex gloves. 'Would you mind lending a hand and then we can talk?'

'Sure.'

'If you pick up the empties, then the rest can get a chance to eat . . .'

Mandy began collecting empty trays and stacking them. He soon began enjoying the work. Most people said thank you or nodded.

'Two minutes,' Father Tony called out to the man with the red backpack at the head of the queue, and pointed Mandy to two empty chairs by the back wall underneath two dental-hygiene posters, one in Spanish and one in English.

The priest sat down, put his hands behind his neck and stretched backwards over the chair. 'This is our fifth sitting today. You're a natural. Why not join us a volunteer for the odd day a week?'

Mandy sat down and rested his legs in front of him. 'I admire your dedication, and when we find Pedro García-Márquez's killer, I might come and help. Not sure about the apron, though.'

Father Tony pulled a face and smiled. Mandy was genuinely pleased to see him – a Brit without a PhD in sarcasm and how terrible Americans were was hard to find in Santa Monica.

'And what about Donna? She told me you've been a tremendous support to her in the past?'

Mandy shook his head, his face almost blushing at the compliment. 'I'm sure she didn't use those words. More like what a terrible landlord I'd been!'

'You can't fool an old hand like me, Mandy. She's a big fan of yours.'

Mandy needed to steer the conversation away from Donna. He was grateful for the priest's help, but needed to ask some questions about the case.

He leant towards Father Tony's ear. 'Are you aware that Lucy Lack has checked out of Shutters, gone AWOL?'

'No. But it doesn't surprise me.'

'Why?'

'She's been under a lot of pressure. I spoke to her yesterday morning before the funeral. She sounded on the edge, so I suggested going back to London. Failing that, coming to work here.'

'You remember the name Susan Green?'

Father Tony closed his eyes briefly, opened them and said, 'The person who wrote the letter addressed to Dominic Young – or should I say the *late* Dominic Young?'

Again, Mandy wondered at Father Tony's perfect memory. 'The man Donna found mutilated on the beach four days ago.'

'Poor kid. Most people would have become hysterical.'

'Not you, though. You took it all in your stride.'

'I'm on pretty familiar terms with death. It doesn't frighten me,' Father Tony replied.

Mandy thought about that for a moment. It made sense. He needed to bluff a little, though, to check they were both on the same page of Lucy's story.

'Can you tell me why Lucy Lack is on the edge? I mean, apart from Pedro's death?'

Father Tony looked at the new line of clients traipsing into the room. 'I would rather talk about this another time.'

'I don't have time, and it may help clear her name – if she is innocent . . .'

Father Tony exhaled and steadied his hand in mid-air as if he was a martial-arts instructor. 'Look, three days before she arrived with me in LA, Lucy's Russian tennis coach – who she was very close to – committed suicide. And strictly between you and me, she's been involved in some particularly nasty blackmail here, which I am not at liberty to talk about.'

'Shall we put the cards on the table and confirm we are talking about the same thing?' Mandy took his phone from his pocket and clicked onto the photo of Lucy in the bondage kit astride Pedro. Then he showed the image with the polo player and Mrs Sternwood.

Father Tony winced at the picture, then turned his eyes away. 'How did you know?'

Mandy chose to tell the virtual truth. It was a risk worth taking. There was something decent about the priest that he trusted. 'I found out that a less-than-charming friend of Pedro's was trying to extort money from them both – threatening to send these photos to his family in Mexico and her colleagues in London. Strictly between us, it was the same man who tried to give the eulogy at the funeral.'

It was Mandy's guesswork, but he was more than seventy per cent certain he was right.

Father Tony blinked, stared up at the ceiling, open-mouthed. 'So that hysteria in church was all about his conscience?'

Father Tony was quick on the uptake and cool under fire as well.

'Bang on the money. Poor man's Helmut Newton regrets trying to sell naughty pictures of a billionaire's son and a pretty futures City trader.'

'So are you saying Sternwood murdered Pedro García-Márquez?' asked Father Tony.

Mandy shook his head, put a finger to his lips and moved closer to the priest. It was time for some quid pro quo.

'Listen, I want to help, if I can, but what else do you know?' Mandy said.

'I can't tell you any more. Not now, and anyway, not until you—'

'When can you tell me?' Mandy interrupted, letting out an impatient sigh.

'I'd like you to do something for me,' Father Tony said.

'And what might that be?'

'Find my client Stevie – he's disappeared off the face of the earth.'

Mandy pulled an irritated expression. This was a murder enquiry, for goodness' sake, not a case to find the alive and homeless. He drew breath and smiled wearily. 'You mean the weird-looking homeless guy you were with when I came here before?'

'Yes. I promised to find him a free dentist to have his teeth sorted out. Homeless people like him don't normally pass up on that sort of opportunity. He's been coming here for eight weeks.'

'Maybe he's simply gone somewhere else.'

'The only thing Stevie wanted was to make peace with his family and find a good dentist.'

'I don't want to be unsympathetic, but I think a lot of these people can take care of themselves far better than you think. If you're that worried, you need the assistance of the men in the black-and-white police cars.'

Father Tony stood up and looked across at Adams. 'They appear to be completely disinterested . . . Too busy chasing down political stuff and drugs . . . The cops don't seem to care. Do you?'

Mandy stared up at a pair of varnished oars tied to the rafters above. A part of him wanted to tell the priest to paddle his own homeless canoe, but because Father Tony had more than stepped up to the plate for Donna, he was prepared to help. Quid pro quo. Mandy liked the fact that Father Tony was tough and the type to put his money where his mouth was.

'OK. I'll make some enquiries and get back to you. And should Lucy make any contact at all . . .'

'I'll ask her to call you.'

Mandy smiled. 'Maybe you'd also be interested in knowing about a club I've set up?'

Father Tony nodded. 'What's it called?'

'The Santa Monica Suicide Club.'

'Not sure about the suicide bit. What's the requirement for membership?'

'A strong interest in survival.'

'Isn't that a contradiction in terms?'

'The club is for people who have been marooned in a metaphorical Siberia. People who know what it is like to feel there is no point pressing the accelerator but decide to keep driving. People who *sometimes* can't stop thinking about taking their own life. It doesn't mean they always have to follow through.'

'I'm intrigued. Maybe I can call you about it on . . . the dragon's number?'

Mandy walked away, aware he'd been talking to a wise man with a sense of humour and excellent memory.

36

5.55 p.m., 18 July

Benny Tan did not want to admit it, but he was beginning to feel rejected. He'd phoned the Los Angeles Country Club people and been told to hold for two minutes, and then was told by another assistant that no decision had been made but to 'please be patient'. Although the woman didn't say it, she certainly inferred that his donation was absolutely *not* a guarantee of gaining membership.

He ran the tips of his fingers over the framed photograph on his desk of the three kids he was sponsoring in Somalia and nearly choked up.

He stood up, careful not to move the three neat piles of bound and certified accounts, valuations and stocktakes, unlocked the 'do not disturb' on his phone and buzzed Kurt, the over-keen new intern.

'My office, please.'

Benny peered at the number on the bottom line of the spreadsheet on his computer screen. The final figure being discussed for the purchase of Fish Farm by Nabokov and the Russian Corporation was $14.4 million. Considering the value of the current stock of fish and the real-estate assets of the store in Santa Monica and farm in Topanga, and how well the business had done recently, the figure was low.

It was a difficult situation and he knew he could not have anything put him on the back foot. He closed down his PC, turned it on again and typed in a seven-letter password. An image appeared, of two workers in waders holding fishing nets on poles next to a line of white polystyrene boxes.

Benny grunted affectionately at the scene. A drop-down menu appeared showing stock, live cams, overheads, breeding statuses and overseas sales books. He clicked on the stock, minimized the screen and opened the sales files. Swallowing the last drops of water from his small bottle of Evian, he tried to add up all the sales printed in a normal type and then all the sales recorded in italics.

It had been suggested by his accountants to use a multiple of ten times sales amortized over the last five years. The figure he had in his head was only $500,000 less than their formula and he could probably live with that. However, the recent demand for hand-reared sturgeon was providing him with real ammunition to persuade Nabokov to shell out more. Not to mention the incredibly successful organic protein fish food Benny had pioneered.

He was a realist, though, and for it to work out, both sides needed to feel they had a good deal.

'How badly do you want this?' Benny asked himself out loud. Whacking the palm of his hand down on his glass-topped desk, he answered, 'I want this agreed by the end of next week – money in my account by September 29.'

There was a knock on the door. Benny got up and opened it. Kurt the intern, almost running on the spot with enthusiasm.

'Mr Tan, you wanted me?'

'Sure. Go get me a copy of the *Wall Street Journal*, a pack of American Spirit and some frozen yoghurt, and ask Janet to come up right away.'

Five minutes later Janet Lee sauntered into his office, without knocking.

'You wanted to speak to *me*?' she asked in an unmistakably sarcastic tone, sitting down in a chair slightly away from the desk.

Benny took out his nail clippers and began work on his thumbs. 'What's wrong?'

Janet stretched her tight black leather skirt down to her knees, crossed her legs and leant back her head. 'Well, you seem to be grooming my successor, for a start.'

'Don't be ridiculous! The kid is just an intern and one who I wish to stay with the company, rather than train up and then see work for someone else. That OK with you?'

'It would be, if I felt you were telling me the truth. I mean, doesn't my position in this company count for anything?'

She brought her clenched fist beneath her chin, the two amber rings on her fingers glinting in the sunlight. Benny knew that she had punched the man running an anger-management course and split his lip open with those rings . . . He wasn't scared of Janet, but his hand still gripped the letter opener on his desk.

'Look, I've told you a million times what you mean to this company. Why do you think you drive that fancy new Range Rover?'

'Because I'm worth it, and you know that! Who else would you get to do all the things that I do? You'd need a small army. You should give me a Range Rover for every day of the week.'

Benny hated moments like these. It reminded him of being married, only

183

worse, because his ex-wife in London was verbally aggressive, never violent. But the secret with Janet was not to show her too much concern or fear.

'You are worth it some of the time, but not when you make stupid mistakes such as the surprise you pulled on the beach the other day. Jesus.'

Janet stood up, folded her arms across her chest and walked towards the window. 'It was a warning to others. It happened. It's done. Can we now move on? Talk about my stock options? I know what you are up to, Benny, and—'

'A warning to others?' He interrupted. 'There won't be any stock options if there are any *others*, get it?'

There was a knock on the door. He ignored it and concentrated on Janet's outstretched hands. 'I want to exercise my stock options in this company. You've always promised but never delivered. Twelve years of my loyalty deserves more. I know you are trying to sell the company from under me, Benny.'

Another knock.

Benny yelled, 'Come.'

Kurt walked in carrying a tub of yoghurt and a packet of cigarettes.

'Saved by the knock, Benny?' Janet said, slipping her handbag onto her shoulder.

'Mr Tan, I think there's something you should know,' Kurt said, putting the yellow pack of cigarettes onto the desk.

'Smoking is bad for you? Was that it, Kurt?' Janet said, peering into the young man's nervous face.

'Ignore her,' Benny said. 'What is it?'

'I've seen a guy on a Harley, with some girl on the back, driving round the parking lot taking pictures of the place. I thought at first they might be crazy tourists or fish enthusiasts, but they came back at least twice, maybe three times. And I'm sure the guy's jacket had Hell's Angel markings.'

Benny took a deep breath.

Janet unwrapped a piece of chewing gum. 'Did you definitely see them in the parking lot?' she said, pushing the gum into her mouth.

Kurt nodded. 'Very sure, yes.'

'Good, well, we can pick them up on the surveillance cameras. How do you know the person on the back was female?'

'They stopped for a few seconds and she took her helmet off . . . long dark hair.'

'Were you intelligent enough to write down the registration?'

There was a pause.

'Yes, here it is,' Kurt said, holding up a piece of paper.

Benny raised his eyebrows at Janet, as if to say, 'I told you the kid was smart.'

Janet grabbed it. 'I'll see where the bike is registered.'

Kurt blushed. 'Oh, I've already done that. My uncle works in the DMV, but don't tell anyone he did this. The bike is registered to a man called John Beethoven Wing, and he lives way up in the Santa Monica Mountains.'

'You didn't have to do that, Kurt,' Benny said.

If Fish Farm needed favours, Benny had his own cops to use. 'Do not do anything like that again, or you will be gone, understand?'

Janet gave a little smile of triumph. 'Anything on the girl?' she asked. 'A photo?'

'No.'

'Kurt,' Benny said, 'here's twenty bucks for your trouble. Can you give us a minute?'

'Sure. Could I have money for the yoghurt and cigarettes? No copies of the *Wall Street Journal* left in any store. So that's nine dollars and twenty-three cents.'

Benny smiled at the audacity and peeled off another ten-dollar bill.

'Keep the change,' he said. 'Nice work. But like I said, don't do anything involving the authorities without my say-so. I have the reputation of Fish Farm to think of.'

Kurt left with a skip in his step.

There was silence for a few moments; then Benny said, 'I'll think I'll handle this one, Janet.'

'No, you haven't got time, and that's why you need me. We'll talk about the options once I've dealt with this and one *other* little matter.'

He looked at the eager expression on her face and wondered if she had become more of a liability than an asset. Maybe Janet and John Beethoven Wing could be involved in the same fatal accident in the mountains? But it was just one of his terrible thoughts he wished he'd never had. Janet was one of the few people he was actually fond of, in a warped kind of way. Not to mention the fact that he didn't know what information she may have divulged to third parties about the inner workings of the business.

'OK,' he said. 'You're right. Once we've seen the footage, why don't we both take a trip out to the mountains and meet with Mr Wing? See why he's snooping around.'

'Or if you don't have enough time, I could sort out a problem on Ocean,' Janet said. 'And leave Mr Wing to you?'

37

7.20 p.m., 18 July

Driving home after seeing Father Tony and Bradley Adams at the shelter, Mandy's brain began to boil over from an excess of information. There were two other places where Lucy Lack could be. And he was hoping that one of them wasn't in England. Gripping the wheel with his left hand, he used his right thumb to locate Wing's number in the 'calls received' section of his cell. Where the fuck was it? Thirty-two calls since he'd met Wing at the tar pits, so it shouldn't be too difficult to find.

Phone held in front of the steering wheel, he dialled one that looked like the right area code. The call connected.

'Springfield Rehab, Malibu Canyon.' He'd misdialled but decided to speak to Donna anyway and pass on Father Tony's good vibes.

'Donna is out running. May I pass on a message?' said the receptionist.

'The message is, "Keep swimming and remember to feed the fish."'

'That's an unusual message. Can you give me your name, please?'

'Don't worry – she'll know who it's from.'

He snapped the cell shut, lobbed it onto the passenger seat. Wing could wait until he got home, whenever that would be. The stop-start traffic was the kind of three-lane holiday traffic Mandy hated. Cars with surfboards, Winnebagos, people carriers reversing out of beachside parking spaces.

His mind was too churned up. The remedy was to go snorkelling and empty his head of the craziness or he was going to explode and end up in a room next to Donna. And that wouldn't do anybody any good, not Pedro, not Mandy.

He drove past the Palisades Beach, where a small posse of surfers in orange board shorts with white surfboards under their arms were standing right where Dominic Young's body had been washed up in its green suitcase.

He was still thinking about Dominic Young and wondering what the hell had happened to Susan Green when he reached his favourite spot on the far edge of Zuma Beach and Point Dume. It was just before eight p.m.

He parked the Amazon next to a VW van and a V8 Mustang in the ten-space lot. Using the open trunk as a screen, he stripped off, changed, grabbed his mask and snorkel, and sprinted to the far side of the cove, where there were rocks and fish to look at.

All the time he kept seeing Susan Green's bright orange hair, like a flame of guilt in his mind's eye. And her swimming-pool eyes – the same blue as the sea at dusk just before it gets lighter than the sky.

He waded in through small waves, until the sea was covering his thighs, dived forward and began swimming crawl, breathing every second stroke, until he felt his usual rhythm. The coolness of the water delighted him, as it had since he was a child. Being submerged was like disconnecting his mental computer: safe, unpursued, not harassed by Jack Russells of doubt, or seagulls shitting questions to which he had no answers yet.

The sea was pretty shallow around Zuma. Mandy believed that if your feet could touch the ground, it wasn't proper, so he swam out until it got good and deep, then switched to breaststroke. He swam over a small cluster of rocks just beneath the surface. There were anemones, sea urchins and almost translucent seaweed, several uninteresting shells, a series of wormholes making an ornate pattern, a light blue plastic bag weighed down by something inside he couldn't see properly and two orange-pink starfish resting on the sand below, one missing half a leg, but the other healthy and complete.

He was glad about the starfish. It had felt pretty barren before he'd spotted them.

For a moment he felt free and at peace in this place, where a strangely shaped piece of rock or sand could be a door to Narnia. Where he could summon up people from his past – his grandparents, his American father, friends from RADA who hadn't made it out of acting alive.

But today, not even in this magic place could he get respite. Today, Susan Green was floating past him, like a dead sailor, dropped from an aircraft carrier, rigid in a starched white shroud, her hair flying free, like glorious orange seaweed, her own letter to Dominic Young clutched in her hands.

That's how he knew it wasn't real. The letter was still at his place. On the table in the kitchen. He tried to concentrate on the cool water passing through his fingers, over his shoulders, along his legs. Anything that would calm him. He did not turn round to check Susan Green had gone. What the hell was it? Some kind of visitation?

Or a sign he should check in with Dr Bates?

Below him, the fish appeared, reassuringly oblivious, in and out of shafts of light from the setting sun. He surfaced, took a deep breath, floated on his back and watched a pair of cormorants in the water in the near distance. It shocked him that he had conjured up Susan Green's dead body in this sacred space. On the beach, a man and a woman were folding a picnic blanket together, while a guy in a white T-shirt and rolled-up trousers, with a cigarette dangling from his mouth, strolled in the surf. Sunset was thirty minutes away and the shadows cast on the sand were long, distinct and beautiful.

He remembered when he was married, his wife greeting him in the kitchen, holding a recipe book and overfilled glass of wine. It was like looking at an isolated photograph with none before and none after – amputated from a sequence. What would it be like to have another wife, a woman, any wife, someone else's wife, back at home? A welcome home, a 'What kind of a day did you have?', and dinner would be ready whenever he was, and yes, she had got the job at the Getty . . . and Aunt Kate from Maine had died, leaving them a summer house and $250,000 . . . The woman looked too much like Lucy Lack for comfort.

This fantasy dissolved in the noise of a white Cessna low overhead, heading for Santa Monica Airport, its wheels ready for landing. High up above the Cessna were two airliners – their jet streams like white chalk being drawn over a blackboard of an early evening sky. He was straying too far away from the case. The image above him was like a classroom reminder to go back and speak to the people closest to the scene of the crime.

His face dried quickly in the last of the sun. New thoughts pinged in his head like unwanted spots of rain on the upholstery of an open-topped car. Quinn the concierge and Wayne Chung from the supermarket, the thoughts said. Quinn and Chung.

Time to get home . . . Swim time was over.

38

10.15 p.m., 18 July

Refreshed by the swim and eating a reheated tomato and mozzarella pizza, Mandy drove to Santa Monica to grab an Irish bull by its horns.

Number 200 Ocean Avenue was relatively quiet in comparison to the techno beats coming from the other end of the boardwalk. He didn't care if Quinn was fast asleep; he could get up and answer some questions in his kimono.

Mandy switched on the hazard lights and reversed the Amazon into a tight parking space. Shit. Fuck. Shit. Crunched the back fender of a Range Rover. He quickly slipped into first gear, wondering if there was any damage. He did not expect the woman sitting inside it to jump out as if a thirty-foot-high tsunami was heading for town.

He straightened his tie, reached into the passenger seat for his torch and got out of the car. The woman was dressed in a leather skirt and had a sharp bobbed haircut. She was shaking her head as if something terrible had just happened.

'You asshole,' she yelled. 'Do you *know* how much this car costs?'

Mandy pointed his torch at the slightly dented fender below the registration plate.

'I'm sorry about bumping into you, but that's what fenders are for, madam. There doesn't appear to be any real damage, so just . . .' He wanted to say, 'Get over it,' but stopped short, still aiming for a conciliatory tone.

The woman's face turned puce. 'No one walks over me, and nobody walks over my boss!' she said, virtually spitting. 'I'm calling the police!'

Mandy groaned. Did he really need this? She was acting crazy. It was late and he wanted to get on.

The woman blinked and hissed like an angry snake, 'I want your name, proof of insurance and your social security number. I'm going to call the cops otherwise.'

Mandy took out his old detective badge and put it within the beam of the torch. 'Madam, I used to be with the Police Department and they don't have the time to look at things like this.'

The long-fringed woman focused her torch on the badge, stepped back, open-mouthed and astonished.

That shut her up. Mandy's torch soon rested on 'Endeavor Investigations'.

'But look,' he went on, 'you can contact me if it turns out you find more damage.' He handed her a card.

The woman carefully placed it inside her purse, time enough for Mandy to glimpse her ID and first name of Janet.

She then waved her torch over the damaged fender and let out a dismissive laugh. 'Sir, you know what? In the heat of the moment, I overreacted. No harm done. My apologies. Have a good night.'

It sounded as if she was reciting something she'd learnt in therapy.

Out of habit, Mandy memorized the licence plate as the Range Rover drove away. Its highly jumpy owner was just the type to try and make an insurance claim, the sort of stupid woman who was going to be trouble. He could smell it.

Mandy climbed the steps to the entrance to Pedro's apartment building and pressed the buzzer marked, 'Concierge.' He waited. Nothing. Did it again.

He pressed the buzzer for a good minute, again zilch. He was beginning to feel like a stalker. A man in his early thirties with round glasses and a shaven head appeared beside him, holding a key on a chain attached to his belt.

'Fuck! You surprised me!' Mandy said, whipping out whatever laminate came to hand first.

The man peered at the ID.

'Can I help you?' The guy had a nasal, Truman Capote kind of voice.

'I'm here to see Quinn, in connection with the Pedro García-Márquez murder.'

The man held on to Mandy's sleeve. 'Oh my God, wasn't that terrible? Luckily I was away in New York . . . I live two floors below Pedro's apartment.'

'Uh-huh. Was there anything unusual about this place or Pedro's visitors?'

'What, in this town? It's all unusual, isn't it? I'm moving back east. You can keep LA.'

'Probably the best place for you,' Mandy said. 'Do you know Mr Quinn?'

The man narrowed his eyes and lowered his voice. 'Between you and me, he is unhelpful, deceitful and one of the most idle concierges I've ever come across . . .'

Mandy wondered how many concierges the guy had come across with which to compare Quinn. Quite a few by the way he droned on. Mandy peered up at the security cameras over the entrance. Their little red lights were dead; they had obviously not been repaired.

'. . . and I've lived in a lot of apartment buildings with concierges, but he takes the cake for rudeness.'

The man leant closer. His breath smelt of breath freshener and garlic. 'I'll take you to his basement apartment, but I'm not going in.'

Mandy followed the man through the door into the lobby. 'Very kind, but I can find it on my own, thanks.'

But no such luck. The bald guy came halfway down the steps to the basement and gave a further two-minute monologue about his whereabouts on the day before, during and after the murder of Pedro García-Márquez, before he left Mandy to it.

The basement was clearly out of bounds to the residents. The floor was covered in yellow lino that hadn't been cleaned for years, the paint on the walls flaking a bit, a musty, uncared-for smell. The concierge apartment was on the right of a huge boiler room and opposite a room that said, 'Cleaning Staff,' on its door. Mandy stared at the word 'Private' on Quinn's apartment. He put his ear against the door, near the spyhole. The TV was on. It was loud. Maybe Quinn was hard of hearing? He pressed the doorbell three times. It was loud enough to wake the dead. He wouldn't need to press it again.

Nothing happened.

Mandy knelt down and pushed open the letterbox.

He could see the flickering light of the TV in the distance and a cream sofa with a long coffee table in front of it. Other than the booming TV, there was a stillness that just didn't feel right. He shifted position, took out the pen from his jacket pocket, propped up the letterbox. There was a random selection of stuff scattered on the sofa: a jumbo bag of pretzels, some magazines and a lotto form.

Jesus!

A large ginger cat was on the coffee table, feasting off a tub of chicken legs and fries; an open bottle of beer stood next to it.

Mandy got to his feet and banged on the door.

'Quinn,' he yelled. 'Quinn. It's Mandy, from Endeavor Investigations.'

Nothing.

He bent down and hollered it all again through the letterbox.

The cat lifted its head out of the bargain meal bucket and meowed.

Mandy lifted the doormat for a spare key – nothing. Ran his fingers above the door frame – nothing. He glanced around the corridor again.

That's when he noticed the door to the cleaner's room behind him was ajar.

He pushed it open. It was pitch dark inside and surprisingly cold. It stank of industrial disinfectant and something nasty and earthy and putrid. He tugged the light cord, but it didn't switch on any lights. He switched on his torch instead. Lucky he'd had that altercation with the crazy bitch in the Range Rover, or he wouldn't have had it on him.

Where would *he* keep a spare key if he were Quinn? The torch flickered up to the top of the door frame, but there was only dust.

To the right of the door was a set of metal shelves with plastic crates full of cloths, cans of polish, roach-repellent and cleaning fluids. He lifted up the nearest crate. No key.

He could hear the cat on the other side of the apartment's door, attracted by his yelling perhaps, meowing and scratching piteously. That gave Mandy the creeps. But the guy was probably in the bathroom or had run out for a pack of cigarettes. And the cat was just a needy, spoilt runt. That was all.

He reached up high in the flickering darkness and ran his hand along the shelf's metallic surface. Something started creaking.

Someone else was in that room with him.

He put his hand on his holster.

'Who's there?' he said. 'I'm armed, so come out with your hands up.'

Nothing except the creaking.

He took out the gun and walked carefully round the shelves.

In the small circle of light, he saw a pair of naked white feet, swinging mid-air.

He flicked the torch beam upwards.

The man they were attached to was hanging from a heating pipe.

Quinn. Still in his white T-shirt, striped pyjama bottoms.

Mandy felt his face go from warm to clammy in one second. A chill. A shock. The tomato and mozzarella pizza forced its way up his throat, straight onto a mop inside a cleaning bucket.

He stumbled out into the corridor, wiped the sweat from his forehead and told himself to pretend he was still a cop, that this was routine. But he had always hated touching the dead. Hated being anywhere near them.

'*Stop being so sensitive, dude,*' was what Terry would say.

Stop being so sensitive.

Fucking great, thanks.

He got up and walked back inside the room, shone the torch up.

Quinn's eyes and head were pointing at an odd angle, like he was staring at something – a note? Someone watching him die?

Mandy took out his cell, switched on its camera and flash. It felt bad but he had to do it. The face looked worse in the light of the flash. Harsh, scared, helpless and sad.

Very dead.

Mandy checked under the fallen stepladder for a note.

There was none.

He didn't think it was suicide either.

The corpse emitted a series of intestinal noises as if it was still alive. Mandy stood up and forced himself to check the eyes again.

But Quinn was definitely dead . . .

Then he spotted something white protruding from Quinn's right earhole. Was it a hand-rolled cigarette? The head of a maggot peeking out? Mandy set up the stepladder beside Quinn's swaying corpse, pulled on his gloves, climbed the ladder and extracted a tiny roll of paper.

He held it in front of his eyes. 'Jesus fucking Christ,' he whispered to himself, 'another one from Chung.'

This time, he wanted evidence. He took out his phone again and photographed the receipt, then rolled it up and pushed it back inside Quinn's ear.

It was time for Mandy to get the hell out. Fast.

He took the stairs three at a time. Outside the building, he dialled 911 and reported the death to the desk sergeant at Santa Monica PD. Then he tapped out a stark text for Terry – 'Quinn is dead' – adding that he needed a super-fast trace on the Range Rover plates asap.

It was only when he sat inside the Amazon and tried to start the car that Mandy realized he was shaking. The smell of excrement and floor cleaner kept returning to his nose like a boxer's smelling salts.

A residue of puke came up into his throat. He opened the car door and spat into a flowerbed. Not a great end to the day.

39

7.29 a.m., 19 July

Mandy squashed the 'off' switch of the alarm with his fist before it started ringing. A glass of water was lying on the bedside table, next to an empty bottle of tequila. He flicked his fingers at them as if they were uninvited guests; they had been the only way he could stop the images of Dominic Young's eyeless body on the beach and Quinn hanging from the heating pipe. His body felt overheated, dehydrated and strangely in need of sex.

The early morning sun blasted through the curtains – heat making matters worse. He leant back on the cotton pillow, as the dream he had had on and off all night flooded back like a treacherous black tide, all disjointed images and pleading faces. Tequila dreams. That was all.

He forced himself into a cold shower. Afterwards, head still reeling, he dressed, went into the kitchen, turned on KCRW and made himself tea, toast and Marmite.

The breakfast show was the usual music, chat and traffic reports. He sat down at the kitchen table, almost willing it to offer up news that Susan Green had been found, dead or alive, and another murder had been discovered on Ocean Avenue. But the top news was that a doyenne of Hollywood gossip, eighty-nine, had died, there was to be a hike in bank interest rates, and the Lakers had played their last match of the summer, beating Orlando Magic.

It made him suddenly feel very unbalanced. Twitchy, and twitchy was not good. He needed to see Dr Bates. He stood up and scratched his head. For an awful moment he thought Susan Green's abduction in front of him and finding Quinn's body had only been something in his imagination. But this was tequila paranoia, not helped by his meds. A tequila-and-meds hangover was definitely worse than any tequila would supply on its own.

Whoever killed Pedro had been there last night. Or someone very close to the killer. Somehow, he felt that was for sure. And he didn't think it was anyone on García-Márquez's list.

But was that just because he didn't want it to be Lucy?

After all, she had disappeared and he had no idea where she had been for the last twenty-four hours. For all he knew, she could've killed Quinn. Although, she'd have needed an accomplice. Quinn was a big guy. No. Not Lucy. Or anyone else on the list – not even the Sternwoods, who were in Mexico.

Something about the Range Rover woman was bugging the hell out of him. Why? She was just another car-obsessed female. A car-obsessed woman right outside a murder scene. Sure.

'There are those unfortunates who cannot or do not recover,' Mandy said out loud as if he was some creepy ventriloquist's dummy. The words rang out in his empty kitchen. Where the hell had that come from? Was he beginning to hear voices?

He stopped and pinpointed it in his memory bank. He'd heard Frank the coroner say it about his time in AA. It was an odd thing to say, especially with twenty years' continual sobriety, but then maybe what he was saying was that not everyone could be cured.

Yet Mandy felt like there was some weird common denominator between him and the Range Rover lady that he, Mandy, wasn't able to see. The Viceroy speed-dating club? Connected to the cops? Is that why she backed off? He knew he'd seen her somewhere before, but where?

Swallowing two gulps of tea, he put the half-finished mug in the sink, unlocked the back door and stood out on the deck above where he had presented the two goldfish to Donna.

The heat and brightness of the day hit him full in the face. He breathed in a hit of almond from his neighbour's tree, some sal volatile that helped him remember where he might have seen the woman before. He walked back into the house and through the front door, opened the already-warm chrome door handle of the Amazon and grabbed a plastic file from the passenger seat.

Back inside his study, he gazed at the two photos he'd taken from Susan Green's carry-on case, and not handed to Broadski and Dent. There it was. In his hand, a ten-by-eight portrait of a smartly dressed, smartly styled woman in her forties. The woman had a desperate look, as if she wanted to be far more attractive than she knew she was. But then, Mandy thought, that'd be the same expression most people had in photographs.

He stared at the handwritten inscription on the right-hand side of the photo: '*Affectionately, Janet.*' Mandy closed his eyes and reran the final words of the conversation with the woman driver outside Pedro's apartment building.

It had been too dark last night for him to be certain about an exact facial match between the photograph and the woman, but it was close. The bobbed hairstyle looked identical. And something in the expression. A woman who still wanted to be hot like a teenager. 'I Feel Good' rang out from his cell.

He yanked it from his trouser pocket. A text from Donna. 'Have you abandoned me? Please come or I will check out and find YOU!'

Mandy let out a worried laugh and fired off another text to Terry. 'Repeat . . . Where the hell is the address for the Range Rover plate? BEFORE THE GIRAFFE BEATS US TO IT.'

That would put a rocket in Terry's pocket. He gathered up the photos, pushed them back in the folder and left them balanced against his computer screen. Eight forty-three. Time to get going.

He was just about to turn out of the driveway when his cell rang again. Agent Anderson.

The FBI guy cut straight to it, no pleasantries.

'Sir? We need to meet.'

Mandy swallowed. 'Is this about Tamara Tyrer?'

'No, another matter. Meet me at four o'clock at the Casa del Mare, next door to the Viceroy. Please do not discuss or divulge this arrangement with anyone else. Goodbye, sir.' Anderson hung up. Polite, courteous but deadly.

Safe inside the Amazon, Mandy pressed 'play' on his stereo and headed off for Malibu Canyon and young Donna. How sane or loopy would she be when he got there?

Springfield Rehab did not remind Mandy of the mental hospital where he had stayed. That place had been straight out of the pre-glasnost Soviet Union, whereas Springfield had sunny-yellow walls hung with bright Mexican tapestries and paintings of rivers and rainbows.

It took him a few minutes to find the day room, but as he pushed open the double doors, Donna stood up from a high-backed armchair. Dressed in old-fashioned pink pyjamas, without any make-up, she looked like a teenager.

Mandy placed both hands on her shoulders, unsure whether to kiss her or not.

'Hug me properly!' Donna whispered.

He held her tight for ten seconds and then broke free.

She pointed to the white jug of coffee, two cups and saucers on the side table. 'Shall I play mother?'

'I'm not sure that role suits you,' Mandy joked.

'Oh, but it does – I want to have a baby.'

Mandy tried not to look too incredulous – last thing she looked capable of was having a child. But then, with Donna, anything was possible.

'One step at a time, eh?' he said, and smiled.

He picked up his cup of coffee, blew on it and sipped, then gestured towards the grounds, hoping to talk about something neutral. God, why was he being so English and restrained?

He knew the common language and what to say under the circumstances. Yet he felt like a parent visiting a child in school or in prison. As though he must maintain a calm and disciplined example, not start admitting to a shared weakness. For goodness' sake. He needed help himself today. What advice could he offer Donna that would be of real use and not just some bullshit to keep the conversation going until he was able to leave?

Exercise. That was good therapy.

'So, how's the running going?'

Donna leant forward, her breasts disturbing her T-shirt and the illusion of childhood she had seemed to be creating. 'No proper running yet. They've got me taking too much brain candy at the moment.'

'Are you managing to do some walking at least? Walking is the thing if you can't run . . .'

She pushed up the sleeve of her pyjamas and pointed to a white plastic watch device wrapped high up on her tanned forearm. 'It's my fitness band, dummy.'

He peered at the instrument. 'Does that also measure how fast and slow you are running or simply how far you have run?'

She pulled a 'dumb question to ask' face.

'Time flies when you're having fun,' Mandy said.

Donna began to whisper. Her voice higher than usual. It creeped Mandy out. But not that much, because he guessed it was something to do with the medication. She pointed to a young guy with a shaved head on the other side of the day room.

'The guy over there is insane. We're in group together. He can't stop taking cocaine, buckets of it, 'cos he thinks his father was responsible for his mother's death. See how everything comes back to your childhood? I shouldn't say that, should I?'

'I don't know,' Mandy said. 'But whatever you say, I would say it quietly.'

Donna pulled at her chin. 'I don't wanna stay here any longer, Mandy. I want to come home with you.'

'I understand that, but remember the grass always seems greener on the other side.'

'Don't give me any more platitudes. I hear one every minute in here, believe me.'

'Yeah, but outside of here is far more of a madhouse.'

'Oh yeah, sure.'

He smiled and sighed. 'Compared to what I have witnessed in the last few days.'

'You're just saying that to keep me here.'

Mandy grimaced as he imagined police photographs of Quinn's drooping head inside a noose and Susan Green screaming in the LAX chapel.

'Sure, Donna. You're right – I am saying that to keep you here.'

They stood up and walked out into the garden.

She knelt down and pulled a handful of grass from the lawn and threw it into the air. 'Thanks for being my knight in shining armour.'

Mandy stopped walking. 'Listen, you are going to have to trust me. You're getting this place for free, thanks to Father Tony and Mr Apple Mac or whoever it is. You won't get this chance again, and the next time your mind chooses to abandon ship, they might send you back home to China Lake and maybe a very different kind of hospital.'

'Now you're going to tell me you know what you're talking about.'

'You need to stay here and disseminate all the bullshit and get yourself in shape. You said it yourself, Donna, it's the last-chance saloon.'

'These people are already driving me crazy. Have you any idea how flipped out some of these rich junkies are?'

Mandy looked at his watch and then at Donna. 'I want you to do yourself a favour and write a diary – a secret blog?'

'Why's that?'

'You never know. It could become a hit,' he said. '*The Diary of a Hollywood Make-Up Artist . . .*'

Donna nodded. 'I'm already doing it and have got a much better title.'

'Oh yeah? What's that?'

Donna smiled demurely. '*Things Go Better with Coke.*'

40

9.45 a.m., 19 July

Mandy had been thinking about Donna and a hundred different things driving back along PCH, yet when he noticed the needle stuck in the red of his temperature gauge, his focus narrowed to the car.

Fuck it.

The Amazon's radiator needed regular topping-up during the midsummer months. That was the problem with old cars: they needed a hell of a lot of attention. Should have refilled before he left home, not hoped the car would stay cool in the wind during the drive to and from Malibu Canyon.

But he hadn't, and from the creaking, it was getting worse. Shit. If he stopped now, the car would heat up even more, the radiator would split in half, and he would be left waiting for a tow truck and be car-less. He needed to keep going and get to a garage. The best bet was nearly five kilometres away: Tassos's Rentabike on Colorado and 17th Street. He owed the cool old Greek a visit anyhow.

Fortunately the next U-turn was less than a minute away. He took it and selected *Fargo* on the stereo, hoping the setting for the music would somehow help keep the car cool. But the sight of a silver Lexus repeatedly appearing in his rear-view – about three cars behind – caught his attention. He steered into a slower lane, dropped some speed and tried to get a closer look at the two dorks in its front seats, suspiciously like Broadski and Dent.

Each time he slowed, the Lexus did too, until it turned off and disappeared up Sunset towards Brentwood. A part of him wanted to go after it and see if the two goons knew about Quinn or had made any progress on Susan Green and Dominic Young.

Not that they were likely to tell him anything. Then the thermometer eased into the far side of the red temp dial with gulp-making certainty. He clung on to the wheel and dialled Tassos to prepare him for an emergency landing at his workshop, wiping sweat from his forehead as his old friend shouted, '*Yassou!* We are waiting for you.'

Mandy grinned as he remembered Tassos's unanswered phone messages.

'Sorry it's taken so long to get back to you! Thanks a lot.' Mandy loosened his tie and upper shirt button, fully aware that the interior of the car was far hotter than the outside.

Silver hair, grey moustache, blue overalls, Tassos stood on the sidewalk in front of the open repair bay flicking his hands like a ground crew technician guiding a plane. Mandy eased the Amazon into the tight spot, got out and walked over to Tassos, who was now inside, smiling at a mechanic working on a dismantled Harley.

'*Kalispera!*' Mandy hollered.

'*Kalimera, malaka!*' Tassos shouted back.

'Will the car be OK here? I need it back pretty badly.'

'Relax. We have to let the car cool down, drain the radiator and then see if it's a leak or something more serious. You look tired, my friend.'

Mandy growled a fake yawn and looked around the workshop. 'Not much has changed, then! I thought you were in the money.'

'Nothing has changed, my friend, except I now pay the wages and insurance of *three* mechanics, not just the one rebuilding the bike there!'

'Business has been good?'

'Eh . . . I can't complain. Every mother in LA wants to ride a Harley. We have another shop in Cross Creek now, and we're even selling Russian bikes too.'

They pushed open the office door, heard the quack-quack welcome of the electronic monitor and walked into the back room of the workshop. There was a desk covered in paperwork, two girlie calendars on a wall, a swivel chair, an old leather sofa and a smell of petrol and cat pee.

'You want coffee?'

'Thanks.'

Mandy smiled. It was good to be out of the heat.

Tassos took out a gas Primus stove and rested it on top of a motor magazine on his desk. He emptied some coffee into a small Greek saucepan, filled it from a bottle of water, lit a match, switched on the gas and – bumph – the coffee was brewing.

'Sit down, sit down!'

Mandy slumped down onto the sofa, trying to remember the name of Tassos's wife, but a quack-quack noise coming from out front saved him the trouble.

Tassos wobbled his head philosophically. 'Eh! A customer – I'll be back. Make yourself comfortable.'

Mandy grunted and smiled, pleased the car and himself were with an old friend.

Like most of his countrymen, Tassos never forgot anyone who had helped him when he first moved to America to start a new life and business. The two had first met nine years earlier, when Mandy was still acting and hoping to land a part in *NYPD Blue*.

Tassos had rented a small garage ten doors down on 28th Street. A slimeball from West Hollywood had been trying to muscle in on Tassos with an old-style protection racket. Mandy adopted a disguise and pretended to be part of the new Russian Mafia. Mandy's grasp of a few key Russian words had helped. And it was before there were too many real Russian Mafiosi to make it dangerous. Mandy could never risk such a thing again. It would be crazy now. Yet Tassos was never bothered by anyone after that.

Mandy sat back in the leather armchair and listened to Tassos speaking Greek with a customer. Within seconds he felt more drowsy and relaxed than he had in weeks.

Ten minutes later the sound of 'I Feel Good' grew louder. Mandy rubbed his eyes and pulled the cell from his pocket.

Terry didn't waste time in getting to the point.

'The Range Rover is registered to a company called Fish Holdings, Inc. at an address in Silver Lake.'

Mandy rewound to how the woman with the bobbed hair and leather skirt had screamed at him before she knew he was a PI. '*No one walks over me, and no one walks over my boss.*'

'Does it mention anyone by the name of Janet?' he asked.

'No, but she is probably some cutie having an affair with her boss and being given the use of the company Range Rover.'

'Maybe she is the boss. Women do run companies, you know.'

'Stop being so sociological, would you?'

Mandy sipped some Greek coffee, spat out something floating on its surface. Terry was back from holiday and being a know-it-all. It was time to bring him up to speed.

'Broadski and Dent are officially working on the case.'

'What? Did the Giraffe tell you officially?'

'Yes, you could say that. I'm also pretty sure he's got Beavis and Butthead tailing me.'

'Get yourself a different car. They're so dumb they wouldn't figure that out for a week. Anyway, I can go and sniff out Mrs Range Rover. Silver Lake is a five-buck cab ride from here. You double-check Quinn.'

'Tell that to his mother. What's the name and address of the guy in Silver Lake?'

Mandy heard Terry light a cigarette, cough and wheeze. It was the one bit of defiance he had left in his repertoire. Mandy wasn't pleased to hear him smoking, but he was happy that they were back on the case and arguing.

Terry coughed a few more times before saying, 'Number 2200 Knocks Avenue. I think that's right next to the Spanish Cemetery. Maybe you should reserve yourself a lot.'

'See you later, dork brain.'

Mandy snapped his cell shut. Something was tugging hard on his fishing line. Picking up the cup Tassos had left for him earlier, he took a few more sips of lukewarm coffee, eased himself out of the armchair and walked out through the door that made the quack-quack noise.

The hood of the Amazon was open, and Tassos was handing a spanner to a mechanic lying on the ground in between the two front wheels.

'Tassos? I need to borrow a car, right now.'

Tassos scratched at his moustache for a few seconds. 'My friend, I have no spare cars, but I have something else . . .'

41

11.25 a.m., 19 July

Mandy revved the 1000cc Kawasaki bike, zipped up the leather jacket, angled the helmet over his head and waited for a gap in the traffic. He made an illegal turn out of the garage and headed east along Colorado. The wind rushed past his face, leaving a smell of dust and petrol. As he opened up the throttle, the power of the engine and roar of the exhaust gave him a thrill.

The bike snaked through the curves of Brentwood up past the summer-lawned mansions of Beverly Hills and on past Sunset Plaza. Coming to a stop at Sunset Boulevard and the construction site of the new Los Feliz Children's Hospital, Mandy remembered when Terry's daughter Caitlin had contracted meningitis and been rushed there. The child was only saved by some exceptional doctors. It was generally agreed between Mandy and Dawn that the stress of it had triggered Terry's cancer. But what the hell did they know really?

He rode on for another twenty minutes, barely noticing the odd-looking churches on the outskirts of Little Armenia. By the time he'd driven further up Sunset towards North Silver Lake, Mandy felt completely able to handle the bike.

He braked as he spotted Knocks Avenue and followed a white arrow sign high up on a wall saying, 'To the cemetery.' It pointed up a short, wide, tree-lined cul-de-sac with several substantial family houses on either side. At the far end of the road was a privet hedge, beyond which lay the cemetery Terry had mentioned.

He pulled his visor down and rode slowly down the road, clocking the Mercedes, Porsches and BMWs occupying the driveways. Save for the whirring noise of a refuse truck, the place was too quiet. Where was everyone?

He drew up opposite the last house on the right-hand side, killed the engine, took off his helmet and dismounted. On the sidewalk next to two wheelie bins was a discreet house sign saying, '2200,' and a less discreet sign saying that the place was protected by a security firm and to 'beware of the dogs'. Number 2200 didn't just have private security; it also had huge metal gates with a security keypad, screen and entryphone built into a side wall. Whoever lived inside was loaded and liked their privacy. It was also next door to a cemetery.

Mandy pressed the entryphone.

A terse voice answered, 'Can I help you?'

Mandy stared into the screen, hoping to catch a glimpse, but it was a one-way.

'I'm sorry to trouble you but I was hoping to speak to Janet. I met her in her Range Rover last night.' He spoke in a pronounced English accent, hoping that the voice, name and familiar make of car would be enough to get him buzzed through the gate.

There was a few seconds' silence, and then the voice said, 'Who did you say you were?'

'Mandy of Endeavor Investigations.' He held his ID to the camera and waited.

A buzzer sounded. The gates opened slowly. He walked down the pebbled tarmac drive. There was a beige three-car garage with its doors closed, a bicycle leaning against one of its side walls. When he got to the steps that led to the double front door, the left-hand door opened and a pair of tanned legs appeared. They belonged to an Asian woman in a short black dress with long black hair and large hands. She was wearing red lipstick, which did nothing for her thirty-something skin.

Mandy held out his hand. 'Sorry, I didn't catch your name.'

The woman did not shake hands. 'Why do you want my name?'

Mandy flashed a business card. 'It's just a routine enquiry.'

She took the card and frowned at it as if it might be infectious. 'My name is Yale.'

'Lovely name,' said Mandy. 'Is Janet at home?'

'No, and my boss is not here. Janet does not live here.'

'This is the registered address for Fish Holdings and the owner of a Range Rover, registration number — Should I wait, or could you tell me when your boss will be back?'

The woman leant her head into Mandy's face and said, 'No, you cannot wait or come back! Now please leave, or I'll call the dogs out.'

She stepped back inside. The door slammed shut.

Mandy didn't fancy his chances with the dogs. He'd had some bad experiences in the past with Dobermanns. Yale had been scary enough.

He walked back up the drive and through the opening set of electronic gates.

The dumper truck was picking up the trash in the street. A man with a Zapata moustache jumped off the truck and ambled to 2200's blue and grey bins.

'Whoa, shit, hold on there,' Mandy shouted, and took a few steps back to the gates, frantically patting his pockets. 'Hey, man, let me look in the orange bag before you throw it. I think I threw a letter of mine away by mistake.'

The man held the bag and dithered.

Mandy handed him a ten-dollar bill. 'Give me a moment?'

The guy held up his hands as if to say, 'Cool, man,' turned to face the refuse truck and lit a roll-up. Mandy opened the bag and sifted through. There were two business-stamped envelopes, both torn into pieces. He stuffed the pieces into his jacket, knotted the plastic bag and gave it to the refuse guy.

'You saved my life there, man. Thanks a lot!' he said, walking back to the Kawasaki.

The refuse guy saluted from the tow bar as the truck pulled away. Behind it – waiting for it to go – was a shiny white Jeep driven by a blonde in a white jacket. As soon as the truck moved, the Jeep parked bang outside number 2200.

Mandy stepped backwards into a gap in the cemetery's hedge. He'd already wasted most of the morning; another five minutes wasn't going to hurt. The driver stepped down out of the Jeep, her face away from him. She was all tight black jeans, sexy pink shirt undone to the top of a black lace bra and shiny high-heel boots.

'Fuck me sideways,' Mandy whispered to himself as the shapely blonde stalked over to the house and pressed the security pad. Like a gravy commercial, the woman's perfume wafted across to where he was hiding. Mandy inhaled Chanel No. 19.

Lucy Lack in retro dark glasses and a long blonde wig. He'd recognize that walk anywhere. The security gates opened more quickly for Lucy than they had for him. Was Lucy a friend of Janet, the lady driving the Range Rover? What else did they have in common – the late Mr Quinn and Dominic Young, whom Lucy claimed to have saved on the plane with Father Tony? The priest had said Lucy's medical skills weren't too hot. Had she been trying to *kill* him?

All he needed now was for Father Tony to appear too and he'd have hit the jackpot. He peered over the closing gate as Lucy walked down the drive, holding one hand inside her bag and swaying from left to right like a model on a catwalk.

He moved to the far left of the gate and took out his scope. The front door was opened by Yale again. But her body language was not exactly friendly. Lucy said something he could not make out, took out some ID and what appeared to be a charity collecting tin from her bag.

What the fuck?

He strained to hear, but he could not pick up a word. She kept showing the tin and a sheet of stickers. The Asian woman kept her arms folded across her chest and began shouting. Now Mandy could hear her all right.

'My boss is away on business. I am the housekeeper. If you want to leave a message, I'll make sure he gets it. We do not give money to people on the street.'

Lucy said something else and placed the collection tin back in her bag.

'No idea when he will be back,' the housekeeper yelled, pointing a remote control at the double gates.

Lucy turned on her heel and made a gesture with her hand that could either mean she would telephone or that she would simply call again.

The housekeeper craned her neck round the door to make sure the visitor was definitely walking back up the drive. Once the gates were opened, she stepped back inside the house porch and closed the front door. Lucy lit a cigarette, took off her jacket, her pink shirt knotted above a bare tanned midriff. A surge of adrenalin coursed through Mandy's body. He strode back across the road, climbed astride the motorbike and waited. Hopefully, the shock of seeing him might loosen her tongue. It had been a while since they last met and touched hands . . .

She ambled towards the Jeep, lost in thought. Mandy held his breath, waiting for his prey to get slightly closer into range. She put her hand in her bag, looked at him, didn't register anything and took out a set of keys for the Jeep. Then she stopped with a jolt, lowered her head and shoulders, turned and stared straight at the bike.

'Mandy! What the hell are you doing here? What the fuck is going on?'

It was difficult to tell whether she was shocked or relieved.

Mandy pointed a finger at his chest. 'What am *I* doing here?'

Lucy Lack stared at him, her fingers covering her mouth.

'It's a lovely spot. Have you been to the cemetery?' Mandy continued.

'I have never been to Silver Lake before in my life.'

'Is that right?' he said with a heavy hint of sarcasm.

She took her bag from her shoulder and held it under her arm. 'Are you following me? Stalking me? Trying to catch me out?'

He swung his leg off the motorbike and stood next to it, moving the throttle back and forth. '*Au contraire*, I've been unable to keep up with *you*. Last time I had the pleasure was when you were sitting next to a retired Hell's Angel at Pedro's funeral. Next thing, I'm reading a note in Shutters saying thanks for the flowers but you've either gone back to London or Mexico. And yet . . .'

'I'm still here?'

She glared at him, clutching the bag in her right hand, fanning her face with the other.

'I wondered if you had made an appointment with Sotheby's valuation department?' he said. It was a cheap trick he regretted as soon as he said it. He'd broken his silence about Pedro's bequest of the Hopper painting. It was intended to be raised in a less tactless, more sensitive way. Pedro was her best friend, after all. He would give her room to ignore it.

Lucy lit a cigarette and took her time to put it to her lips and inhale. She looked straight into Mandy's eyes and said, 'Who knows whether that will you're referring to was ever witnessed. Personally, I *very* much doubt it. OK?'

She threw the cigarette onto the road, crushed it beneath her boot and headed for her Jeep. He felt like more of a shit, but something was telling him the time had come to show Lucy the two images saved on his phone he took in Eduardo García-Márquez's study after the funeral.

Clearly Lucy knew how to wear different wigs. But what the hell was she doing wearing one in Silver Lake?

Mandy stepped away from the bike. 'We can sit and talk inside your car. It's got air-conditioning.'

She pulled herself into the Jeep, locked the doors, turned on the engine and half wound down the window. She stared straight ahead, avoiding his eyes. Mandy angled his head close to the open driver's window.

'The air-conditioning will work a lot better with the windows closed,' he said. 'Want me to show you how?'

'No, I'm happier with you on the outside.'

He looked at her angry face and smiled. She took another cigarette from a packet on the passenger seat and lit it.

'OK, I'm going to ask you three questions,' he said.

She exhaled a plume of smoke. 'I don't really give a shit what you ask.'

'Mind telling me where you stayed last night? Another hotel?'

She smiled wearily and shook her head, held her hand up as if to say, 'Why, and what the fuck?' but then shrugged and started talking. 'After the funeral I stayed with Wing. He has a place with a guest suite in the mountains and you may have heard I was banned from attending Pedro's wake by his mother . . . Mrs Fucker.' She dragged hard on the cigarette.

Mandy completed her sentence. 'So Wing stepped in and provided a much-needed port in a terrible storm.'

'Yes, that's right. Kind of him, wasn't it?'

He wondered if it was worth asking what had happened between them prior to that, but decided against it for the time being.

'So are you going to stay there or in Santa Monica? What happened to going back to London or Mexico?'

'I've got some unfinished business,' she said, tapping ash into the ashtray. 'Wing didn't come back last night, didn't answer calls or texts. I got a little freaked, called a cab and checked into a hotel.'

Mandy wiped sweat from his upper lip. It didn't sound too good about Wing.

'Not Shutters?' he said.

'No.'

Mandy grunted. 'Loews?'

'Not after what happened last time.'

'OK, so why are you here in Knocks Avenue?'

'That's four questions.'

'Never been too good at arithmetic.'

'Fuck you, Mandy. Why did you send me those flowers?'

He felt himself blush. 'Probably because I was a little drunk after the funeral.'

'Jesus! Listen, I am really angry about what you said about me and the fucking Sternwoods. Don't you get it? You should be stalking them, not me, and finding who killed Pedro. I thought you were supposed to be one of the good guys. Stop harassing me!'

She wound down the window some more and thrust the collection tin out. Mandy took it and studied the exterior. A home-printed label: 'Please give generously to the Ocean Park Homeless Shelter.' A bleached-out photo of Father Tony and Adams squatting besides two homeless men had been glued round the tin. He pulled out his wallet and dropped a ten-dollar bill in the tin and passed it back to her.

It was time to be straight with her about the images he now had of her and the Sternwoods in his phone. Yet he didn't want to lose touch with Lucy again – she was both his prime concern and his prime suspect. He couldn't afford for her to storm off in a fit of pique and disappear. Tracking her down had been harder than he'd thought.

'Could you finish answering why you're here?'

She pushed the collection tin back into her bag and gripped hold of the steering wheel.

'Father Tony recommended I did some volunteering. Take my mind off things?'

'And that meant being in Silver Lake, where there are about three and a half homeless people?'

'I am not dealing with clients, Mandy – I'm fundraising, and in case you didn't know, there are a lot wealthy people living in Silver Lake.'

'Plenty more in Santa Monica and at Shutters.'

'Look, I happen to have a list of names of people who might be sympathetic. That's why I'm here. Why are you here? Following me, instead of nailing the Sternwoods. What a total waste of time.'

To his surprise, tears had appeared at the edges of her eyes. She looked vulnerable. But only for an instant.

Of course he wanted to believe her, but something bugged him about even the tears. There was something else in the pot that he hadn't even smelt yet.

'We can go and talk about what I've discovered about the Sternwoods over coffee maybe,' he said. 'And maybe then you can tell me why you're really here?'

She put on her seat belt. 'Are you deaf? I came here to see the man who lives here about donating, but he's not here. OK?'

'Was that the wife you were just talking to?'

'No, it was his housekeeper. If you are not following me, why are you here?'

Mandy paused to think of a phoney reason and then decided on the truth.

'Quinn the concierge at Pedro's was found dead last night. I had a scrape with someone's car outside and their car is registered to this address.'

Lucy shook her head. 'I can't deal with any more death.' She paused. 'Just tell me what the fuck you *think* you have discovered about the Sternwoods and me.'

'Sure you want to know?'

She took the last drag of her cigarette and stubbed it out in the ashtray. 'For Christ's sake.'

Mandy pulled the phone from his pocket and rested it on the glass of the open window, Johnny Sternwood's nice group photograph on the screen facing inwards.

She lifted up her sunglasses and leant forward, blinking at the phone as if she was looking at a photo of a baby in a cot. 'Can I have a look?'

He pushed the phone through the gap in the window.

As if she was trying to read a text in bright sunlight, she held the screen up to her eyes. 'It's frightening what people can do with PhotoShop these days,' she said coolly.

It wasn't the reaction Mandy had expected.

'Mind telling me where you got this from?'

'I'd rather talk about that over a cappuccino.'

Before Mandy had a chance to react, Lucy tapped the 'delete' key with her finger, rolled her eyes and lobbed the phone back through the window, so that it clattered onto the road. 'Fuck off, Mandy. Don't you dare ever come near me again!'

He felt the Jeep jerk backwards and he fell over onto the sidewalk as Lucy reversed in a 180-degree arc, tyres screeching, and roared off down Knocks Avenue.

'Don't do anything stupid!' Mandy shouted as he grabbed his cell, pulled on his jacket and helmet, and kick-started the bike.

42

11.50 a.m., 19 July

Lucy Lack was a faster and more skilful driver than Mandy had imagined. Maybe he still had some old ideas about females' driving abilities, especially blondes, even if it was only a platinum wig. But by the time he'd ridden out of Knocks Avenue and turned onto Sunset, the white Jeep was way ahead in the distance, and he'd been thoroughly disabused of those. Lucy had balls, skill and verve. She weaved between the inner and outer lanes, undertaking and overtaking to get ahead like a boy racer from an estate back home.

His helmet visor up, Mandy turned the throttle; the Kawasaki shot past seven, eight, ten, twenty cars. Wind pummelling his face, he pushed his weight down on the back of the saddle, leant into the curves and focused on the road and on the blonde in the Jeep. Fuck! Why had he handed her the phone? And why had she been wearing a wig? Was she embarrassed to ask for donations for the homeless? Surely nobody would recognize her in Silver Lake.

There was a screech of tyres as a Chrysler in front slammed on the brakes. Mandy swerved left, front wheel inches from the car's fender, smell of friction in the air. He shouted, but the driver was jabbing his left hand towards the left-lane exit sign.

Fuck.

Mandy dropped back. Lucy Lack gained fifteen seconds. He steered round the outside of the car, aiming to have a clear passage down the double yellow lines. But he had miscalculated, and the wind coming off the car hurtling past in the opposite lane blew him sideways. He'd been away from bikes for too long.

He tucked back into the lane and shifted position on the saddle. The Chrysler turned off, leaving a space.

Luckily Lucy was obviously not going to deviate from Sunset. She said it was the first time she'd been to Silver Lake, and if that was true, it was a sure bet she'd stay on Sunset all the way to Santa Monica. Wide, glamorous, billboard-bedecked, two-lane Sunset was the comfort route for anyone who didn't want to use the eight-lane freeways.

He reckoned she would most likely head straight to Venice and try to punch Sarah Sternwood in the kisser, then do something far worse to Johnny's breeding equipment. He didn't blame her for wanting revenge. Trouble was, she didn't know Johnny and Sarah Sternwood were in Mexico City receiving attention from Mrs García-Márquez's private clinic. García-Márquez confirmed the bad dealings between Sarah Sternwood and Pedro, so that stacked.

But what if she wasn't heading out to the Sternwoods' mansion? Wing had disappeared – just Wing doing a bunk from a needy Lucy, or something more sinister? If she drove towards 6th and Wilshire, then there was someone else Lucy could be seeing, and Mandy's stomach clenched a little at the thought: Adam Pollock.

Pollock had been hanging around Shutters the other day. Was that the slimy git she'd hired to dish the dirt on him, Mandy? Worse, had she kept Pollock on to find the killer? Instead of him?

He readied himself to ride out onto the yellow line; up ahead, the white Jeep was caught in a right-turn-only lane, wedged between cars. A clear gap, so easy; just a twist of the handle and he was two cars behind her.

He pressed the Kawasaki horn, loud and shrill. Lucy reacted immediately, checked the rear-view and then stared straight ahead, cigarette hanging from her mouth, holding the wheel like she was in a racing car. She kept revving the engine, readying herself for a gap, for someone to let her pass into their lane. He'd chased bank-job drivers with worse skills than hers, but then they were nearly always chopped up on coke, and Lucy was stone cold.

He tried to inch his way between the two cars ahead of him, but they were too close. The heavy bike started to wobble; he stamped both feet onto the ground. Lucy gave the ghost of a smile at that.

She turned the Jeep so it was just jutting into the outer lane. He wheeled the bike backwards to get back and alongside her. Some arsehole started hooting. He ignored it, manoeuvred the bike and roared off. But Lucy was already over the other side of the lights. Cars swerved round her. She was driving like her life depended on it. But what on earth did she think *he* was going to do to her?

He put his head down and raced across the light. It turned red. The speedometer tilted between eighty and ninety; mess smacked into his sunglasses. A hundred.

Then he was next to the white Jeep, trying to get Lucy to slow down. She shouted, 'Piss off!' and threw the cigarette from her mouth, directly at him

211

through the window. It hit the zip of his leather jacket, small bright embers splintering down his chest.

'Stupid bitch!'

He took his right hand from the throttle and flicked at the hot ash. Lucy shoved the stick shift into second and accelerated away. He pulled over onto the inner lane, slowed right down.

Beaten.

In the distance, a small white hand flipped him the bird out of a white Jeep window. Great. Some car was hooting and flashing their lights right behind him. He had a bad feeling it was an unmarked police car. He snatched a glimpse into each wing mirror: Broadski and Dent right behind him, waving their fat fingers in the Lexus.

43

Midday, 19 July

Benny Tan drove his BMW down PCH listening to Randy Newman's 'I Love LA', his cell nestled in his shirt pocket. An American Spirit burnt in the ashtray.

Today, he'd had a breakfast meeting downtown with Nabokov and two of his top number crunchers in the swanky Biltmore Hotel, no expense spared. To his surprise, Nabokov had behaved impeccably, and the two accountants were polite and civilized too. He'd particularly liked when the older one said, 'It's going to get tough out there, Benny. A good time to cash in and let a larger corporation take the strain.' That guy had a brain like Benny's. Sure, there was schmoozing, but still, it had gone better than he expected.

For one thing, nobody challenged the accounts or suggested he 'better cut us a better deal'. All that was left was to finalize the goodwill figure.

'We're not that far apart,' Nabokov had said with a shrug. 'Insert it into the agreement and let's sign the contracts in two days' time – contracts ready for perusal tomorrow.'

Fifty per cent on signing, followed by two equal tranches on 1 November and 1 December. Benny took a drag on the cigarette, lowered the window and fanned the smoke out with his hand. It would be a disaster if they knew that he was desperate to sell, but he'd kept his cards close to his chest. He allowed himself a little smile. Let people smell your fear and you are finished. He turned the music up and drove on.

The car was going no faster than twenty-five miles per hour when the cell vibrated against his chest. Even so, he pulled over. Growing up in Canada had taught him three things: you can never be *too* careful; safety must come first; and good manners cost nothing.

He stared at the text. 'Need to talk, asap. Possible problem. Janet.'

He extinguished the cigarette between his fingertips, flung it through the window and, with his left indicator flickering, drove on.

After all the years Janet had worked for him, he knew that when she used the words 'possible problem', there was a definite problem. She was the best employee he'd ever had, but recently he was wishing she would take early retirement. That whole bad business with that big-mouthed thief Dominic Young.

As he turned into Sunset and then North Channel Road into Fish Farm's showroom, he told himself not to jump to any conclusions. He was glad the signs saying, 'We Support Dentistry Sans Frontiers,' had been taken down, but winced at a bucket and sponge sitting beside the dental van in the corner. He parked the BMW in its spot next to Janet's Range Rover. All eleven company cars were in, including Dick's brand-new Ford pickup.

He waltzed through the electronic doors of the entrance, waved good morning to the showroom staff and walked over to Kurt.

'Do me a favour and stop that van being washed in the main parking lot,' he said. 'Take it down to the carport space by the basement entrance and clean it so thoroughly I'll be able to see my face in it – use bleach.'

'You got it, sir.'

Benny marched up the polished wooden stairs. If that intern played his cards right, he could be in line for promotion. He padded down a corridor past his own office and swiped his card down the side of a security door. It opened to reveal five people plugged into headsets taking orders. There was a smell of industry about the place, and at the farm, that Benny was proud of.

To one side, Janet Lee sat inside her glass cubicle in a grey business suit, speaking on the phone, tapping a keyboard and staring into her monitor. He knocked on her window, held up his cell phone and pointed to its screen.

'My office, now!'

He swung into his own office, filled a paper cup from the water cooler and drained it in two gulps. Then he turned to Janet – already sitting on the chair in front of his desk.

'So let me get this straight. The guy, a private investigator who crashed into your Range Rover last night, came asking to see *you* this morning at my house in Silver Lake?'

An image of a solemn-faced Nabokov and his two accountants shaking their heads and leaving the breakfast table shot into his mind.

Janet folded her arms, her face slightly flushed. A sure sign of guilt with Janet.

'Correct. Yale called from the house and read out the same business card he gave me last night. Remember we registered the car to the holding company?'

Janet knew better than to second-guess the boss. Benny nodded, sat back behind his desk and examined the file Janet had put together on Private Investigator Mandy. The guy sounded like a loser: nationality, British; ex-Santa Monica Police; lived alone with a tenant on Castellammare Drive; divorced.

There was no doubt Janet Lee was Benny's most thorough and hard-working member of staff. That's why she was so well paid and why he hadn't got rid of her over the Susan Green and Dominic Young fiasco.

Trouble was, he'd allowed her too much authority and it had gone to her head. Janet was becoming a loose cannon herself, and one for whom he could not afford to continue making excuses.

'Where did this accident happen?'

'About ten o'clock last night on Ocean. I was tying up some loose ends, like you asked me to.'

Benny let out an angry sigh. 'Contrary to what people say in Hollywood,' he said, 'there *is* such a thing as bad publicity, and right now, I don't need any at all.'

'Is that because you are selling the company, Benny?' Janet said icily.

'I've worked out a stock deal for you, Janet. I'm having the agreement drawn up right now. Should be ready in less than a week,' he lied.

Janet Lee hugged herself and let out a sigh of gratitude. 'I have always tried to do my best for you.'

'I know you have, and I'm going to show you how much I appreciate what you've done. Now, can we get back to this man Mandy?'

Janet wiped a tear from her eye. 'Sure.'

'How much do you think he knows?'

Janet's face contorted into a frown. 'He knows diddly. It's just a coincidence. I'm playing safe, that's all.'

Benny Tan picked up the letter opener on his desk and stood up. 'I don't believe in coincidences,' he said, slapping the letter opener hard against the desk. 'This could be a disaster.'

'Could be a coincidence; doesn't have to be a disaster,' Janet said, crossing her legs.

'We are going to have to meet Mr Mandy, especially if he doesn't work alone.'

'Trust me, he's a lightweight, a store detective, more used to keeping tabs on celebrities. Honestly, he's a weirdo with a bad credit rating, a loner driving a Swedish car twenty years older than our new intern . . . It's just a crumby coincidence—'

'He can't be that dumb if he figured out how to find the house,' Benny interrupted, pointing the tip of the letter opener at his throat. 'Precisely the sort of person we do not need prodding around here.'

Janet stood up, plucking at the pleats of her grey trousers. 'Bringing him in could draw too much attention to us – make the problem seem bigger than it is. The guy just needs a shock to warn him off.'

'I'm interested in immediate containment. I don't want any *shock* that can

215

be discovered by members of the public walking on the beach, or anywhere else for that matter,' Benny said, rubbing his eyes with the palms of his hands. 'Be subtle, and don't get carried away.'

44

3.35 p.m., 19 July

Mandy took a slug from a cold beer wrapped in a paper bag. It felt good to be back sitting on the leather upholstery of the Amazon, watching the girls playing volleyball on Santa Monica Beach.

Broadski and Dent had been virtually rear-ending him since he lost sight of Lucy and the Jeep. It was a humiliation that he frankly could've done without. But that was how it was. He tried throwing them off with a dummy right-hand turn on Robertson, before a sudden switch left onto Santa Monica Boulevard. He finally managed to lose them good and proper by riding the Kawasaki into a hidden side entrance into Tassos's garage on Colorado.

So, OK, it was a little embarrassing, but he'd got the two goons away from Lucy Lack. Unfortunately, it had taken a chunk out of his day, not to mention his adrenalin, and now he didn't know where Lucy Lack was either.

He'd taken the now cooled-down Amazon to Venice, just in case Mr and Mrs Sternwood had returned home. Two letters, some junk mail and three copies of the *LA Times* were inside their mailbox, no rattlesnake. No broken windows and no hate messages daubed on the front door. So Lucy did not appear to have called round after all. The realtor's 'House for Sale' sign was still nailed to the top of a wooden post by the front gate. He needed to move on.

So he'd high-tailed it to the homeless shelter, tuned into KCRW playing 'California Girls' on Harry Shearer's *Le Show*.

'Speaking of girls,' Shearer interrupted the record, 'I am happy to announce that the show received a call from the manager of the Veil to say that singer Susan Green is safe and sound in rainy old London and reforming the band. Apparently she'd forgotten to take her shot of diabetes insulin . . .'

Mandy had switched off the radio and driven on, trying to figure out if it was possible or even likely that Green could have flown to London. Of course, when she disappeared, her passport, wallet and tickets were in her handbag, so maybe, yes, she had taken a later flight. But it didn't quite add up. And reforming the band without Dominic Young? It seemed unlikely.

He'd got to the homeless shelter with only a bit of time before he was meant to be where he was now – waiting for Anderson. Four or five clients were at the tables, none of whom Mandy recognized. But no Lucy with her tin and ten dollars of his money. Bradley Adams stepped out from behind the counter, wearing a dark striped apron and a pair of reading glasses, looking like he belonged to a cooking article in a Sunday magazine.

'My favourite priest here?' Mandy asked.

'Working the night shift for St Monica's – still upset about Stevie.'

'Stevie?'

'The missing homeless guy.'

Mandy grunted. He hadn't done anything to help the priest find the guy.

'Lucy Lack work here today?'

'Miss Lack? She did some washing-up in the kitchen and went off sunbathing, or was it fundraising?'

Adams seemed slightly drunk. Maybe there was another side to him that only came out when he was intoxicated.

'Do you know where she's staying?'

'Not on the beach, I imagine.' He laughed at his own joke, leant inside the kitchen door, brought out a packet of Marlboro Lights, handed them to Mandy. 'She left these, if you want to give them back to her. Want to know what colour underwear she was wearing?' There was a knowing smirk on his face.

'Not interested right now, thanks.'

Outside the building, Mandy's fingers pulled a book of hotel matches from Lucy's pack of cigarettes. The Comfort Inn, 26th and Santa Monica Boulevard. Rather than phone the hotel, he wanted to visit himself. His meet with Agent Anderson was due to kick off at ten past four, but not at the Viceroy as planned. 'We need to move the location,' was all the guy had said. 'A man carrying a white electric guitar will meet you by your car opposite the pier and escort you to the new meeting place. OK?'

Mandy didn't care if he was met by a Klingon playing a banjo, just as long as there was no trouble with the FBI.

Twenty-five minutes before curtain up.

He drove fast all the way back up Santa Monica Boulevard until 26th Street. The hotel was white and pink. He left the Amazon under a concrete carport. The Jeep was in the corner, the blonde wig on the back seat, the car keys dangling in the ignition. He opened the door, took them out and dropped them in his pocket. Then into the hotel. The sparse reception desk was manned by a man in his sixties in a crimson Comfort Inn blazer that looked anything but comfortable.

'Do you have a Miss Lucy Lack staying here?' he asked, flashing his PI licence.

'She is a guest of the hotel, but she's busy right now in our conference room.'

Mandy pictured Lucy Lack being interrogated by Broadski and Dent. 'I have something important to give to her for that meeting.'

'First on your left and then first on your right – can't miss it.'

He followed the directions until he came to a glass-bordered teak door. He looked through a side window into the room. On the middle of a table, a rifle with telescopic sights was lying next to an empty gun case. Lucy Lack sat on one side, and on the other the cream-suited figure of Private Investigator Pollock. Terry might be right about Lucy's innocence, or lack of it, after all.

45

3.55 p.m., 19 July

The sight of Lucy Lack, arms folded, conducting a business meeting with the smooth-talking Adam Pollock temporarily knocked the wind out of Mandy's sails. He dropped the Jeep's car keys at the reception desk and walked out, telling the old blazer man on reception, 'No message, no nothing.'

'When in doubt, do nothing' was what old Grandfather Mandy used to say. So he'd driven back down to the pier, parked up close by and taken a beer from the cool box in the trunk. The truth was, he was in shock. Lucy, a gun, Pollock. Gun, Pollock, Lucy. Pollock, Lucy, gun. However he ran it, it didn't look good. Even worse, he felt like a cuckolded prick.

As he drank the last drops of beer, an athletic, good-looking black guy with short dreads leant against the hood of the Amazon. Mandy was about to hoot the horn at him when the man lifted up a cream-coloured Fender.

'Follow me.'

The guy carried the guitar by the base of its neck. Mandy sniffed the sickly smell of hot dogs, candyfloss and marijuana. It was comforting somehow. He raised his sunglasses to read the sign over the pier entrance fifty yards away.

YACHT HARBOR

SPORT FISHING BOATING

CAFE

A platoon of people were turning into the pier, as another came out – it was an obvious place to get lost in a crowd. Was that Anderson's idea?

They walked past the entrance, alongside a line of parked cars, until they reached a Winnebago that took up two spaces. Four mountain bikes were attached to the rear doors and a satellite dish to its roof.

'Is this it?'

'One moment.'

The black guy gave a half-smile, touched an earpiece in his right ear and muttered something. Twenty seconds and the door to the Winnebago buzzed open; a set of steps dropped down. Mandy took a deep breath and climbed up, clenching his fists.

Anderson, dirty cream suit, no tie, was waiting just inside. 'Please walk right to the end,' he said.

He had a plain wedding ring on his finger and a livid scar on his neck where the collar hung open. A bullet, or a stabbing? Maybe even a chemical burn.

'Apologies for the subterfuge, but even Casa del Mare next door to the Viceroy became unsafe and we haven't set up an office down here yet.'

Mandy followed him, stooping slightly under the low ceiling, past two casually dressed guys on swivel chairs using a remote to switch between a dozen monitors. Two of the screens were on the main entrance and rear exit to the Viceroy.

Anderson motioned Mandy to sit down in the driver's chair while he took the passenger seat and closed the cab door behind them. He pulled out a foldaway table, produced two small bottles of water from a tiny fridge, handed one to Mandy, set the other down on the table. The windscreen was heavily tinted, and there was a portable fan hanging from the rear-view.

'We can't run those computers and air-con at the same time,' he said, putting the cool water bottle to his forehead. 'And people think we're over-funded!'

Mandy opened his bottle and took a gulp. What the hell did the guy want from him?

'I am going to come straight to the point and speak candidly, sir.'

Did FBI agents even call their kids 'sir'?

'OK,' Mandy said. 'Please do, as it's hot and I have other stuff to do today.'

Anderson took a breath, held it, exhaled. 'First up, everything that we are about to discuss is *sub judice*, should be treated as secret or classified, and must not be disclosed to anyone.'

'Anyone ever at all?' Mandy said, coughing and clearing his throat.

Anderson picked up the beat and stared more intently. 'That includes your ex-partner, Terry, from Monterey, Fabienne and your housemate.'

'Donna, who is currently in Malibu Canyon, and even my mother from—'

'Oxford. It's our job to be well briefed on our sources. I will tell you when you can talk about it when the time comes. There are benefits of information from us for you. Do you agree to our terms?'

It was like being asked if he wanted a final card at poker when he had a fifty-fifty chance of winning and losing. Fact was, the odds in Santa Monica were worse. There wasn't much choice, so he nodded. Anderson took a moment to compose his thoughts and said, 'Tamara Tyrer was not, repeat not, involved in any political organization. She was simply a part-time hooker with a proclivity for visiting Russians. She was in the wrong place at the wrong time and a bullet destined for the deputy attorney general's head ricocheted into her chest.'

'So why am I going to be a good source for you?'

Anderson gave a humourless laugh. 'We're investigating intelligence that the Viceroy murders were committed with the backing of a criminal organization.'

'Still doesn't tell me why I'm here.'

'The organization is Russian – we believe they are working with an inform-ant inside the police.'

'LAPD, or SMPD?'

'Maybe the former, maybe closer to home.'

'Care to elaborate?'

'No.'

Mandy nodded. 'I'm afraid I'm out of touch with the Russian Mafia.'

Mandy stood up, leant his hands on the enormous dashboard and peered out through the window.

'Look,' Anderson said, 'I need information from you about colleagues in the SMPD. All the way to the top. And you know that cops don't like to tell us about other cops.'

'Damn right they don't.'

Anderson took another swig of water. 'OK,' he said. 'We believe there is serious corruption, and I am not talking about getting a free plate of spaghetti and meatballs at Luigi's every Friday night.'

'I must go and look for Luigi's,' Mandy said. 'I missed out on all the free stuff.'

'Maybe that's why there are people in the SMPD who'd like you off the scene.'

'Maybe so.'

Clarence Spider was the name he guessed was on Anderson's tongue. It was certainly the one on his own. It wasn't exactly a surprise.

'Is there any way for you to get us information?' Anderson said. 'Ex-colleagues?'

Mandy pictured Terry's expression on being asked his opinion.

'Most of them don't like me . . . British ex-actor and now a PI. Plus I didn't exactly leave with a heroic fanfare.'

'You had a breakdown and a whole heap of shit.'

Mandy smiled at Anderson's research and stared through the windscreen at the cool dreads guy tickling the strings of the Fender, his other hand slowly tapping the fretboard.

'Anything at all,' Anderson said. 'And maybe we can give you something. Nothing big . . . but . . .'

Mandy sucked in a lungful of air. He hated being reminded of the kiddy-porn case, and even more that any tosspot with reasonable security clearance could read his file.

'OK,' he said. 'You must have access to the membership of the Speed-Dating Club at the Viceroy . . . Did anything odd or a strange name come up? A guy called Dominic Young, or Lucy Lack, Susan Green, Johnny or Sarah Sternwood, for example?'

Anderson opened up a laptop, typed in a password, clicked on various files and stopped. 'Susan Green? Yes, she was a member, been going there for about six months. Dominic Young, Lucy Lack, Sarah and Johnny Sternwood, no. None of these people are relevant, believe me.'

'Maybe not to you and the Viceroy case.' Mandy stood up. 'I'll see what I can find out about the SMPD for you. No promises.'

Anderson nodded.

'One more thing,' Mandy said. 'Do you think I should have been looking at drug cartels in Mexico or any other foreign nationals for the García-Márquez murder?'

Anderson shook his head, upended the last of his bottle of water into his mouth. 'The Agency is not able to help in that area, sir.'

He scribbled on a blank business card and handed it to Mandy. 'Use this number if you have a helpful piece of information.'

Mandy moved towards the exit and called out over his shoulder, 'I'll be in touch.'

46

6 p.m., 19 July

'Meet me outside the Alhambra at six p.m.,' Terry's voice message started. 'I want to be entertained but not talk about Dawn, Florida or cancer.'

Mandy texted back, 'OK,' and in the time he had left bought some supplies from Continental, drove up Olympic to 12th and parked across the road from the Alhambra's blue neon sign. He was trying not to think about Lucy Lack and Adam Pollock, and was wondering how he could bypass the subject of the FBI with his old partner.

Terry was already there – leaning against a doorway, smoking a cigarette and gazing into space. Blond hair shorn, in long black shorts, loafers, no socks and a white loose-hanging shirt, one finger holding a jacket over his shoulder.

'Dude!' Mandy called through the window.

Terry raised his arm, straightened up, took two long puffs on his cigarette and threw the butt down a storm drain in the gutter. Mandy got out of the car and crossed the road. He could tell from the rubbery face and lopsided way in which he was standing that Terry was back on the steroids. Florida had clearly not been much of a holiday.

The Alhambra was a run-down cellar bar that had not been redecorated since 1975. The only Spanish thing about it was its name and the overplayed Gypsy Kings CD in between the tequila and the Jack Daniel's. Lonely people, ageing hookers and dangerously lost tourists made up its clientele.

They shook hands, said nothing and walked down the run of cast-iron steps. The place stank of forty years of smoke, mothballs and booze. Feet sticking to the orange carpet, probably older than them, they squeezed past some empty tables to get to the bar.

Two chubby Puerto Rican hookers, the wrong side of thirty, peroxide hair thick with hairspray, looked up from the other end of the bar, smiled and carried on talking. Terry sat down. Mandy slid onto the neighbouring bar stool.

The barman slouched over and scratched his stubble. 'What you having?'

'Coke.'

'Johnny Walker and water,' said Terry. 'Go easy on the water, no rocks.'

The barman repeated the order to himself and swung round to prepare them. Someone pressed 'play' on the bar's ancient jukebox. '*Bamboléo.*'

'*Hola, señor!*' the girls called out.

'Come on, girls, shake it!' Terry said, getting up.

The hookers slid off their bar stools and began dancing, arms aloft. Terry had long thought he was John Travolta. Mandy hated dancing, always felt like a self-conscious seal at a circus. But he enjoyed watching other people dance, their moves, their expressions.

He looked across at the hookers' swaying backsides and imagined them fifteen years before. Hot, horny and hopeful. Not like now, with probably only a few years left to go, if that. Terry didn't look too good either – red in the face and sweating, but what the fuck – he was laughing his head off. Enjoying himself as much as a frisky eighteen-year-old.

For the length of '*Bamboléo*' – and he hadn't realized just how long that track really was – Mandy watched the trio gyrating and grinding on the temporary dance floor, while slowly drinking his Coke.

The bartender called over, 'Another round?'

Mandy nodded, said, 'Yes, and add a double shot of brandy to the Coke, thanks.'

Terry sat down next to him, out of breath from the dance, took two sips of his whisky, clapped his hands and coughed for a minute. The chest and underarms of his shirt were stained with dark pools of sweat.

'You know what?' he said, leaning over towards Mandy. 'I don't want to die! I am not going to die. Too many things I want to do and see with my two girls.'

Mandy couldn't tell if Terry was being sarcastic or serious.

'You're sounding like Pacino in *Scent of a Woman*,' he said, hoping Terry would talk about something else.

Terry laughed and downed the remaining whisky. 'I meant it, you asshole!'

Mandy took the new drinks from the bartender, handed Terry his and drank two large gulps of his Coke and brandy.

'Listen, cut all the dying baloney. I thought that illness and death are not on the agenda, remember? Cheers!' He raised his glass in a toast.

Terry raised his glass too. 'Cheers!' Mandy banged his glass on Terry's so hard they nearly broke.

Terry finished his drink, grabbed a cigarette from his packet of Marlboro and pushed it between his lips.

The barman came over. 'I'm sorry, buddy, but the law is the law,' he said, pointing upwards to two security cameras attached to the ceiling over the bar and the cash till. 'I'll get canned if they see you smoking.'

Terry held up his hand in a 'stop' sign and took the cigarette from his mouth. 'No problem, man. I'm just giving my lips something to do while my friend drones on about his life. He even paid for the drinks, right?'

'That's correct, he did,' the barman said.

Terry fanned his sweat-soaked shirt, waved to the hookers and readjusted his position on the bar stool. 'So how goes it, bro? You winning?'

Mandy poured some peanuts down his throat and decided to leave the FBI stuff to last – didn't want to get sidetracked into talking about politics and the police, not when Terry was loaded.

'I'm getting closer but haven't nailed it yet.'

'Dude, you're not even two weeks into the investigation. Catching a murderer can take months, even years.'

'I haven't got years.'

'How did it shake down in Silver Lake?'

Mandy pulled out the two torn envelopes he'd taken from Knocks Avenue and joined them together on the bar. 'By sheer coincidence I discovered these . . .'

'In the trash can outside the house?' Terry smiled, winked and read out the address on each envelope. '"Mr Benny Tan, 2200 Knocks Ave . . ." and "B. Tan Esq., Fish Farm, North Channel Road, Santa Monica . . ."'

'Yes, so he's the guy who owns the house and the Range Rover.'

'And the tropical fish place in Santa Monica – Dawn's sister is nuts about it. Man, she loves those little blue ones.'

Mandy hadn't known Dawn's sister was a fish-fancier.

'You've been there?' he said.

'No, but apparently the place is coining it big time, so I'm not surprised the guy lives in Silver Lake.'

The barman set down another bowl of peanuts.

Mandy pushed the bowl towards Terry, cleared his throat and said, 'I'm trying to figure out why some woman working at Fish Farm should be parked outside 200 Ocean and leaving just about the same time as Quinn was murdered.'

Terry tapped his cigarette against the bar, packing the tobacco tightly. Old habits die hard.

'Maybe Quinn was so disappointed with the tropical fish she delivered he decided to end it all? Totally possible in this town of nuts.'

'Thanks for the insight, Terence.'

Terry scowled, knocked back a belt of whisky. 'OK, Professor, so she was working late. People work late these days – customer service – things can be delivered late as you like. Anyway, why are you so sure Quinn didn't kill himself? Did you get a time of death? Spoken to Frank yet?'

Mandy shook his head, grabbed a handful of peanuts and swallowed them. He wanted to tell Terry what a dickhead he'd been for not following up on Quinn sooner, but it was too late, and though Terry was back talking the talk, he looked like shit, so he shelved it.

'My gut says Quinn was murdered, but there weren't any signs of struggle when I found him. I couldn't get in the apartment, so it was difficult to tell.' Mandy paused to extract a piece of peanut stuck in his teeth.

'I don't believe that Janet woman was delivering tropical fish. Something weird about her and even weirder about the house in Silver Lake. Quinn's death was made to look like suicide. Probably by the same person who filleted Dominic Young and Pedro García-Márquez. Someone who was also a loyal customer of a Chinese supermarket.'

Terry leant back on his stool. 'You saying it's my fault now? Why didn't I chase Mr Quinn quicker?'

Terry was gravitating between being pleasantly boisterous and becoming an ugly drunk. Mandy guessed the mood was in part because he'd had a shit time in Florida and partly because he more than knew he wasn't cutting the mustard on the investigation front. Stage-three cancer was taking its toll on his mind.

'I'm not saying that. And you know it.'

A few moments of silence, broken by Mandy choosing 'Nutbush City Limits' on the jukebox. One of Terry's favourites.

'Now that's a great record. Thanks, fucker!'

'Guess who I just met with?'

'I don't know – Queen Elizabeth the Second?'

'J. Edgar Hoover would be closer.'

Terry raised his finger in the air. 'Bartender, could we have two more drinks and whatever the ladies are having too.'

The barman nodded in the two hookers' direction. Both girls raised their empty glasses.

Mandy leant towards Terry. 'And that's not all. Are you ready for this?'

'Surprise me.'

'Lucy Lack. And a scuzzball PI.'

'Told you she was up to her neck in it.'

'That's not all. She checked out of Shutters, to stay with a retired Hell's Angel friend of Pedro who has now disappeared himself, so she's sought solace at the Comfort Inn.'

'Comfort Inn from Shutters? And she's been fucking a friend of poor dead Pedro?'

'I didn't say fucking, did I?'

'Stop being so English – why else would she be with someone like that?'

Terry's mood had switched to pumped up and angry; whisky often brought out a destructive streak.

Mandy shook his head. 'Forget that – there's more. I went over to the Comfort this afternoon; she was in a meeting room with Adam Pollock. Do you remember him?'

'Why the fuck's she talking to him?'

'Don't know. Pedro? Revenge on the Sternwoods for their photo shoot? She's not a killer, though.'

He didn't mention the rifle on the table between her and Pollock.

Terry downed his whisky in one, shrugged and slowly wiped his mouth with a handkerchief. 'Yeah, but she might have hired a killer. You're getting obsessed with her and in the wrong way. You're letting this woman walk all over your judgement.'

'You don't know what you're talking about.'

'When are you going to stop running after the wrong fucking girl, you jerk? You know the FBI statistics – seventy-five per cent of male homicides are committed by a spouse, girlfriend or family member. Maybe your Lucy Lack didn't pull the trigger, but she had a hand in it . . . She's got a fucking Hopper painting *and* a house out of it, hasn't she?'

Terry swayed on his bar stool, put his elbows on the bar and rubbed his eyes. That normally meant he was past gone and running out of gas for the night. On three whiskies? And steroids? This was not a good sign.

'Dude, did you go to another bar before meeting me here?'

Terry stood up and finished his whisky in one hit. 'Why the fuck not? I've got a wife and family who are bugging the shit out of me and a tumour the size of a mouse.'

There wasn't just anger in his voice; there was fear. Mandy breathed out slowly, put his hand on Terry's shoulder.

Terry was swaying.

'Can I come and stay at your place for a few days? I need a break. We can crack this case together. What do you say?'

'Are you off your head? Stay at my place when you've got all that room service at home? You're crazier than I thought . . .'

The bartender set another whisky and a Coke on the bar. 'Compliments of the two ladies.'

They both swung round, hands raised in thanks, but the women had supped up and left for the night.

Terry took a generous sip from his new whisky. Mandy didn't touch his Coke. He stood up and leant on the bar with two hands.

'How much do you think someone like the Giraffe earns a year?' said Mandy.

'Depends whether you are talking officially or *unofficially*,' Terry said.

'Do you think he's straight? I think he's a seriously weird fuck myself,' Mandy said, lifting the glass of Coke to his lips.

'A "weird fuck" is a polite description for that control freak. He has no kids, no wife, just him.' Terry paused to wipe his mouth on the back of his hand, then carried on: 'My guess is that he doesn't need any extra money – just likes to get even with a few people, that's all. Maybe if it weren't for Fabienne, he'd get even with you.'

Mandy thought about this for a moment.

'I never did that weird fucker any harm. Wish I had.' He added a cynical laugh.

Terry nodded. 'The wife being murdered is what made the Giraffe tick the wrong way. That's the reason for him being such a fuckhead. Get it?'

Suddenly Terry yawned, folded his arms on the bar and laid his head on them. He was totally bushed. Mandy looked at his watch: twenty past seven.

He asked the barman for the check.

A good sleep and knowing that Dawn and the kids would be back soon and old Terry would be Detective Insightful again. No harm in hoping.

'Hey, dickhead, there's a Swedish taxi outside. Not forgetting a great-looking English driver offering you a free ride back to Echo Park.'

Terry didn't lift his head from the bar. 'Broadski and Dent are far more likely to be putting their hand in the chum, if you really want to know,' he said. 'I can probably think of one or two others, providing I can smoke in your precious car . . .'

'Keep talking and smoke as many cigarettes as you like.'

47

9.30 p.m., 19 July

The drive back to Terry's house in Echo Park had reconfirmed what he liked and respected about Terry: his resilience, humour, eventual reliability and ability to fall asleep, snore and totally forget he'd been roaring drunk. But Terry living in Donna's old room was never going to happen. For all of his bad-tempered discontent, Terry was a marshmallow on the inside – he loved Dawn and the kids too much to spend any real time apart from them.

Three minutes from home and revving the engine at a red light on PCH, Mandy punched in *The Long Good Friday* on the stereo; a saxophone began playing in a minor key. It was the moment in the film when the gang leader realizes there is a Judas in his organization. Mandy gazed at the deep, shimmering ocean and swallowed hard as he imagined Dominic Young's dead body inside the green suitcase, floating on its surface.

The lights changed; he turned into Castellammare Drive. The security light from the phoney garage shone on the Amazon's bonnet as always. He pushed the front-door key in the lock. Two things were odd. The door was not triple-locked and no cat with its hungry meow.

A small shark swam into the shoal of endorphins in Mandy's head. He stepped back and looked down at the gravel drive. Nothing seemed disturbed. There must be a perfectly logical explanation as to why the door was unlocked. Yet he definitely remembered triple-locking it when he left that morning.

Inside, apart from an odd smell, reminiscent of a dry cleaner's, nothing was out of place. A stack of DVDs and paperwork were on the glass coffee table just as they'd been for months; the cushions were still spread on the sofa and armchair. Mandy spotted his reflection in the polished TV screen.

He flicked the TV onto CNN, muted it, went into the kitchen and took out a pack of sausages from the fridge. It felt like someone else was inside the house – a loud silence that brought the hairs up on the back of your neck. He ignored it. Stabbed holes in both sides of the sausages with a fork, put them in a pan, added a dash of oil, lit the gas and left them to it.

Still. It was odd. Sausages usually meant the cat appearing. He went to the back door, unlocked it.

'Ned!'

No sign.

He walked onto the upper deck and down the steps. His own heart thumping; speeding road hogs on PCH; wafting laughter as people said goodbye at the end of a party; parrots cackling in the trees. The smell of sizzling sausages wafted down the steps to the lower floor like a siren calling . . .

He rattled the handle on the guest apartment. 'Anybody there?'

No, the door was locked and nothing moved through the bedroom window but pitch dark.

'What the hell are you worrying about?' he muttered to himself as he climbed back up the rickety wooden steps.

In the kitchen once more, he flipped the sausages and turned down the heat.

Time for a shower. He stank of the Alhambra.

He opened the door and switched on the bathroom light.

Ping. The light bulb died. Fuck, he'd forgotten to buy any. He cursed, kicked off his shoes, pulled off his tie and shirt, threw them on the floor, stepped out of his trousers and shorts, and remembered where he'd put some candles left over from a bad dinner date two years ago. Showering by candlelight – how Lucy Lack would approve. He padded into the kitchen, naked, knelt down on the sticky floor by the cupboard under the sink, pulled out a candle, pushed it into an empty wine bottle. He lit it and shuffled out of the kitchen along the hall and into the bathroom. He balanced the candle on the toilet seat.

Then he leant into the shower. Something dark caught his eye. He yanked the curtain back, grabbed a candle and held it up.

'No! You bastards!'

He swung round, put the bottle down in the basin and covered his mouth with his hand.

It was his cat, Ned, hanging in a noose from the showerhead.

He lifted the cat up from underneath, loosened the electric flex away from the curved pipe of the showerhead. The noose was tightly coiled round Ned's neck; the fur was silky-smooth but not warm. The cat's pink tongue was hanging out of the side of his mouth, green eyes staring straight ahead.

Mandy placed a clean white towel on the bathroom floor, laid Ned on one side and covered him with the other. The motionless body, so completely still, had a small, sticky trickle of blood oozing down its chin. Someone had done this in the last four hours.

He ran into the office, grabbed a pair of pliers, rushed back and cut the noose from Ned's neck. It was only then that he saw the beige luggage label tied with a single piece of string to Ned's collar. '*BACK OFF.*'

He stood looking at the label, veins and arteries pumping with injustice and rage. The creature he had fed and looked after for twelve years, the one thing that had stayed with him, through thick and thin.

'And vengeance shall be mine, and vengeance shall be fucking mine,' he said. He couldn't stop – kept repeating the phrase more and more loudly, first like a prayer and then like a chant. An enormous pressure of anger was about to explode. He stood up and threw the wine bottle into the bathroom mirror. It shattered and fell into the basin. Shards ricocheted into Mandy's legs; one lodged in the black fur of the cat's right ear.

He picked up Ned and held him in the folded towel like a child. It was only a cat, he kept telling himself, just a cat. But it didn't feel like that.

He chose to bury the cat in a spot beneath the branches of his neighbour's almond tree. It was one of Ned's favourite places to sleep. The parched summer ground was hard as rock, so he hosed down the earth and realized, too, that the best way of digging a two-and-a-half-foot hole was take a swig of tequila every time he dug out a spade full of earth.

One foot down, he stopped digging, took a slug of tequila and texted Donna that Ned had been killed on the road in front of the house. Ned was the closest thing either of them had ever had to a friendly room-mate. At least she had the two goldfish to keep her company.

A text pinged back almost immediately.

'Jeez, Mandy, I'm not allowed to call but am bawling my eyes out. That's the worst shit I've heard all year. I'm praying for the big furry guy – he was the best!'

Mandy exhaled in relief, wondering what Donna might have done if he had told her the cat had been hanged.

Eventually, after completing the burial and having drunk nearly half the bottle of tequila, he came inside. He walked into his office, teary-eyed and yawning, and switched on his desktop.

Clicking onto three search engines at the same time, he put in 'Fish Holdings', 'Fish Farm, Inc.' and 'Fish Farm UK'. A website emerged for the first two, and a link to a Scottish salmon and mussel farm for the UK entry. In addition, further down the list, was the annual companies' statutory and fiscal report that every company in the US was obliged to file.

Mandy scratched his balls as the files unfolded. Then he found the correct site. Fish Farm Santa Monica *and* a reference to Fish Farm Holdings, but no address. It was an expensive, smart, clearly laid-out website. He ignored 'Fish',

'Price Plans', 'Welfare & Maintenance', 'Location' and 'Delivery Service', and clicked on 'History & Achievements'. Fish Farm was a sizeable business with a long history, boring awards for hygiene, helping disabled people, men returning to the community from prison, and donations to a charity called Dentistry Sans Frontiers, which sounded like a bad joke from *Saturday Night Live*.

Then he saw the name 'Janet Lee, Vice President' next to a photograph of the lady with the Range Rover, except in this picture she was smiling. The nut with the odd hairstyle. He clicked on the name 'Benny Tan, Chairman and CEO' – he was late fifties, well groomed, Chinese American, perfect teeth and cheesy smile.

He stood up from the computer and lifted files and papers on the desk, checked beneath the computer and printer but still couldn't find the photos of Susan Green and Janet Lee. Categorically, unequivocally, he had left them by the computer yesterday morning and now they were not there. He checked the bathroom, bedroom, upended the cushions on the sofa, opened every kitchen drawer and cupboard, even the gummy carpet underneath his desk, but the file of photos was nowhere to be seen.

His mind started to race. Where the hell were the García-Márquezes? They must have returned from Mexico by now. He remembered the protocol and texted Miguel.

Then he went back to his list of possible hangmen. Spinning an empty beer bottle, he came on Lucy Lack hiring Adam Pollock to kill Ned . . . Why? Why would she say, 'Back off,' like that? Was he getting too close? No. If anything, she had hired Pollock to find out who killed Pedro and where Wing had disappeared to. And also more than likely to protect her backside when it came to the family and their accusations that she'd used undue influence on Pedro to bequeath her the Hopper and the cottage in Mexico. Why the hell hadn't she asked him? Why ask that bullshitting clotheshorse Pollock? Had he really upset her that much, or did she just think he was too thick to find the killer?

If she was going to use Pollock to drop the Sternwoods further down in the shit, find some dirt that would stick to the palate of a juror, he could live with that. Mrs García-Márquez was hanging their arses out to dry right now in Mexico City anyway. He wiped his eyes, stretched his arms over his shoulders, breathed out.

Could it be a García-Márquez – one who did not want him to get any closer to the truth than he already had? Alfonso or Miguel or Mrs García-Márquez sprang to mind. That family certainly had its share of skeletons in walk-in closets. No. Stop going down that road again. They were the ones who'd lost their son and brother. He took a long pull of tequila and kicked over the empty waste-paper bin.

Who would want the photos and to warn him off? Janet Lee was ticking quite a few boxes. She had to be a serious contender.

Terry's calm-but-annoying voice came into his head. '*Dude, you're not even two weeks into the investigation. Catching a murderer can take months, even years.*'

Mandy grunted, pulled open the middle desk drawer and retrieved a pack of index cards, took out a marker pen and created new cards for Pedro, Dominic Young, Quinn and Ned, all with the word '*Deceased*' at the top. On different-coloured cards, the people who were missing: Susan Green, Wing and, for good measure, Stevie, the guy Father Tony was always banging on about who was missing from the shelter.

Just looking at the pile of cards he remembered something. The free dentist Father Tony had mentioned regarding the homeless guy, Stevie, who needed—

Fish Farm. Supporting your local dental charity.

That would tie a few people together.

But how?

He rearranged the cards on the desk. And added one card that said, 'Alfonso?' on it, and, 'Drugs?' Hell, maybe Alfonso had killed Pedro just because Pedro kept trying to get him clean? People had killed for less.

Mandy padded back into the sitting room, lay down on the sofa and switched on the TV. What the hell had happened to Scottish Ray? He tapped out a text saying, 'Ray, you lazy bastard, send your report immediately, please,' and pressed 'send'.

Within two minutes he'd received a reply: 'On the case! Check your email in twenty minutes.'

Mandy pictured Ray scurrying around his flat, assembling bits of hand-written notes he'd stuffed in trouser pockets to put together the information. The tequila and emotional energy used in the aftermath of Ned's death made him feel heavy and tired. He crashed out into a deep sleep, wondering why anyone would harm his old cat and how there would never be another one.

6 a.m., 20 July

He woke five hours later, CNN blaring and Fox playing in the bedroom. Both stations were still running with the 'mystery of the Viceroy motive'.

He made himself feel better by yelling, 'How about talking about who killed my cat!'

He sighed and got up, his head killing him from tequila and anger, brushed his teeth and shaved in the kitchen sink, unwilling to even look at the shower. It was difficult to stop thinking about why anyone would want to kill Ned. He needed to distract himself, change the subject. So he strode into his office and sat down in front of his computer. He clicked on his inbox and highlighted Scottish Ray's email report. Mandy read it aloud, overdoing a Glaswegian accent to cheer himself up.

To: Mandy
From: Scottish Ray
Subject: Lucy Lack
Date: Slightly later than anticipated

OK, Big Man,
You're certainly getting your money's worth from me! I've been travelling all over London and am completely knackered. All right for the likes of you, sunning yourself on the beach, no doubt! I went to the City and found the pub where all the Steel Bond traders drink after work. I explained I was a writer/ director researching a film about difficult women working in the City – did they know any? It worked like a treat! They totally believed me and it didn't take long to get three of them to spill the beans on our subject.

Found out your girl is currently suspended on full pay pending a disciplinary hearing – financial irregularity? No one sure but no way is she a senior trader . . . She's a junior and prone to exaggerate her status. Reputation of a hothead with balls . . . temperamental, hard-working, not good with sexism – punched two male colleagues in the three years she's been there but remained in the job. Not known for buying a round or ever stumping up loose change at the casino they visit.

Sorry to disappoint you but sadly no porn form at all. Nothing, nada, nix, and I know all the right and *wrong* places to check. Clean as a whistle, not even a photo on Facebook. So I went to see her mother in Battersea. Two-bedroom flat, nice road. Mum as highly strung as a cello, dotes on her daughter. Didn't know anything about her being suspended from work. Does now! Found out Lack has paid all the bills, mortgage, mother's clothes and holidays for the last seven years, put herself through university at same time. The kindest girl on two legs. Father buggered off when she was a kid, yada, yada. More boyfriends than you could shake a stick at – only one American for the last four years – but hasn't met the right man. I said I knew a couple of candidates but Mum said, 'Forget it,' as most men are bastards, especially ones from overseas. Before I left, she showed me photos of Lucy. When am I coming over to stay? Classy or what!
Hope this helps. Want me to keep digging?
Och aye, from your faithful pal in London,
Ray

235

Mandy printed a copy and stood up. Beneath Ray's jocularity lay the makings of a highly effective snoop, capable of loosening the tongues of the most hard-hearted of people. His weak points were clichés, amphetamines, Internet dating and expensive hotels. The email left an odd taste in Mandy's mouth. He'd not forgotten that Lucy Lack had hired Pollock to report on his personal life. That had pissed him off, yet the gall of it had amused him.

Using his own private eye made him feel as if he'd been cheating on his wife, read someone's private diary. How stupid was that? Why did he feel like that? All is fair in love and war, isn't it? Hearing about Lucy's domestic circumstances was damning. But however noble she was in taking care of her mother, there now appeared to be even more of a motive for her to see Pedro dead. Borrow against the Hopper painting, pay off the Sternwoods, two fingers to the disciplinary hearing to go hang, and buy her mother her own flat. She was sorted and had enough cash and a cottage in Mexico to last for the rest of her life. Perhaps María García-Márquez's instincts were correct. Lucy Lack was a bloodsucker, roadkill dressed up as prime steak. Pedro was dead, so who was she planning to shoot with the rifle?

Before he'd finished reading Ray's report again, two calls came into his cell one after the other – why the fuck did he ever have two lines?

It was seven thirty-four. He hadn't even brushed his teeth.

Donna again . . . The other: Eduardo García-Márquez.

The text to Miguel had worked.

He pushed 'answer'.

'Donna, hang on, or I'll call you back?'

He switched to García-Márquez.

'Mandy' – García-Márquez sounded tired – 'I'll come straight to the point. My wife and I are at Santa Monica Airport, refuelling in more ways than one, and I wondered if you could get over here for a progress meeting.'

It was the last thing he wanted to do, but the guy was paying him.

'Sure. What kind of plane?'

'Gulfstream G550, parked near the control tower. We have to leave in less than two hours. My wife is unwell.'

'I'll be there in half an hour.'

He reconnected to Donna.

'I'm back. So what's up? You OK?' Mandy said.

'Do you want to know where the best smack deals are being done in Santa Monica?'

'I might do. How did you come by this information?'

Donna lowered her voice. 'Look, they'd go mad here if they found out I was snitching stuff I'd heard during the NA meeting last night. Right?'

'Yes, but I am not making you do that. You're going to tell me something because it's in the public interest and you want to be a part of that, right?'

'Next thing you're gonna tell me is that this call is being recorded. I love it when you manipulate me like that!'

Mandy shook his head and smiled. 'Donna, fuck off and give me the facts.'

'Well, maybe everyone knows this, but I sure as hell didn't.'

'Knows what?'

'That there is some little market where spaced-out, Ferrari-driving smack-heads go to score their shit. Best prices, super-fucking-duper best merchandise and easy to park. Comes in by plane every fortnight at the local airport, on a Cessna Skylab or something – they'll cut your balls off if they know you know.'

'Have these guys been clean for a long time?'

'No! Three days clean now and going nuts – hence the offloading.' Donna almost squealed. 'But these guys have been buying in bulk by the kilo from a Chinky market on Cloverfield. They talk like they're dealers to Hollywood A-list, top hotels, the polo set and art world. Make any sense?'

'Are you sure about all this and the Cessna?'

'Two of the guys here *used* to own planes there. They lost all their dough doing smack and were moaning about *their* dealer having all their money now and the same plane to boot. Do you get it?'

'I get it, and thank you. Your reward will be in heaven, if not before.'

'That cat better be in heaven. Did you bury him in the garden?'

'Yes. In the shade of the almond tree.'

'Aw, that is so great. You know what? I think you really loved that cat and . . .'

While Donna cooed about Ned's death, Mandy interjected the odd word but let his mind connect Chung and the receipts found on Pedro, Dominic Young and Quinn.

It made sense.

Wayne Chung had not just been unforthcoming; he'd been downright evasive about the CCTV footage – just like Quinn. It was time to play hardball. The more Donna talked, the more Mandy wanted to drive round to the store on Cloverfield and punch Chung in the throat.

By the time he'd left the house, he felt electrified to have a target to aim at last.

48

8.45 a.m., 20 July

'Nice plane, if you've got the money,' the information guy said, pointing to a sixteen-windowed, pearl-white jet parked a hundred metres away at the end of a line of smaller planes near the control tower. Mandy nodded and headed over.

He flashed his ID to the barrel-chested security guard and ran up the steps. Although he didn't expect the door of the plane to be opened by a uniformed hostess, he was surprised to be greeted by Mrs García-Márquez, wearing a black hunting jacket and jodhpurs and holding a Polaroid camera.

'Smile, please!'

Mandy thought about getting paid. The camera flashed.

He stepped inside, pulling the heavy door shut behind him.

'Is Signor García-Márquez on board?'

'No, he is off the board but returning in about a quarter of an hour,' Mrs García-Márquez said.

She unsteadily pulled the Polaroid print from the camera and waved it in the air. 'I like these old things, don't you?'

The brandy fumes on her breath were enough to anaesthetize a horse.

Mandy took hold of the photograph and peered at it, buying time to determine whether his host was utterly sloshed or on something more serious. It wasn't a good Polaroid. It resembled a poor man's Lucien Freud.

Mrs García-Márquez snatched back the picture.

'I'm keeping a record of everyone coming aboard,' she said, sellotaping Mandy's Polaroid up onto a luggage locker with ten others, all equally blurry.

'Great idea,' he said, looking down the cabin for her husband or any members of staff.

'It's not a bad old bird as planes go. Of course, you probably have a much better one yourself, don't you?'

He grinned. 'I travelled in one a few times, but not with such nice people.'

'Ah, flattery, Mr Mandy, will get you everywhere.'

He flashed a fake smile. He wanted to bring up Alfonso's love affair with heroin and how Pedro had tried to help, the Sternwoods and, for good measure, to drop the name Chung. But it was a waste of time because she wasn't listening. She was jabbering and rapping about the plane's attributes and sounding like Stan in *South Park*. Mandy grabbed hold of the headrest of a seat and zoned out.

The plane was vaguely similar to the one he and Terry had travelled in on their last case four years ago. Both planes were privately owned and furnished with wide seats and sofas, and there the similarity ended. The sixteen wide cream leather armchairs in the García-Márquez plane resembled an expensive hairdresser. The decor was modern nouvelle, save for a crucifix hanging beneath a portrait of Pedro on one wall and a couple of polo mallets balanced over two seats. The other jet had been a much larger Boeing, but far older, its carpets and seat covers stained and badly worn. The other big difference lay in the personnel, and the use of film cameras to make porn shows with barely teenage girls.

'Don't you think, Mandy? Don't you think?'

Mandy jolted back into the 'now'. Valeria García-Márquez had stopped gabbling and was on the move, pulling herself along the aisle by the headrests, aiming for the captain's cabin. She came to a stop, picked up a white hairdryer from a seat and crouched down as if she was a cop holding a gun and thought Mandy an intruder.

She dropped the stance after a few seconds, then carried on speaking as if nothing had happened.

'I take it you know about Josefina's friend Quinn?' she said.

It was the first thing she had said that made any real sense. But Josefina's *friend*? The nanny?

Mandy scratched his eyebrow.

Keep calm.

'Yes, I know about Mr Quinn.'

He cleared his throat and straightened his tie. 'When did you all return from Mexico?'

'We have not all returned, Mandy. Pedro and Johnny and Sarah Sternwood are still there.' Mrs García-Márquez smiled a tight smile.

Like everything else she had said, it was convincing in tone but ultimately didn't make sense. Circuits inside her brain appeared to be shorting out and producing lucid but illogical bits of speech. If he hadn't witnessed her behaviour at her son's wake, he could have felt quite sympathetic.

'Mandy, I know what you're saying and how clever you are. But don't go

239

shooting your mouth off or you could end up biting the hand that feeds you. And my husband has very big hands, doesn't he?'

'Big hands, yes, Mrs García-Márquez.'

'*In vino veritas*, Mandy, eh, don't you agree?'

'Quite so, Mrs—'

'He left this for you.'

She reached inside her hunting jacket and pulled out an envelope.

He took the envelope and peeked inside. It contained a cheque. 'Thank you.'

'My husband decided to go to Mass at St Monica's. He hasn't come to terms with Pedro's death, poor man. Goodbye, Mr Mandy.'

She pointed the hairdryer at the exit as if she was holding a Colt .45. He needed no second bidding: in seconds he was out of the door and down the steps of the plane.

At the bottom of the steps, he felt sick. Shaky. He crouched down behind the staircase in spitting distance of one of the tyres. Electric flashbacks of the clapped-out Boeing 727 four years ago and the child-porn gang illuminated his brain. His arms were restrained by two bodyguards. Terry already handcuffed in the seat by the emergency exit three rows behind. The pornographers cheering on a buck-toothed man to ease down the pants of an unwilling thirteen-year-old girl.

'Go on! Go on do it, do it . . .'

Mandy head-butted the two thugs behind him, flicking his head back so hard their faces exploded in blood and gristle. Then he grabbed hold of the buck-toothed man and, taking his head in both hands, yanked it round till his neck snapped. Even now Mandy could hear the sound of it breaking. He hadn't known that he had it inside him to be so angry.

But that was then.

He looked around him. The 'now' – Santa Monica Airport, surrounded by the wheels and landing gear of private planes. The sharp smell of aviation fuel. A woman dressed in a white tunic and a security guard were running towards the plane.

The woman was carrying a chrome tray, a white cloth over its contents. It didn't look like room service. A broad-shouldered man dressed in an immaculate dark suit walked briskly past the medic towards him. Three other people in the distance. Mandy stood up, breathed out as he recognized the suited man as García-Márquez and walked towards him.

'You OK? You look shaken up,' García-Márquez said.

'Your wife is a bit distressed in there.'

García-Márquez placed a sympathetic hand on Mandy's shoulder and barked some instructions in Spanish to the medic. Miguel, María and Alfonso

García-Márquez joined them from a black sedan, all looking pale.

'I'm sorry but we have no time now,' García-Márquez said. 'I wanted to have a conference, see if there was something we hadn't covered about Pedro. But my wife is very sick and we must take her to Minnesota, where she'll be taken care of.'

'I'm sorry.'

García-Márquez stepped beside Mandy so that he would not be overheard by his children.

Mandy angled his head to catch the look in García-Márquez's eye. It was steely and dark, not the type of man to be on the wrong side of.

'And if you were thinking that my wife could have killed Pedro, don't think it. She may not have been the best mother to him, or any of them, but she's not a murderer.'

'I never thought that she was,' Mandy said truthfully.

He could hear Mrs García-Márquez shouting and swearing inside the plane. The medic and security guard rushed up the steps like a SWAT team.

García-Márquez forced a smile, stepped away and put his arm around his daughter's shoulder. 'Find Pedro's killer, please. Few things matter to me but my children, as you may have understood – dead and alive – do. *Adiós.*'

Mandy walked away from the family and their gleaming plane towards the main airport building. He did not look back, even when he heard the aircraft door open and Mrs García-Márquez shouting, 'Don't touch me, you ugly bitch!'

Five minutes later he was outside Chung's on Cloverfield, listening to Bernard Herrmann's 'Taxi Driver' and wishing he had a Trebor mint. There was a bitter taste in his mouth: a mixture of images of Ned, Valeria García-Márquez and, far worse, the teen-porn case. Not a pleasant flavour.

And damn, he had to meet Frank at the morgue in less than an hour's time. He put his hazards on and ran into the store. There were only three or four people, and a shop assistant pricing tins with a labelling gun.

He walked up to the open till. 'Chung here?'

'Mr Chung's not here.'

Mandy squeezed his fist, itching to punch someone. 'Wayne Chung?'

The girl didn't take her eyes off the open cash drawer. 'He's away too.'

Wayne Chung came out of a stockroom.

'Hello! Wayne!' Mandy called out. 'Apparently you're away.'

Chung looked up, trying to figure out who was calling him. But before he had time to focus, Mandy was up next to him.

'Great to see you after all this time,' he said, spun him round and pushed him straight back into the stockroom, locking the door behind them.

'What's this about? You were the man asking about CCTV?' Chung said, frowning. His hand twitched, near his pocket. Mandy beat him to it and pulled out a small gun, a shiny black .22 with a pearl handle. A Ladysmith. Mandy smiled.

'And one or two cash receipts – that's right. I knew you had a good memory . . . Now shut up and sit down.'

He pointed to a chair with the Ladysmith. Chung eased his shaking legs under the table. On it were a stapler, a grey file, a large-screen laptop; against the grey wall behind it stood a new safe, three feet high, with a large dial, one giant tin of soya and two freezer chests – the type you choose ice cream from.

Each one was locked with two silver padlocks.

That must be some very expensive ice cream.

On the right-hand side of the room, four CCTV screens showed the shop, interior and exterior.

'You can make this easy or you can make this hard, Chung. There's no need to be nervous. You know why I'm here. Three of your cash receipts have been found on people who have been murdered.'

'We're a popular store.' Chung was staring at the safe and the refrigerators, sweat pouring off his forehead, though the air-con was near freezing.

Mandy held up the crumpled receipt that he'd found in Dominic Young's nose. 'Recognize it?'

Chung blinked and kept staring at the safe.

'Hey, why d'you keep staring at the safe? Afraid I'm going to rob you?'

The man gave a nervous grunt, leapt from the table and rammed his head into Mandy's chest. Mandy tensed his body just in time and brought his knee up into Chung's nose. Blood spurted. The man screamed out in pain. Mandy pinioned his hands with a pair of old cuffs, forced a handkerchief into his mouth and sat him back down on the chair.

He searched Chung's pockets, found a set of keys.

'Safe, or freezer?' he asked.

Chung did not reply.

Mandy smiled.

'Freezer first.'

He opened the padlocks on the left-hand freezer. Inside were two stacks of white polystyrene boxes that smelt of fish. He opened one. Empty. So was the next. This was pissing him off. Who the hell kept empty boxes in a padlocked freezer? He picked up the rest, shook them. Same weight, also empty.

Christ Almighty. Had he made a big mistake and overstepped the mark with Chung? Broadski and Dent would laugh till Christmas if he got a battery and kidnapping rap.

Shit.

He closed the lid and stepped away just in time to see Chung shaking his head in admonishment. Jesus. Had he really fucked up here?

A sixth sense made him push open the lid of the freezer again. Examine one of the boxes. On its side. He could just make out the word 'TOANGA.' Topanga? Where Susan Green said she took Dominic Young to try and return whatever it was he'd stolen.

'Nothing in that freezer. Before I try the safe, I'll have a quick look in the other one.'

Chung rocked in the chair, blood dripping from his nose; it sounded like he was about to suffocate.

'It hurts, doesn't it? I hate it when it happens to me.'

Mandy unlocked the second padlock and opened the freezer.

Chung toppled off the chair, the pens from his shirt pocket falling onto the floor, and started to crawl towards Mandy.

'Wayne, I thought I told you to remain seated?'

Mandy kicked him hard on his right elbow.

Chung doubled up in agony.

'One moment, please,' Mandy said, as his hand burrowed deep inside the freezer and pulled out two brown plastic slabs. 'I don't remember finding anything like this at my local store. I've obviously been going to the wrong place.'

He forced the man back into the chair, placed the receipt and one of the slabs of heroin on the table and sat down opposite.

'Now, let's cut to the chase. Of course, I realize you don't know how the freezer came to be filled with bags of heroin. Personally, I'm not interested, but the cops will be, and they're going to be here in five minutes.'

So saying, he pulled out his cell and texted the code for a drug bust and the address to the desk sergeant at the SMPD.

Chung shook his head defiantly.

Mandy pulled out the gag. 'Tell me about the receipts and where those boxes go in Topanga Canyon.'

The guy looked at the receipt and shook his head. 'No way.' He pushed the receipt away with his cuffed hands as if it contained explosives.

Mandy picked it up and held it up to the light. For the first time he saw something imprinted on the back – an impression from someone writing on top of a pile of receipts. He had never noticed it before – it had always been crumpled. Pedro's receipt didn't have an imprint: he'd checked that one. He laid the receipt flat, picked up a pencil from the floor and shaded the back of it. It revealed a twelve-letter clue: '*DOG FOOD CHAIN.*'

He placed the receipt back in his wallet.

'What's the "dog chain" all about?'

A high-pitched siren was blaring up Cloverfield. He stood up, bent down and pulled Chung towards him by the lapels on his jacket. 'What's it mean?'

Chung's face went ashen. He shook his head, let out a deathly sigh and shook his head again, beads of sweat covering his forehead. Then he seemed to crumple.

'Chain is trying to frame me, but he's not as smart as he thinks he is.'

'Who the hell is Chain?' Mandy pushed the barrel of the gun in Chung's right ear.

Chung swallowed.

'One night after we'd closed, he came in from the airport demanding food for his dogs. Because he was very aggressive, I said, "Forget it – it's too late. Go home." He became angry, but still I didn't let him in. Since then he's tried to involve me in his terrible crimes. The guy's insane, totally crazy.'

'Who does Chain work for?'

Wayne Chung exhaled through his mouth and looked up at the ceiling.

'Did Chain like eating tortilla chips? Was he a regular customer?'

Chung's eyes widened with fear. He lifted his fingertips and shook his head. Mandy knew he wasn't going to get any more but gave it one more try.

'I am going to ask you again – who does Chain work for?'

Chung looked away. Mandy guided the stub of the gun down to Chung's mouth. It was crude but necessary. Chung's eyes bulged. He then opened his mouth and stuck his chin forward, like a baby wanting food. The guy was terrified, and it wasn't of Mandy.

He'd obviously said too much, and wasn't saying any more.

Mandy replaced the gag, nodded his appreciation, removed the handcuffs and left the packet of heroin and the small handgun just out of reach. Ignoring the sullen looks from the checkout girl, he walked out through the busy store.

Outside, a squad car screeched to a halt and two young cops leapt out. They were the rookies from 200 Ocean.

Mandy jumped into the Amazon. As its engine started, he heard one gun-shot. A small calibre, exactly like you'd get from a .22 Ladysmith.

Whatever Chung knew had gone with him.

He pictured the rookies discovering Chung's body and a freezer full of heroin. Three cherries on each of their fruit machines – promotion toot sweet. But the guy who really mattered – or the woman – was whoever Chung had been so afraid of.

49

White rubber boots squeaking on the white tiled floor, Mandy pushed through the swing doors of the morgue. Frank and Foxy were working on a cadaver, which smelt pretty bad. He'd decided not to mention what had happened at Chung's. He still didn't want Frank or Foxy being linked to him taking evidence from a crime scene. Maybe the receipts he'd found on the corpses of Quinn, Pedro and Dominic Young were coincidences, but it was far more likely to be the calling card of a killer. Whatever they were, he was saying nothing to no one right now.

'This is a surprise. We thought you'd left town,' Frank said sarcastically, without taking his eyes from the slimy grey brain he was easing out of the body's skull.

'Hey, Mandy. Long time no see,' Foxy said, emptying the contents of the stomach into a large glass jar, holding a suction hose as if it was a vacuum cleaner.

'Busy City Arizona?'

'Yes, you could say we are maxed out!' Foxy said, gesturing to two other shrouded bodies horizontal on a table behind her and snorting a giggle.

Mandy chuckled politely, adjusted the mask over his nose, took a deep breath and tried to look at the ID tag tied to the dead man's toe.

'Would this be Quinn, by any chance?'

Frank dangled a retractor over the skull cavity. 'You're a bit late,' he said. 'Foxy already did that one pretty well all by herself, didn't you?'

The hot redhead turned to Mandy, pulled down her mask and smiled. 'Six o'clock this morning. First one I have ever done from top to bottom, start to nearly finish.'

'Meaning Frank applied some finishing touches?'

Foxy smiled. 'You have to have the master's approval or it wouldn't be right, would it?'

'So what was cause of death?' Mandy said, catching Frank's tired eyes watching him.

Foxy raised her eyebrows towards Frank. 'OK to tell him?'

Frank shrugged. 'Sure. Why not?' he said.

'Cause of death was strangulation, asphyxiation. He hanged himself, but not very professionally.'

'There seems to be a lot of hanging going on in Santa Monica at the moment.'

'Why do you say that?' Frank asked.

Mandy stepped towards the autopsy table, yanked down his mask for ultimate impact and said, 'Because somebody hanged my cat last night.'

Foxy let out a cry. 'No!'

'Yes. In my bathroom using electric flex.'

'Jesus!' she said. 'How awful. You must be devastated. How old?'

'Twelve.'

Frank shook his head. 'There are so many sick people around.' He rubbed his gloved hands together and said wistfully, 'Do you think it was Donna? Revenge of a sick puppy?'

'Donna? She loved that cat.'

'Not so long ago you thought she was a witch. They like killing cats.'

Mandy pictured naked Donna sipping coffee in his bed. 'Don't worry – she was asleep in Springfield Rehab in Malibu Canyon. I checked.'

'So someone else is trying to put the frighteners on you? Or some sick random prank?' said Frank, pressing his scalpel into the left lobe of the dead man's brain.

'The first, I think . . . Unless it was someone's idea of helping me cut down on my grocery bills.' Mandy forced a sarcastic smile.

Frank didn't react.

Mandy continued, 'There was a "back off" note attached to the cat's collar. I think it's connected to the Pedro García-Márquez and Dominic Young case and—'

Frank held up his hand for silence. 'Listen, you should know that Broadski and Dent are due here any minute. I know they are looking for your blood, so maybe you should scram,' he said.

'Appreciate that,' Mandy said, smiling at Foxy.

She smiled back at him.

'There's nothing I can do to stop them,' Frank said.

He sounded pissed off, like he'd been reprimanded over something.

'Frank, have you got time for a coffee?' Mandy said.

'I don't think the folks in Café Rebublica would be too pleased to see me like this.' Frank pointed to his blood-spattered gown.

Mandy laughed. 'You've got a point. I'll go and have one on my own,' he said. 'But are you sure Quinn wasn't murdered?'

Frank scratched his withered ear and looked over at Foxy. 'Tell him what you found.'

Foxy wiped her nose on the sleeve of her gown and turned to face Mandy. 'Quinn was going to die anyway.'

'How come?'

Foxy looked over at Frank. 'He had grade-one leukaemia and there was no evidence of treatment. He would have been dead in less than a year.'

'Can you have leukaemia and not know about it?'

'Other problems like prostate or pleurisy can obscure it for a while.'

'Wonder if anyone else knew about that?'

'On the record, there's nothing to say Quinn didn't hang himself. Maybe found out about his disease and decided to end it.'

'But . . . ?'

Foxy opened her mouth to speak, but Frank spoke instead.

'You need to get going, Mandy. Broadski and Dent are going to be here any second.'

Mandy looked up at the clock and back at Frank. 'Frank, are you OK?'

Frank pulled down his mask again and pointed at his face with the scalpel. 'I'm fine, but overworked and underpaid, that's all. Now, for your own sake, get the fuck out of here.'

Mandy stepped out of his morgue clothes, changed his boots and departed the mortuary trying to remember when he had heard Frank swear before. He was an old-school guy, clean and serene, and prided himself on not 'cussing' about anything or anyone. Maybe something or someone was putting pressure on him, or maybe it was just a really bad day at work. Whatever, it didn't sound right. Frank also seemed in too much of a hurry to get him out of the place – just because of Broadski and Dent? Granted, they might have said some harsh words about him, but even so, Frank was the assistant coroner of Santa Monica. Didn't that mean something – even to those two creeps?

It all felt wrong. Frank swearing? Frank telling him to leave? He walked one block in the heat to the Café Republica. He needed a caffeine fix.

The place had six high chrome don't-hang-around tables inside, the kind you couldn't sit at because they didn't have any seats. There were three customers but all wanting takeaway, and two baristas. Mandy positioned himself with a clear view of the entrance door, spread his notebook on the table, ordered a large iced cappuccino and checked his phone.

The phone call was to Fabienne; she sounded tight-lipped.

'I can't talk because someone's nearby.'

He pictured her in her office, her back to the Giraffe, standing close by.

'Someone hanged my cat in the shower yesterday.'

'You're kidding!'

'No, I am not. Know anybody who hates me or cats?'

'Oh my God, who the hell would do a thing like that? What does Terry think?'

'I don't know yet, but I will in a minute.'

He heard the Giraffe moving in the background. Fabienne lowered her voice. 'Come over for dinner tonight. We can go for a walk on the beach with the dog and talk then.'

'Sure,' Mandy said. 'I'll try to be there before sunset.'

He closed his cell and took a deep breath. The waitress ambled over and set down a glass of iced cappuccino on the table. A gust of warm air from the café door being opened, followed by the whiff of aftershave; Broadski and Dent in blazers, blue jeans, open-necked white shirts and shades. Both ordered a latte and Danish.

Whatever they came to see Frank about hadn't lasted long. Maybe they were picking up Quinn's post-mortem report.

Dent rested his arse against the back of a chair and scowled, while Broadski leant an elbow on the table and said, 'You want to shoot the shit with us, buddy? Pool our information and share in the reward?'

Mandy just smiled. He wanted to smoke them out.

Broadski and Dent shrugged shoulders – an old-school comedy duo.

'Does Fabienne kneel beneath the table and blow you, like Foxy does Frank when he's cutting up a stiff?' Broadski said, with a sneer.

The coarse remark from such a lowlife rocked Mandy hard in the gut. But he didn't react. What Fabienne was, or wasn't, to him was none of their fucking business. He gave a big grin, adjusted his sunglasses.

'Is it something you dream about, Broadski?' he asked. 'Told your rabbi?'

Dent gave a snort of laughter. Broadski looked angrier than he'd expected the remark to make him.

'We're not all nut jobs,' Broadski said. It was a lame comeback.

'Is Fabienne here?' Dent said, moving his finger in and out of his mouth.

Mandy looked at Dent as if he was a piece of shit on the sidewalk.

There was a certain confident tone in their voices, like they'd eavesdropped on Mandy's call with Fabienne.

'I think you'll find she's at work,' Mandy said, 'working for your boss, in fact.'

'Too bad,' Broadski said.

There was an uncomfortable silence.

Mandy drank half his iced cappuccino. How to proceed? Goad them about their lack of progress on Dominic Young, how he managed to lose them when chasing after Lucy Lack, or the Lakers' recent defeat? They were not even incompetent has-beens, more like never-beens. Both desperately holding on to their jobs, hoping for early retirement so they could pay off their mortgages, move somewhere shit like Miami and set up as private eyes.

He resented them, not only professionally but because of the type of people they were.

'I hear . . .' Dent said, his mouth full of Danish, 'I hear it wouldn't go too well for Fabienne if she lost her job.'

Mandy drained the last of the cappuccino and wiped his mouth with his hand.

'Guys . . .' Mandy paused, 'you should be working as diplomats, in somewhere like Afghanistan.'

Broadski smirked. Dent looked temporarily intrigued.

Mandy extended his grin by a few millimetres; he had to stay calm until they revealed their real intentions. If they really knew about Fabienne giving him info, she could face disciplinary action, and probably lose her job and any prospect of police re-employment.

Broadski held his hand close to his mouth as he angled a toothpick into a gum.

Dent said, 'Mandy, we all know this conversation isn't taking place, so let's put the pussy on the table.'

A fuse blew inside Mandy's brain. He shot forward, grabbed Dent by the throat and squeezed hard. Mandy knew what he was doing, knew his own strength when it came to his hands.

Dent's face turned puce, dark as a cartoon beetroot.

Broadski took a pace towards them, had his cell out of his pocket and shouted, 'Hey!'

Mandy gave him a rugby hand-off. 'Did you break into my house yesterday, Dent?'

Dent shook his head, pulling at Mandy's fingers.

'No way,' Dent stuttered, face swelling, eyes straining in their sockets. 'Don't be crazy.'

'Any more crazy than you already are,' Broadski said, with a smirk. He pushed open his jacket and put his hand on a large holstered gun.

'Let him go before I fucking hit you over the head.'

Mandy loosened his grip on Dent's neck. Dent gulped in air and kicked his pointed shoe hard into Mandy's thigh. It hurt, but it was worth it.

Dent stepped away to the café window, took several breaths and rubbed his blotchy throat.

'We have not been in your house. You are barking up the wrong tree,' Broadski said with a brief smile.

Like some petulant drunk, Dent ran over and threw a punch towards Mandy's head. Mandy stepped back and the blow landed on his shoulder with a loud slap. He felt his knuckles tingling for action, more blood rush to his already overheated face.

Broadski yelled, '*Leave it!*' stepped over to the worried-looking café owner and flashed his police badge. Mandy and Dent nodded to the owner that everything was OK.

'Just a stupid misunderstanding,' Broadski said, dropping a ten-dollar note in the staff gratuity tin.

When he returned to the table, he shook his head and drew breath. 'Mandy we don't *need* you. We thought we could save us all some time by collaborating a little, was all . . .'

Mandy walked over to the counter, asked for a glass of iced water, got it and drank it straight down.

'So you want me to share my information?' he said.

'Yes.'

'And then you tell me what you know and then we catch the killer?'

'Absolutely,' Broadski said. 'And then go to García-Márquez and ask him to divide the reward in two?'

'There are three of us, Mandy. But whatever works – you're the point of contact.'

This was the weirdest meeting of all time. In some ways, it no longer mattered if Broadski and Dent were bullshitting him or simply trying to muscle in on the reward. He'd never share it with them, and they'd sure as hell never share it with him.

'OK,' Mandy said. 'Lucy Lack has hired PI Adam Pollock to investigate the García-Márquez murder.'

Dent took his hand away from his throat and caught Broadski's gaze.

'Why did she do that when she knows you are on the case? Aren't you cutting the mustard for her?' he said.

Mandy shrugged. 'I'm employed by García-Márquez, not her.'

'Oh yes, that's right. And that's why you were chasing her on that fancy motorbike.' The two detectives pointed at one another.

'And you were following me to find that out?'

Broadski and Dent looked blank.

Mandy wanted to steer them away from Lucy.

'She is going back to England and leaving everything in Pollock's hands.'

Broadski pulled a face that actually amused Mandy and said, 'I wouldn't like to leave *anything* in his hands.'

Mandy smirked in agreement. It looked like they'd bought the bad steer.

'OK, next up,' he said. 'Mrs García-Márquez flew off in a private jet this morning to a clinic in Minnesota.'

'Why'd she do that?' Dent said.

Broadski broke his toothpick in two. 'You think she's involved?'

Mandy tapped his fingers under his chin. 'Up to here.'

The smile dropped from Broadski's face. 'How do we know you're not shitting us?'

'You don't, but it's a small town and you've got the Giraffe on your side.'

Dent placed his fist on the table. 'You could be setting us up. What's our guarantee?'

Mandy laughed, desperate to squash Dent's face into his empty plate. He wanted anything they had on Susan Green. He'd given them her suitcase, for fuck's sake, so where was the quid pro quo? But oddly they didn't seem too bothered about that investigation. Wonder why? The García-Márquez reward? Or something else?

'So what are you going to tell me in return? What happened to Susan Green? Is she dead or alive?'

Dent scratched his nose. Broadski drank the last of his latte. There was no response. He needed to provoke one.

'Terry always said you were a couple of self-interested fakes.'

Broadski pushed his face close towards Mandy and said, 'The best thing that ever happened to your pal Terry was getting sick. Nothing against the guy personally, but *he* was the fake.'

'Oh yeah, is that so?'

Dent took a noisy bite of his Danish. 'Yeah, it is. He was the kind who only survived by putting in long hours and kissing ass. He's a fucking pussy.'

'What did you just say?' Mandy said, pushing his face close to Dent's nose.

'I said, Terry from Monterey is nothing but a fake and a pussy. Got something to say about it?'

Mandy thought about it for two seconds.

He swung his fist as hard as he could into Dent's ribs. The sound of bones cracking was unmistakable. The punch was at just the right angle. Dent yelped like a fox whose leg was caught in a mechanical trap.

Broadski shook his head and lashed out, scraping the trigger of his gun down and across Mandy's scalp.

Everything went black, and stars came out. It stung like fuck, but he didn't go down. He flicked the gun out of Broadski's hand with his left arm. As it clattered to the floor, a waitress yelled, 'Watch out – it might fire!'

The manageress pulled the waitress behind the counter.

Mandy used his right palm to perform a well-balanced judo push to Broadski's chest. He fell like a rotten tree.

As he made for the door, Mandy reckoned as a meeting to share information it hadn't gone too well.

Outside, on the crowded sidewalks of Main Street, Mandy's head began hurting. He dismissed the thought of returning to Frank for some medical attention. Anyway, Frank had been weird, neurotic, trying to warn him off.

Mandy pressed a white handkerchief to the top of his head and then looked at it. A three-inch-long patch of blood. Nothing life-threatening, yet the pain was getting worse.

Back inside the Amazon, he checked his cell. There was a new message. 'Sorry for running away yesterday. I am going back to London tonight and want to see you before I go. You know where I am. Lx'

He set off for 26th Street, front tyres screeching as he made a U-turn.

50

1.15 p.m., 20 July

Fine jets of water fell on Benny Tan's head as he took a late-morning shower in his office bathroom. After stepping out of the shower, he dried his arms, legs and torso, then towelled his head fifty times until his hair was bone-dry.

The last two hours had been the most stressful he had experienced since taking over the business. Chung shooting himself had nearly been a disaster. It was only thanks to Chung's staff's quick thinking that a slab of merchandise had been removed from the table where Chung lay dead. But when the cops managed to break open the two freezer compartments and discovered the remaining slabs of heroin, the game was nearly up. Fortunately, everyone connected to the store stuck to the same story. They knew nothing about it at all. The one who might have known *something* was their dead boss, killed by an intruder firing a pistol into his head. It was fanciful but was going to give Benny enough time to do what he had to do.

Benny pulled on black underwear, socks, short-sleeved shirt and a $1,400 suit that Yale had helped him choose at that expensive store in Silver Lake.

'You look like a serious tycoon about to sign a big deal,' Yale said when he tried it on. Benny grunted. Yale might be a freak, but she was loyal and content with her lot, not grasping for more all the time. Unlike Sonia Chung.

He'd phoned Wayne's wife earlier, to make sure she said the right thing to the police. Not that she was likely to mess up, but he'd heard she was a hard-nosed, money-grabbing bitch. 'I'm so sorry for your loss, Mrs Chung. Wayne was a good man. You must be—'

'Angry that he did it without making any arrangement for me and the kids to know his online passwords for the bank and how to pay the household bills. It's going to be a nightmare, Mr Tan.'

Benny scowled into his phone. He knew exactly what was coming next. Sonia Chung was an old-school hustler, a former croupier working in Orange

253

County on a fake passport – her lucky day had been meeting lonely Wayne at the blackjack table.

'Mr Tan, Wayne's death puts me in a very difficult position. I may need to look at changing the way the business is run . . . maybe look at taking a good cash-advance payment from a new source.'

Benny clenched his fist. There was no way she could know about Nabokov, not unless the bearded Russian or one of the accountants had got to her already – which he doubted. Why would they? But there were plenty of other players to deal with on the board. On the very day the deal was going to be signed, he could not afford to have any leaking taps.

'Would one hundred and fifty thousand dollars in cash make your life more bearable, Mrs Chung?'

'Oh, Mr Tan,' Mrs Chung trilled, 'thank you for your kindness and sympathy at this difficult time. My children and I were thinking of taking a trip overseas to get over Wayne's death. A hundred and fifty thousand in cash or banker's cheque and four business-class seats to Beijing would see us straight.'

Benny weighed up what was at stake.

'Dick will call round with the money,' he said, 'which you can either bank here or take with you. Best to catch the next flight, at three thirty. Dick will take you to the airport and make sure you are safely on the plane.'

Mrs Chung was profuse in her appreciation. But she was still a worry. The distribution deal through the supermarkets was sweet, easy and watertight, and worth $4 million in turnover. In hard terms, thirty per cent of the business he was selling to Nabokov. After ten years it would not be easy to replace, especially considering its proximity to the airport, North Channel and Topanga. Chung's was a vital part of the business and Benny could not afford to have any problem with it – today of all days.

Benny shook his head at the memory and stepped into new leather brogues, elegant but slightly tight. He'd bought them that morning after an early visit to the farm in Topanga. He'd been there to check everything was shipshape for the signing party – proper Russian vodka and top-grade caviar . . .

He'd worked out a good cover story for Nabokov – Chung just discovered he had a terminal illness and had thought it better to limit his family's suffering by killing himself now. It was credible. It would emerge that the staff had got it wrong about the intruder. The family could back it up.

The only remaining problem was the man seen speaking with Chung immediately prior to the 'suicide'. The young policeman had identified him: Mandy of Endeavor Investigations, the same guy who'd driven into Janet's Range Rover. Janet had said he was a loser. But he didn't seem to be too much like a loser given he'd been in two places connected to Benny in a couple of days.

He closed the bathroom door, walked over to his desk and pressed the phone code for Dick. It took a few rings before he answered, and – as ever – he was driving. Dick sounded cheerful.

'Yo, Benny. I have the hundred and fifty gee in the glove compartment and heading downtown.'

'OK. Make sure you see Mrs Chung and her children go through the departure and security gates. Get that right and there's a bonus waiting for you. OK?'

Benny hung up, made a note about the bonus and ticked off an item from his mental list of staff members who he needed to keep vigilant that day. Dick Chain and Janet were two of the inner circle left to compensate. Moving his mouse, he clicked through the CCTV screens on his desk. In the downstairs showrooms, fifteen to twenty customers were gazing at the aquariums, while another six were queuing at the tills. Not bad for a weekday lunchtime in July.

Clicking onto reception, he spotted Janet, in high heels, white blouse and a short dark skirt, greeting customers as they came in from the car park, hands clasped together over the gold buckle of her Gucci belt. Benny sighed. There was no one better in his organization. If only she didn't have such a short fuse. Despite the fuck-ups and the badly unresolved issue with the private invest-igator, he had decided to give her a piece of the business after all – which, providing the deal went through, and subject to her signing a total confidenti-ality and non-disclosure agreement, would net her in the region of just over a million dollars – an incentive to stay silent in anyone's book.

Benny followed Kurt on the monitor, wheeling a customer's trolley through reception past Janet out to the car park and loading up their car. No weird visitors on motorbikes out there today, Benny thought, as he waited until Kurt returned and then buzzed down and told him to take over the customer-greeting duties while Janet came to meet him by the piranhas' tank in two minutes.

'Sure thing, Mr Tan.'

The kid was so grateful; he was starting to get on Benny's nerves. Nothing he could do about that, though, not yet. He took out a large brown envelope from his briefcase, pulled out a document and stared at the front page: a legal share transfer agreement he'd had his lawyer in Silver Lake draw up overnight. It was a contract between himself as owner of all Fish Farm shares and Janet Lee, transferring 7.5 per cent of his shares to her in return for a nominal pay-ment of $750 – the same amount he'd spent on his new shoes. After all, 92.5 per cent of $14 million is better than 100 per cent of nothing, Benny reckoned.

When he got downstairs, Janet was waiting by the fish food display. He walked her a few yards down a 'celebrity' aisle of octopuses and conger eels, and stopped beside the well-lit piranha fish.

'I know what you are going to ask,' Janet said, tapping her finger on the glass of the tank. 'How come this Mandy guy was at Chung's? Am I right?'

But Benny was only half listening. Two chattering customers pushed their shopping trolley into the aisle and someone turned up the volume on the new Coldplay album Benny bought the staff as a present. He shook his head at Janet, stepped closer and spoke into her ear. 'Let's go in the back and talk. I can't concentrate here.'

He swiped his security pass down the side of the chrome door with frosted portholes, waited for a click to sound and then pushed it open. He gestured to Janet to follow him down the narrow corridor leading to another chrome door.

Halfway along it, Janet cleared her throat and pointed to the ceiling. 'Could we not go to your office and talk?'

Benny looked at Janet and inwardly laughed. He was not going to give her everything on a plate. If she was getting 7.5 per cent of the business, she needed to be reminded of the importance of keeping the company secure from rogue forces. He needed to hear her re-pledge her loyalty to him, not just because of the Nabokov deal but for his, Benny Tan's, future too.

Janet knew more than anyone where the bodies were buried. Signing a contract of confidentiality, given the circumstances, would not cut the mustard for him. He needed to feel her loyalty, but more importantly he needed to feel safe knowing she could not afford to disclose information to third parties.

'Why don't you like it down here? I don't get it,' he said, giving her a little smile that he hoped was affectionate and friendly.

Janet pointed to the emergency exit and then downwards towards the basement.

'From a security, hygiene and moral point of view, I think it's wrong for us to keep those things here. I really do.'

'Did you say "moral"?'

'Yes, I did, Benny. I think everything should be incinerated.'

She was upset, he could see that.

He put his hand on Janet's shoulder – it was much softer than he expected. 'Let's go and sit down in the dental people's coffee room – there's no one there.'

Benny reversed back up the corridor and pushed through an unmarked door, switched on some fluorescent lights. The room had a glass-and-chrome table, six grey padded chairs. Glasses and two bottles of water were laid out on a tray. Janet sat down. Benny sat across from her. He upturned two glasses and undid the top of the bottle of water.

'Drink some of this and tell me exactly what's on your mind. I want to make you happy, not upset.'

Janet stood up, rested one hand on the table. 'Benny, I'm forty-three years old, I don't have a pension or any money hidden away, my elderly parents are finding it difficult to pay the bills, let alone look after themselves, and . . .' she paused, 'when I called round at Mandy's house, I found documents showing he's being funded by the García-Márquez family – the Mexican avocado and mobile-phone García-Márquezes – and, and, and,' she stuttered, 'he somehow had gotten hold of photos of me.' She squeezed her eyes shut. 'Photos I stupidly gave Susan Green . . . How did that man get his hands on them?'

Photos of Janet and Susan Green. That was a loose end Benny hadn't heard about before. And no wonder. A big fat loose end.

Benny beamed a reassuring smile at Janet and fanned his hands to her to sit down. Once she was seated and sipping from a glass of water, he said, 'I'm only interested in solutions today, not problems. I don't have the answers to all your concerns, but this might help your situation and motivate you to get the missing answers . . . Check it out.'

Janet narrowed her eyes and scratched her head. Benny slid the share certificate documentation over to her side of the table. Janet read the first lines of the document, occasionally muttering certain words out loud. Benny drew a doodle of a big dog with a pencil, snapping the stub of it as he pondered Janet's poor judgement in giving Susan Green photographs of herself.

Janet began to cry. Benny started to explain the takeover with Nabokov. Janet stopped crying.

'It's nothing less than you deserve, Benny. But I am completely overcome, and shocked. Thank you so much. It means so much to me,' she said, her hands clutching at the table top.

Benny stood up and as a way of reciprocal body language held on to the table too. 'That's over one million dollars coming your way, Janet. We are due to sign the agreement tomorrow or even this evening, providing we can keep our heads screwed on.'

A loud knocking at the door threw Benny off track.

Janet looked over at him. 'You expecting company?'

Benny shook his head. 'Come in!'

The door opened and stepping inside the door frame was a red-faced Kurt.

'Sorry to interrupt, but there were two messages for you, both urgent.'

'Well, what were they?'

'Mr Nabokov said to tell or ask you to be at the Viceroy Hotel at four this afternoon. He said you would know. That's it, sir.'

Janet shot Benny a knowing shareholder nod.

'And the other message?' Benny said.

Kurt read from a scrap of paper. 'Could you call Mrs Zimmer in the secretary's office of the LA Country Club? She didn't say what it was about.'

257

Benny was pleased about the last message. The Los Angeles Country Club had come good at last. But he was less happy about a breach in Fish Farm security.

'How did you get into this section, Kurt? Your card has limited access.'

Kurt looked pleased. 'I learnt how to adapt swipe cards at college . . . You just need the right information from a basic card.'

'Is that the only one you've made?'

'Yes, sir.'

'That sounds like you've been using aptitude and initiative to me, but don't ever do it again. We have levels of security for a good reason. Get back to greeting, please.'

Kurt looked down. 'I'll change it back, sir,' he said, and closed the door behind him.

'Jesus,' Benny said, putting the top back on the bottle. 'That was a little too close for comfort.'

'He's a liability,' Janet said. 'I worry about him.'

'What? Do you think our intern is connected to the guy on the motorbike?' Benny said, tightening the cap on the bottle of water.

'I guess anything is possible.'

'But what happened to the biker in the end?'

'That guy?' Benny said with a smile. 'Oh, he's on the farm and soon will be adding some protein to the sturgeon.'

'Ah, the farm . . .' Janet nodded sagely. 'And the girl with the long hair?'

'What girl?'

'The one on the back of the motorbike Kurt saw in the parking lot.'

Benny picked up the unsigned share certificates and waved them in Janet's face. 'You'd better check that out. We cannot afford to have anyone running around who could damage this deal.'

51

1.45 p.m., 20 July

Mandy blinked for several seconds. A breeze was blowing through partly drawn curtains, and there was a jet flying overhead, his head on clean-smelling pillows and his body on a salmon-pink bedspread. Where the hell was he – hotel, hospital or clinic?

On his left a wall and to his right a table, on which sat a glass of water, a lamp and a beige telephone. Within touching distance an identical double bed, on which his socks, jacket and tie lay scattered. He looked down: unbuttoned shirt, suit trousers and bare feet.

There were dabs of blood on his fingers and pillow. That's right – the smack on the head. The skin on his right knuckles was broken again. Must have hit somebody. He winced, swung his legs onto the floor, scanned past closet, chest of drawers, old-fashioned TV, stopped at the blonde wig on the large suitcase full of folded clothes. The case was balanced on a narrow pine table; next to it a small basket of cookies: 'Welcome to the Comfort Inn.'

Lucy Lack. He was in Goldilocks's bed. What a lucky, or stupid, bear.

One forty-five – must have been out for at least an hour. He got up, opened the curtains and looked down at the turquoise pool three floors below.

A tanned woman in white cap and black bikini was swimming breaststroke. He yanked out his cell and re-read Lucy's message: 'Sorry for running away yesterday. I am going back to London tonight and want to see you before I go. You know where I am. Lx'

His senses reconnected and he was back on the planet. He couldn't remember getting to the car park off Main Street from Café Republica, but driving up Colorado, 26th Street and Santa Monica Boulevard to the Comfort and parking close to a white Jeep, that was hazy but present.

So where was Lucy? Where was the rifle he'd seen on the table in front of her with Pollock? The sun shone too brightly; he shut the curtains. In the

259

dimness, a feeling overtook him that Lucy was behind him, with a loaded rifle. He let the fantasy live for a few seconds before turning round. No one there. Nothing but the suitcase, all packed up ready to go.

He pushed open the bathroom door. It was tiny – a quarter of the Shutters en suite. Yet in two respects it was absolutely the same – seventy-five unlit night lights on the bath surround and a huge photograph of Pedro in a frame. There was a faintly sickly smell of skin cream.

Mandy peed carefully into the toilet bowl and flushed. He cautiously lifted both ends of the cistern lid and looked for the dismembered rifle. Zilch.

His bloodstained handkerchief was on a glass ledge above the basin, along with several bottles of painkillers: Oxycontin, Vicodin, Tylenol Extra Plus and a small plastic spray of liquid Valium.

He spurted some on his finger, dabbed it on his tongue and twigged. She had held a glass of water and several pills in the palm of her hand, pink nail varnish, gold bracelets round her wrist – 'Here, take these.' He remembered jerking his head back to swallow the pills. Yes, painkillers and Valium – enough to fell a giraffe. No wonder he'd been out for an hour.

He went back into the room, picked up his phone and sat on the bed. Where the hell was she? Tried her UK cell. Off. Nothing from Terry on his cell either. Lazy fucker must be still sleeping, or maybe he was with his girls. Mandy hoped so. He tried Terry's number again, got the answerphone. Someone knocked.

He leapt up and opened the door. Lucy stood in a white sleeveless cotton dress holding up a brown paper bag from a deli and a smaller one from a Green Cross pharmacy.

'Mind if I come in?' she said. 'Feeling better?'

'I wasn't sure where the hell I was when I woke up.'

As if it was the most normal thing in the world, she pointed to the suitcase and said, 'Could you move that so we can use the table underneath? I can sit on the bed and you can use the chair.'

'Sure.' He lifted the suitcase and placed it on the floor.

A minute later he sat opposite her with a cheeseburger and fries in front of him. He picked up a thick chip, dunked it in some ketchup. Lucy drank from a water bottle. Light beads of sweat above her lips glistened in the light seeping through the curtains.

'It's boiling out there,' she said. For the first time since he'd met her, she didn't just look strawberries and cream but happy and relaxed.

'It's always warmer when you get away from the coast. No ocean breeze.'

'That's why I've got the curtains half closed.'

'Are you not going to eat?' Mandy said, biting into the cheeseburger.

'I'm not hungry.'

It was odd how pretty girls never seemed to eat.

'Mind telling me how I got here?'

'Reception phoned to say there was a man not making much sense and asking for me in an English accent.'

'You figured?'

'Had to be you. I brought you up here, gave you some painkillers and stayed with you while you slept – for a while anyway.'

She emptied the pharmacy bag onto the bed, picked up a packet, read the label and then took out a tube of cream. 'I'd better wash my hands.'

He watched her shapely backside and legs as she walked into the en suite, her hands fiddling behind her head tying her hair into a bunch.

Swallowing a mouthful of burger, he said, 'I'm fine. It's very kind, but no need to go to this trouble.'

She walked in, holding cream and some gauze. 'Don't be stupid – septicaemia can kill people. This is the strongest antiseptic gel I could find. Now hold still – I'll try not to hurt you too much, just a bit for flashing those nice photos at me maybe . . .'

He felt her warm body press against his shoulders and her hands push gently through his hair. He felt his body tighten and relax.

'Hope this doesn't sting too much,' she said.

He moved his back closer into her, dropped his napkin, so his arm touched her leg as he brought it back to the table.

'Didn't you become a doctor on the plane and help Father Tony save Dominic Young?' he said.

Her fingers stopped padding the wound. She let out an awkward laugh. 'Bloody Tony told you, did he? Promised me that he wouldn't tell anyone, cheeky priest. Lucky I like him so much.'

'So?'

She laughed again. 'Stupid, really. I sometimes do stupid things. I don't know why. Well, I do know why, but . . . yes, I pretended I was a doctor on that plane.'

'Why?'

'I like to feel needed.'

'And you and Father Tony saved the guy's life, right?'

'Yes, but the only medical training I've had is a first-aid course in the Girl Guides.' She stopped again and sniffed.

Mandy found her hand and stroked it. 'I won't tell anybody.'

'Thanks.' She squeezed his hand back.

Both of them kept their hands there long enough to know their flesh touching had not been an accident. She pulled away first, but he felt her body relax, soften into him more.

'What do you think about Dominic Young? Wouldn't it have been better if he'd been left to die on the plane than to end up as he did?' Mandy said.

'Is that a trick question?'

'No, I want your views . . . irrespective of any investigation.'

'I hope this whole conversation is irrespective.'

It was a fair point. Mandy nodded, and out of nowhere with no plan, he twisted round in the chair, took hold of her shoulders and kissed her. Afterwards he leant back, smiled and noticed her pink lipstick, soft skin. Her sparkling green eyes were smiling back at him.

'Where were we?' Mandy asked. Half dazed.

'Dominic Young.'

'Well?'

'I'm sorry about what happened to him, dead on a beach, but I'm glad he didn't succeed in killing himself.'

'Why? Isn't it everyone's right to choose?'

'Perhaps.' She thought about it for a moment. 'When you're old or have a terminal illness, or you're about to be massacred and raped by an invading army. Not because your boyfriend or girlfriend has dumped you – that's just stupid.'

Mandy shrugged and gave her a knowing look. 'You're right, Lucy. You don't want to end your life because of someone leaving you. But in my experience, people who commit suicide, or consider doing it, or even those who are faking it are people who have a lot going on under the surface that they need to work out. But then, I've been around for a hundred years, and you're only in your twenties.'

'Tony said you'd set up the Santa Monica Suicide Club?' she said. 'How do you become a member?'

'It's a club for people who decide *not* to kill themselves but to stick with it. Doesn't mean you have to be a battery-powered smiling saint instead either. It's a club for survivors. So far, you're pretty well qualified to join.'

He fell silent, torn between more questions and kissing her. A distant voice warned him about traps and weapons. But it was Terry's voice, not his. Blood was pumping fast round his body; he was horny and drunk without any alcohol. He could smell her sex.

She ran her hands through his hair.

He leant back and curled his arm around her legs, gently twisting her body so she ended up sitting sideways on his lap. They kissed, more intensely and more passionately. When they stopped, she grabbed hold of his chin, smiled and then slapped him hard on his cheek.

Perhaps it was a warning. He gave her a mild slap back and kissed her on the neck. She gave him a pretend shocked look.

'Quits?' he said.

'Quits.'

They kissed again.

'I hate to say this,' Mandy said at last, 'but I need to get one or two things straight between us.'

She swivelled her backside on his lap.

'It's OK – I get it.'

'Good. I have to have some answers.'

'And I have to wash this antiseptic off my hands.'

She got up. In front of the doorway, she said, 'I need to answer certain questions too; it's a way of purging myself. I had a weird epiphany last night.'

He could hear her wash her hands and dry them.

'Sounds very Father Tony. Were you with him?' he called.

'No, Pollock,' she said, walking back into the room.

'I know,' he said.

'He thought you'd probably figure it out.'

Mandy grunted. The guy must have seen him through the window. He prepared a disparaging remark about Pollock, but swallowed it.

She picked up a French fry, sprinkled salt on it and popped it in her mouth.

'The reason I let you in my room is because of Pollock. He said you were one of the best, that you have backbone, and integrity.'

Mandy squirmed. 'Must have me mixed up with someone else,' he said, stroking the shoulder strap of Lucy's dress. 'It was Pollock who gave you the dirt on me too, wasn't it?'

'Yes, and I'm sorry about that. I was freaked out and feeling under attack and very alone.'

'So why hire him in the first place? Not just for little old me? I guess it was to find the killers or get enough dirt on the Sternwoods so they ended up doing six hundred hours of community service in South Central?'

'Nice idea. Let me imagine and savour that thought.'

She bent her head forward and moved it slowly from side to side. 'I get a stiff neck whenever I think of those bastards.'

He put his hands on her shoulders and began kneading the tight muscles. 'I'm the best in the business.'

'Which business is that?' she said, letting out a long sigh.

'I'm in the happy-ending business,' Mandy said with a laugh.

Lucy chuckled, and allowed her shoulders to relax. 'Yeah, you're really good at this – powerful hands and fingers.'

'Should have done this for a living. So come on . . . why did you hire Pollock?'

'I was trying to tell you when you came to my suite in Shutters. And then you pressed every single button when you went off on the Sternwood bisexual-orgy slant.' She paused; her head drooped as though she was considering something.

'One night about six months ago, shortly after Pedro had refused to bail them out again after their crappy business failed, they invited us over for dinner. I should have known something was wrong, because sleazy, polo-playing Memo, Pedro's mother's godson, happened to be there too. They plied us with poppers, champagne cocktails and plates full of delicious-tasting lobster and crab. It was only later that I discovered the drink and mayonnaise were spiked with Rohypnol and Viagra. Not that the Mexican polo player needed any assistance – bloody pig. Anyway, the delightful little dwarf Sarah Sternwood asked us all to play a game of fancy-dress charades in which we had to invent names of imaginary porn stars.'

Mandy suspended the massage. 'Think of the name of your first pet and add it to your mother's maiden name?'

'Mine was "Sooty Brazier", and that's as pleasant and innocent as it got.'

The request for zero TV pornography in her suite at Shutters was now making sense.

'This led on to us actually being characters in a pretend porn film. And of course, Mrs Sternwood omitted to mention that Johnny was secretly photographing it all.'

'You should have seen that coming,' Mandy said.

'I will next time, believe me. And yes, before you ask, to my shame, things did get way out of hand. But not quite as bad as those photos suggest.'

'What about Pedro and the polo player? Was that blow-job photo faked?'

Lucy shook her head. 'No, that was the trouble – it was real. Can you believe it? Poor Pedro didn't know his food had been spiked. He hadn't had sex for two years.'

'So when did the coercion or blackmail begin?'

'They met Pedro one Sunday lunchtime a week later at a place in Malibu. Sarah put the photos on the table as if they were publicity stills for a movie. Johnny then asked Pedro if he would like to donate two hundred thousand dollars to their new charity.'

'What he really meant was bail them out of the shit because their house was on the line for their business?'

'Got it in one.'

'A bad spot for Pedro. Did he pay up?'

'No! I wanted him to. That's what we rowed about. I said that although they were despicable scum, it would be far better for him and me if he settled. They also knew someone who knew my boss's home address in London.'

'So?'

'He refused point blank, said he would not be blackmailed under any circumstances. I was too ashamed to tell you the whole story when we met at breakfast. Anyway, what does it matter now? Once they knew he wouldn't play ball, they sent photographs to my boss in London, which resulted in me being suspended with a formal warning.'

'And losing your job would put you and your mother in desperate straits.'

Lucy angled her head round to look at Mandy. 'I didn't tell you any of that. How did you know?'

'I've done my research. I'm not a bad detective.'

'My mother is the exact opposite of Mrs García-Márquez. She is kind, loving and tolerant, but not able to cope on her own.'

'She depends on you?' Mandy said, gently squeezing Lucy's shoulder.

She cleared her throat and carried on. 'That's why I came to see them at Loews that time. I offered them three grand, all I had left, but they refused. Not long before Pedro was murdered, they threatened to send photos to Mr García-Márquez too. That would have really blown all his fuses.'

'And did they?' Mandy asked, already knowing the answer was affirmative.

'Pedro told them he didn't care what they did as he'd already sent them to his mother. But yes, they probably did. Stupid fuckers. I guess that's one of the reasons why I was turned away from the wake.'

Her story was stacking up fast with Scottish Ray's report. A couple more hoops to jump through and then he could apply a full-body massage and relax.

'But didn't you already know that Pedro had left you an Edward Hopper painting in his will? Didn't he tell you or let you know? With that sort of financial muscle, you could have blown the Sternwoods out of the water, surely?'

It was a good multiple question designed to flush out the truth. He squeezed her hand to help her answer. Lucy didn't hesitate with her reply.

'Pedro told me about the cottage and painting a few weeks ago. It was a ridiculously big gesture intended to stop me from worrying about never having enough money.'

'Wow, he really did like you one hell of a lot.'

Lucy unclamped her hand from his. 'Some people do like me.'

Mandy inwardly winced at Lucy's hurt face and took hold of her hand. 'I get that.'

She let out a long breath. 'I told Pedro he wouldn't be dying for a long time, so it wouldn't make any difference; I'd still worry – it's in my blood. Also that I didn't actually want his money, just enough of my own. Anyway, I didn't take it that seriously, because I also guessed with a family that powerful, it would only be a matter of time before that particular will was declared null and void or claimed never to have existed.'

'I'm sorry to keep up the questions, but why stay at an expensive place like Shutters if you're worried about cash?'

'Good question. It was partly pride, because I wanted the family to believe I had my own money, but also because I was really upset and wanted to stay somewhere nice.'

'So you hired Pollock to find out that the will had been witnessed?'

Lucy shook her head. 'No, that wasn't the reason. I guess you were bound to find out sooner or later . . .'

'What?'

Mandy cleared his throat. He'd finally reached the edge of Niagara Falls.

'I hired him to find my father.'

Mandy's heartbeat increased, but his massage did not falter. He rubbed her warm skin over and over, and thought about what she'd just said.

'Didn't you say he lived in Canada?' he said eventually.

'He moved to California years ago but never told us, pretended he was still in Vancouver.'

'So what else did Pollock find out?'

'That he'd done some bad things, theft, violence – and that doesn't even include what he did to my mother. But also that crime does pay – he's stinking rich, changed his name and has been living in the lap of luxury, while we ate baked beans . . .'

Mandy slipped the straps from each of her shoulders. 'So did you tell Pedro? Is that why his mother thinks you're trailer trash?'

She shook her head again. 'No, she doesn't know. I already felt very ashamed that I didn't have a father, let alone one who was a lowlife. They already thought I was trailer trash and only wanted their son's money. I told him in the end, a month before he died, and he was brilliant – "Water off a duck's back," he said. "If it helps you to meet him, then let's find him."'

'And he was the one who suggested Pollock?' It would explain why García-Márquez Senior hadn't been so keen on the smarmy git and had hired Mandy instead. 'Was it Pedro's idea?'

She sighed. 'Yes,' she said. 'But Pollock took weeks to come up with anything. Pedro was dead before he found the fucker. That was what I was really doing in Silver Lake yesterday – looking to collect something different from money.'

'Jesus,' Mandy said. He rested his fingers on Lucy's bare shoulders. 'Please tell me you're not saying that Benny Tan is your father, are you?'

She frowned and nodded slowly. 'I am saying exactly that, yes.'

'Do you know what he does for a living?'

'He sells tropical fish on North Channel Road.'

'You've been there?'

'Wing took me a couple of times, but we didn't go in.' She let out a tearful laugh. 'Not enough bottle, that's my problem.'

'And then Wing disappeared . . .'

'Yes.' She took a gulp of air. 'Got a bad feeling about that.'

Mandy pondered the idea. 'What happened to the rifle you had with Pollock yesterday afternoon?'

She took his hands off her shoulders. 'You saw us?'

'Didn't want to intrude.'

'I kept it.'

'Christ,' he said. 'You don't even have a permit for it, do you?'

'So?' She shrugged. 'Anyone can get a gun here. Even school kids.'

'Can I trust you?' he said.

'Can you trust *me*? Why else would I tell you all this?'

She got up from her chair, turned round and unbuttoned the front of her dress so her white underwear was clearly visible. 'Look under the bed.'

He knelt by the side of the bed, ran his arm underneath it until he felt the coldness of the thick metal rifle barrel. He eased it out, hooked the trigger guard with his finger, stood up and set it down carefully on the window ledge. He felt his heart beating harder. He exhaled with a whistle and swung round.

Lucy was sitting on the salmon-coloured bedspread hugging her knees.

Waiting.

He looked at her bare olive skin and unbuttoned his shirt. His cell phone, on the floor where it had fallen from his pocket, began flashing and to play 'I Feel Good'.

'What the fuck?'

'Leave it,' she said, lying back across the bed.

He winced but answered the call.

Father Tony.

'There's an emergency at 1600 Montana Avenue. I need you here right now.'

The priest's voice had a nervous, 'I'm not kidding' quality.

Talk about bad timing.

52

3.52 p.m., 20 July

Benny Tan poked the parking validation ticket into his breast pocket and strode up the stairs of the Viceroy. Eight minutes early. The intern had not taken the name of the meeting room, so he'd been early enough to find out.

'Be right with you, sir,' the receptionist called out.

Benny mouthed, 'No problem.'

He looked around at some of the grand antique furniture, or reproductions. It was good quality. He remembered importing stuff like that from China, back in Canada. Of course, his stuff had all had hidden compartments, but then probably a lot of the originals did too. Where else would people have stashed their valuables before banks?

'Excuse me, sir. Sorry for keeping you waiting. May I help you?'

'I am here to see Mr Nabokov – a private room?'

The man peered down at a register and stabbed his finger on the page. 'The Windermere Suite on the seventh floor. Shall I have someone show you up?'

Benny shook his head. 'No need.'

At the elevators, he bowed and grinned when the next two arrived, crowded with tourists, but declined to join them. When an empty one arrived, he darted into it and pressed 'close' before anyone else could step inside.

When he reached the seventh floor, he pressed 'fifteen', and then 'eighteen'. Why was he feeling nervous? Why did it matter if he was a few minutes early? Just he hated unscheduled meetings like this.

Was Nabokov going to spring his chairman and directors on him? He could handle that. He could handle anything. As long as the Russian wasn't backing out of the deal.

He did a quick breathing exercise to stop his mind's negativity. It was odd to be on the same floor the two gunmen had stayed on before they shot Griswold, the deputy attorney general. He rode back down to seven and stepped out, hoping to fuck that the Russian hadn't changed his mind.

He was outside the Windermere Suite – at exactly four p.m. The door opened and he was inside, arms in the air, frisked by two bodyguards. Dumb asses – he never carried a gun to a meeting. If you had to do that, in Benny's world, you'd already lost the upper hand. If someone wanted to kill him, they would. Having a gun himself was not going to act as a deterrent.

'Mr Nabokov is waiting for you outside, sir,' one bodyguard said. 'The girl will bring you a drink.'

The other pulled open a glass door that led onto a terrace overlooking the sea. The smell of ozone and the heat were acute as he walked into the light. Nabokov was getting up from a chair at the far end of the terrace. Two men sat opposite on a cushioned bench, their backs leaning against the terrace railing.

Broadski and Dent.

What the hell were they doing there? Benny'd only met them once before, and that had been once too often. Standing next to them two other guys in suits. Big guys, confident. They looked familiar, but not in these surroundings.

Nabokov walked towards him holding his arms out wide, as if nothing was wrong. 'Benny! Wonderful! Please come and join us.'

Benny shook hands. 'Good to see you, Dimitri.'

Using his hand to shield his eyes from the sunshine, he went over to the table, sat down and nodded at the big guys in suits. A tall, sallow-looking girl, early twenties, walked onto the terrace with six glasses of iced mint tea. Everyone took one and drank a few sips.

When the waitress departed, Nabokov leant forward. 'Now, I don't want you to think I've tricked you into coming here this afternoon, but up until about four hours ago I thought everything was plain sailing.' He gestured at Broadski and Dent.

'Carry on,' Benny said. There was a silence, filled by cawing seagulls and children shrieking down on the beach.

'We appear to have a plumbing problem,' Nabokov said, rolling his hand towards one of the men in jackets. 'The officers will explain.'

Both men lifted their shades.

Benny drained his mint tea and waited.

Broadski held up the palms of his hands. 'The boss asked us to come this afternoon. We've been around as cargo for a couple of years now, but as of last week have been upgraded to club. If you want to check it out with the man direct,' he said, holding his phone up in the air, 'I can patch you through straight away.'

Benny stared into Broadski's eyes, shook his head, wishing he'd brought Dick Chain along.

'Tell me the problem,' he said, 'and I'll see if I have a solution.'

Broadski held up his phone and showed two colour photos.

'There is a squealer about, someone who's been leaking information, telling tales outta school. Initially, we thought it might be someone in the chief of police's office, but now we've narrowed it down to two other people – maybe both. Take a look at these females.'

Benny squinted at the phone's screen. The faces were hard to make out in the searing light, but one was Janet. The other was cute, pouting with attitude and long blonde hair.

'The blonde,' Broadski said, 'is a fruit loop called Donna who lives in Mandy's house and went snooping on the beach the other day and discovered Young's trunk. One of our sources in a rehab place heard her blabbing to him on the phone about buying heroin from your Chung. The other you already know.'

'How did the guy in rehab know she was speaking to him?'

'How many guys do you know called Mandy?'

Benny nodded slowly. He wanted every bit of time so he could squeeze out of the situation.

Broadski increased the size of the images on his cell phone. 'Janet and Donna – sounds like an ice cream, doesn't it?'

Benny took hold of the phone and clicked back and forth between the images. *Et tu, Janet.*

But could he trust that Broadski and Dent had got it right? What better way to fuck up an organization than to sow discord? What if Janet wasn't a Judas at all? Why would she squeal? She had too much to lose, especially after he'd agreed the stock option. Had she been boasting at her hairdresser's? Had she squealed before he'd offered her the stock option? Had she doubted him? Had she betrayed him?

'Loose lips sink ships,' Benny muttered to himself.

He handed the phone back, stepped over to balcony rail, gripped hold of it and stared out to sea. Everyone was waiting for him to say something. They could wait. Janet wasn't a traitor, though she had been an idiot about giving photographs to Susan Green. And yet it was her fault that Dominic Young had ever been a part of the equation. The stupid bitch . . . He'd felt something was wrong this morning, and now the more he pieced things together . . . Maybe she'd deliberately crashed her Range Rover into Mandy? No, she loved that car almost as much as she loved licking Susan Green's pussy.

Benny turned back round and felt like a high-court judge about to pass the death sentence. 'I want to know two things before I go any further,' he said.

'Tell us.'

'How the fuck did you two cops know about the deal going on between Nabokov here and myself?'

Dent stepped forward. 'The boss told us this morning, or was it last night? We were told on a need-to-know basis only.'

The 'boss' could only be one of two people in Benny's book – an associate of Nabokov or someone high up in the cops. Benny didn't want to lose face by making out he didn't know. He just wanted the deal to go through and be out the other side.

'Second,' said Benny, 'what about Mandy? How do we stop him?'

'We had a frank discussion with him earlier today. He's like a bear with a sore head that'll chase after anything now. Grab hold of the Donna bitch, the snitch in rehab, and use her as bait to lure him in and deal with him from there, a two-for-one deal.'

Benny turned to Nabokov. 'Do we have a deal once these problems are taken care of?'

'Absolutely,' Nabokov said. 'It's ready to sign, but not with informers and an ex-cop floating about the surface.'

'I want to sign the agreement tonight at Fish Farm.'

'Benny, I don't have a problem, so long as the plumbing gets fixed beforehand. OK?'

'Are we agreed, then? You deal with mine, and I'll deal with yours?'

The two cops nodded. Nabokov smiled.

Broadski handed Benny a piece of paper. 'Your one's staying in Malibu Canyon.'

Benny folded the paper into his pocket and got up to go. A late afternoon drive along PCH would help him to think more positively.

He was also glad he wouldn't have to do Janet.

53

Mandy gripped the brass doorknocker in the shape of a lady's hand and rapped it against the door. Despite being run-down, the house had to be worth way more than $2 million. Every fibre in his body wanted to be back at the Comfort Inn with Lucy, but it would have to wait till later.

It was a full minute before Father Tony answered, shook Mandy's hand and offered a double grunt by way of a greeting. Judging by the gritted-teeth smile, he was stressed.

The sound of a woman wailing came from the back of the house. The tone of the wail was familiar. It went with marigolds, a crucifix and a statue of the Virgin Mary: Josefina.

The priest gestured for Mandy to follow him through the hallway, lit by small red icon candles beneath crucifixes and framed pictures of the Virgin Mary, into a cloyingly warm sitting room.

Josefina stood up from the floral-patterned sofa and almost curtseyed. She was in a shapeless brown dress that looked like it hadn't been washed for weeks. Her eyes were swollen, and her mouth twitching like she'd overdosed on diet pills. In her hands, which were trembling, was a framed photo of Quinn. She set this down on a coffee table, next to another group of portraits of the García-Márquezes. The room smelt of old diapers and burnt food. A box of Kleenex was balanced on the armrest of the sofa.

'I'll be in the kitchen if you need me,' Father Tony said, walking towards the door.

Mandy sat down and smiled sympathetically, hoping the woman would sit down too. But she began to rearrange the photos on the table, every so often stopping to stare at the large crucifix on the wall. He looked at the photograph of Quinn and wondered if he was looking at the missing piece of the jigsaw. He was about to find out.

'Father Tony said you needed to get something off your chest, Josefina,' he said, putting a hand on her shoulder.

She nodded. 'I do, but I need my picture of Pedro to give me the courage.'

Mandy stood up and walked over to the window overlooking the backyard. It consisted of withered marigolds, a hammock and a small statue of Jesus nestling behind an empty paddling pool.

Josefina found what she was looking for: a silver-framed photograph of Pedro. A young, smiling Pedro, taken when he was eighteen or nineteen. Still looked like a nice guy.

Mandy cleared his throat. 'So are you ready now to tell me what happened?'

She tightened her grip around the photograph.

'Quinn was a bastard,' she said. 'We met at the Catholic Singles Club. He is the only man who danced with me.'

Mandy could imagine how Quinn must have charmed her. The guy was a sleazeball but hadn't been bad-looking, and if he had an ulterior motive, maybe he could be charming too. With Pedro, Miguel, María and Alfonso not needing her any more, the old nanny must have been very lonely. She must have put her own life on hold for those children, he realized. Quinn was her version of romance.

'So you started seeing each other?' he said.

She nodded. 'For three years he pretended he loves me, but really so he could get his hand on this house.'

'That must hurt,' Mandy said. 'But how did Quinn think he'd get this house from you?' He knew, but he needed her to confirm it.

'*Señor*, this house was to be given to me because I bring up Alfie. And I have worked for the family since I was fourteen-year-old *chiquita*. Forty-two years! I was told it was mine, but then they give the house to Pedro. Then Pedro says he will give it to me. And then Pedro changes his mind. I trusted them – when they say they do something, I think they will do it. *Sí, señor*, you agree?'

'It must have felt like a betrayal,' Mandy said. 'So what happened?'

'Pedro came to me one day and say, "I've been told to only leave you the house for the rest of your life, but you'll always have a roof over your head."'

'So you don't own the house but can live in it as long as you want?'

'Correct, *señor*.'

'Sounds like he was being weak.'

'Weak, *señor*? Pedro is often weak. All of the children are except the girl. I say, "Why you not stand up to your father?" But he say his mother made him. That woman! After all I'd done for her children.'

'So you killed Pedro?'

'No, no. Never!' She broke off. She was struggling to speak. 'I never harm

Pedro,' she said. 'Never. He was also my child. Weak but beautiful, and a big heart. I never stay mad at him for long.'

'But Quinn did? He wanted revenge, didn't he? And at first he said he was going to get revenge because you had been cheated. But then you saw that he wanted things for himself?'

'You are right, *señor*.' Tears began streaming down her wreck of a face again. 'Why did I let him make me?'

Mandy cleared his throat. 'What did he suggest? Did he make it sound like it was only what anyone else would do? Perfectly normal considering what had happened?'

She bit her lip and nodded. 'Quinn said we take something from Pedro as big as the house. He said he knew a man who help. I thought we take the painting.'

'The picture of the girl in the café?' Mandy decided to play down the value. 'Worth over half a million dollars.'

Josefina screwed up her mouth as if she'd just tasted sour milk. 'I said it's no good to take – because it looks so miserable. I know it is worth something: Pedro always show it to people. But is it worth so much?'

'Maybe more,' he said. 'Five or six times more. So, the helpful man – did you know who the guy was?'

'Dominic? An Englishman.'

Jesus Christ. Dominic Young? Susan Green's ex-boyfriend, the corpse on the beach, was meant to have been Josefina's knight in shining armour?

'Have you been asked this by anyone else, anyone from the police?' Mandy asked.

'No, *señor*.'

He took hold of Josefina's liver-spotted hand. It was clammy and bony. 'Good. Don't tell anybody else – it's important. You won't be safe if anyone else knows.'

She clutched at his hand like a starving child.

'Now,' he said, 'the man or men were not interested in the painting, were they? Tell me what happened.'

She dabbed her eyes, began threading her rosary through her fingers. 'Quinn tell me it go wrong, but he tell me how after the funeral. He tells this man Pedro's blood group – rhesus negative.' She looked sideways at him. 'I had to know all the children's blood groups, *señor* – in case of accidents.'

Mandy stood up and scratched the back of his head. 'So,' he said, 'Quinn told Dominic that Pedro had a very rare blood group and he suddenly became really interested?'

Josefina leant forward on the sofa. 'I don't know, but next thing another man call him and say he do the job as Dominic has to go see his mother.'

'Do what job?'

She held up her hand, sucked hard on her teeth and continued, tears running down her cheeks. She could not bring herself to look at him, or at the photograph of Pedro.

'Quinn let them in while Pedro was still sleeping. He didn't know Pedro ask Russian girl to come to clean because Lucy arriving from London. The girl has a key because Pedro sleeps late. The two men tell Quinn things all wrong. By mistake they silence her.' She lost control here. Her eyes found his; she was begging him not to make her say it.

'Go on,' he said.

'They silence Pedro for good; they kill the girl to make it look like she killed herself. She is nineteen years old. Quinn got five thousand dollars and they said more later, much more, but he must keep mouth shut. Quinn scared. They brought down a white box – like fishermen use for their catch . . . Quinn say it make him feel sick. But they give him the money later . . .'

'A business opportunity where people are killed in the process?'

'*Sí, señor*. Someone wanted something enough to pay a lot of money.'

Fuck. Did she know that Quinn had been dying of leukaemia? Maybe the old bastard had been trying to get the house or the money for her after all?

'So Quinn thought he'd found a way of earning good extra cash?'

'Yes. I think he want to set up in business with this man and the English boy.'

'Did he disconnect the security cameras in the lobby?'

She nodded. 'Yes, that and letting them into the building. He is a TV repair man: he knows about cameras.'

He took his cell from his pocket and put his hand on her arm. 'Quinn is in a better place now.'

She crossed herself. 'I doubt that. But may God have mercy on his soul.'

He bowed his head respectfully, using his right thumb to make the photo full screen. He needed to be certain she had not taken part in Quinn's death.

Holding the phone close to the light, Mandy said, 'Here's another sad picture.'

She stared for two or three seconds at the image of Quinn's lifeless head, let out a guttural moan, bent down and vomited into her handbag.

Mandy walked back into the kitchen. Father Tony was seated at the table, arms folded across his chest, like an expectant parent.

'How is she?'

'Queasy, but quite calm considering I just showed her a photo of Quinn's body.'

'Why on earth did you do that?' The priest closed his eyes and shook his head.

Mandy opened the refrigerator, found a Coke, ripped it open and took several gulps. 'I needed to know how involved she is.'

'And did showing her that tell you?'

Mandy nodded. 'Think so. She threw up.'

Father Tony shrugged. 'A guilty person might be sick too.'

'Sure, but she was shocked and surprised. You can't fake that. She hadn't seen it before. It was all news to her.'

'And did she confess she killed Pedro?'

'No. Because she didn't. But she told me what really happened, or what happened according to what Quinn told her.'

'Do you think I have a duty of care to tell the police what I know?'

Mandy pictured Broadski and Dent, and laughed. They hadn't exactly been too worried about any duty of care regarding Pedro.

'I don't think you are obliged to disclose anything right now, but I reckon as her priest there might be one or two issues and a hefty penance.' He finished the Coke.

'So what happens to Josefina?' Father Tony said.

'Police enquiries will probably conclude Josefina didn't have any intent to harm Pedro. She's old and had poor taste in men. Quinn wasn't only trying to steal her money; he was also dying of leukaemia.'

'Did Josefina mention that just now?'

'No, Frank, the assistant coroner, told me this morning.'

He crumpled the Coke can against the tabletop and said, 'Thanks for tipping me off like you did.'

'I'm going to see if she's all right. Have you got to go somewhere?'

Mandy wiped some sweat off his brow and fingered the car keys in his pocket. 'I've got an appointment to see some fish.'

54

6.50 p.m., 20 July

During the short walk from Josefina's house to the Amazon, Mandy phoned Lucy at the Comfort. She picked up immediately, sounding anxious. 'You OK? What about Tony?'

'Everything's fine with him. Stay where you are and don't answer the door to any strangers. In fact, only answer the door to me. I will be back soon.'

'How long will—'

Mandy didn't answer and drove off wondering if Lucy was reading a magazine on the bed in her underwear. Or was she waiting behind a locked bathroom door wearing a bathrobe, scared and slotting bullets into the rifle?

He parked close to Fish Farm on North Channel Road, checked his loaded gun in its holster and got out of the car. His heart was pounding. He tightened the knot in his tie and out of nervous habit shined his shoes on the back of his trousers.

Purple clouds obscured the setting sun and cast dark shadows over the Fish Farm building. The area around its entrance resembled a black lake of shadow. Three cars left in the lot and none of those was a Range Rover. Just a silver Prius, a beat-up Honda Accord and a shiny black Ford pickup with a large, empty dog cage in its rear.

The double doors of the showroom opened automatically. Inside, there was a reception desk and, through another set of doors, a circular sales counter with four cash tills. A woman with flabby arms in a kaftan was handing a credit card to a dark-haired salesman. Mandy guessed she was the one driving the Prius. Another salesman, in Fish Farm overalls and a baseball cap, was stacking shelves with boxes of fish food – the bashed-up Accord. Did that mean the salesman was the owner of the Ford, or was there someone else in the building? Someone with big, cageable dogs?

The place was lit by ceiling spotlights and other recessed lighting, sophisticated and calming, over four lanes of two-storey fish tanks. Mood music was playing that he recognized but couldn't identify. There was a glass-shuttered doorway to the left with a sign saying, 'Staff Only,' and what looked like a flight of stairs behind it. Were there more bubbling fish tanks up there or Tan's office?

The shelf stacker emptied his box of fish food and disappeared through one of the 'staff only' doors. It looked like everyone else had gone home. There hadn't been any lights in the upstairs windows when he walked through the car park.

The sales assistant held up his hand and leant over the counter. 'Sir? The store is closing in six minutes. It's an hour earlier than usual because of a stocktake.'

Mandy took two paces towards the counter, holding up his hand too, noting the name on the badge pinned to the assistant's short-sleeved shirt. 'That's fine, thank you, Kurt. I'm not going to be long.'

'Well, I'm here if you need anything, sir.'

Mandy grabbed a small supermarket trolley from a short line of them by the desk and wheeled it purposefully down the first aisle of aquariums.

The tanks were humming with electricity and bubbling from oxygen feeds. A few suction and beeping sounds, the place could double as an intensive-care ward. Running his finger along the cold, damp glass of each tank, he began to enjoy the colours of the almost unreal fish, ducking down to peer under every third or fourth tank to see if anyone else had come in – Janet Lee, Tan or the goon who had taken Susan Green.

Halfway down the final aisle, he pulled his finger away from a brightly lit tank where conga eels pressed and slid their coils against the glass like they wanted to be free, to push through the glass.

'Three minutes till closing, sir,' Kurt, the sales assistant, called.

He reached a red security rope protecting two tanks like important paintings in a museum. These were obviously celebrity fish. Two long-jawed barracuda swam in one, flicking their tails, aware and disturbed perhaps by the razor-toothed piranhas darting about in the other.

Mandy pressed his nose to the glass; a ball of piranha raced over, tapping at the cold surface like hornets crashing into a windshield on the freeway. He noticed something more interesting than the celebrity fish – a small corridor connecting to an emergency exit. Halfway along it, a chrome door with frosted portholes. 'Staff Only.' Behind him, the sales assistant was texting with his head down.

He parked the trolley, tried the door – locked. A swipe-card mechanism by the side of the door. Mandy peered through one of the portholes. Behind this door, another 'Strictly No Entry.' Only, the 'strictly no entry' door was ajar – kept open by the corner of a white polystyrene box just like the one he had seen in Chung's office.

The Chinese writing and the stencilled word 'Topanga' down one side proved it wasn't a coincidence. Mandy's gut had been right. There was something more to this place than pretty-looking fish. Four dead people had all led him to this store, with its rare and pricey fish. What else did it have down there?

Mandy suddenly felt the fear.

He took three deep breaths.

His mind filled up with Susan Green anxiously explaining how her ex-boyfriend had been caught stealing from his employers and how she drove him to Topanga to make amends. Chung, Topanga and Dominic Young – Fish Farm and heroin.

Yet there was a more complicated crossword clue to solve, a cryptic one.

Mandy sniffed the air, slid his fingers along the glass sides of the tank, dropped down on one knee and dragged the palm of his hand across the vinyl floor. The surfaces were entirely smooth, not a speck of dirt. Why was the place so scrubbed, so polished and spotless?

Was this where Chung and Tan's syndicate cut the heroin and packed it into the polystyrene boxes for the wholesalers?

Above him, the music was interrupted.

'We will be closing in one minute, ladies and gentlemen.'

There was only him. And he didn't feel much like a gentleman. He walked towards the cash tills in a kind of daze, emerged by the white plastic counter and deliberately banged the trolley against the front of it. The young sales guy, Kurt, looked up. He couldn't have been more than twenty years old.

'Hi, sir! Did you find what you were looking for?' he said, sales grin back on his face.

'Quite a place you have here, Kurt.'

'Wow, are you English?'

'That's right.' He looked at his watch. 'Yes, I'm visiting from the University of Oxford, been here a few months teaching at UCLA.' Mandy grinned at the young man.

'You're kidding!'

Kurt looked genuinely impressed. He needed just the right amount of bait.

'Yes, I'm doing some research about the world's best fish and pet shops.'

'Awesome!'

'I take it Benny and Janet are not here right now?'

'You know Mr Tan and Janet?'

'We've spoken a few times; they've always been very helpful.'

Kurt cracked the slightest of smiles. Mandy spotted an opening.

'So this is quite a big operation, then? You sell to other places, not just customers who turn up here?'

Kurt checked they were not being overheard. 'Here we have two floors with a hundred tanks on site, some with saltwater fish, some with fresh.'

'But are there more than two floors?'

Kurt nodded. 'Mr Tan has a great knowledge of fish, very good at selling fish to existing and new markets too. Customers like fish that are exotic, erotic and neurotic. Funny, eh? He's really successful. Fish Farm even has its own farm where fish are bred.'

Mandy's spine tingled.

'In Topanga?'

Kurt smiled and nodded.

'Topanga Canyon Road?'

'No, it's not there.'

'Which road is it?'

'I'm sorry – it's not company policy to say where it is.'

'No problem, I understand. I'll ask Janet when I next bump into her.'

Kurt held his phone up to the light – checking the time; a security swipe card was wedged down the back cover. Mandy watched carefully as Kurt replaced it on the counter.

'It's past seven, sir, and security are strict here,' Kurt said, 'I'm afraid you'll have to make your way to the exit . . .'

'You couldn't just tell me the cost of a single piranha? I think the price is on a label on the tank.'

'Wait right here.' Kurt ducked under the counter and walked past the 'Fish Food' display, gliding along the polished floor towards the middle row of tanks.

Mandy leant over the desk, grabbed hold of Kurt's phone. 'Don't go to too much trouble!' he called out.

'No worries, sir, just getting it now.' The boy's voice came from deep within the maze of tanks.

Mandy pulled the security card out of the cell-phone cover, slotted it into his pocket and retuned Kurt's cell to the counter.

Then the speakerphone on the counter crackled. 'Kurt! You should be cashed up by now.' The voice was gruff and Texan. That couldn't be *Tan*, could it? Sounded more like someone from the Deep South than LA.

Mandy stepped back from the counter, fighting the thought that he'd been spotted by the owner of the truck with the dog cage in the car park outside.

He didn't like dogs any more than he liked dead bodies.

Kurt sprinted back over and picked up the handset.

'Sorry, Dick, just dealing with our last customer.' Turning to Mandy, he said, 'Single piranha is three hundred and fifty dollars, sir.'

The voice came over the speakerphone again. 'Yeah, the store is closed now, so the customer will have to leave the building.'

Dick sounded like a redneck, just the type to own the Ford pickup. Mandy placed a folded twenty-dollar note into Kurt's top pocket and held up his hand mouthing, 'Thanks a lot.'

Kurt mouthed, 'Wow,' and picked up the receiver again. Mandy could hear Dick chewing Kurt's arse over something down the receiver. Time to get moving.

'Thank you. I will definitely be coming back,' Mandy called over his shoulder, as the electronic doors closed behind him.

Dick. Dick Chain?

He got back double quick to the Amazon and drove down to the ocean, parked up, took a beer out from the trunk and sank into the driver's seat to quench his thirst and contemplate. Necking the beer as if it was sacred, he thought whether to go home and regroup or drive straight back to see Lucy Lack at the Comfort. Bearing in mind it appeared that he now had clearance to land on her salmon-pink bedspread, it wasn't a difficult choice.

The beer sank into his stomach, nice and cold, and satisfying. The ocean swayed. A perfect moment of silence.

Then his phone vibrated. He tried to ignore it.

But it was flashing 'Dawn'.

Terry's wife never, ever called him unless it was something urgent. Urgent, bad or an emergency.

55

8.15 p.m., 20 July

Mandy followed the nurse to the couch in the only quiet corner of the emergency room. It was newly built and unfamiliar. The place looked like it could have been a motel but with drapes and plastic screens for walls, mobile drips and oxygen machines instead of room-service trolleys. Plus the stench of vomit, disinfectant and antiseptic.

A bearded doctor, white coat and stethoscope, greeted him. 'Presumably you've done this before.'

Mandy took an actor's deep breath. 'Yes, but this guy is my ex-partner, so it's a little different,' he said.

'I'm sorry.'

The doctor guided him down the curtained corridor, jerked one of the curtains back sufficiently for Mandy to step inside. 'I'll come back in five minutes and see how you're doing. Take your time.' The curtain was pulled shut behind him.

Mandy stared at Terry. He was dressed in unfamiliar white pyjamas like a large child, lying perfectly still in a freshly made-up bed. His blond moustache was drooping slightly around the sides of an unsmiling mouth. It was as if he was pretending to be dead, seeing how long he could keep it up.

Mandy touched the side of Terry's face. It wasn't cold, as he'd expected, but still warm and dry. The skin of his folded hands and neck and face was faintly blue.

He knew the discolouration was due to anoxia, a lack of oxygen in the bloodstream. He picked up the medical chart, glanced at it and put it back again. It didn't help. He had a speech in mind, a mixture of W.H. Auden and something from John Donne. But he couldn't even open his mouth to speak.

He stared at Terry's hands: his watch, wedding and signet rings were missing. He guessed they'd been taken, one each for Dawn, Caitlin and Alice. He hoped so, anyway.

He wanted to leave but felt he should stay as long as possible. Respect was far easier in death than in life. 'Anticlimactic', 'final' and 'empty' were the words he associated with death. You forgot everything that had been pissing you off about the person. They were gone. And you stood in that enormity. Knowing you could never enjoy being pissed off at them again.

He sighed, leant on the back of the chair by the bed and willed him to open his eyes, to announce that it was all just a joke.

'Not nearly as good as it's made out to be, is it, Terry?' he whispered. It didn't sound like his voice. 'Don't worry, I'll make them weep at your funeral.'

Tears began to course down his cheeks. He knelt by the bed.

'Thank you, friend and partner. Thanks for not selling me or yourself down the river when the going got tough. I am appointing you president of the Santa Monica Suicide Club. I'll do my absolute best for Dawn, Caitlin and Alice. Keep the room next to yours up there reserved, will you, please? I'll write to you, somehow.'

Terry's eyes didn't move, didn't open, and he didn't smile.

Having thanked the crash team and the doctor in charge, Mandy stood outside on the hospital steps, feeling life was pointless. To think he'd been about to put a hose to his own exhaust pipe just before Fabienne had called him about Pedro's murder. And now he was alive and Terry – who'd always just wanted to live – wasn't.

Shit. Shit. Shit. Fabienne.

He'd completely forgotten. He pulled out his phone and tapped out a text. 'Sorry about dinner. Terry dead.'

He pressed 'send'. It didn't read that well. But he couldn't bring himself to write anything else.

He walked down the hospital steps.

56

8.35 p.m., 20 July

Mandy drove slowly up Santa Monica Boulevard towards the Comfort Inn. He resisted the temptation to revisit the Alhambra and get drunk, even ignored the vibrating cell phone in his pocket. A blunt wave of sadness was pounding his solar plexus. It was like being a kid again, like the time when his stepfather hit him so hard on the head he'd been unsure whether to cry or throw up. He brought the Amazon to a stop by a bank of empty parking meters outside an anonymous office block. There didn't appear to be anyone around. A random thought occurred about the dead bodies he'd seen in the last few weeks and how he hated touching them. Yet somehow, the one he never wanted to see, he hadn't minded touching.

He kept the engine running, his foot stroking the accelerator, almost as a way of preventing himself from sinking into despair. He leant down and pulled out the bottle of Martell wedged beneath the passenger seat. The bottle was half full and only to be used in emergencies. This was an emergency and he needed anaesthetic. He took two generous slugs and then another two, and returned the bottle back under the seat. Seeing Terry lying dead in hospital had been surreal, and even though he'd shed a few tears by the bedside, angry thoughts were catching up with him. Something like a fishbone was lodged in his throat, telling him there was a connection between Quinn being involved in Pedro's murder and finding Terry dead in hospital. He knew that he should have dealt with Quinn himself and not left it to Terry. What the hell had he been thinking? The guy had been trying to fight off cancer, for God's sake, and hadn't needed the added stress of chasing down some lowlife concierge on Ocean. He banged his head against the car window. It was too late for recriminations. Terry was dead.

Mandy gripped the steering wheel hard, cleared his throat and sniffed like somebody snorting coke. He had made a decision. There would be no mourning Terry, no wallowing or anger over his passing – not until he'd nailed the people ultimately responsible for Pedro García-Márquez's death. The score had to be settled. Terry would have approved of the arrangement and would have done the same for him. Touching the black-and-yellow-spotted squash ball lying inside the open glove compartment, he looked up at the fading light of the pale mauve mid-evening sky and drove off.

57

Some minutes later, Mandy stood with his arm around Lucy Lack. She was staring solemnly through the open window of her room at the Comfort. The surroundings were quiet save for the electrical hum of the fridge, a police siren in the distance – no one was swimming in the pool down below. Her handbag and suitcase lay neatly on top of the salmon bedspread; the bed had been perfectly made up. No sign of crumpled pillows or the lunch they had enjoyed earlier, only the remains of a black coffee in a cup and a saucer full of cigarette butts balanced on the windowsill. Judging by the 'do not disturb' sign hanging outside the door, the clean-up operation had not been done by room service. She was no longer wearing the white dress but the same cashmere V-neck jumper he'd seen her wear in Shutters and a pair of black jeans and loafers.

He had tried to sound matter-of-fact when telling her what Josefina said Quinn and his friends had done to Pedro, but his voice cracked when adding the bad news about Terry. There now seemed little point in withholding the information that her father was most likely connected to Pedro's death.

'You're joking?' Lucy said, as she began to weep.

'I'm afraid not. I've just paid a visit to his store.'

The crying turned to uncontrollable guttural sobbing, with her arms folded across her chest, each hand holding on to each shoulder as if she was preparing for the brace position on a plane. Her grief was coming from deep inside.

Mandy stood with both hands on her heaving shoulders, aware that he was intruding on something intense and private. Strangely, Lucy's howling made him feel more composed and determined to get back to work. He strode into the emptied bathroom, grabbed a handful of toilet paper, came back and gave it to Lucy. She stopped crying, uncrossed her arms, then let out one more sob, turned away from him, blew her nose and was silent. Mandy lit two of her Marlboro Lights, handed one to her and began smoking one himself. She took it but didn't take a puff of the cigarette and let it dangle limply between her fingers.

He leant forward and exhaled smoke through the window. There was no doubt having sex would be a great comfort, a reward, something they deserved to share after each other's bad news. But he was also aware her bags were packed and the moment had passed. It was time to say goodbye, for her to return to London and for him to get back to North Channel Road. Maybe they would meet again in the future, in another place, in another time.

'Probably best to blow the smoke outside – we don't want to set off the fire alarm,' Mandy said with a slight smile, trying to sound cheerful.

'I don't care,' Lucy said, 'if the Santa Monica fucking fire brigade and ten police cars get called out.'

He touched the side of her face. 'I know what you mean, but that wouldn't help right now.'

She took a long drag, blew the smoke into the darkness outside and turned to Mandy. 'I didn't think you were coming back. No point in being here any more.'

'Is that why everything's packed up?'

'Obviously,' she said, staring forlornly at the suitcases on the bed.

Mandy pulled a face. 'I was always coming back, but shit happened. Do you know what I mean?'

Lucy slowly nodded and gently placed her fingers on his lips.

'Look, I didn't know Terry, but I'm so sorry for you. Pollock told me how close you were to him, and what can I say? Death is just such a fucker . . . but at least . . . he wasn't murdered.' She started crying again.

He squeezed her hand until she composed herself.

The cell in his pocket vibrated. 'Sorry,' he said, 'but it might be a text from Dawn, Terry's wife. I should have called her. Damn it!'

He peered at the call screen and read out the caller's name: '"Nancy, Donna's Sponsor."'

Mandy took a second – 'Nancy who?' – and then read the message. Thank God it was written like an email.

'I'm slightly freaking about Donna. She was taken out for a drive with a "family friend" at around 6 p.m. but has not returned to Springfield. No response from her cell. Is she with you? Has she made contact? Do you think we should phone the police?'

'Fuck!' Mandy shouted as he texted a message back: 'Was she driven off in a silver Lexus? Did anyone see?'

'I'll check and call you back.'

He let the phone slip from his hand. Donna, Donna, Donna, whatever are you doing?

Lucy knelt down by the bed and pulled out the rifle. 'I'm coming with you.'

'No, you are not. Go home. It's too dangerous here. Now give me the rifle.'

'No. I'm keeping hold of this and I'm coming. I know how to look after myself, Mandy.'

'Not in that way, Lucy, believe me.'

A text pinged back from Nancy.

Mandy read it out. '"The car was a black BMW station wagon."'

'That's the same car my father drives,' Lucy yelled, grabbing hold of the rifle and her car keys and heading for the door.

'OK. Let's go,' Mandy said, stubbing out both cigarettes in the saucer.

58

9.30 p.m., 20 July

Mandy watched Lucy bring the Jeep to a silent halt in the shadows of the Fish Farm car park. She got out of the car and walked towards him, the rifle hanging from a strap over her shoulder like a fashion accessory.

'I have a right to be there and no one is going to stop me,' Lucy had said angrily, as she marched out of the hotel. 'I'll be your assistant if you like, but don't treat me like a child.'

Other than locking her in the hotel room, there was no way he could have stopped her from coming, not when she had a loaded weapon in her hand.

The temperature outside had dropped to sixty degrees, but it was hardly cold. He flashed the Amazon headlights. She walked over, slipped onto the passenger seat and quietly shut the door. Mandy took the bottle of brandy from under the passenger seat, swigged two mouthfuls and offered it to her. She shook her head; he pushed it between her lips till she swallowed a large gulp. Despite the glow on her face, he could tell by the pulse in her slender neck that she was scared. And she wasn't the only one who was nervous. Mandy reached in front of Lucy and took out Terry's squash ball from the glove compartment. He put it in his pocket for good luck, inhaled deeply and recited: '*Do not go gentle into that good night, Old age should burn and rave at close of day; Rage, rage against the dying of the light.*'

Dylan Thomas's words stiffened Mandy's resolve but were not helping Lucy's shaking hands or nerves.

'I've been thinking,' she said. 'Why not call the police and get them to see if this Donna is inside?'

'Don't trust them, not the local cops anyway.'

'How about the not-so-local ones?'

Mandy eased Anderson's FBI card out of his wallet. 'Make a note of this for use in emergencies only. I'll give you Frank's as well. He's the assistant

289

coroner, well connected, and a sensible guy. And here's Fabienne, who *should* help.'

Lucy tapped the numbers into her phone and handed the card back to Mandy.

'Copy these as well,' he said, handing her numbers for Nancy, Donna's sponsor, Donna's father in China Lake, the duty doctor at Springfield and Tassos.

She did so.

He pointed over his shoulder. 'Let's get on with it.'

'You know what?' she said, her voice shaking a little. 'I don't care about my father. I'm over it really, if I'm honest. It was terribly important to me to know who he was and where he lived, if he was married again, children and all that, but I don't care now if I never meet him. I couldn't give a shit, in fact, so why not just forget this?'

'No, you owe it to Pedro and to yourself to be here. Hold on tight.'

Mandy's stomach began churning again, a PowerPoint presentation of images: Terry laughing, Donna, Terry dead, Donna bruised and in the back of a car. He wound up the window, leant over and squeezed her hands. 'I have to do this – there's no choice: someone's life, and other people's lives are at stake.'

She nodded. 'I just have a very bad feeling about this.'

'Try not to have a bad feeling and listen to me,' Mandy said. 'Whatever happens, stay inside the car with the doors locked, and text me the second anyone or anything unusual turns up.'

Lucy held up her cell. 'Got it.'

'Now keep checking in with the clinic and Nancy to see if Donna has made contact or been found. Also look at the Google map of Topanga – for any places big enough to have fish-breeding ponds. And if you feel it's getting too scary or weird, don't call Pollock, call my friend Tassos. He'll come, no questions asked.'

'I'm not going anywhere until I see you get back in the car.'

Mandy looked at her and shook his head. She might have found where her father lived, but she was hardly Cagney or Lacey. Lucy was a fatal combination – sexy, stubborn and scared.

She shivered. 'Do you have a heater in here? I'm cold.'

He turned on the engine, revved and slid the heater controls to 'on'. They hadn't been used for a long time, not since he and Terry had gone one winter to Monterey to see where Terry had grown up. Terry inside his old classroom, pulling faces at the desk where his teacher used to sit, ringing the school bell, hitting an imaginary strike with an imaginary baseball bat.

Mandy held his eyes shut and thought of Terry's motionless body in the hospital bed. He shook his head.

He would not revisit that scene.

He grabbed his torch from the back seat, ran his hand down the side of Lucy's face and got out of the car.

One minute later he stood by the entrance to Fish Farm and looked across the empty car park. There was little traffic on North Channel, the odd car passing, the odd motorbike. Light from the two overhead lamps spilt onto the hood of the Amazon. He could see Lucy inside, arms outstretched on the steering wheel, the glow of a cigarette in one hand, holding her phone towards her face like a hand mirror in the other.

He forced himself to smile, patted his gun and the iron bar inside his jacket pocket and took out a pair of latex gloves and the swipe card he'd stolen from Kurt. He put the gloves on, took a deep breath and slid the card down the mechanism in the door frame. There was a click and the entrance doors parted, the thick glass sliding apart with a sigh. He stepped inside; the air brushed his neck as the doors closed behind him.

The place was dark. He gripped hold of his torch, shone it along white walls and ceiling. The doors to the showroom pushed back and remained open. He walked through.

The room smelt of almonds and body odour. Strange. It seemed larger than before with just the buzz-buzz hum of electricity from the pumps and green baby lights over the tanks. The bubbling, whirring and hissing noises coming from the tanks still reminded him of hospital.

He put his gloved hand on the counter where he'd spoken to Kurt. There was an odd purple fluorescence within each of the cash tills.

He flicked the beam of light over the door saying, 'Staff Only,' walked over, swiped the mechanism. It opened. He ran up the stairs three at a time, on the balls of his feet as close to silent as his bulk could manage. At the top, a suite of three glass-walled offices.

One was larger than the other two, with expensive modern furniture and half-drawn Venetian blinds on three sides. The corner spot had to be the boss's. He went in and sat down in the high-backed chair behind the glass desk with its large white computer; the car park's lights were coming through the window at the end of the room.

He had his bearings now. He took the iron bar from his pocket and rested it against the keyboard of the computer. Next to the desktop, a cheesy photograph of a group of African kids smiled up. Not exactly what Mandy had expected from Tan. There were no drawers or paper files, no clutter but a silver letter opener.

Tan must have everything on computer. Password-protected. He switched it on and, while it was warming up, walked around the room examining the stuff on the walls: a mounted wall speaker, a half-unfurled Stars and Stripes, endless health-and-safety certificates and two framed photographs of Tan in a tuxedo shaking hands with the Clintons.

Mandy shone the torchlight on Tan's face. No way did Lucy's green eyes match Tan's dark ones. But the mouth, nose and chin were virtually identical. Christ. Stop. Stop it. The girl in the car park outside was not phoning her estranged father so he could kill him right now. The sins of the fathers did not always become their daughters'.

The beam of the torch hit a half-open door behind the desk. Inside was a windowless bathroom. He went in, closed the door and switched on the light. It was mirrored, spotlessly clean, scissors and nose-hair trimmer on the side of the basin, a large pile of towels on the floor.

The sight of a toilet made him want to pee. He unzipped his flies and stood over the bowl. A green box of matches from the Viceroy Hotel was lying on top of the cistern. He picked it up and shook the box. Nothing. He pulled open the empty matchbox drawer; someone had neatly printed six words: 'Whenever you run out, call Nabokov.'

Mandy repeated it. Viceroy Slayings, heroin, big money greasing palms, dead Russian girls at their cleaning jobs.

'Whenever you run out . . .' Run out of what? *Fish?* Unlikely. *Matches?* Fuck off. *Money?* More likely. *Heroin?*

Even though he didn't know who Nabokov was yet, he knew Tan was up to his neck in far more than tropical fish. Heroin didn't get into polystyrene packing crates all by itself.

He pocketed the matchbox and urinated over the toilet seat, the lid, the cistern and the surrounding carpet, up and down the pile of towels and finally left a dark yellow pool of piss in the square white basin of the shower.

A slightly more civilized variation on the normal calling card burglars liked to leave. Tan was a prick, had treated his daughter appallingly and, in case they never met, Mandy wanted him to know what he thought of him. He zipped up.

A dog barked.

It sounded unpleasant.

And close.

Inside the building, or where Lucy was waiting? He switched off the bathroom light, checked his cell under the desk light. Away from the bathroom, the text alert beeped. Shit!

A man drove into the car park, waited a few seconds and drove out again.

He hurried to the window, heart pounding, but the car lot was empty.

Time to get downstairs. The PC had booted up. He sat down at the desk, yanked the keyboard towards him.

'Bigfish', 'Lucy', 'Lucylack', 'lucytan', 'fishy', 'bennyfish' he rattled off. None of them worked. He heaved himself out of the chair and was about to shut down when he decided to type in one more word: 'Topanga.'

Open sesame – a screensaver of Benny between four ponds, behind him a large modern building, the top storey's four cubes arranged at odd angles. Mandy reached for his cell and took three or four pictures. The photo looked like it was taken in Topanga overlooking PCH. He flicked to 'most recently viewed'. Russian Holdings Corporation, Moscow and Fish Farm. He clicked the file open.

It was an undated contract of sale between the two parties. The dog barked again. The registered office for Fish Farm was not Benny Tan's house in Silver Lake, or North Channel, but an address in Topanga. He emailed it to himself and, for safety's sake, pressed 'print'.

Printout in hand, he stepped down the stairs and back into the showroom. The room felt swollen, its bubbling pipes louder, the air clammy like a greenhouse with the heat full on.

He walked to the middle row of aquariums, keeping the beam of the torch away from the windows but illuminating each tank as he went.

'Sorry to wake you,' he whispered as a joke. Then stopped dead.

Something had moved behind him.

He flicked the torch off, swung round and scanned the tanks. He held his breath. Something splashed on the surface of a nearby tank.

It splashed again and stopped.

He crept on, past octopuses, conger eels, barracudas and piranhas, to the chrome door.

'Staff Only.' He took out Kurt's swipe card. He swiped it down the reader, waited for the click and pushed inside, shutting it silently.

He stared out through the porthole back into the showroom.

Had he been mistaken? Just nerves?

Or was someone in here with him?

Nothing moved in the dim green light of the tanks. Nothing but the metallic flickering of the prize specimens.

Shaking his head to ward off the spooked feeling, he passed through another door – 'Strictly No Entry' – propping it open with a fire extinguisher. The lino floor smelt like Quinn's basement.

He flicked the torch back on; a half-open door to his right, a corridor ahead with an emergency exit at the end and another doorway six feet to the left. 'Authorized Personnel Only.'

That must be the one.

He swallowed, made his tongue push some saliva around his dry mouth.

Heartbeat rising, he pushed at the door. Locked.

If there was anybody in the building, they already knew he was there. If there wasn't, then it would make no difference. He imagined Donna's blonde head between the two bastards who'd taken her and threw himself at the door, left shoulder first. He'd done it a hundred times when he was a cop. The pain would pass.

There was the noise of the lock giving way and wood splintering. Behind the door, a stairway. He pushed another fire extinguisher against the smashed door and began to climb. Down into a darkness that was not just an absence of light but an absence of soul. He tried to find that funny.

On the first step.

Something metallic scraped along the floor behind him.

He swung round, lifting the gun out of his pocket as if he still did it every day of his life. By instinct.

The fire extinguisher was no longer wedging the door. The door was closed.

Nothing to worry about.

The extinguisher slid. That's all.

He put the gun back in his pocket.

Terry voice spoke in his head: '*What's the worst that can happen to us, dude? We'll be fine.*'

If someone else was in the building, it was too late to worry. Just get on with it. Let it play. Too late . . .

He clicked on a light switch.

The basement was maroon-painted concrete. Two black doors either side of a hallway. He pushed open the door on the right, pulled on a hanging cord and four fluorescent tubes lit up a large room with another door at the far end of it: 'Emergency Exit.' Useful.

A long metal table like a hotel kitchen table stood dead centre. Fish or heroin? A coiled hose, a vacuum cleaner and a fetid smell he remembered from a disused public swimming pool.

He wiped the palms of his hands down the sides of his jacket, adrenalin pumping, chest, throat and underarms leaking sweat. It wasn't just fear; it was the smell, that rancid, neglected smell.

He ran to the far end of the room and checked the emergency exit's peephole glass. The door backed out onto a loading bay and a shiny black Mercedes van. Access on the opposite side of North Channel, either via San Vicente or Neilson Way.

His cell vibrated. He opened the message: 'Black Ford pickup in car park . . . Leave NOW.' He pushed the door. But the emergency exit wasn't moving . . . No swipe card required, no exiting through the back door. Jesus.

He took a running leap at it, shoulder first. But it didn't move. It was made of stronger-grade stuff than the door to the stairs that he'd shouldered. So Tan trusted most of his workers, then. Or he knew they were scared of him . . .

He tried again. The door fought back. His shoulder hurt like hell.

Back out into the hallway, he strained to hear noise from above.

Nothing.

He started walking – quieter than a panicking rush – up the metal stairs. Fuck it.

Every fibre, bone, muscle in his body was telling him to get the hell out of there while there was still time; another part – maybe Terry's part – was screaming to go back to the last door.

The door he hadn't seen behind.

It didn't have a swipe reader. But it was the same shoddy door as the stair entrance. He kicked it three times with all his fury and strength. It buckled and cracked.

Inside the room, something stopped him from pulling the light cord. He didn't know what. A whispering sense of dread; there was something inexplicably evil about the room. His torch and the light from the corridor. That was enough.

The room had wooden shelves floor to ceiling on both sides.

A chill ran up his spine and over his head . . . The shelves were full of rucksacks, backpacks and cases.

He took several breaths, tried to argue with the feeling, failed and made himself do what he didn't want to do. Stay. Look. Witness.

He played the torch beam over the shelves, bulging with personal belongings.

Treasures. Some bags had badges sewn on them; some had dirty and defeated-looking peace signs; some were organized, with gym shoes tied to their straps.

He stood swallowing the stale body odour, rotting food, damp clothes. Inside the bags was the sum total of people's worldly goods, even their lives – all trussed up and going nowhere. It was like the bags were the people themselves.

What the hell were they doing there? And where were their owners?

He walked further into the room and shone the torch along the middle and top shelves. The bags on the top shelf were covered in dust. Those on the lower shelf looked cleaner, more recently abandoned. A few still had labels.

He swivelled a label sewn into a shoulder strap of a pristine pink rucksack. 'Tracy and Snowy, 45 Chestnut Tree Avenue, Lakeside, Des Moines 50317.'

Santa Monica was a long way from Idaho – 1,700 miles, to be precise.

And one caught his eye. A red bag with 'Broken Pack on a Broken Back' scrawled on it in marker pen.

The guy with a dog in the queue of the shelter.

He hadn't really listened to Father Tony carping on about the homeless disappearing. But it was making sense now. If you could call it sense.

Mandy shuddered.

He understood now.

All that was left of them was the unique scent on their clothes.

A door clanged open above him.

No mistaking it this time.

He turned off his torch and crouched. Yanked out his cell and photographed each shelf and saved them under 'Fish Farm evidence' to make it easier to find if he didn't make it. He loaded them into a message, and for safety's sake, addressed it to Frank and Fabienne, then pressed 'send'. Someone would eventually figure it out. If the damn thing would send it. No signal. The curse of the basement.

A dog barked from somewhere up above him, definitely inside the building. Fuck. Stay calm. Get out of here.

He closed the door of the room of bags softly, as though it was sacred, and ran up the metal stairs.

Three things were different in the showroom: the overhead lights were on, a white polystyrene box was balanced on the sales counter near the cash till, and the sound of two panting dogs was coming from the middle aisle of aquariums. They weren't Chihuahuas.

Movement on the far right-hand row of tanks. A large guy in a white T-shirt and black leather suit emerged from behind the celebrity tank. He was between fifty-five and sixty, big – six foot four and two hundred and fifty pounds, built like an American football player with dyed brown hair to his shoulders and red blotchy skin. He was holding a short-barrelled pump-action shotgun in one hand and two dog leads in the other.

Worst of all, he was not in a hurry. That was always a bad sign. The guy wasn't panicked in the least.

Mandy just stood there eyeballing the guy and taking in the position.

'Hi, there,' the guy said, friendly as fuck. 'Hope you like dogs.'

Then the guy pointed the double barrels at him. 'That your car outside, sir? The red Swedish beater?' His accent was a little like Fabienne's, but less refined. Texas redneck.

'Yes, that's mine.'

Maybe Lucy had had the good sense to hide or drive away before this oaf started asking questions. He hoped so.

'She's a beauty – if you like cars that can't really do anything. You live on Castellammare Drive and your name's Mandy?' Southern Man said, with a parody of a smile.

296

'Yes, and are you Dick Chain, by any chance? A good customer of the late Mr Chung and with a talent for writing on the back of receipts?'

The guy yanked on the straining leads and gave a wry smile. 'That's right, Mandy. I'm here to escort you to our other office, to meet our CEO.'

'Good. I want to meet him.'

'The boss said to let you know there's a young friend of yours waiting there, but best not tell anyone about it, so hand me your phone, please.' The creep held out his wriggling fingers.

'A young lady friend of mine, perhaps?' Mandy said, easing the safety catch off the gun inside his pocket.

'Maybe.'

Chain laughed. It was a very relaxed laugh. Worryingly relaxed. 'Now, this baby has both barrels loaded, and once they've had their muzzles removed, my two dogs can disable a running man within about seven seconds. So don't think about it and let's do this nice and easy, yes?'

Mandy hooked his finger through the trigger of his gun and wrapped his hand round the handle.

'I am going to take it easy,' he said. 'And I like dogs too much to harm them. Pit bulls are my favourite breed. It was you who punched me out in the chapel at LAX, wasn't it? Always happy to put a face to the bastard who did that.'

Chain shrugged. 'I prefer Labradors,' he said. 'As a pet. But for getting results, it's pit bulls every time. Now, sir, stop fucking with me. Put your hands on top of your head and walk slowly towards me. Any screw-up and I'll shoot your dick off.'

Mandy pulled his left hand out of his pocket, attempting to hide the fact he was trying to lift his gun out with his right.

Chain dropped behind the tank. 'Have it your own way,' he said.

Mandy started moving towards the cover of the counter. The two pit bulls thundered towards him — tubes of muscle and rage, claws sliding and scraping along the polished floor, tongues hanging between powerful jaws, teeth bared, flecks of spittle and foam.

The first ran into Mandy's leg and bounced off, collecting a kick in the ribs with a howl.

Rage, Mandy thought, not pain. The dog's chest had been solid muscle.

The second launched itself into the air and sank its teeth into his right forearm, with a squelching, sucking sound Mandy had never heard before. The dog held on like his arm was some form of prey. The dog's weight dragged his hand down to the ground. The pain kicked in.

He shook, but the dog just increased its grip. Jaws tighter than ever. Teeth biting deeper into the flesh.

297

'Fuck!'

Chain stood up and laughed. 'Good boy,' he said. 'Fetch him over here. Come on, sweetheart. Good Boysie. Come on, sweet darlin' . . . That's right – drag him over. Come on.'

Chain's pervy dog talk sounded exactly like the porn makers on the plane. The red switch flicked in Mandy's head. He pulled out the iron bar, lifted it high and rammed four inches of it into the clamping dog's eye. It shrieked, blood spurting – the eye was messed up. Boysie fell to the ground and shuffled towards its owner, slipping on the bloody floor and crapping itself. But Mandy had forgotten the other pit bull. It sank its teeth into the back of his thigh.

No time to register the pain.

Chain was jogging towards him, pump-action cocked at chest height.

'You hurt my Boysie,' he was shouting. Tears, actual tears, running down his acne-scarred face.

'Thought you preferred Labs,' Mandy said, holding his gun unsteadily in both hands. Gouts of blood running over the polished metal. Dog still chewing the back of his leg.

Kill or be killed.

Mandy aimed at the guy's chin, squeezed the trigger twice.

The bullets hit him in the neck, blew a socking great hole in his throat, blowing him backwards, the jugular spouting blood. He landed spread-eagled on the side of a toppled fish tank.

Mandy looked down at the dog still attached to the back of his knee and shot it through the head. He killed the injured one with a bullet to the heart. It had been in terrible pain, and Mandy hated that.

The gunshots and smashing glass reverberated around the room like a car crash.

Mandy didn't bother to ask the guy any further questions. Blood was pouring out of his ears, nose, mouth and throat – the impact had made him bite through his tongue. He kicked away the shotgun, bent down and pulled out a wallet from Southern Man's jacket pocket.

A California pilot's licence indicated, 'Richard Chain.'

Dick Chain.

The receipts.

Chung's.

The dog food.

Why hadn't Chain pulled the trigger?

Someone else must have wanted Mandy alive.

That was good news. Hopefully.

Fact was, he was alive, and Chain and his dogs were dead. He shuffled to the sales counter, grabbed hold of the white polystyrene box and got out of the building before he threw up.

59

10.55 p.m., 20 July

Mandy spewed his guts over the front of the Ford pickup, gripping the sides of the hood as he did. Blood was dripping down his arm, soaking his shirt sleeve and flowing out of the back of his leg too. The thought of the dark hole in Chain's throat and the bits of dog brain on his shirt made him retch some more.

After spitting and wiping his mouth clean, he took off his jacket and limped back to the Amazon. Providing he found some painkillers and stopped the bleeding, he could carry on. He fell onto the driving seat.

When he came round, his eyes focused on an orange flashing light.

A perfumed hand stroked his forehead. 'You're going to be fine.'

Lucy Lack.

'Hello, my friend. Have some Coke – and take three of these.'

Tassos.

Sitting on the back seat.

Mandy took the pills and swallowed then with a long swig of Coke. There was a thick dressing on his arm, and Lucy was trying to bandage his leg.

'Hey,' she said. 'When I saw that big guy with a gun walk into Fish Farm with those two dogs, I freaked – called all the numbers. Tassos was round the corner. Thank God he had a first-aid kit in the breakdown wagon.' Lucy snipped the ends of the bandage. 'Anderson's on his way with some back-up – ETA ten to fifteen minutes.'

He pulled his cell from his jacket, clicked on the photo of Benny Tan's screensaver and handed it to Tassos. 'Recognize this place? Somewhere in Topanga . . .'

Tassos took it. 'There are two or three roads with big houses like this overlooking the ocean on the PCH side.' He shrugged. 'Could be any one of them.'

'Fuck. I was hoping it would be obvious.'

'Maybe in the morning it'll be easier to spot,' Lucy said, rubbing Mandy's neck with her hand.

'She's right! My friend, you should go to the emergency room and get those wounds looked at.'

Mandy ignored him. 'Did you look up Topanga on the Net?'

Lucy shook her head. 'Too scared.'

He put his hand inside his pocket and took out the printout from Tan's desktop. Then he pulled open the polystyrene box and snatched at the remains of a despatch note inside.

'Bingo,' he said. 'Two delphinium and one tiger fish for an address in Singapore sent from Fish Farm Topanga, 2199 Brookside Drive. Same address as on this printout – third turning on the left up Topanga Canyon Drive.'

Tassos peered over Mandy's shoulder. 'You sure?'

'I was hired three years ago to find a missing German shepherd for the owner of a house up there. I never found the dog, so I hope it's not the same guy.'

He put his left arm around Lucy's shoulders and squeezed. 'I have to do this alone. It's safer if you follow with Tassos in the recovery truck.'

She nodded.

He leant across, opened the door and she stepped out of the car. 'I've put my rifle behind you, just in case you need it,' she said. 'It cost a fortune, so it ought to be good.'

Mandy smiled, then looked over at Tassos in the rear-view. 'No discussion, just your help.'

Tassos shrugged. 'No problem. Don't drive too fast – we'll follow you.'

Mandy eased his feet over the pedals, fired up the engine. He waited till Tassos was outside the car, then called through the window, 'Tell Anderson I'm heading for 2199 Brookside Drive, Topanga.'

He pulled out his gun – the handgrip still sticky with his own blood – slapped it onto the passenger seat, shoved the gearstick into first and took off.

301

60

Mandy sped past the turning for Sunset, necking the bottle of Martell to deaden the pain from his wounds. The exit for the Getty and Castellammare flashed past. Down from fifth to third to second, engine racing. Back up to fourth, slowed the old car to eighty before it had a heart attack. One hand on the wheel, he leant behind and pulled up the rifle and slotted it in the well of the passenger seat. It had a six-bullet chamber, for hunting deer not humans. '*Whatever works,*' Terry said in his head.

He slowed down and looked in the rear-view for Tassos's recovery truck. Nowhere in view. Not as turbo-powered as Tassos always boasted . . . but that was what Mandy wanted. No danger for Lucy, or Tassos. This was his responsibility. His call. He owed that to Lucy. Only one name was on his mind now: Donna. Why the hell had they taken her?

He turned off the brightly lit PCH into the relative darkness of Topanga Canyon Drive. A petrol tanker on full beam nearly forced him off the road. A sign pointing left for Brookside Drive high up on a curved overhead street-light. He used his uninjured arm to swing the wheel into Brookside, killed the engine and freewheeled to the far end of the road.

The road was a cul-de-sac with grass banks, white picket fencing and ten-foot concrete walls round the bigger estate entrances. He remembered each house had a steep driveway. The missing German shepherd had been from 216, the same three digits as his mother's phone number when he was a kid. The hairs on the back of Mandy's neck and arms bristled, and his mouth dried. An owl hooted; a donkey brayed louder and louder as if it was being brutalized. Nope. Mandy had never liked Topanga.

He took another swig of brandy, pulled up the handbrake and took a breath. The time to meet the CEO was now.

Out of nowhere a roaring. A big car behind him. Headlights on full beam.

A massive jolt. The Amazon slammed forward. His head hit the windscreen, his chest the steering wheel. Winding him. No air.

Fuck!

Some maniac had driven into him. He gasped, open-mouthed, chest heaving. Head throbbing, half conscious. The headlight beam blinding him. Then a 'pop' sound as the vacuum in his lungs broke and he could breathe again.

He spun round. It was the dark bulk of a Range Rover, but he couldn't see who was driving. Had to get his bearings – booze, painkillers and adrenalin were all fucking with his head.

The Range Rover rammed into the Amazon again, steamrolling it along the road, like a stock car at a demolition derby – effortlessly bulldozing him towards a concrete wall. There wasn't time to jump. He grabbed the rifle, flicked the safety catch, aimed at the middle of the back window and let off two rounds. The butt kicked back hard into his shoulder. Glass shattered. Cold air and gun smoke filled his lungs. The Range Rover increased speed.

He yanked the steering wheel hard down left as far as it would go, slammed both feet onto the brake. The effect was instantaneous – the Amazon jackknifed into a 180-degree turn. The rear end smacked into the wall with a terrifying metallic crash.

Beside him, the Range Rover careered into the wall. Two heads flicking forward and back like two crash test dummies. Broadski and Dent.

Mandy kicked open the passenger door, grabbed the torch and shone it through the Range Rover window. The detectives had not been wearing seat belts. It wasn't a great look.

Despite a broken nose, badly split lips and his right eye hanging down his cheek like an oyster, Dent was breathing. Which was more than could be said for Broadski. Judging by the blood trickling from his ear, motionless head and blank eyes staring at the indicator stick, Broadski's cerebral cortex had been severed – even at that little speed, it could happen. Mandy wiped his mouth with the back of his hand.

What the fuck were they doing there? Were they the tip of the corruption iceberg or just stupid? However much he'd disliked them, Mandy had too much faith in the SMPD to think they'd ever do something like this.

'*Sucker,*' Terry's voice said. '*Nice guys come second,*' followed by a roar of Big Daddy laughter. Then he was gone and Mandy was alone with the badly mangled Dent and the dead Broadski.

Headlights lit up the road – Tassos's recovery truck.

'I've called Anderson,' Lucy shouted through the window.

Mandy nodded. 'Stay here,' he yelled, and ran through the entrance to 2199.

The high metal fence and gates were the same colour as Tan's house in Silver

Lake. Two signs – 'Service Entrance' and 'Private Drive' – pointing at different driveways that curved 150 metres round a low-lit lawn covered in small warning signs on long spikes saying, 'Trespassers will be prosecuted.' The front and roof of the entire house was floodlit. Maybe they were expecting somebody.

It was a modern building, with floor-to-ceiling windows on the ground floor, and above that, a floor consisting of four connecting cubes set at angles to one another exactly like the photo on Tan's computer at North Channel Road.

To the far right of the house, four outbuildings, all of them bigger than a usual suburban garage.

Keeping to the shadows – easy when someone throws so much light about – he walked towards the various cars in the driveway: a BMW estate, one old but familiar-looking Mercedes, the same Honda Accord he'd seen before, a Dodge Cruiser and a Lincoln. He guessed the BMW was the car Donna had been in for her magical-mystery trip.

All the ground-floor windows were seeping light through long blinds. He thought he could hear people inside, shouting, laughing. They sounded drunk. In the distance, the sound of sirens – Anderson's FBI team?

He took the safety catch off the handgun and stepped onto the path, noticed several heavy-duty air-conditioning units had been stuck onto this side of the house like magnetic fridges.

He coiled his finger round the trigger of his revolver, cocking his ear close to the wall to try to hear what was being said inside. He could hear only blurred, muted voices.

At the rear of the house, he stepped onto a terrace – the house was elevated, higher ground at the back, with a basement. Behind him, dark, lapping water – the fish ponds from Tan's screensaver.

He looked up at the large window on the raised ground floor, blazing light. The windows were all too high on this side of the house. He couldn't even see a door until he spotted a black Mercedes van parked at the top of a ramp at the far end. He scanned the long wall for an entry point. It was weird – a line of closed windows but no doors. Access to the building had to be down the ramp, probably through an underground garage.

But he needed to see who was inside first.

There was a huge terracotta-coloured tub with a dead olive tree two windows down. He grabbed its plastic rim and dragged it beneath the well-lit window, clambered onto it – every inch of his injured body complaining – and leant onto the window ledge so he could see into the room.

It was a high-ceilinged kitchen with light blue walls. A large, dark-haired man with a beard was standing at the far end of a dining table raising a glass of wine to two heavy-set Slavs sitting either side of him. Bodyguards. A flushed

304

Kurt was between Beardy and the Asian woman from Silver Lake – Yale. To her right, a white-haired man built like a bull, who Mandy was pretty sure was Chain's silent partner, the guy who'd helped kill Pedro and take Susan Green from the LAX chapel. There was a spare place next to this man that nobody had claimed. Janet Lee or Dick Chain, Mandy guessed.

Someone in surgical scrubs wearing a toy Schwarzenegger mask on their face came in. He couldn't tell if they were male or female. Maybe this was Janet? Yale jumped up, held up two hands with bright red-painted fingernails and yelled something.

Whoever was inside the mask seemed to agree and picked up a glass of wine. Then as if it was a game of charades, Arnie stepped behind the bearded man and placed a pistol to his head. Yale stopped smiling. Kurt froze. The two bodyguards began to go for their guns but changed their minds. It all went very slow. Like time was freezing. For a split second, Mandy was more fascinated than shocked.

Arnie kept staring at the five people watching him, gun still held to the temple of the bearded man. The eyes behind the eyeholes dark and empty. He said something to the kid, but then caught sight of Mandy and fired two shots at him, shattering the window.

But Mandy had already jumped down and was running to the other end of the house where the van was parked. The sirens were far closer now. But he couldn't wait. He needed to find Donna before Arnie did.

He ran down the ramp, into a twenty-foot-long tunnel. At the end were the grey metal doors of a goods elevator. To his right, a set of double doors wedged open by a medical trolley that led to a pink corridor. He ran down it. A door with a handwritten sign that said, '*Despatch*.' The writing was beautiful – elegant calligraphic italics. Someone cared about something here – just not about human life.

He went in. In the middle of the room, a black-bedded operating table was positioned underneath an overhead examination light. A bank of glass cabinets containing surgical instruments stood against the side wall emitting an ultraviolet light. To the right were two metal sinks.

Three white polystyrene boxes taped and sealed with sterile wrapping tape stood on the operating table. Same as he'd seen in Chung's and the basement in Fish Farm, Santa Monica.

The final movement of *Swan Lake* was playing through ceiling-mounted speakers. It was a piece Mandy normally liked. He spread his hand over the cold work surface, increasingly aware he was not alone. At the far left of the operating theatre, an archway led to a small room shaped like a tiny chapel.

He made himself walk through the arch. Inside, three shrouded bodies lay on gurneys. The place reeked of old antiseptic, like a mortuary he'd once visited in Marrakesh. A large blue electric bug exterminator hung from the ceiling above.

Someone was walking in the corridor above the one Mandy had run down. He went to the first gurney and took hold of the green sheet. The body was female. He pulled the sheet off the face. He knew by the big orange hair it wasn't Donna.

Susan Green was naked, her arms were crossed over her breasts, and down from the sternum to her belly button was an upside-down 'T' of uneven stitching.

He put back the sheet.

There was the clunk and whir of a descending elevator. He covered his mouth with his left hand to try to block out the smell of death and exposed the next body. It was a skinny redheaded guy. His eyes and mouth were still open and terrified. The guy's long, tattooed arms were hanging by his sides. He had the same stitching on his torso.

Mandy cursed. He'd found Father Tony's homeless friend, Stevie from Texas.

He replaced the sheet and turned towards the door. There was an echo of the lift gates being opened and closed. The game was nearly over. Without thinking, he ran his hand over the last shroud and took it away when he realized it was the shape of a petite woman. Donna?

He hesitated. Someone was locking the doors down the corridor, whistling the same Tchaikovsky that was playing on the overhead speakers. Mandy took his pistol and stuck it inside the belt of his trousers. Then he took hold of the green sheet, lifted it away from the third body and felt himself go cold.

It was the woman with the Range Rover, Janet Lee. How did the number two of Team Tan end up dead?

Then he realized the whistling had stopped.

He winced as he felt the cold butt of metal press into his spine.

This had to be Tan.

'I always had you down as a respectable businessman, Benny, not this sort of thing.'

'No good looking for someone down here – they're all dead. Don't turn round, and hold your hands up where I can see them.'

It wasn't Tan. It sounded like . . . *Frank?*

Mandy felt a professional hand scurry under his armpits, round the back of his belt and inside his pockets and take the pistol from his belt.

'None of this was supposed to happen, Mandy. I didn't intend it, but that jerk Tan was taking this outfit somewhere I didn't approve of.'

Yes, that was Frank's voice loud and clear.

Mandy stared up at the electric fly exterminator and pictured the room with the backpacks in the basement of Santa Monica. He jerked his head round.

The assistant coroner of Santa Monica had pushed the Arnie Schwarzenegger mask up on his forehead.

'Frank?'

Good old Frank.

'Eyes straight ahead until we get upstairs.'

Was this some kind of awful practical joke? He hoped so.

'Frank, you're one of the good guys,' Mandy said. Where was Anderson when he needed him? 'What the hell are you doing here?'

'Everything in good time. Keep walking.'

Mandy faked an easy-going laugh.

'I don't want to sound like a corny movie, but there are a large amount of FBI people about to burst through the door.'

'What's done is done.'

Frank sounded weird; his breath smelt like he'd been at the mescal. A loud banging started. It came from the metal door that opened onto the ramp. Muffled shouts echoed down the tunnel. Unless Tan had some other secret army, it wouldn't take long before the place was secure . . . But Frank still had a gun. And Donna.

'Move!' Frank yelled.

Mandy shuffled down the corridor with Frank poking the gun hard into his back.

Frank pulled open the elevator gates. Mandy stepped in; Frank followed and pressed the button for the top floor. The automatic pressed over Mandy's heart. Three bad years in Vietnam had taught Frank how to use a pistol. No doubting that. The elevator set off with a jerk.

'Careful now,' Mandy said. 'Let's not have an accident. You don't really want to kill me, do you?'

Frank didn't reply. Keeping his hands up above his shoulders, Mandy stepped sideways so his back was against the wall. Frank's forearms, green surgical vest and neck were splattered with blood. Yet his face looked the same as it ever did – upright, friendly and decent.

'Frank, you got mixed up in this by mistake. The mask doesn't suit you. Can't we talk, please?'

Frank changed his grip on the gun and smiled. '*Please?* Ah, you always had such manners – more than I can say for most people in our line of work, right?'

The elevator pinged as it reached the top floor.

Frank motioned with his gun to open the gates.

Mandy stepped out onto a thick white carpet and into a bright, open-plan office. Four blue-and-grey work stations complete with headsets, keyboards, screens and vases of flowers. The room was lit by spotlights.

'This is where the orders and sales get made,' Frank said, letting out an impatient sigh, as if he was either proud or ashamed of something. 'Everything is computerized. Every organ that is extracted is barcoded and put in the computer to find a host or a sales match. Providing the customer is within thirty-six hours' flying time of LA, they can get whatever they want. Nothing is wasted; any surplus flesh or unwanted parts are fed to the fish in the ponds.'

He sounded like the gravel-voiced salesman in the TV ad selling Chevy pickups.

Mandy had a terrible taste in his mouth. Where the hell was Donna? He was afraid to ask.

'And what about Tan and the people who work here?'

Frank sat down on the side of a desk and angled the gun away from Mandy for the first time. 'Tan is next door waiting for us. The other people who work here are at home, quite normal and start, like all of us, at nine a.m. and leave at five p.m. Just a job to them.'

Mandy sat down, stunned by what he had just heard. He opened a desk drawer, saw some papers and looked back over at Frank.

'Do the Giraffe or Foxy know about this?'

Frank retrained the gun on Mandy. 'The Giraffe is a self-serving chameleon. He knows something of what's been going on, but is a master in covering his tracks. Foxy doesn't have a bad bone in her body. She's completely naive. You should take her on a date.'

'I'm more interested in Donna. Is she around?'

Frank grunted sadly, lowered his eyes, shifted himself off the desk and pointed through the open window overlooking the front lawns. 'She's in the trunk of my car.'

Mandy jumped up, open-mouthed. 'What?'

Frank pointed the gun at him. 'Sit down, you idiot. The last person I wanted to see hurt was Donna. Benny used her to get you here and then wanted me to harvest her.'

Mandy cupped his hands round the bottom two corners of the computer screen and flung it across the space between two desks. It caught Frank across his face and shoulder, knocking him hard against a wall. After a few seconds Frank recovered and picked up his revolver but didn't shoot. It was like he was immune to the pain, even with a crimson gash from eye to mouth.

'I always said you could be good at this job, but nobody believed me,' Frank said, as if they were watching a ball game together. 'Relax – Donna has a bottle of oxygen. She'll be OK for hours.'

Frank paused to take off his surgical gown, hat and gloves. He glanced across at Mandy. 'You know how it is. The department treated me like garbage for thirty-five years, suspending me that time, always saying I was going to be promoted, keeping me on the edge. I kept panicking about money, and in the end did a few more homeless jobs for Benny – so what? Did anyone miss them? Then he asked me to do some old criminal types, but they weren't healthy enough. So we moved onto the premium market, healthy organs from the healthy. Targeting healthy individuals, people with good genes, and then matching the blood types to pre-existing orders. Russians and Arabs were paying top dollar. Californian finest is what brings the money in . . . It's all locked into the special hard drives of those computers over there.'

'Frank, what the fuck happened to you here?'

'I never meant to stay involved with Tan. Five years ago – it was supposed to be a one- or a two-off, that's all. Making some money on the side while cleaning up the city of lowlife was one thing, but then selecting decent, well-bred, well-meaning citizens is quite another. Tan went mad, don't you see that?'

'I understand or am beginning to,' Mandy lied.

He wanted to bring up the subject of Terry never finding a kidney and how Terry was now dead. But an instinct for survival overrode it, and Frank seemed to want to speak.

'A big part of me wanted you to discover the bad guys, and I suppose me . . . But all the time I was being pressurized by the two blackmailing Lakers fans not to break ranks.'

'They've gone for the big sleep now,' Mandy said, 'so it doesn't matter. But then I thought you were the man with principles and integrity, so I guess I've been a sucker all round. Over twenty years of AA – what the hell happened to you, Frank?'

Frank shook his head. 'Nobody's perfect, Mandy. I like to think I've earned your respect back tonight. You see, I couldn't let Tan go through with the deal. It was Nabokov and his Russian Corporation who assassinated Griswold and Powell at the Viceroy. It was their way of saying, "Back the fuck off," to the deputy attorney general. Only a matter of time before they start taking over businesses, hospitals, banks, indoctrinating our children and trying to change our way of life. Russians don't care. Never trust a Russian. So I did the right thing – I went a little crazy, a little medieval Polish on all these bastards – all except the two kids. You'll find my signed statement on my bedside table. I don't want to say any more.'

Frank was drunk but still in control. He gestured towards a door with frosted glass Mandy hadn't noticed before. 'Open it, Mandy.'

Something felt wrong about the invitation – as if it was booby-trapped with explosives.

Mandy stepped over to the door, watching Frank and the gun all the time.

309

'There's no need to knock; just go in.'

Mandy gripped hold of the handle, opened the door and walked inside. A desk light shone on a bottle of vodka. Then he gulped.

Just behind the desk there was a stepladder where you'd expect a chair to be. A man – Mandy recognized as Tan from the photos – was standing on the top step. A noose was tight round his neck, his mouth taped, his legs bound together, his hands handcuffed and clearly visible pointing under his chin as if in prayer. The noose was taut and hanging from a wooden beam in the ceiling. Frank must have used a separate ladder to hook the rope round the beam and tie it in a special knot beneath.

'My turn to be corny, I'm afraid,' Frank said, picking up the end of a long piece of black flex attached to the stepladder and tying it to the door handle.

Frank yawned. 'In the old days, if you had a bad tooth, you used to tie a piece of string round it and the other end to a door handle and then slam the door. Benny's dental people took out a lot of people's teeth who didn't really need them taking out.'

Mandy stepped back. He could hear car doors slamming outside and several men shouting, 'Move!' Agent Anderson had arrived at last and driven onto the lawns below.

Frank cleared his throat, smiled a fatalistic smile, closed the door behind Mandy. Immediately the flex sprang tight and the stepladder creaked and began to topple. Tan screamed through his gag and managed to grip hold of the ladder with his feet for a moment longer. Then it wobbled and fell away. The man was falling. Mandy ran over, smashed the vodka bottle against the side of the desk, jumped up, lifting Tan's flailing legs into the air and severed the rope above his head with a broken piece of glass. He then let Tan fall to the floor – lucky to be alive.

Behind the door came the loudest gunshot.

Mandy jumped down from the desk and yanked open the door. He froze as he watched Frank's body crumple to the floor, his face side onto the carpet, eyes shut, blood oozing from his temple, past his shrivelled ear, down his cheek into his open mouth.

The building appeared to be shaking with the early tremors of an earthquake. Whether it was really happening inside Mandy's head or because an FBI SWAT team were charging along the corridors downstairs didn't matter. Mandy didn't care. He knelt down and pulled out a set of Mercedes keys from Frank's trouser pocket. He kicked Tan hard in the leg to make sure his bindings were still secure and then ran to the elevator, slammed the gates shut and pressed the button to descend.

Clutching Frank's car keys in his hand, he took deep breaths and tried praying, telling himself like a frightened kid that everything was going to be OK – or at least nothing more could go wrong. The surfeit of adrenalin overrode the pain from his leg and arm. The elevator hit the ground floor with a bump. Mandy heaved back the gate. In front of him, five flak-jacketed FBI agents pointing automatic weapons.

'*Freeze!*'

Mandy raised his hands in the air.

'Drop your weapon and place your hands on top of your head. Make a move and we'll shoot.'

Anderson ran up the ramp from outside, reached the elevator.

'Back off,' Anderson shouted. 'He's with us.'

'Thanks,' Mandy said, leaping up. 'Tan's upstairs with . . .' but he still couldn't say it, couldn't quite believe that Frank had been part of all this. 'There's a kid who might still be alive in the kitchen.'

He charged outside, hurtled round the side of the building, past the plastic tub with the olive tree. A stocky FBI agent with an Uzi ran alongside him. Mandy's thigh began to burn with pain. The painkillers were wearing off. He gritted his teeth and punched his own thigh. The first stab of pain dropped him to the ground, but then the adrenalin started to kick in again and he staggered up.

'The Mercedes,' he said to the stocky guy. 'She's in the trunk.'

Mandy ran towards the old Mercedes, dragging one leg behind him, the other guy sprinting ahead. The pain in Mandy's leg was almost unbearable.

'There,' he shouted.

Three car keys on the ring. The first key wouldn't fit; the second key wouldn't turn. There was an ominous silence from inside the trunk.

'Donna!' he shouted.

Jesus, was this the right car, or had Frank just been lying and Donna was packaged up in the three polystyrene boxes on the operating table? Please God, not this time.

'Donna? Christ, answer me, would you?'

Last key in the lock, a click and he popped the trunk.

She was still clutching the oxygen mask to her face.

Mandy put his hands underneath her tiny waist and slender legs, and lifted her out of the car like she was the most precious thing he had ever touched. She was still warm. He pressed her close to his chest and rocked her back and forward like a baby.

'Can I have some help here, please?' he shouted. 'Can I have some help?'

311

61

2 p.m., 24 July

There was no view of the aerobics class from the Giraffe's office window that lunchtime because the blinds were drawn. The air-con for the whole building on Main Street had been out for three days now, a technical gremlin no one could fix. Two rotating floor fans whirred and blew supposedly cool air around the office. But it was like a ship's boiler room. Mandy wondered if someone was having their own payback day.

'I suggest we start in three minutes and conclude as quickly as possible,' the Giraffe said. 'Before we all expire.'

Dressed in a dark suit and polo-neck sweater, he held a white police index card in one hand with what appeared to be a list written on it, and a cup of coffee in the other. No one replied. It was clear why they were there and that things were going to come to a head, whether they liked it or not.

Sweat ran down Mandy's back as he shifted his position on the leather sofa, trying to look composed. The stitches in the wounds on his legs tightened like they were about to snap every time he sat. The temperature wasn't helping. The wound on his arm had started to weep and had been re-stitched the previous day. God bless the UCLA emergency room on 14th Street. The re-stitching had hurt like hell. But when he revisited the room where Terry died, the pain had been far worse.

Anderson sat on a chair, one leg balanced on the other, left hand flat on the arm of the sofa, a polished wedding ring glinting in the sunlight on his finger. O'Dowd, the dreadlocked guy, was in a suit and tie. He sat behind the Giraffe's desk typing with two fingers into a laptop. For a two-finger typist, he was pretty fast. Everyone was carefully avoiding eye contact with Mandy.

'Cream with your coffee?' Fabienne asked Anderson.

'Yes, please.'

Mandy smiled. 'White with one.'

The Giraffe handed his empty cup to Fabienne for a refill without even looking at her. Fabienne filled the cup.

'Will that be all, or do you need something else, sir?' she asked. She appeared to be operating on autopilot. Her face looked thinner. Mandy reckoned she must have lost weight – and similar to Donna, she hadn't been a big girl to start with.

Donna had said Frank hadn't hurt her at all, not physically. But being trapped inside the trunk of the car, not knowing where you were, or what was going to happen next would scare the shit out of anyone, let alone Donna. It could have easily pushed her over the edge, but for some reason best known to Donna, she was OK. Mandy was proud of her. She was back in Springfield feeding her goldfish and telling everyone she met about her ordeal and how it was *really* just like being in *On Stranger Tides*.

Mandy smiled and then shuffled uncomfortably in his seat. The minutes when he thought Donna might be dead had been among the worst in his life – and there were a fair few to choose from. Still, now was now, and it was only a matter of seconds or minutes before Anderson told the Giraffe he was under arrest. Well, that was what he thought was going to happen. To confirm to the others his cell was switched off, Mandy peered inside his jacket pocket and deftly checked the red light of its recording device was glowing.

The Giraffe held out a long, paternal arm towards Fabienne. He was showing her far more concern than usual.

'Come in and shut the door and sit down. I want you to be a witness.'

Fabienne sat down next to Mandy.

The Giraffe coughed and then spoke. 'I'll get straight to the point.'

Fabienne also coughed, her hand straying to the scarf round her neck.

'Mandy,' the Giraffe said, 'you took the law into your own hands and tried to blow us off the scent so that you could claim the reward and run round town saying you're the biggest private dick since Philip Marlowe.'

Mandy grunted and shifted forward.

If this was going to be a humiliation session before he was handcuffed, he wasn't having it. He'd sooner deck the guy and fly back to England with nothing than take any more of the Giraffe's shit.

'Marlowe didn't actually exist,' he said. 'He's just a character out of a book – I thought you might know that.' He felt Fabienne's hand take hold of his arm.

'Best if you hear the Chief out . . .' she whispered.

The Giraffe gave her a thankful look. 'You're lucky to have that woman sitting next to you, so listen up. We're going to make you an offer that you'd be very unwise to refuse.'

Mandy stared at the Giraffe's throat. It was jutting in and out like a turkey.

So that was it – he was about to be stuffed. A whitewash that seemed to be being supported by the Bureau, with the Police Department taking the spoils.

He disappeared inside his head, like when he was a kid trying to ignore his stepfather, so he only half heard the Giraffe's complaints about procedure and tampering with evidence, withholding information from a police investigation . . .

'All of which could lead to you being charged with accessory or complicity to murder,' the Giraffe was saying. Mandy heard that loud and clear. 'And that doesn't include the priest, Father Tony. He's now being investigated. He could face deportation.'

Mandy cleared his throat and patted the phone in his pocket. 'Am I really hearing this? I think if people knew the truth, they'd be baying for your blood. How about the assistant coroner of Santa Monica, let alone your ace detectives Broadski and Dent? Jesus Christ!'

There was silence. Fabienne was dabbing her nose with a tissue.

'Well, no one said life was fair, did they?' the Giraffe said with a faint smile.

Mandy wanted to punch him.

'May I say something?' he said, getting to his feet and looking at Anderson and O'Dowd for a fair hearing.

'Be quick,' the Giraffe said.

Mandy began: 'Before you send me out into the Gaza Strip with a swastika painted on my forehead, let me remind you that *you* recommended me for the job. Eduardo García-Márquez was the guy who hired me and set the parameters for the reward. And it was me who unearthed Benny Tan as being behind the killing of his son and a few other people too.'

O'Dowd suspended his high-speed typing to swig from a small bottle of water. The Giraffe stifled a yawn and smiled at Anderson as if he was Mandy's long-suffering guardian.

'Wake up and smell the coffee, Mandy.' The Giraffe peered at the index card on the mantelpiece.

'Gentlemen, I'm going to the bathroom. Please tell Mandy the terms of the deal. Tell him if he accepts the arrangement, there's no reason his new private detective agency won't begin to thrive in this town. Otherwise . . .'

The Giraffe let the threat hang in the air for a moment. 'I'm retiring in six months and I want my exit to be clean as a hound's tooth, not reeking of shit.'

The Giraffe strode off, closing the door behind him.

Anderson ushered Mandy to sit down.

'This is a matter of national security, so there is going to be compromise and most of it will be yours. The Chief wants this to be seen as being solved by the SMPD alone, and that Broadski and Frank Polanski were killed in the line of duty. The Bureau's position is that we don't want to complicate matters by making public the involvement of the assistant coroner and the two detectives. It's not strictly a federal matter, and we have bigger fish to fry, Mandy. Sorry. We wanted to eliminate Nabokov, the Russian Corporation and Tan. We got what we came for.'

'What's the proposal about the reward offered by Eduardo García-Márquez?' Mandy said, looking directly at Fabienne.

Anderson took a big breath and said, 'The reward is to be paid into a special charity for the families of fallen officers, after making over a generous sum for your expenses, Mandy. Twenty thousand dollars.' Anderson grimaced. He obviously thought the amount was a kick in the teeth.

Mandy laughed. Fabienne fanned her face in disgust. Twenty thousand would barely cover his debts. Anderson wiped the palms of his hands together.

'This proposal sucks and you know it,' Mandy said.

Anderson looked behind him at the door and shrugged. 'Choice one: you could be charged with aiding and abetting, withholding evidence and maybe even involuntary homicide. Charges might also be brought against the Greek man, the Mexican nanny and certainly against the alleged daughter of Tan.'

'What on earth would you charge Lucy Lack with? She knew nothing about her father's activities.'

'I'd guess aiding and abetting a break-in, being a foreign national in possession of a lethal weapon, withholding evidence – the Department would find something, you can be sure of that.'

'Do you want me to make you a counter-proposal?'

Anderson folded his arms. 'No, this is not open to negotiation.'

Mandy forced a smile onto his face. So this is what it feels like to be the fall guy. He pictured Lucy's shocked face on being arrested by federal agents at LAX, wiped sweat from his upper lip and stood up, not caring about the pain.

'Feels like it's not only my leg that's been stitched up,' he said. 'But seeing as we are all sitting cosily here together, one question . . .'

Anderson loosened his tie and nodded. Mandy fingered the phone in his pocket.

'When we met for the second time, you said you were investigating police corruption.' Mandy stared straight at the Giraffe's desk. 'At the highest level. What happened to that enquiry? You can't mean that Broadski and Dent were in this alone or that Frank Polanski was their puppet master? Frank hadn't always been like that. I promise you that . . .'

O'Dowd closed the lid of his laptop, looked sympathetically at Mandy and spoke for the first time. 'Best to look upon this as losing a battle so we can all win a war.'

'Sure, but why is it me who has to lose the battle?'

Anderson gestured, 'Stop,' and pointed to O'Dowd. 'Tell the Chief that he is required.'

O'Dowd nodded and stepped out of the room.

Anderson sighed, lowered his voice. 'Giraffes have the highest blood pressure in the animal kingdom and definitely some of the unhealthiest of colons. So don't quit before the fat lady has finished singing.'

Mandy and Fabienne looked at one another and said nothing. Mandy sat back down on the sofa, feeling vaguely stupid that he'd leapt to his feet in the first place. They listened to the whirring of the two floor fans in silence until the Giraffe and O'Dowd came back into the room.

Anderson gestured for the Giraffe to sit. Then, as if announcing the crop report on TV, he stood behind the chair he'd been sitting on and paused a few seconds to ensure he had everyone's attention.

'Deputy Attorney General Griswold was murdered by two Vietnamese,' Anderson began, 'contracted by the Russian Corporation – a business owned by Nabokov and an organized-crime syndicate based in Siberia – lots of ex-KGB and some of their former prisoners . . .'

'The kind with full-body tattoos – stars on their knees,' Mandy said.

Anderson nodded.

Mandy rewound to what a drunken Frank had told him in Topanga about never trusting Russians. Why did he think like that?

Anderson continued, 'Griswold wanted to make his mark by pushing through legislation against money laundering and taking a stand against organized crime, especially from Eastern Europe. He and Sergeant Powell were shot dead to send a clear message to government law-enforcement agencies that these people are prepared to be ruthless.'

'But Broadski and Dent weren't part of the Russian Mob,' Mandy said. 'That I don't believe – they've got far tougher and brighter people themselves.'

'That's not true, nor were Broadski and Dent working for the assistant coroner. We know that from Dent's testimony we got from him before he died. They were largely working for themselves and *someone* in the Police Department.'

'So it was a business opportunity that drew them into the Russian–Tan deal?' Mandy said. He remembered the documents on Tan's computer. Tan had been about to sell up and retire – so he could live as a member of the LA Country Club and not a psychopathic freak.

'Tan met Frank five years ago at a benefit for UCLA Hospital. Their paths crossed the following year at a Republican fundraiser. Tan liked Frank Polanski because he had skills and friends at his favourite club. Tan needed a link to the Police Department to provide a source for homeless people or cleaned-up addicts.' He shook his head. 'Seems they shared the same views on cleansing the city of bums and illegals.'

Fabienne surreptitiously tapped Mandy's hand. It was all making sense to her.

'It boiled down to this,' Anderson said. 'We subpoenaed Tan's company bank records and triple-checked the statement Frank left at his home. Frank was on the Fish Farm payroll in return for part-time surgical duties. Tan was exporting those extracted body parts for transplant use in Asia and Russia—'

Mandy interrupted, 'And exporting them in the same white polystyrene boxes as his live tropical fish and importing heroin in the same boxes back here. But I think we already figured that out, didn't we?' he said, grunting sarcastically. 'And answer me this, Agent Anderson, if you know everything, why did Frank have such a hatred of Russians?'

Anderson held up his hands in astonishment. 'Didn't he ever tell you?'

Mandy shook his head and sighed. 'I wouldn't be asking if he had, would I?'

Anderson drew breath and appeared to modify his voice to grave. 'Frank's grandfather was one of the eight thousand Polish officers executed by the Russian secret police in the forest at Katyn in World War Two.'

'Frank hadn't been born.'

'No, but his mother never got over the loss and took her own life when he was eleven years old. It affected him badly, and over time, especially when the truth of it came out, he became obsessed that the massacre was the root of all the unhappiness in his life. He has over thirty books on the subject in his apartment, and over twenty documentaries.'

There was a silence.

It was like finding the missing piece to a jigsaw. The answer made total sense to Mandy, especially considering what he felt about his own grandfather. Now was not the time to contemplate such things. He repeated the word 'Katyn' to himself and carried on with his complaints.

'And what about justice for Pedro or his family? Just another cover-up?'

The Giraffe grunted impatiently. 'It's a "take it or leave it" situation, Mandy. The García-Márquez family know Chain and Quinn killed their boy; that's all they wanted to know, not the ins and outs of it.'

'Bollocks!' Mandy said.

The Giraffe pulled a document out of one of his desk drawers. 'Look, just sign this. It's a statement that Frank, Broadski and Dent were all killed in the line of duty and that you are grateful for the amount of the reward we've offered you.'

'Twenty grand?'

The Giraffe leant his long body and face over Mandy. 'Yeah,' he said, 'twenty thousand bucks is twenty thousand more than you had a month ago. Suck it up.'

Mandy stood up, cleared his throat and straightened his tie. 'Stick it up and blow it out of your crooked arse,' he said.

He closed the door quietly behind him. No need to slam it – his words were still ringing in the astonished silence. That was the thing: none of them had imagined he might say no. To them, twenty grand was better than nothing. But sometimes, just sometimes, nothing was the better option.

By the time he hit the street, Mandy realized he had no car in which to get home. The Amazon would be in intensive care at Tassos's garage for several weeks, maybe more. What the heck? It was a beautiful day, and a cool breeze was blowing off the ocean. He did not want to hail a cab or rent a bike or car from Tassos. He quickened his pace down Main Street, fully aware it would not be long before the Giraffe or Anderson's men came after him. He kept calm and told himself to travel anonymously, in a way he normally never did. And provided he didn't look back, they wouldn't get to him. Above all, whatever happened now, he was pleased with himself for saying what he said and leaving. Connecting a hosepipe from the Amazon's exhaust and placing it inside the car now seemed an impossibly crazy thought from his past. How different it was to have choices. In the distance, he saw an empty bus stop.

Amid a shimmering heat haze two hundred metres ahead, he caught sight of a big blue bus waiting at a bus stop. Despite the heat and the stitches in his legs, he ran for it, just like he'd done as a schoolboy in Oxford. Once aboard, he paid the fare to the driver, and using the tops of the tough plastic seats as ballast, walked to the back and sat down. Two backpackers and three boogie-board-carrying teenagers were the only other passengers on board. They were all silently staring out towards the sea. As the bus trundled past the tall, sway-ing palm trees on Ocean, Mandy looked up at the white stucco building where the late Pedro García-Márquez used to live. There and then, he made two promises: to find the family of the dead Russian girl he'd discovered in Pedro's apartment and to find two black kittens for Alice and Caitlin, daughters of the president of the Santa Monica Suicide Club.

The pneumatic doors of the bus opened at the stop at the bottom of California Avenue and Pacific Coast Highway. The three chattering teenagers jumped off the bus and raced onto the beach. It was only then that Mandy pressed 'audio playback' on his cell and held it tight to his ear. His damaged knee jigged up and down as he realized he had successfully recorded the entire conversation that took place in the Giraffe's office.

He breathed in the ozone and allowed a smile to spread across his face. That recording was his protection and evidence, the bargaining tool he needed to negotiate his future. He quickly emailed an attachment of the recording to Eduardo García-Márquez and also to Scottish Ray for safe keeping.

The bus continued in the direction of Malibu. Mandy looked at his phone again and scanned for new messages or email. There were four: one was from Donna, one from Father Tony at St Monica's and one each from Eduardo García-Márquez and Lucy Lack in London. Each one had an intriguing request. But instead of responding immediately, he switched off the cell and walked to the front of the bus. The next stop was Point Dume.

He removed his shoes and socks, hung his jacket over his shoulder and walked barefoot across the sand to the spot where he'd often swum. He undressed, hid the phone and wallet inside his shoes and ran into the shallows of the ocean. Mandy wanted to taste the saltwater and see the fish swimming beneath its surface. In particular, he needed to find the starfish with the missing leg he'd seen before.

He took a huge deep breath, stepped forward and plunged head first into the sea.

'Keep swimming,' he told himself. 'Just keep swimming,'

Acknowledgements

I am grateful to the following people for providing invaluable support and succour while I wrote this book.

Jon Beecher, Janice Burns, Laura Collins, Karl French, Jim Greenberg, Mathew Hamilton, Ianthe Jacob, Anthony Keates, Christopher Monger, Toby Moorcroft, Brian and Sue Potter, Mark Robbins, Peter Robinson, Nigel Ryan RIP, Carol Tidy Walker, Clare Tupman, Sarah Tyrer, Janet Walsh, Sophie Wilson, Bradley and Diana Wood, Patmos Squash Club, The Artist Studio, Tim, John and Annabel at Whitefox, All at Les Amis de Bill, Jane Villiers, Matthew, Tania and Kelly at Sayle Screen, The Vagia Café, Patmos, The Beirut Lodge, Ted, Norman and Syd (two boss cats and dog)

www.santamonicasuicideclub.com

Instagram: SantaMonicaSuicideClub

Twitter: @jcthomasauthor

www.jeremythomas.co.uk

Facebook: Jeremy Thomas Author

www.samaritans.org

Lightning Source UK Ltd.
Milton Keynes UK
UKOW04f2221170316

270372UK00003B/80/P